CW00970004

THE MURDER OF CROWS

An Inspector Vignoles mystery

Stephen Done

The author asserts the moral right to be identified as the author of this work. All rights reserved. No part of this publication may be reproduced, stored in a retrieval system or transmitted, in any form or by any means, electronic, mechanical, photocopying, recording or otherwise, without the prior permission of the author. This book is sold subject to the condition that it shall not, by way of trade or otherwise, be lent, resold, hired out or otherwise circulated without the author's prior consent in any form of binding or cover other than that in which it is published and without a similar condition including this condition being imposed on the subsequent purchaser. © Stephen Done 2008

British Library Cataloguing in Publication Data:
A catalogue record for this book is available from the British Library
ISBN 978-1-904109-198

Published 2008

The Hastings Press
PO Box 96 Hastings TN34 1GQ
hastings.press@virgin.net
www.hastingspress.co.uk

Set in Garamond
Cover design by Bill Citrine
Printed by Printondemand-worldwide, Peterborough

THE MURDER OF CROWS

An Inspector Vignoles Mystery

~ ACKNOWLEDGEMENTS ~

I would like to thank those who have helped, advised and encouraged me along the way, and all my family, close and extended, and especially Irena, for the continuing love and support. Sincere thanks go to Bill for another splendid cover design and to Helena of the Hastings Press for all the support, advice and hard work in preparing the text. Thanks to David Brown for permission to reproduce 'Finmere' as the frontispiece. More of David's excellent and evocative railway pictures can be obtained from the Hayrack Gallery at www. hayrackgallery.co.uk.

A special thank you goes to everyone who bought *Smoke Gets in Your Eyes* and in so doing, made *this* book possible. Also to Sarah Glynn and the staff and pupils of Chenderit School, Middleton Cheney, for turning my first book into a stage production. Such support is rare for a new author and is much valued.

A number of excellent books have been consulted to help provide background to this story, but in particular *Never Again: Britain 1945-51* by Peter Hennessy (Penguin, 2006) and *Austerity Britain 1945–51* by David Kynaston (Bloomsbury, 2007). Thanks to J. M. Dent & Sons Ltd for permission to use lines from *The Flight of Birds* by John Clare and from *A Christmas Carol* by Christina Rossetti.

Stephen Done

~ AUTHOR'S NOTE ~

The former Great Central Railway really did run between London Marylebone, Leicester Central, Nottingham Victoria and onwards north to Hull, Manchester and Birkenhead. It was later operated by the London & North Eastern Railway, then by British Railways, but sadly most of it was gone by 1966–7, a victim of Dr Beeching. Woodford Halse really was a major railway junction with a large engine shed and goods' marshalling yards, and many of the railway locations featured also existed.

However, there was never a railway detective department and considerable liberties have been taken with reality to create this work of fiction — and it should be read as such. Any similarity to persons living or dead is unintentional.

~ ABOUT THE AUTHOR ~

Stephen Done was born on 3rd August, 1960. On his eighth birthday, whilst living in Scarborough, he declared that he wished to become a steam engine driver, only to be advised that British Railways was scrapping steam the very next day. Unfortunate timing. So he took up writing about them instead.

A museum curator, he has worked at the Bristol Industrial Museum, Cyfarthfa Castle Museum and has been curator of the Liverpool Football Club Museum since 1997. He is a keen birdwatcher and railway modeller and enjoys a pint of real English ale.

Stephen can be contacted via the website: www.inspectorvignoles.ukwriters.net or via his publisher.

or Mum

In the bleak mid-winter
Frosty wind made moan,
Earth stood hard as iron,
Water like a stone:
Snow had fallen, snow on snow,
Snow on snow,
In the bleak mid-winter
Long ago.

Christina Rossetti, *A Christmas Carol*.

~ CONTENTS ~

Prologue

THE MURDER OF CROWS

January 1947

The murder of crows had feathers blacker than the mouth of Catesby Tunnel.

They were perched along the looping garland of telegraph wires running parallel to the railway tracks, hopping and flapping from one wire to another, making croaking and cracking noises that rattled around the deep, but otherwise silent, railway cutting. The land lay still. The wind had finally dropped, leaving undisturbed the fresh snow caught upon the black-etched lines of the tree branches, and only the birds' movements sent showers of fine powder from the sagging wires to the drifts below.

The crows watched and waited, impatiently flapping a wing or making small jumps along the wires as they looked for any chance of food: searching for a small rodent stopped dead by the cold far from its cosy nest, or a rabbit, chilled and starved to the bone, its last hope of food buried beneath impenetrable layers of snow, now crouched into a furry ball, eyelids drooping as merciful sleep lulled it away from life in this frozen land, soon to become the crows' next meal.

Snow had fallen, snow on snow.

Two emboldened jackdaws were strutting confidently around the railway tracks, turning their heads in jerky movements to fix their sapphire-blue eyes on the ground, pecking speculatively at any small object welded by ice to the hoary sleepers. Wires squealed as they pulled a signal into action, fighting against the deep frost caked upon the little pulley wheels that carried the wires from the distant signal box. The yellow-and-black signal arm groaned and pointed its twin metal fingers skywards. A deep rumble started to resonate through the frozen ground, the wooden sleepers quivering slightly under the feet of the jackdaws as the rails raised a fragile, glassy, ringing sound. The tunnel mouth exhaled a blast of air that smelt of wet loam and sulphur as the sound of a panting beast became clearer. Huffing and hissing, with fast-measured beats that ricocheted and roared around the tunnel walls, it drew closer. The jackdaws, without even a glance at the tunnel, flapped slowly into the air with long, easy wing-beats and curved across the dimming sky towards the skeletal trees in the fields above the cutting.

The crows, taking this as their lead, leaped into the air like so many pieces of burnt paper swirling above a bonfire as the snorting iron horse thundered out of the tunnel, whistle blowing in a wavering, mournful blast that carried far across the iron-hard land.

The locomotive was streaming steam and its pounding motion was wrapped in clouds of white that swirled around the trailing carriages, dipping and diving between the bogies until finally the last shreds were torn into tiny fragments and melted away into the air. The engine was a rich, apple green, startlingly fresh against the white of the snow, and rimed in frost where the steel was not warmed by the roaring fire in its belly. The smoke clouds collecting around the cab were flashing in reds and oranges as the barely-visible fireman shovelled more coal into the open firebox, looking for all the world like a devil stoking the fires of hell. The driver leant out of the cab window, cap pulled tight down over his forehead, squinting at the signal arm, flecks of snow stinging his eyes and cheeks.

The train rattled past, a fine spray of snow swirling briefly around the rails before the land settled back into its frozen stillness. One by one, the crows circled above the railway cutting, watching the train stream past like a tiny model, then glided back down onto the telegraph wires, eager to see if the passing train had shed any crumb of food or disturbed some small creature from its lair. The piercing eyes of the jackdaws drew them in still closer; a ragged black vanguard, swooping and curving in graceful patterns just feet above the rails then, flapping and stalling their flight, they dropped down upon their long legs into the powdery snow. A chorus of excited cracks and croaks started up from the watching crows, like a sinister audience urging the jackdaws on.

Their luck was in.

Chapter One

'The Way You Look Tonight'
Frank Sinatra

Detective Inspector Charles Vignoles, accompanied by his sergeant, John Trinder, were walking as briskly as they were able along a snowy lane, using the compacted tyre tracks made by a farm tractor as narrow pathways. These preformed tracks notwithstanding, theirs was still a slow and stumbling progress. The base of these ruts was frozen into either a polished surface of pure ice like slippery brick that threatened to send them flying, or was formed into irregular lumps and bumps of hardened snow that caused them to stub their toes and lose balance. This was still preferable to trying to wade their way through the virgin, powdery snow that seemed to fill the narrow lane to bursting in gently heaving billows of brilliant white.

It was already shaping up to be the coldest and snowiest winter anyone could remember and promised to become even worse. There was talk of such a winter in the days of Samuel Pepys, but this was distant history, and as some wags were happy to point out, nobody ever froze because of what was written in a history book. The consensus was that they had never felt anything like it before, and they were freezing.

A little snow had fallen during December, but the initial romantic euphoria of a white Christmas soon paled as the stark reality of acute austerity measures and rationing bit even harder as the bitter-cold winds from Archangel blew in from the north. Even if the sun shone — and it seemed to do so all too rarely — it brought no warmth to break the iron-hard grip of the cold and, to make matters worse, the apparently complacent Minister for Fuel and Power had finally admitted that coal reserves were dangerously low and might soon run out; the government threatening that electricity would be rationed to just a few hours in the mornings and evenings, with heavy fines for those tempted to ignore the ban. And as January progressed into its third week, the mercury was continuing to drop whilst the storm clouds were gathering on the Arctic Circle, ready to make their move upon Britain, and even the most optimistic meteorologists were struggling to find any news to cheer its bleakly despairing people.

Could it really get worse? The cold and the threatened heavy snow were the unvarying topics of conversation in every meat and bread queue, in every bar and darkened office and on every railway platform and tram stop. A conversation might start optimistically about football, but then Saturday's abandoned fixtures soon brought them back to talking about snow, the perishing cold, the rationing and the lack of warm winter clothes. Housewives standing outside in tiresome queues might talk at first about the latest Ministry of Food recipe for 'Baked Squirrel', but soon such unappealing solutions to the food shortage drew bitter complaints — "Well how the bloomin' 'eck are you suppose to catch 'em? They run up trees like a flash!" — and so the talk would return, yet again, to the struggle to secure even a scrag-end of mutton or a rubbery piece of stewing steak after long hours in front of dimly-lit and poorly-stocked shops.

And every night further layers of frost and ice built up on that formed the night before, until the whole country was frozen close to standstill. But the frost and ice, though an inconvenience, was not the real problem. It was the terrible, scything winds that caused the most distress. These were winds that blew the snow into deeper drifts and which cut through each layer of clothing, seeming to unpick each stitch and then slide icy fingers inside the thickest of coats and warmest of gloves. It was a wind that rendered the brightest of fires futile and made each bedroom unwelcoming, with bed sheets impregnated by damp and offering but a miserable escape from the chills of the day, despite multiple hot water bottles. And it was this wind that threatened to bring a white invasion force to Britain. A silent and pale army that could paralyse and overwhelm the population more completely than the still freshly-remembered flights of Heinkel and Dornier bombers a few years before. And so the people of Britain huddled down against the massed assaults of lack and want, unemployment and imminent bankruptcy, drab clothes and drabber food in an unravelling Empire.

It was for this reason the two detectives were grateful for a temporary lull in the wind that Friday morning as they trudged away from Finmere station towards the former R.A.F. airbase. Since the end of hostilities this airfield had been converted into a temporary transit camp for displaced persons, which in the case of Finmere D.P. Camp, was about two hundred Polish families, all of whom had fled their country and were now homeless and in need of assistance to rebuild their lives. Many were probably wondering if it had not been a mixed blessing to end up in a country that seemed to be struggling, and possibly failing, to get back on its feet.

Neither officer was particularly looking forward to the visit, and having to walk three miles or more from the station did little to lighten their mood. Taking the police Rover had never been an option, as the roads would have been impassable to anything smaller than a truck or tractor. Even if they had been clear, they lacked sufficient petrol coupons to make the journey, and after a particularly unfortunate incident in April last year in which the precious vehicle had been abandoned without petrol, Vignoles had found his ration monitored and audited with pedantic precision by his chief superintendent. The car was strictly off-limits.

'Brrr, it's just so damned cold...' Trinder spoke through the folds of his scarf.

'It is a nipping and an eager air.'

Trinder raised his eyebrow and looked at Vignoles.

'*Hamlet.*'

'Nipping and eager? Bloody freezing, more like!'

'And if *The Times* is to be believed, there's worse coming.'

'Please, no. I've about had enough of this cold.'

'It's those northerly winds that are the worry: straight from Siberia or thereabouts and set to bring us an unwelcome, and very late, Christmas present from Uncle Joe.'

'Stalin? Phaa!' Trinder spat out the words with contempt, although they were somewhat deadened by his muffler, 'that man and his sidekick Molotov are making life hard enough already from what I've read; we hardly need anything else from their God-forsaken country.'

The sound of their feet crunching through the snow somehow seemed to emphasise Trinder's point, 'Things really are pretty bad, aren't they? We're in real danger of a crisis. I hear they called the troops in to sort out the meat drivers' strike in London.'

'A bad show, that. Yes, I fear this could be — to quote yet more Shakespeare — *Our winter of discontent.*' Both men fell silent for a while as they contemplated the twin threats of an uncooperative Soviet Union and a worsening winter. 'How much further is this place?' The scarf wrapped tightly around his neck muffled Vignoles's voice.

'Another mile or so, I reckon. It just feels like a much longer trek in this snow.'

'You can say that again.' Vignoles blew a stream of white breath out through the woollen fabric, seeking to gain a few moments of warmth around his lips. It served only to mist his silver-framed glasses. 'We could never have got the car down this road.' Vignoles sounded like he was trying to convince himself. 'We would have been bogged down, for sure.'

'Agreed. At least the trains are still running, though they are having the Devil's own job keeping the points operating. I don't know if you saw the traffic reports this morning?' Trinder glanced across at Vignoles, 'the delays were horrendous last night after that freeze.'

'I noticed. When you think of the men working on the lines all through the night to keep them clear, we should admit that our little walk in the country doesn't seem quite so bad after all.'

In truth, Vignoles did not mind the fresh air and was glad of an excuse to escape the filthy smog of Leicester. A yellowish fog had grown steadily worse in recent weeks as everyone stoked their fires with whatever they could find to burn, and this was mostly the poorest grade coal and salvaged refuse from the many bomb sites; usually damp wood covered in noxious paint. Now, something called an 'inversion' was holding this stinking air close to the ground and choking its poor citizens as a cruel repayment for trying to warm their houses. So, Vignoles was enjoying the way the countryside was rendered magically beautiful by the snow, but his feet were damp and achingly cold. He was also wondering if their journey was little more than just a symbolic gesture, and a rather heavy-handed and unwelcome one at that, serving no real purpose.

'I know you feel that we could have let uniform deal with this, maybe even given it over to the civvies; but this is the third time this family has been caught stealing coal from railway property, and this Major Duffy chap hinted that they have been up to more than that. He specifically asked that we put some pressure on them and try to nip it in the bud.'

Vignoles glanced across at his sergeant, who was walking with his shoulders hunched, staring before him whilst choosing his footing with care.

'What sort of stuff? Food? Or does he think they are working something like a ration book swindle?'

'He was vague. He knows about the coal — but so do we, as it was one of our officers who caught them red-handed — but he seems to suspect more. I suppose that's why he called us in. But he could be fed up by now of the railway police always on his patch.'

'Fair enough. There's plenty of pilfering and black-marketeering going on, that's for sure. So, do we give them the full treatment? Make them realise that we're on their backs?' Trinder looked across at Vignoles.

'Actually, we must tread carefully. Rather like we are on this dratted ice.' Vignoles wobbled slightly as he momentarily lost his footing. 'These people are not prisoners, even though they live in a camp behind barbed wire. They are as free as you and I and deserve the same level of restraint and respect. Nonetheless, they have been caught stealing. However, privately I might confess to having some sympathy with their plight, holed up as they are in accommodation that must be worse than useless in a winter like this.'

'Yes.' Trinder pondered Vignoles's words for a moment. 'You're right; it must be awful in those horrid little huts. Bloody freezing.'

'Exactly. But there again, many others are also freezing across Britain, and robbing coal from one source just denies someone else. It's a very serious situation with the coal reserves, and even a few shovelfuls here and there are just not acceptable. Whilst I speak with them, have a little sniff around and see if anything else looks suspicious.'

Trinder nodded by way of a response.

A few steps further along the snowy road they passed beneath the spreading arms of a large tree, and as they did so both men stopped simultaneously as a small, brightly-coloured object dropped out of the branches in front of them. So light and insubstantial was it that no indentation was made in the snow. It was a tiny bird, wings folded close to its body and eyes closed shut as if asleep.

Vignoles bent down, carefully slid his gloved fingers underneath and lifted the bird in the palm of his hand. The yellow, black and red feathers were shining like a jewel.

'A goldfinch.'

'Is it dead?' Trinder bent his head forward to look more closely.

'Yes. Frozen solid, poor thing.'

'It just fell out of the tree? How extraordinary.'

Both men exchanged glances. 'The birds must be really suffering in this weather. No food. It's very sad.' Vignoles placed the bird gently back upon the snow beside the thorny skeleton of the hedgerow.

Trinder looked up into the branches above them. 'There are more up there. I wonder which will be next.'

Vignoles also looked upwards. 'Let's hope there's a thaw soon. That's all will save them, I fear. Wait a moment whilst I try to get my pipe fired up. If I can... just... get my fingers to work, that is.' Vignoles pulled down the scarf from across his face, fumbled inside his coat and extracted a pipe and a round tin of Ogden's Nut Flake. Trinder removed his gloves and pulled a packet of Black Cat cigarettes and some matches from a pocket of his coat, expertly flaring a match and proffering it to Vignoles.

'A new pipe?'

'Yes...' Vignoles puffed quickly whilst holding the match to it, '...Anna bought it me for Christmas. Heaven knows where she managed to find it.' He produced two more short puffs until the bowl was glowing orange, and then held the pipe out, the better for Trinder so see and allowing the sergeant to lean forward and light his own cigarette from the burning tobacco.

'Nice. Looks expensive.'

'I dare say. Anna likes things of good quality and tends to look at the price tag last of all — inevitably to my cost!' Vignoles grinned. He looked at the pipe appreciatively. 'Still haven't really got used to it yet. Been using the old one at work until now as a new pipe needs to mellow in a while, but so far it tastes pretty good. How did you both spend Christmas? Somehow I've allowed weeks to pass with my head filled with work and never asked the question. Most remiss of me.' The two men continued walking as they talked.

'Violet and I had Christmas Day together. We even managed to find a duck to roast.' Trinder shot a sideways glance at Vignoles, who raised an eyebrow in response. 'Violet has a friend in Woodford Halse who's a farmer; I think he shot it. Anyway, it was gratefully received.'

'A definite benefit of her living in the country.'

As if to underline the point, a pair of gadwall flew overhead. Both men watched them pass with thoughts of roast dinner close to mind.

'Indeed. And you will never guess what Violet got me for

Christmas? A real cracker of a present, I must say.' Trinder did not wait for Vignoles to reply. 'A genuine recording by Sinatra of *The way you look tonight*. It's one of those V Records the G.I.s brought over with them. Super rare.' Trinder's enthusiasm was shining through as he talked. It was common knowledge that he was an avid collector of music and an expert on most of the dance bands and their singers.

'I am not sure I have heard of these V Records.'

'No? They're American-made: once the States entered the war they forbade their artistes to excessively profit from it — the war that is — by making too much money from songs that caught the public imagination. But the U.S. government also actively encouraged music-making to lift morale.'

'Just like our Vera Lynn did for us here.'

'Exactly. The U.S. paid no royalties, just a fixed fee for each recording. The records were then distributed free, or for a few dollars anyway, amongst the U.S. forces. After the war they were supposed to destroy them all so that the artistes could then re-issue or re-record these wartime cuts on a normal commercial basis. As result, this is a rare survivor.'

'How on earth did Violet find it?'

'Impressive, eh? She *is* very good at finding bargains — she loves trawling through bring-and-buy sales and the like, and she saw this on a market stall — lots of the Yanks are selling off stuff before they make the trip back home. You can pick up all kinds of things nowadays.'

'That's true.' Vignoles was thinking of the racketeers and spivs that seemed to lurk on every street corner and skulk into pubs.

'But sergeant, is this record not a little, shall we say...' Vignoles paused a beat, '...illegal?'

'How? A Yank selling a record?'

'Did you not say that the records should all be destroyed once the war ended? And, as that was a good eighteen months ago...' he winked. Vignoles enjoyed making fun of his sergeant.

'I think those instructions apply in the U.S.A., but surely not here?' Trinder's voice lacked conviction.

Vignoles grinned at his sergeant who was, despite the cold, blushing pink. 'John, old chap, don't look so worried. I don't imagine that Uncle Sam will be knocking at your door and I don't see Frank Sinatra or the Three Jive Bombers struggling as a result, either. Actually, it was a very thoughtful present to buy someone like you. Violet put an awful lot of care into selecting it.'

'Gosh, yes. It was really something special.' Trinder's face lit up into a broad smile.

'And, you know, when someone puts that much care into choosing a gift for someone they have known for quite a time, because, let's face it John, you and Miss McIntyre have been walking out for nearly a year...'

'...Nine months.'

'Long enough.' Vignoles grinned knowingly at Trinder before continuing. 'Don't you think it tells you a lot about how they feel?'

'Well, yes. I suppose it might.' He made an unconvincing job of sounding bemused by the question. 'Yes, it does. But I think one must be careful not to presume too much and jump to conclusions.'

'Indeed not. But there again, sometimes one can be too discreet. One should be careful of appearing uninterested. Fortune favours the brave, as they say. And nine months is positively cautious, old chap.'

'Our circumstances are not the easiest for marriage, if that's what I think you are talking about. What with Violet living in Woodford and still supporting her daughter...' He tailed off.

'Indeed. But things can change. If there's a will, there's a way.'

Trinder made no response, just looked ahead whilst drawing upon his cigarette.

'And I am being too inquisitive. My apologies.' Vignoles also fell silent for a few moments before continuing. 'Ah, if I am not mistaken that is the lovely Finmere D.P. Camp ahead. We had better look up this Major Duffy first, then tackle the Walentynowiczes. That should be a challenge — like pronouncing their name: I was practising all last evening.'

※　　※　　※　　※

Whilst the two railway detectives approached Finmere Camp, Miss Vera Harding was taking a cup of tea in the refreshment room at Nottingham Victoria. Before the war this would have been a splendid and comfortable place to while away the time, and it still retained the scale and grandeur of a station with aspirations, but now its cavernous roof, spanning platforms and railway tracks, was still missing most of the glass, removed as a precaution against the Blitz. As a result, the platforms were now cold and icy, with an unpleasant draught licking around the legs of the many waiting passengers. The cavernous tunnel that loomed at one end of the station, with its deep, stone retaining walls, did nothing to lessen the feeling of dankness and, with the overcast sky prematurely casting an evening gloom around the smoke-blackened buildings, it was a depressing place to stand.

It was for these reasons that Miss Harding preferred to escape into the comparative warmth of the refreshment room. This was illuminated by hissing gas lamps and was made steamy by the two chrome urns boiling on the counter. Food was scarce and the glass cabinets upon the counter were as bare as old Mrs Hubbard's cupboard. If this was a not clear enough message, a large poster on the wall proclaimed in bold letters: 'Don't ask for bread unless you really want it'. However, hot water and tea was, thankfully, still plentiful and Miss Harding felt snug as she clasped a cup in her hands. She just hoped that, when her train did eventually arrive, it would have heating that worked, as the warming effects of her tea were never going to last the journey.

Miss Harding was a pretty, smiling, twenty-four-year-old typist recently engaged to be married. She would not have considered herself showy, but she still tried to keep herself looking smart and modish, despite the very best efforts of the government's mean coupon allowance, the lack of almost any clothes to buy and the long, tiring hours she worked. But she was feeling particularly good that afternoon, as this was a chance to enjoy her latest pride and joy: a lovely new winter coat.

She smoothed one of the sleeves, appreciating the feel of the fabric, then flicked a speck of coal from a lapel and checked that her brooch was still in place. This was a stylised tiger lily, fashioned from scraps of cream felt and carefully flecked with spots of orange dye to imitate the colouring of the flower, all set off by a dark green stem and leaf. The brooch was something she had made one evening by following an idea in *Woman and Home* magazine, and she was quite pleased with the effect, but now wondered if the leaves were lost against the colour of her coat. She shrugged; it was a minor detail as the coat was really the main attraction. This had been run up from a blanket, but quite expertly, by a local dressmaker, and really looked a treat. The blanket was pure wool and she had been lucky enough to strike a good deal with the spiv hawking it. As a result the coat was of a slightly longer length than she had worn in years, and the lapels eased just a touch wider than most, and taken together with an outrageously expensive hat — at least it seemed so to Miss Harding on her meagre wages — she felt like a million dollars, as they would say in her favourite American films.

As she crossed her legs, she observed with a quiet sense of satisfaction that, after much practise, the gravy browning and eyeliner pencil had done a pretty decent job of emulating stockings and she was pleased with her handiwork. Yes, all things considered, she was looking and feeling good and filled with excitement about the weekend ahead.

She was travelling south to Banbury to meet her old school friend Heather Spencer. They had seen each other so infrequently in the last few years, what with travelling discouraged and the unforgiving hours they both worked, but Miss Harding had managed to convince Mr Brown, one of the legal partners, to allow her the afternoon off. Her first half-day in maybe a year, but so valuable, for she could now travel down in good time and spend all the Friday evening with Heather. Maybe they could go to the pictures? She loved the cinema: the whole theatrical build-up to the main event with the Movietone newsreels and the desperately bad B films. It would be warm and snug in the cinema as well, making it the perfect escape from the cold outside.

Looking at the clock, Miss Harding saw it was approaching the time she had been given for her much delayed train, so she finished her tea, gathered up her small travelling case, umbrella and handbag and braced herself for the icy world outside. The platform was now surprisingly empty, having shed its crowds in the time she had been in the refreshment room, and she wondered if perhaps she'd got the platform wrong. She considered it better to double-check and so walked over to a smartly-dressed young woman wearing a long navy coat with silver buttons and a peaked cap proclaiming that she was an L.N.E.R. station porter.

'Excuse me, is this right for the Banbury train?'

'Banbury? Let me think... yes it is, but not directly. You'll need to change at Woodford Halse. This is actually for London. But it stops at Woodford for your connection,' she smiled warmly, 'though I fear you might lose the connection to Banbury, as it's running late. I suggest you make enquiries when you get to Woodford. The timetable is quite shot to pieces.'

'What's new?'

'Yes! We have no bananas, either.' They both laughed. 'I'm afraid it's all too common now, what with the track worn out by the war and this weather we're having.'

'Dreadful, isn't it? I've never known anything like it. And they're predicting far worse.'

'Heaven forbid! I don't think I can stand it to get any colder. And they're having such a problem keeping the lines clear. If it's not the snow, then it's the ice. That's the problem today, frozen signals near Sheffield, apparently.' The porteress smiled.

'Ah, I see. I *will* get to Banbury, though?' Miss Harding bit her lip.

'Oh yes. Just an hour or so late, and that's pretty good going these days.' She grinned optimistically. 'And here comes your train now. Let me help you with your case...'

A grimy engine slowly clanked past them, wheezing and panting and sending soft curls of steam around their legs. Miss Harding noticed that it was a colour that defied definition and looked very woebegone; however, the distinctive brass nameplate, depicting a fox leaping over letters that proclaimed 'The Quorn', caught her eye.

'What an odd name.'

'It's a hunt, so hence the fox. We have lots of these engines through here and they're all named after foxhunts.'

'Oh, how gruesome.' She pulled a face, being no lover of hunting, but then smiled in response to her helpful new friend, who was now explaining that the indescribably dirty carriages were not the normal type that she could expect on the London train.

'With so much disruption they must have dragged these awful old things out today. They don't even have corridors.' The porteress was holding a narrow wooden door open for her. 'No chance of a restaurant car and I'm afraid; no conveniences, either.' She gave another apologetic smile as Miss Harding stepped into the narrow compartment that consisted of just two long-cushioned seats facing each other with another door and a pair of windows at the far side.

'Not to fret; it seems warm, at least, and that's the most important thing right now.'

'Change at Woodford — don't forget!' The young woman

closed the door and stepped back, looking along the train to see if anyone else needed assistance.

Having placed her small travelling case and umbrella neatly in the luggage rack, Miss Harding watched the porteress walk briskly a few yards along the train and then stop abruptly. Steam rose in slow, white curtains in front of the window and at times masked the view, rendering the uniformed woman shadowy and indistinct. A guard's whistle blew. The engine gave a short 'toot' and she felt the carriages rock slightly as the engine started to take the strain. A loud whooshing sound was followed by a deep bark as the engine made its first real pull.

As the view started to slide slowly past the window, she was suddenly aware of a running figure approaching her compartment through the steam. Her friendly porteress shouted and waved her arms, but then stopped and put her hands on her hips in an attitude of disbelief as the door to the compartment was flung open, and a short, fat, panting man spilled into the narrow space. He brushed against her knees, forcing her to swing her legs to one side to allow his bulk to squeeze past her, uncomfortably close. The man slammed the door shut and shuffled along until he flopped heavily down upon the seat diagonally opposite hers, a small canvas bag with carrying handles, like those used by a tradesman such as a carpenter or plumber, bounced down onto the seat beside him, rattling with a metallic sound as it did so.

'Gosh. Just made it!' His breathing was short and laboured. 'That was a bit of luck.' He grinned at her, his small eyes like little black currants behind his thick-lensed glasses. 'I very nearly missed it: it's late, you see. Should have been here forty-three minutes ago. And yesterday it was thirty-four minutes late,' he took another gulp of air, 'a most confusing state of affairs. Can't rely on the timetables these days. What is the world coming to?' He seemed to be talking aloud to himself and Miss Harding remained silent. 'But it's my lucky day.' He stared at her with a disconcerting intensity and grinned.

She mumbled something indistinct by way of response and tried to fight down a feeling of resentment that this large man had suddenly invaded her space. The trains were nearly always so crowded these days that she realised she had already started to harbour selfish thoughts of having the compartment all to herself.

Reaching for her handbag she extracted a carefully rolled-up newspaper, whilst trying to remind herself that the man had as much right to enter the compartment as she. But his beady gaze was somehow too long and arresting, and it made her feel ill at ease. She sought the safety of the open paper, lifting it high so that it masked the man and, with this flimsy wall between them, tried to forget that he was there.

The train was gathering speed, chuffing with regular beats and spilling clouds of steam along the outside of the carriage window so that she could see very little. With the barrier of newsprint raised on the other side she was hemmed in all around and was forced to read a long article about the chancellor, Mr Dalton. It was on the state of the economy and was rather tedious and complex, though she did laugh silently at the poor chancellor's inopportune comments, which the paper was enjoying repeating with great relish: Dalton had told the House of Commons that 'the shortages and frustrations which still afflict us will disappear like the snows of winter, and give place to the full promise of springtime'. Fat chance of that.

Miss Harding forced herself to continue reading, as she was convinced that the eyes of the man were boring into the paper. If she were to lower it or even turn a page, she felt sure that his piggy-gaze would meet hers. The more she tried to quell this belief the more convinced she became that he was staring in her direction. She tried to listen for any movements to help gauge what he was doing. His breath had been laboured at first from running, but now it had settled and he seemed curiously silent and inert.

Oh, bother the chancellor and his finances! She could not bear to stare at the same article any longer and would have to risk turning a page. She would do it quickly with her face set in a mask of impassive indifference. That way, if he were looking her way, he would meet no encouragement to engage her in conversation. She did so, and as the flimsy paper wall dipped slightly she took a furtive glance across the compartment.

The man was sitting very still, with forearms resting on his knees and head drooping towards the floor. He had untied his polka-dotted neckerchief and held this loosely in one hand. He might even be asleep. The steam heating was leaking slightly and sending slow, leisurely drifts of vapour curling around his thick legs and torso. It looked as if he were steaming after a long run or smouldering like a lazy bonfire. He looked surprisingly peaceful and not in the least bit threatening. There was also a strange and pungent aroma now filling the carriage. What was it? Soap? Yes, it was coal tar soap. It was a smell of cleanliness.

Miss Harding felt her foolish fears collapse like a house of cards. He might not be the most attractive man to look at, but that was just her silly prejudice. He was clean and apparently sleepy after an honest day's toil. She now found the image of the steaming and resting man rather amusing. Relief flooded through her, and after some further turning and folding she happily looked to the society column, placing the paper more comfortably upon her lap and even smiled to herself, laughing inwardly at her idiotic thoughts. Thank goodness she had not made them more visible!

A short while later she stole another fleeting look and saw that he had still not moved: the poor man was dozing in the warmth of the carriage. And she was the one looking at him. Really, she needed to be far less suspicious of others and so, now feeling more relaxed, she started to enjoy reading about a Hollywood party hosted by Humphrey Bogart and Lauren Bacall.

※   ※   ※   ※

Major Andrew Duffy was a young, fresh-faced man with fair hair and a narrow moustache. His uniform was ironed and pressed into creases so sharp they looked dangerous, but it was hanging off his thin, angular frame as if a size too large and — whilst immaculately clean — it also betrayed signs of fading and fraying. A classic case of 'make do and mend'. The major's shoes were burnished to a shine that would have dazzled if the sun had been out. His fastidiousness was ironically and rather pathetically offset by the dilapidated and ruinous surroundings of Finmere D.P. Camp, which had presented a sad and depressing sight to Vignoles and Trinder as they trudged through the open gates.

Major Duffy's office was situated in a utilitarian building so typical of wartime airfields, with small, metal-framed windows set in walls painted in shades of cream and green but now furred with damp. Ancient brown linoleum that smelt of disinfectant lay upon the floors. The roof was clearly not watertight, judging by the tea-coloured stains spreading out in ominous rings upon his office ceiling. It had all seen better days and, after being abandoned by the R.A.F., there was little doubt that every expense that could be spared had been in turning the camp into a temporary home for its lost and displaced occupants. The major had attempted to rise above this decrepitude by keeping his office scrubbed, polished and as tidy as a monk's cell. It presented itself as a model of British Army efficiency; though whether this was a continuation of Duffy's own personal standards of grooming or just something to fill in the time due to a lack of any real work was debatable, for as he entered the room Vignoles spotted a Raymond Chandler paperback lying on the major's desk, incongruously at odds with the regimented orderliness surrounding it, and Vignoles had formed the impression that this had been put down, somewhat hurriedly, immediately prior to their arrival.

Certainly the major was pleased to have company, fussily settling the two of them in timeworn armchairs and fortifying each with tea in ill-matching cups, as if he were hoping for a long and cosy chat with friends. Duffy also appeared only too happy to spend the first few minutes talking about the weather, the recent nationalisation of the coalmines — something he seemed averse to — and the ever worsening rations and would have probably moved onto discussing the Palestinian and Indian situations, if Vignoles had not pulled him up short.

'So, major, about the Walentynowiczes: have they been a problem before?'

'Ah, yes, of course, must crack on with the matter in hand.' Major Duffy smiled and then sat back in his chair, which creaked as he did so. 'The Walentynowiczes...' He appeared to be stalling for time, which gave Vignoles an ominous feeling. 'Getting to be a bit of a bother all this business with the coal thefts. With the fuel crisis developing, this is of course a serious matter.' He paused before proceeding in a cautious manner. 'But look here, they're decent people, you know. I'm the first to want to see discipline and law and order upheld and I can see that they have clearly crossed the Rubicon, so as to speak...'

'But?' Vignoles looked at the major quizzically.

'I can't see any real badness in them, inspector.'

'But they were caught red-handed, stealing coal from the merchant's at Finmere station. Stealing is a crime and it should be punished. We've been far too lenient, to be frank.' Sergeant Trinder spoke in a calm but forceful manner, making it clear what he thought of the situation.

'Of course: you are correct.' The young major paused. 'Look, I like to think I run a tight ship here and having the railway police sail by is not quite my idea of doing so. But I would like to advise caution and sensitivity, that's all.'

Vignoles suppressed a smile at Duffy's wayward simile, located as they were virtually in the epicentre of England, as far from the sea as possible in a former air base run by the army. 'And we are the very model of sensitivity.' Trinder made a noise that might have been a snort as Vignoles spoke. 'We are not here to be heavy-handed, but, as my sergeant has pointed out, we have actually let them get away with just a ticking off before. This was possibly a mistake and the magistrates' court could be beckoning this time.' He paused for a beat. 'Tell us a little more about the family and then we shall go and pay them a visit.'

'The father, Jozef, keeps himself to himself. Probably won't say a lot — he might not say anything in fact — and sometimes makes out he doesn't speak English. In fact he can get by perfectly well: he has been doing some odd bits of work around the area and seems to manage all right.' Trinder was writing in his notebook as the major was speaking. 'His wife, Ludwika, is a quiet, kindly sort. Now, she really doesn't speak a word of English and lets her daughter, Kat, do the talking.'

'Kat? She's the one our men accosted taking the coal?' asked Vignoles.

'That's the girl. Katarzyna to be correct; but everyone calls her Kat or Katy.'

'Thank the Lord for that — these Polish names are getting me into a right muddle.' Trinder was staring at something in his notebook with an air of growing exasperation.

'They take a bit of getting used to but you'll soon get your ear in, with a little practice.' Trinder made a sound like 'humph' and rubbed out something with the eraser on the end of his pencil.

'Kat has some spirit about her and does most of the talking for the family. I concede that she is perhaps a bit wilful and stubborn — but there are worse crimes.'

'Like stealing?' Vignoles pulled an ironic half smile and then motioned for Duffy to continue.

'Yes. Indeed.' He coughed lightly. 'Then there is little Adam. He's just a typical eight-year-old. Quite bright and does well in his lessons.'

'Nothing more? It all rather sounds like two young people

chancing their arm to help keep warm. I thought I understood that you were worried about some black-marketeering?'

'Ah yes. Well...' The young major looked a little discomforted. 'It's just a suspicion; I have no evidence as such.' There was a pregnant pause as Vignoles waited for him to continue. 'And upon reflection I think I rather allowed myself to speak out of turn. A mistake, perhaps.'

'So now you don't suspect the family are dealing and trading illegally?' Trinder looked annoyed and took to contemplating his sodden boots, which were creating pools of water upon the major's lino.

'Look here, I have a feeling that within the camp some — how shall I put it — *trading* takes place, and I wondered about Jozef. But then I suppose I wonder about any number of them at times. Probably all without any firm basis. The problem is there are always some odd chaps hanging around with bags full of what I am quite sure are contraband goods. But it's so damned hard to keep tabs on them all. And you know how these fly-by-night types are. You can never pin a flipping thing on them.'

Vignoles nodded, but said nothing.

'So things do go on here and, frankly, at times it puts my back up. But then I remember that these people are not prisoners. They are free to meet with whomsoever they want.' The major stopped and took a breath.

'Even if it involves illegal trading?' Trinder asked the question.

'Maybe there is, maybe not. It's hard to be sure. It's everywhere these days, isn't it?' The young major looked slightly uncomfortable, 'what with the Walentynowicz kids getting repeatedly caught taking coal, I fear I might have jumped to conclusions. The father and a few of the other chaps go off each day to — well, I don't exactly know where — in their beaten-up old van and seem to come back with tins of food, cigarettes and goodness knows what else.' He exhaled deeply. 'But I'm pretty sure they are actually working and so maybe they're just pooling their ration cards and coupons. Dammit, if they get the odd basket of eggs for doing an honest day's work, why not? But something in my head made me put two and two together and...' He tailed off.

'And make five? You're having second thoughts?' Vignoles raised an eyebrow.

'Perhaps.' Major Duffy spread his hands wide and gave a wry grin.

'I see.' Vignoles sighed heavily, also thinking about his wet feet and ruined shoes. He tried to take another slant upon what was looking like a wasted journey. 'So, no other problems?'

'No, though you can't have failed to notice that this place is not exactly Buckingham Palace, even if some comedian has painted a sign to suggest just that and nailed it over his front door.' All three men smiled companionably. 'Conditions are pretty rough here, y'know? I have so few options open to help make things better for them. I have just enough coal to last us until the end of the week! We're in a pretty tight spot and some of them are, quite seriously, liable to freeze to death.' He ran his hand through his hair in an expression of frustration. 'On top of that, the ruddy gas boiler's playing up; that provides hot water for the communal washrooms, not to mention the one in my own quarters. But I shouldn't grumble, I suppose.' Duffy smiled grimly and spread his hands in a gesture implying futility.

'I can imagine it's tough, though it seems that perhaps you have called us here on rather a wild goose chase. However, we are best able to judge if there are any grounds to your suspicions.' Vignoles took a breath. 'We shall not take any more of your time.' He stood up, extending his hand to the major. 'Hopefully our being here might just put a stop to their foolishness and we won't have to bother you again.' 'Nor trudge all the way out here in snowdrifts', he thought to himself.

After taking directions from Major Duffy, Vignoles and Trinder walked into the camp along a wide road lined with rows of identical, single-storey huts, each with a pathway cleared of snow and curls of filthy smoke rolling from the blackened stovepipe chimneys. The corrugated iron roofs retained irregular clumps of snow and were rimed with frost, as if an artist had scumbled white paint over the edges of the metal sheets, and picked out every detail with startling clarity. Each hut had a porch with a little pitched roof above the door and, in an attempt to soften the starkness of the architecture, some of the occupants had added thin plywood decorations in the form of wooden panels in a mock-Tudor style to the little gable ends, or provided hand-painted house names, some of which were wonderfully inappropriate, including the 'Buckingham Palace' that Major Duffy had referred to. They read out the names as they walked past; Arcadia, Blenheim Palace, Marble Arch, The

Empire State Hut and then the one they were seeking — the last along that particular wide road — Mandalay.

'So this is the *Road to Mandalay*? It's not much to sing about, is it?' Trinder stood and looked around at the low, mean buildings, the leaning telegraph pole, the rusting metal windows fogged with condensation and the black Humber motorcar jacked up on bricks, missing its wheels and filled with cardboard boxes of what looked like old clothes. A solitary crow perched on the drooping telephone wire and eyed them suspiciously.

Two small figures wearing winter coats with big buttons down the front and wrapped in brightly-coloured knitted scarves, gloves and bobble hats were standing at the far corner of the hut, each holding an icicle that was at least two feet in length. One of them brought the thicker end of the glassy rod level to his eye, holding it as if it were a rifle and fixed a bead on Trinder, then made a sound that mimicked a gunshot and travelled across the chill frozen air. The two children then laughed and scampered out of sight behind the hut. The crow flapped away with a rusty croak.

'And it's hardly Arcadia either. I just wonder if the new prefabs are much better.' Vignoles pulled a face. 'But everything looks worse on a raw day like today. Let's get this over with.'

Vignoles walked up the path and, as he knocked on the door, a loose pane of glass rattled in the frame. The door was immediately opened and he saw a young, tall and slim girl, whose sullen face did nothing to detract from her startling good looks. Her hair was raven black and it framed a beautifully-sculpted face with high cheekbones and a mouth shaped in a perfect cupid's bow, despite her attempt to force it into a scowl. Vignoles sensed she had been expecting them, perhaps watching for their approach through the steamed-up windows, and that her expression and demeanour had been affected deliberately for their benefit.

'Good day, miss. I am Detective Inspector Vignoles and this is Sergeant Trinder of the London and North Eastern Railway police, detective department. May we come in?'

The girl did not answer but stepped back slightly and nodded her head towards the interior of the hut, which Vignoles took as an invitation for them to enter. It felt warm, but only in contrast to the deep cold outside, and Vignoles was sure that after the initial relief of stepping inside had worn off it would not feel so welcoming. The air was damp and the windows and walls streamed with condensation. The room smelt of laundry, cooked cabbage and pungent wood smoke, yet was also laced with something bitter that stung the eyes and throat.

Vignoles looked around the room and saw a woman in her forties who was wearing a neat, well-tailored, fawn-coloured dress, a knitted cardigan buttoned tight to the collar and a pinafore tied around her waist. She also wore a headscarf, which was another indication that the hut would not feel so warm after some time within. She was rolling out a rectangle of pastry on a wooden kitchen table and assembling what looked and smelt like a meat and potato pie. This must be Ludwika.

She looked up at the two men, gave a worried smile in acknowledgement of their presence and showed her floury hands as an excuse to continue rolling out the pastry. A short man with a jowly, rotund face, the curves of which were echoed by the shape of his belly, and with thick, dark hair slicked back over his head, walked slowly across the room towards them. He was wearing a dark suit with a maroon knitted tank-top beneath and a tie in a generous and well-formed knot. When he extended his hand in a cautious welcome Vignoles noticed that he wore an elegant and probably expensive watch. He fought down an irrational suspicion as to why such a man might have a watch worth a good fifteen pounds.

'Jozef Walentynowicz?'

The man nodded half-heartedly, in response.

'I'm Detective Inspector Vignoles and this is Sergeant Trinder, of the London and North Eastern...'

'Tak, tak. I know.' He waved his hand to signal Vignoles to stop his introduction. 'We expect you.' He promptly turned away, walked over to the stove and stood with his back to it between two wooden clothes horses draped with wet clothes. Pulling out a pack of cigarettes he proceeded to light one. He made no indication that his visitors should take a seat on one of a number of ill-assorted chairs around the kitchen table. Mrs Walentynowicz continued to work on the pastry with exaggerated diligence, but shot a glance across the table at the two detectives. The atmosphere grew oppressive in the dank, stinging, pungent air.

'We need to talk with you about the recent theft of coal from Finmere station by Miss Walentynowicz. As you know, this was not the first such time she has been caught taking coal and we have so far, shown leniency towards Katherina.'

'Katarzyna.'

Under the father's unflinching gaze, Vignoles was annoyed with himself for mispronouncing her name. 'Sorry, Katarzyna. But this cannot happen again. If there is a repeat, then make no mistake about it, we will refer the case to the juvenile courts.'

Jozef Walentynowicz smoked slowly and thoughtfully, staring at Vignoles with an expression the detective found hard to read. Perhaps he had not understood what had just been said? Then, leaving his cigarette in his mouth, he bent down and picked up a zinc bucket from beside the stove. It was filled with grey ash and pieces of clinker and he tipped it slightly forwards so that the contents were visible to the officers.

'Take it! We finish now. Haha!' He proffered the bucket of ash and grinned, the cigarette bouncing upon his lip as he talked and his eyes twinkling mischievously.

'Mr Walentynowicz, I do not think you are taking this seriously. Theft of coal — any theft — is a crime, and will not be treated as a laughing matter by a magistrate.'

'We freeze! You want that for us, eh?' He placed the bucket back on the floor. 'My family cold. Very cold. We must do something. Is warmer in prison, eh? My children are warmer there?' He shrugged and then started to walk towards the back of the room. 'Pffa!' He opened a side door. 'Katarzyna talk with you.' And with that he walked outside and slammed the door behind him, but not before Vignoles had caught sight of an axe resting on a large block of dark-coloured wood with fresh chippings surrounding it on the snow. He immediately realised what was producing the strange odour that filled the air: they were burning an old railway sleeper, which would of course be heavily impregnated with creosote. The realisation made his eyes sting even more sharply.

Vignoles turned towards the sullen girl and attempted a smile.

'Miss Walentynowicz, we are not here to be unpleasant, but we really do need to talk to you about what as happened. You must understand that, no matter how tough things are, you simply cannot take coal that is not yours.'

The room fell silent except for the occasional spit and crackle of the wood in the stove and a faint, wavering whistle of a distant train. Vignoles noticed that Trinder was walking around the room looking at the food tins on the cream-painted shelf unit beside the sink, occasionally lifting and inspecting one and in so doing attracting the sidelong glances of both women. The younger one shrugged and looked at the floor, pushed her hands into the cardigan she was wearing over her thin, blue gingham chequered dress. She had a narrow woollen scarf tied tightly around her neck. Her mother said something in a quiet but querulous voice that had a sad, high-pitched note to it. Her daughter rolled her eyes in response, but then fixed them upon Vignoles.

'What you want? That policeman told me it was wrong when he stop me. I was sorry and we give the coal back. So...?'

Vignoles found himself taken off-guard. He was not at all sure what he did want to say to this young woman. Major Duffy had initially implied that something rather more serious might be behind this incident and then appeared to retract the statement; so now here he was confronting an apologetic seventeen-year-old and feeling rather foolish. She was clearly no hardened criminal or racketeer.

He was startled out of his thoughts by Miss Walentynowicz speaking at him, her eyes flashing and the words issued staccato fashion as if from a gun. 'We need coal, wood, anything! We can pay you for coal. We have money — we're not stupid, poor peasants, you know!' She darted forward and pulled open a wooden drawer in the side of the kitchen table, from which she extracted a purse. 'Look! Here, we give you money for coal.' She held out a crisp ten-shilling note, 'this is enough for few bags, yes?'

'Oh no, we don't want your money.'

'You want more? OK, OK, I understand!' She was nodding in an exaggerated manner. 'We must pay double — anything just to keep us warm...' She started to tip some coins onto the table and a few dirty coppers rolled across into the fresh flour her mother had sprinkled on the surface. She was breathing hard, the anger boiling inside. Some strands of her hair escaped a pale blue clip that held it to one side of her face, the effect making her look even more wild and angry.

'Please stop! You misunderstand why we are here. We do not want anything from you. Put it away.' A silence fell.

'I'm sorry...' She suddenly looked contrite and glanced at the floor, her cheeks flushed. She seemed to deflate like a balloon. 'But we cannot even buy any coal. Don't you see?' Her voice was quieter, but still laced with emotion. 'We have money and yet we freeze! Everyday we see trains full of coal and none of it for us. It's crazy.' Her anger was burning itself out almost as quickly as it had flared up, soothed perhaps by her mother, who was now speaking softly and quickly, placing a hand on her daughter's shoulder as she did so. Mrs Walentynowicz continued in an imploring voice, looking at Vignoles, and he understood the meaning if not the words.

The inspector nodded and then smiled, hoping to diffuse the situation whilst still feeling acutely embarrassed. 'And I am sorry. The situation is very bad, I know. But I'm not from the Ministry of Fuel and Power and so I cannot discuss why coal is so scarce. But you must toe the line, just like the rest of us.' Vignoles paused and then tried a lame joke, 'We must all "Shiver with Shinwell and Starve with Strachey", it seems.' The two women stared blankly at him. 'The law is the law, and you must abide by it.' He coughed and turned as if to leave but stopped. 'And another thing; you should be careful about burning railway sleepers. The creosote on them is dangerous and the fumes could kill you.'

'It was old and the men were throwing it away.'

'I don't doubt that and I am not accusing you of theft, but it's really not good for fuel. It is highly poisonous...' Vignoles tailed off, realising that he had little to offer the family and wishing he were no longer there. Sergeant Trinder meanwhile had been continuing his circuit of the room and now attracted their attention by holding up a stack of cartons of Lucky Strike cigarettes.

'Who bought these?'

'Tata. Why?'

'It's an American brand. Not what I would expect.'

'The Yanks sell them. They sell anything.' She brushed the stray hair away from her face. 'Sometimes he even gives things away. He's nice like that and helps us a little.' She then muttered something in Polish that probably translated as 'unlike British policemen' and looked squarely at Trinder. 'Why is that wrong?' She spoke softly now, her anger all used up and her face displaying a tired sulkiness.

'He?' Trinder noticed the change from plural to singular.

'The man — the men, I don't know,' Miss Walentynowicz waved a hand dismissively. 'They are pilots or something.'

'I see. The same goes for the tins of meat, all marked U.S.A.F?'

No one answered and Trinder shrugged. Perhaps it was only fair that the American servicemen shared out some of their stores: they had plenty, by all accounts. 'Their very own version of "Lend-Lease", eh?'

'I don't understand.'

'Forget it. But as you say, they'll sell anything.' Sergeant Trinder carefully placed the cigarettes back and straightened up, taking a deep, weary breath as he did so and looking at Vignoles. 'I'm finished here.'

'We shall say good day to you. I very much hope we shall not have cause to meet again. If you make the mistake of taking any more coal, I am afraid we shall press charges. Put your trust in Major Duffy and his men and you'll get by. Just don't be tempted to take things that are not yours — please!'

Vignoles placed his hat back on his head and adjusted his scarf in preparation for the biting cold. With a final glance around the room and the two women watching him, he stepped outside.

Chapter Two

'CUANTO LE GUSTA'
Carmen Miranda & The Andrews Sisters

As Heather Spencer walked towards the gloomy booking hall at Banbury station, an express train travelling northwards thundered past in a stream of wailing steam. The engine's deep, Brunswick-green paint and shiny copper glinting in the pale light of the gas lamps complemented perfectly by the chocolate-and-cream coaches that trundled behind in a rattle and a rumble and a mist of snow kicked up by the back draught. As the express swept away beneath the road bridge, it left little clouds of almost iridescent steam that gently swirled and fragmented into ever-decreasing powder-puffs of white that magically dissolved into nothing in the dying embers of the winter afternoon.

Miss Spencer glanced at her watch and saw that she was optimistically early. She walked over to a narrow, round-arched window cut into the dark-wooded panelling of the ticket office, bending slightly so that she could speak to the woman behind the counter through the similarly-shaped hole cut in the glass.

The ticket clerk looked up at her approach: 'Can I help you?'

'I hope so. I am here to meet a lady who is travelling down from Nottingham. I wondered if the trains are delayed? And if so, when I might expect her?'

The ticket clerk smiled sympathetically and nodded. 'Nottingham, did you say? What time train did she take?'

'I have it here: I wrote down the times and the connections of her train on the back of an envelope.' Miss Spencer extracted a letter from her handbag and slid it under the little glass archway. The ticket clerk glanced at it for a few moments, looked at her wristwatch and frowned.

'I fear she may have missed her connection at Woodford. The trains running to London are all a bit delayed. But if you can wait a moment I shall just double-check.' With that she slid off her high, wooden chair and walked towards the back of the office. Miss Spencer was able to see her speaking to another woman, seated at a desk with a microphone placed at its centre, with a pile of timetables and papers surrounding her. The clerk nodded a few times in response to something the station announcer said, then returned to the window with her face set in an apologetic smile. Miss Spencer already knew that it was not going to be good news. 'Yes — as I feared — this beastly snow is causing the usual chaos. They're having all manner of problems today and her train — the London train — was awfully delayed.'

'But she will get through?'

'Oh gosh, yes!' the clerk winced sympathetically, 'she'll get here all right, don't you worry. She's at Woodford, that's my guess. With luck she will make the next connection.' The clerk checked her watch again. 'Hopefully she'll be on the six forty-five. Why not take a seat in the refreshment room? They have a jolly good fire going, as the local engine drivers like to give them a shovelful from their engines every few hours.' She grinned mischievously. 'But don't let on.'

'Mum's the word!'

'I can't promise they'll have much to offer, but the tea's good.' She gave another winning smile.

'Oh dear, I thought as much. You rather come to expect it, don't you? '

'What? The delays or the lack of food?'

'Both!'

The two women laughed.

'But I actually meant the delays to the trains.'

'She's a friend?'

'Yes. Vera is my very dearest friend. But we've not seen each other recently and I'm impatient for her to arrive.'

'It will all be forgotten once you get home, put the kettle on and sit down for a good natter. I'm sure you will have a lovely weekend.'

'Thank you, we shall.' Miss Spencer walked deeper into the decrepit building following a wooden sign with a pointing finger that indicated 'Refreshments & Ladies' Waiting Room'.

Banbury station was a rim place to contemplate spending any significant time in on a dark and raw evening such as this. The gas lamps dangling from the blackened wooden ceiling seemed to cast no light at all and only added to the sense that this was a building mired in years of sooty smoke and blackout paint. The now-rickety wooden construction had been designed by Brunel sometime in the very distant past, and might even have been considered grand in its day, but was now a sad and pathetic monument to the great engineer. It was slowly but surely rotting away, with some of the timber cladding missing, and what remained was ill fitting and inviting of draughts. The thick wooden supporting columns appeared to have been gnawed at their bases by huge rats, whilst there was a worrying list to some of the walls that created an odd sense of being off-balance or intoxicated. It could surely only be a matter of time before the whole train shed would collapse to one side in a heap of rotten timber. There were great, gaping holes in the canopy that spanned the running tracks, and what glass it once held had long since been removed, ensuring that it now provided ineffectual shelter from the bitter wind that seemed permanently to whistle along the platforms. Some of the porters would swear that the wind was whipped right off the Urals and straight down platforms one and two. The hunched passengers, standing there in their layers of coats and cardigans, hats and scarves, would not have disagreed.

Miss Spencer was grateful to find sanctuary inside the refreshment room, which did at least manage to present an appearance of faded glory, an effect enhanced by a cheerfully roaring fire and the smell of toast and hot soup. The walls were studded with enamelled signs advertising products now scarce or impossible to buy since rationing, whilst a radio glowed in the corner, playing something lively.

Well, if she had to spend a little longer waiting for Vera, then this was not such a bad place to do so, thought Heather Spencer. The tea was strong and she greedily set her eyes upon a solitary sugar cube that had been placed on the saucer with a wink by the pretty waitress. Such a small pleasure, and yet one that now had the ability to quite cheer the whole day. How she longed for the days to return when she might order a fresh cream cake or a sugary doughnut without inducing the incredulous laughter of those serving behind the counter.

She settled down in a deep leather chair and took out the paper. The song on the radio was something vivacious and cheering by Carmen Miranda, and it brought a whiff of a hot Mexican night into the room. Miss Spencer laid her paper on the table for the moment, sat back, took a sip of the sweetened tea and smiled to herself. Despite the rationing and the bitter winter, and even with the annoying delay to Vera's train, it was good to be alive.

❖　　❖　　❖　　❖

John Beeby was an odd man and was liked by few who met him. He was considered strange, or at least a bit peculiar, perhaps some even found him unsettling. He had no friends to speak of, and only one or two who would tolerate him occasionally for a cup of tea at the same table at lunch time or allow him to sit near them in a pub and bore them with his endless monologues on timetables and bus route changes until they could take no more and made excuses to leave.

What Beeby thought of his fellow workers, neighbours or those he met during his working day, was unknown, because no one ever bothered to ask him how he was nor sought his opinion on anything, with the one exception of using his impeccable memory of public transport timetables for their own convenience to save time looking them up themselves. Certainly Beeby liked things to be done in a very particular way, one which did not always sit comfortably with his fellow workers. He liked order, and had what might be considered an obsessive love of timetables. His collection stretched back many years and was carefully aligned in date order upon his bookshelves, and it was to these he looked to find order and direction in the chaotic world that surrounded him. Conversely, he detested any kind of delay or alteration to his plans. He was attentive to time and detail, using these twin guides like handrails as he made his way through the swaying, wavering uncertainties that assaulted him each day, and if despite his best laid plans and well-maintained wristwatch he was to miss the tram that he had pre-determined would take him to work, then he would be thrown into near panic, his equilibrium upset, and he would need time to revise his daily transport strategy.

He was a tradesman, a gas fitter, and there was plenty of work, in fact far too much, what with the many bomb-damaged premises to fix up and everything in a terrible shambles. Even working every hour of the day and night would never hope to meet the demand. He worked for a large company with contracts across Nottinghamshire, Leicestershire and even down into north Northamptonshire, and could be sent almost anywhere within this area, and so he always tried to plan his visits in advance and with meticulous detail, which always caused unkind amusement amongst the other men in the company. Well, they could laugh if they wanted, but his boss saw the benefit. Oh yes, Beeby was the star performer, meeting more deadlines than two of the other slackers combined.

Why? Because he planned his work carefully by plotting everything down to the last detail in his little notebooks.

But, of course, it didn't always work out like that. Other people were always doing unexpected things that got in the way of the smooth running and order of his life. Like calling in sick and forcing him to suddenly take over someone else's job, giving him little time to reorganise and plan his day. Why were people so thoughtless? Today was one of those annoying days, and he'd had a few near misses that morning. Two of his customers were not there when he arrived, making him wait to start work and threatening to throw his timetable into complete disarray. They blamed the weather, of course, but Beeby was smart and had factored delays to the trains into his planning. Why could no one else ever do this?

However, it was not just other people that upset his ordered world. He had been a bit foolish with regard to catching the London train and that had been down to his own over-confidence. He should be more careful as that glass of stout had nearly cost him dearly. Fortunately he had managed to jump onto the moving train, but it had shaken him up and he'd needed to compose himself for quite some time afterwards. However, his luck had held and it had turned into a *most* satisfying afternoon.

Beeby smiled to himself whilst looking deep into his reflection in the mirror above the sink in his bedroom, his hands unconsciously smoothing his shirt and feeling around his neck. That reminded him. Suddenly he pulled a face and turned away, rubbing his hands as if stained with a spot of some persistently sticky substance that refused to be rubbed away.

Something was wrong.

He felt an unease growing inside and realised that he was trying to avoid admitting that all was not as it should be. He wanted to savour the unexpected delight of the late afternoon, but instead he was becoming tense and his palms were sweating. He disliked this sensation, it made him feel dirty, and so despite the cold he ran some more icy cold water over them as he stared back into the mirror, peering through the rash of black spots in the silvered backing that made it look diseased, and into his own eyes. His breath clouded the glass. He needed a bath. But this was part of his problem: the bathroom was engaged. That Mr Blenkinsop was taking a bath and, as everyone who shared these digs knew, he usually took a good hour over his ablutions, despite the line painted low on the side of the tub in glossy red enamel that ensured your knees and most of your body remained exposed to the steamy chill of the bathroom air. But why was he taking a bath tonight? It was most odd. No, it was worse than odd; it was most inconvenient! All the lodgers had set times and days and Mrs Tipping was most particular that they adhered to them, so why was Mr Blenkinsop breaking the rules?

Beeby rubbed his hands together again, the soap hardly dissolving in the near-frozen water into the basin, and a gnawing sense of panic started to disturb his stomach. Then he remembered that he needed a shilling for the gas meter and he only had a two bob bit and a few tanners. Why had he not thought of that earlier? He felt another wrench in his tummy. Another mistake. There was nothing for it: he would have to go back outside and try to get change from the pub on the corner. He was now feeling angry and irritated as his routine was in severe danger of being irrevocably disrupted. It would spoil everything and render the whole *experience* with the girl pointless. He needed that bath to bring some warmth into his frigid little room then, with the lock turned in the door, he would have a mug of cocoa and then, and only then, could he allow himself to properly remember her.

He stomped out of his room, cursing silently. Oh, blast that irritating little man! Why is he in there? Beeby shot a lingering, hate-filled look at the closed bathroom door and the curls of steam that slipped beneath rendered yellow by the light of the single bulb inside. A sound of sloshing water and the tuneless singing of Mr Blenkinsop just reinforced the injustice of the situation. How could he make five inches of bath water last so long and sound so enjoyable? Beeby walked down the cramped stairs, his slow, heavy tread making each step creak despite the worn carpet, until he encountered his landlady, Mrs Tipping, in the hall.

'Is something bothering you, Mr Beeby?'

He stood stock-still and stared at her, his fingers digging into his palms, hoping the pain would keep the voices in his head at bay. He failed to answer her for a few moments and his silence seemed to stretch into an eternity marked out by the slow tick and clunk of the grandfather clock that loomed its dark presence over the two of them.

'Well? Cat got your tongue? You certainly seem out of sorts, I must say!' She had a sharp, penetrating voice that carried through the whole house.

'I, er, I was just thinking to have a bath, but Mr Blenkinsop seems to be doing so...'

'Of course he is. It's *Friday*. You *know* that Fridays are his night. You can't just go taking a bath just when you feel like it, Mr Beeby.' She stressed his name aggressively, 'Hot water costs a lot of money and the government are telling us to save power. I can't go letting you run hot water just when the fancy takes you. There is a routine, which you must stick to. And if you don't mind me saying, you seem to give yourself more than enough attention with those bars of soap you keep buying. Cleanliness is to be applauded, but I do think you exaggerate.'

She gave him a harsh look and a sudden sniff that barely concealed her disapproval, deliberately inhaling a whiff of the scent that was oozing from Beeby to reinforce her point. 'And soap is getting scarce. You should do your duty and moderate your use.'

But Beeby was not listening. Friday? How could he have got it so wrong? He had somehow thought it was Thursday — his bath night. But of course; he had taken a bath last night, and yet somehow, with all the alterations to his day and then striking so lucky on the train, he had got muddled. He'd seen his chance, acted upon impulse and really not thought it through. Acting on impulse was something he almost never allowed to happen. He despised people who did that kind of thing. He swayed on his feet and rubbed his brow.

'Are you all right? You seem to have quite taken a funny turn.' Mrs Tipping stared at him without a trace of kindliness and more from a fear that he might be sick upon her carpet.

'I, er...oh.. no. I am fine, Mrs Tipping. A long day, that's all. I just need to get a breath of air and a shilling for the meter.' He forced a smile.

'You are a strange fish. Well, you make sure you get yourself right. I can't be doing with people being ill in my house. Have you been drinking?'

But Beeby's mind was spinning and he virtually sleepwalked his way out of the house and along the narrow pathway of cleared snow on the pavement towards the pub. The gas lamps were glowing with a pretty halo of frosty light. A car swished and crunched along the road, its yellow headlamp beams illuminating Beeby. His eyes were dazzled momentarily and he stopped in his tracks.

It was all ruined. Here he was, back in the raw night air looking for a shilling change and no chance of a bath for another week. He continued to walk, forgetting to enter the pub, his slow and heavy footsteps pulling him forwards, one foot after the other. He watched his shoes break through the crust of frost and find a secure footing on the treacherous pavement. He kept his pace regular, refusing to allow any deviation in the metronomic precision of his stride. He sought calmness through this regularity and by pushing the nails on his scrubbed-raw fingers into his palms, the pain helping keep his demons at bay.

He needed to review the afternoon's events: if he had got such a thing as the day of the week wrong then perhaps he really had done worse and made a graver error of judgement? And now the handbag would have to go. Perhaps he should not risk keeping anything. He stared at the many footprints embossed in the snow on the pavement as he strode onwards along dim streets shrouded in a feint, frozen mistiness.

Perhaps he might allow just one small item. It would be such a waste otherwise. But was it too much of a risk? Could he be sure that Mrs Tipping didn't poke around his things when he was out? He stopped walking for a few moments and wiped his brow, which was clammy, despite the cold. In doing so, he looked at his handkerchief and that reminded him of yet another problem that was worrying him: his missing neckerchief.

He walked long into the night, a solitary figure in a dark overcoat with hands pushed deep into the pockets, head down, hat brim pulled forward as if to shade his eyes from the weak lamplight. His pace was even and measured like the slight puffs of mist from his breathing. His focussed progress and ration-defying plumpness exuded a sense of calm and normality that he did not feel, but rendered Beeby all but invisible and unmemorable to any other passer-by still outside in that unwelcoming Nottingham night.

✳   ✳   ✳   ✳

Heather Spencer was now feeling a mixture of frustration and growing concern. Vera had still not arrived and it was now quite ridiculous to even think that she would before morning. The last connecting train from Woodford Halse had long since arrived and departed. It had been all but empty, except a tall and desiccated elderly man. Miss

Spencer had plucked up the courage to speak to him. Had he seen her at Woodford? Perhaps she had been sitting on the opposite platform and missed the train? But he had quietly pointed out that Woodford had been deserted, and with just two platforms to choose from and helpful staff to advise, it was highly improbable that her friend had missed the last train. With a sinking heart she watched him walk away. A stranger, and yet he had seemed like a tiny glimmer of hope, linking her to Vera on that distant station. But now he was walking away and leaving only a deeper sense of darkness and emptiness.

The refreshment room had long closed, but the ladies' waiting room at least had a fire of sorts and would remain open all night, though it was deserted. Miss Spencer sat alone on a padded and buttoned leather bench, a copy of *Picture Post* on her lap, and tried again to re-read the same stories. She looked without really seeing, at photographs of Princess Elizabeth and Prince Philip of Greece and read the story of their blossoming romance. She sighed, tossed it to one side, flung her head back, stared at the ceiling for a few moments then closed her eyes. She really didn't want to count how many hours she had been there. And where was her friend?

Miss Spencer tried to think of possible explanations, her mind running through each variation time and again, hoping that one would satisfy sufficiently to calm her nerves. She must have missed the Woodford Halse stop and continued on the train to a later station and only then, realising her mistake, got off at — who knows where? She had then probably found that there was no connection back to Banbury. That had been the analysis offered to Miss Spencer by the friendly ticket clerk. One of the porters had also suggested much the same and had tried to encourage her to return to her home, offering that if she left a telephone number they would call through if her friend arrived before morning. She had not wanted to leave, however, and she had no telephone number to offer. She just could not believe that Vera would not step off one of the now worryingly infrequent trains that huffed and clanged and whistled their way into the station.

To make matters worse, Miss Spencer began to imagine that Vera had, by some accident of fate, managed to get on a train that stopped at the small Merton Street station situated alongside the main Great Western station that she was presently waiting in. She had wasted energy dashing across to this odd little building with its curved wooden roof on the infrequent occasions that a train had arrived. This served only to make her colder and her feet wetter and to increase her sense of frustration. Trains at Merton Street were sad little local affairs and all were disconcertingly empty of passengers. Knowing nothing about railways, she did not really understand why two stations sat side by side in this way, but presumed it had something to do with what railway company owned it. What she did know was that it was all very confusing and inconvenient.

Back at the main station there were still trains passing, but her optimism was repeatedly dashed by discovering that these seemed always to be from Paddington or Bristol, Oxford or Birkenhead or some other place that — according to the chirpy porter — it was apparently impossible for Vera to have transferred onto.

Miss Spencer had even telephoned Vera's fiancé, Dennis Ferens, from the cubicle in the booking hall to see if he had heard from her, but he was not at home and his landlady had been terse and unhelpful. This just increased her feelings of isolation and insidious worry. She toyed with the idea of trying to call Vera's parents, but she remembered that they also had no telephone and relied upon their neighbours, whose names she could not remember; in any case, it was now past eleven-thirty and far too late to disturb them. This would just needlessly worry them, as surely they could not possibly know what station Vera was stranded upon.

There was nothing for it. She really would have to return home and try to get some sleep. Then, refreshed, she would come back bright and early the next day. Yes, tomorrow is another day, and it will all work out for the best. Miss Spencer adjusted her coat, re-wrapped her scarf and braced herself for the long walk home as she crossed the dim booking hall and went out into the night. Outside, the frost was sparkling on the ground like millions of tiny diamonds.

And as she made her lonely way home, at that very moment in distant Marylebone station, a railway porter whistled a tuneless melody, drained his enamelled mug of the last of his tea and collected the two items of lost luggage that had been handed in earlier that evening. The small travelling case and umbrella were both old, but of decent quality and well cared for; they would be sorely missed by their owner. He had placed them in the porters' office earlier, but they had nagged at his conscience as he had drunk his tea so he decided that before his shift finished he would lock them away in the lost property office, where they belonged. The stationmaster would only give him ear-ache over the matter if he didn't. He barely glanced twice at the case and its neatly-written luggage label that bore the inscription: Miss. V. Harding, 12 Formarke Road, Nottingham.

Chapter Three

'JACK, YOU'RE DEAD'
Louis Jordan & his Tympany Five

Reginald Stevenson was walking the line near Catesby Tunnel. He was checking that the many rods and pulley wheels that operated the signals and points were not clogged by snow and ice and that the oil lamps were still burning behind their coloured glass windows at the top of the signal posts. It was cold and bitter work and his hands and feet ached constantly as a consequence. He'd worked on the railway most of his fifty-six years and he'd never known it so bad. Maybe it was his age, but he was really feeling the cold this evening.

The sky had been like a sheet of zinc all day, both featureless and oppressive, and the iron-hard ground was jarring his knees and ankles as he trudged slowly beside the running lines. Now it was dark, though the snow gave off a strange, otherworldly glow that at least made it easier for him to see where he was walking. Every few feet, Stevenson swung his long-handled hammer to shake the snow from the little pulley wheels that guided the signal wires. Sometimes he had to stop and give them an extra whack and a dollop of glutinous oil from the pot he held in his other hand. The oil was really getting too viscous in the cold and needed a warm-up beside a friendly fire. So did he.

He stopped and looked along the line at the distant, twinkling red light of a signal. It was not so far now until Charwelton. The awful, dark depths of the tunnel were behind him and pretty soon he could seek warmth and respite at the station and pass an hour or so thawing out along with his oil pot. He smiled: the thought of a round of toast and some tea cheered him. But he was used to the long and arduous hours and even the solitude was not really oppressive. In fact he rather enjoyed the periods of time when it was just himself, the railway lines and the birds and animals in the fields. As if on cue, a barn owl screeched in the distance, its eerie voice carrying across the snowfields.

Stevenson approached the signal and looked up at the tall post and the icy metal ladder that led to the tiny platform that gave access to the lamp and the mechanism that tipped the signal to 'clear' and back to 'danger'. Leaving his long-handled hammer at the base, he pushed the carrying handle of the oil pot further along his left arm and started to climb. It was slippery and the air immediately seemed to feel even rawer as he ascended the treacherous rungs.

'Hell's bells, can it really get any flipping colder?' He puffed out clouds of white steam as he hauled his stiff limbs into action. 'Bloody hell!' he cursed out loud as his foot slipped and banged his shinbone on the unforgiving ladder. 'I should have been a bloody signalman. Bloody cushy job on a night like this, sitting in a warm bloody signal box, whilst mugs like me do the real work!' He vented his annoyance to the surrounding fields and the owl screeched as if in reply. He then managed a smile at the oddity of that and leant against the narrow metal rail around the platform, gently easing his feet into a safer position and scraping the thick rime of frost from the wooden floor with his boots. He dabbed oil onto the signal mechanism, careful to keep his hand away from the joints and cranks in case the signalman moved the lever and set it into motion.

Despite his cursing, Stevenson actually rather liked signals. He liked the way they clanged into position and how the wires would fizz and twitch beside the tracks as they were pulled. There was something reassuring and calming about these intricate wires and pulleys and the twinkling lamps and the jutting arms. The fact that a man somewhere distant animated the signals gave them a strangely human aspect. They were almost alive and able to reach far down this deserted, snow-filled line and direct the movements of trains. Though the signalman could not see nor hear Stevenson as he stood on his precarious, crow's-nest of a perch, they were nevertheless connected.

He waited to see if the signal would move and that his oiling had indeed kept the mechanism working. Looking down the line into the murky distance, Stevenson could just discern the soft billows and folds of the steam of an approaching train, for even in the dark of that night the snow seemed to make the steam luminous. The beat of its exhaust started to hammer across the open fields, reverberating and echoing on the resonating ground. He cocked his head and listened for the little fluttering sound of the wires, then watched as the cranks smoothly started into action and the arm raised towards the sky, clanging and then bouncing briefly before coming to rest.

The approaching train was now much louder, its syncopated swing-beat first colliding with its own echo in a confusing jumble, but then finding a complex counterpoint that ricocheted like a machine gun. Stevenson remained where he was, for he enjoyed the drama of a passing train when perched high above the ground on this land-locked crow's nest. It would be frowned upon by his boss, but he'd spent enough years on the line to know what he was doing. Anyway, it was a small pleasure and in this searing cold any tiny joy was to be seized upon.

The engine was cocooned in white steam and pushing a jet of exhaust high into the sky before it tumbled down way over to one side to lie like a blanket of fog over a huddle of sheep. Reg could tell that it was a passenger train from the pools of warm yellow light that spilled onto the bright reflective ground, touching the smooth undulations of the snow with gold. It was good to see the carriage lights liberated like this after so many years of blackout. It was an attractive engine on the front, but it looked too small for the massive train it was hauling, though its six-coupled wheels gamely pounded the track and made the signal post shake as it passed. The train was incredibly long and looked full to bursting. Stevenson wondered that they could not have drafted in a larger engine for the job. He tried to read the nameplate and thought it might have been 'Hartebeest'.

He watched as carriage after carriage trundled below, the windows affording him a perfect view of the many dozing servicemen and women inside and of a sleeping family with a child nestling against each parent; businessmen travelling first class were smoking cigars with sheaves of papers on the table between them and he could see that the corridors were crammed with trunks and cases and standing passengers smoking beside the small, open windows. He tried to count the carriages and reckoned there were fifteen, at least. The yellow light spilling out of the windows dipped and fell across the snow and, as Stevenson looked towards the rear of the train, caused him to suddenly narrow his eyes and peer harder at something that caught his attention beside the track some distance away.

It was hard to say what it was and the passing lights were all too brief to give him a good view, but he was intrigued. He was unsure how he had even spotted it, but years of walking the line had made him alert to anything out of the ordinary and his perfect eyesight had caught a flash of something lying there.

The things people threw off trains. He'd seen all sorts in his time — not all of it pleasant, either. The rubbish people seemed to feel compelled to jettison with no thought to the railwaymen who had to pick it up! To be fair, he'd found a fair amount of money as well — loose change mainly, but a ten-bob note and even a pound on one occasion. But whatever this was, this was something bigger than usual. Probably just a branch of a tree bent low by snow, but he'd check it out as it looked close to the signal wires and that was never good.

As the last wisps of smoke and steam curled around him, he eased down the ladder and back onto the ground. He clicked his lamp back on. The long years of working in the total darkness of the blackout had so improved his night vision that he only used this when there was something needing detailed inspection or when negotiating a tunnel. The beam swung across the snow as he walked and he flicked it repeatedly towards the object of his interest. At first Stevenson still continued to check each set of pulley wheels as he advanced, but as he came closer his attention was drawn completely away from his work. He felt his breathing quicken and his leaden legs started to move in a stumbling trot. He squinted to resolve the image more clearly and then having done so, wished that his eyes had fooled him and that it would just turn into a fallen limb of a tree.

But there could be no mistake. He was only a few yards away, and brilliantly illuminated by his lamp were a pair of human legs rising, bizarrely and improbably, from the smooth and undisturbed snow. It was a woman, and from the position she was lying in she must be unconscious — or worse — after a fall from the train. She was on her back, and her head and torso were pitched steeply downwards into a deep drift of snow filling a ditch at the side of the running line, leaving only her legs sticking up and out of the snow in a most inappropriate manner. He put down his hammer and oil can and sprinted forwards with long, heavy strides, all tiredness suddenly lifting from his limbs. He stopped short and stared down at her, his lamplight caressing her legs, which were thrown apart by the fall, her stockings clearly visible up her thighs, her dress and petticoat raised to her hips in thick folds. Stevenson flicked the light away and pulled back in shock. He didn't want to look and yet he found himself unconsciously drawn again to follow the line and curves of her legs to the dark shadow beneath her scrunched-up dress, then up her body until the snow that had tumbled upon her formed a slight mound and obscured his view of her face.

He squeezed his eyes shut for a moment then re-opened them, a tightness starting to form in his gut. 'Miss?' His voice was just a croak and he needed to cough to clear his throat. He tried again and louder, 'Miss! Are you all right?'

But he knew that she was not, and with his head pounding and starting to spin he edged closer and peered towards her face, reaching forwards to shake one of her arms that had been flung wide onto the drift. He frowned and his breathing stopped. The snow was oddly dark and stained and disturbed by numerous small indentations that formed crazy patterns and marks upon the otherwise virginal snow. 'Oh, Jesus! No, no!'

He recoiled backwards and stared up into the leaden night sky, hoping to erase the image burnt into his eyes, welcoming the harsh coldness that seemed to scour his eyeballs. He then screwed them shut in a vain attempt to eradicate the sight. The head of the young woman was thrown back with her hair rolling in thick drifts on either side, her hat long gone. A scarf gagged her mouth. But it was not even this distressing sight that made Stevenson fight to keep the nausea down, it was that her eyes had been violently removed, leaving bloody sockets and dried rivulets of blood down her cheeks to form pink blooms of colour in the snow like a garland of funeral flowers.

'Jesus, Joseph, Mary and all the saints preserve us.' He turned and stepped a few paces away, glanced once more at the terrible sight and then vomited into the snow. He stood bending over with his hands on his thighs and gulped in some keen air, eyes screwed shut. After a few moments he stood up, steadied himself and made the sign of the cross.

The poor woman needed attending to. That she was dead he knew was obvious and that she had lain there undiscovered for some time seemed evident. He needed to alert the authorities immediately, but most important of all, right now, she could not be allowed to lie there exposed to the world, humiliated and degraded beyond what she had already suffered.

He thought first to move her body, but then stopped himself, realising that the police would want to see her exactly as he had found her. But she must be covered. He didn't care what they said: it was not right to leave her like that. He looked around him in a futile search that revealed only snow and gleaming railway lines, and so he unbuttoned his heavy overcoat. He was but a few miles away from Charwelton station and calculated that if he kept up a quick enough pace he should be able to get there before hypothermia set in.

He spread the coat carefully and respectfully over her face and body, pulling it as far over her legs as it would go. Then he started to move in a lumbering jog, his heavy, hobnailed boots swinging in loping strides towards sanctuary, happy to put as much distance as he could between himself and the terrible sight.

Chapter Four

'I DON'T KNOW ENOUGH ABOUT YOU'
Peggy Lee

Vignoles was awakened from a deep sleep by the telephone ringing in the hallway downstairs. He opened his eyes and stared, unseeing, into the pitch black of the bedroom for a few moments as he tried to place where he was. His mind swam back towards reality, reluctantly letting go of a blissful dream of eating a huge roast goose with all the trimmings. He groped a hand across to his bedside table and clicked on the lamp. The bulb was weak and almost ineffectual, but perversely it now felt glaring in its sudden intensity. The telephone meanwhile continued to ring downstairs. It could only be police business, as they knew to keep ringing until he finally answered.

Anna stirred beside him under the weight of two blankets and the thick counterpane that each night threatened to either smother them or keep them snug — twin objectives that were never quite fully met. She mumbled something and Vignoles gently kissed her forehead by way of reply and in little more than a whisper advised her to stay sleeping. She gave a slight smile and snuggled back into the escape of sleep. He felt a pang of envy, then swung his legs out of the bed and searched for his slippers as the intense cold in the room jarred him awake. There was the scent of damp in the air, ever present since the weather started to turn chilly back in November. Wrapping his paisley-patterned dressing gown around him, he switched off the bedside lamp and made his way across the pitch-black room, felt around the bedroom door for the brown Bakelite switch of the landing light, then descended the thickly-carpeted stairs, remembering to avoid the penultimate step, which always squeaked unpleasantly and which he always promised Anna that he would fix — one day.

He picked up the phone, steeling himself for what was coming. If the call could not wait until morning then it would be something serious.

'Yes?'

'Detective Inspector Vignoles? I have a call from the L.N.E.R. police department. Do you wish to accept it?' The clear, clipped pronunciation of the operator was strangely calming.

'Yes, thank you.'

The line clicked and a man's voice urgently cut in.

'Sir?' The voice continued without waiting for the obvious affirmation. 'Sorry to disturb you, inspector, but we have a body. Beside the track near Charwelton.' It was P.C. Blencowe, who was on the night watch in the office at Leicester Central station.

'Ah... Oh dear. What circumstances?'

'A young woman. She must have fallen off a moving train.'

'Fell? Any more information?'

'I've not got the full details, but actually it seems possible that she was thrown off.'

Vignoles took a sharp inhalation of breath, 'Why do you say that?'

'From the way she's lying in the snow.' He stopped for a moment. 'But actually sir, there's something else...' Blencowe's voice had a strained edge to it.

'Go on.'

'The man who found her, well, he was in a bit of a state by all accounts, and of course I can only tell you what he said as it was retold to me by the stationmaster at Charwelton and he was also a bit sleepy on account of his being woken up so early and so I can't be sure that what I am saying is correct, but...'

'Yes, yes, Blencowe, get on with it, man — what are you trying to tell me?'

'She's been mutilated.' He paused. 'Her eyes have gone.'

A brief silence fell again, with just the quiet tick of the mantle clock in the parlour and a few whirrs and clicks along the telephone line. Vignoles could not hear, but sensed the presence of the operator listening in on the line. He could imagine her horrified expression. He coughed lightly, and the small click that followed immediately revealed that she had disconnected herself from this shocking conversation.

'Gone?' he continued, not referring to the eavesdropping operator.

'That's what he told me. Blood everywhere. A horrible sight, apparently. It's quite shaken him up. The man who found her, that is.'

'I presume a doctor has confirmed all this?'

'Yes. I believe they roused a local man from Charwelton and he confirmed her dead.'

'I'm coming straight over. Call Sergeant Trinder and get

him in double-quick time. We'll rendezvous at Leicester and travel on to Charwelton together. In the meantime, get back onto the stationmaster and tell him to detain whoever found the body. Do we know who it was?'

'A Mr Stevenson. He's a lengthman.'

'Tell him to stay put until we arrive.'

Vignoles replaced the receiver, all feelings of tiredness blown away by the news. He walked into the dining room, turned on the light and walked across to a set of low bookshelves. These were their latest acquisition, made of pale wood in a new and stylish design, and he reached for his well-thumbed copy of the Bradshaw timetable and another weighty book on the top shelf that detailed goods' workings. Sitting at the angular dining table — yet another recent investment — Vignoles quickly skimmed through the pages, occasionally glancing up at the wall clock. He made a few notes of train times on the back of an envelope that had brought his latest corporation rates bill, and then closed the books. He stopped and stared pensively at the curtains drawn across the windows for a moment, then quickly took the unpaid rates bill out of the envelope, flipped it over and wrote a quick note to his wife. He propped this against the vase filled with dried, everlasting flowers that Anna had picked last summer and went back upstairs to dress.

✻   ✻   ✻   ✻

A few hours later, Vignoles and Trinder were drinking much-needed mugs of tea in the guard's van of a milk train that was giving a decent impression of racing towards London. With flakes of snow still falling and the sky heavily laden with dark clouds, dawn had failed to bring any cheer to what promised to be a difficult morning. Both men were hungry and longing for a hearty breakfast, but that prospect seemed a long way off. The guard was a quiet, self-contained man who seemed to take the presence of the two officers in his van with unhurried equanimity. He had simply spoken to the driver in advance of starting away from Leicester Central about their un-timetabled stop along the line near Charwelton water troughs, and then said and done little else. Vignoles was glad that the guard was not pestering him with questions that he would not have been able to answer, even had he been willing so to do.

Vignoles always tried to prepare himself in advance of visiting a crime scene rather as an athlete might concentrate his mind before a race; focussing on all the angles and questions that the scene might raise. He took the time he had now to remind himself about some of the small details and surprising facts that had later helped him solve previous cases, and in so doing he was, with any luck, sharpening his sleep-dulled senses and quickening his deductive powers. As it was, with the early hour of his rising and the gentle swaying of the van as it trailed behind the speeding train, he felt himself now in danger of being lulled to sleep.

He glanced across at Sergeant Trinder, who was also manfully attempting to fight off sleep as he sat on one of the hard wooden benches that ran the length of the side of the van. Trinder's head would droop and nod forwards, then he would snatch his head upright and open his eyes in surprise, but his vacant expression gave the game away. The now almost-empty enamel mug of tea slowly slipped from Trinder's grip and clattered to the floor, making the sergeant start.

'Eh?' He looked around blearily, then down at the mug on the wooden floor and the small pool of tea. 'Sorry. Must have dropped off.'

Vignoles grinned at Trinder, pleased for the wake-up jolt it had also given him and took this as a cue to stand up and stretch. Catching the guard's attention, he asked how much further they had to go.

'Not far now. We're just approaching Catesby Tunnel. You want dropping on the far side, is that right?'

'That's the information we have. Two men should be guarding the spot and they'll give lamp signals for us to stop. The body should be covered up.' Vignoles added the last statement in answer to the long look that the guard gave him.

'It's a dreadful thing that she's just lying there... makes you wonder.' The guard gave no further indication of what he was wondering, and none was needed.

'The dark has at least helped on that score.' Trinder had also stood up and was yawning.

'Then at least we can thank the winter for something.' Vignoles rubbed his hands together near the little stove in the corner, trying to absorb some of the welcome heat it offered. The van however was suddenly filled with a sharp blast of icy air as the guard stepped out on to the small veranda at the far end and peered along the train for a better view. He ducked back inside and pulled the door closed.

'Here we go, guv'nor, Catesby.'

He suddenly grinned and moved over to join Vignoles beside the stove. 'She seems to be steaming well, so we'll be out of it in no time; doesn't pay to get stuck in a tunnel at the back end. Like Dante's blinkin' inferno, it is.'

At that moment, before Vignoles had time to wonder whether he was surprised at the guard's literary reference or not, the sound of the train suddenly changed and they were slammed by a shockwave of air. The noise levels rose sharply and the percussion beat of the engine started to echo and reverberate all around. The pale, dawn light was easily snuffed out, heightened by the curls of choking smoke that started to ease their way under the doors and swirl around the wooden cabin. Vignoles could feel the sulphur on the back of his tongue and the sharp, pungent smell of coal that pricked at his nose and stung his eyes; the whole effect was alarming, with the train roaring and screaming as it progressed ever deeper under the ground. It was a strange and disorientating feeling with nothing visible beyond the windows, trapped in a rocking and jolting wagon filled with smoke and assaulted by hammer-blows of sound. The guard was correct; Dante could have found similarities to his vision of hell.

But Vignoles was surprised to feel exhilarated by the elemental violence of the experience. He thought about what it must be like upon the semi-open footplate of the locomotive, where everything would sound so much louder and the brick lining of the tunnel passing just an arm's length away from the men standing and swaying there. Despite the grimness of the task that lay ahead at the other end of the tunnel, he found himself grinning and resolved to ride the footplate of an engine one day and to repeat the journey.

After a few minutes the sounds diminished and the sickly, dawn light reappeared as they exited the tunnel in a swirl of grey and white smoke, accompanied by a long note upon the whistle. The engine shortly afterwards sounded two short 'crows' that Vignoles assumed to be an acknowledgement of a hail from the trackside. The guard stepped back onto the veranda with Vignoles and Trinder following, and by leaning over the side they could discern a red lamp being waved from side to side far ahead by one of two black figures etched against the white snow. The train was slowing, and one of the loco crew was looking back down the train at the guard, who was acknowledging the signal with his hand.

Once the train had hissed to a halt, the two detectives stepped briskly down onto the trackside. Vignoles looked up and thanked the guard, who silently nodded in acknowledgement but did not glance towards the covered shape lying nearby. He quickly waved his green flag for the train to restart. The plume of white exhaust towered forty, maybe fifty feet up in a great mushroom cloud above the white landscape as the engine hissed, whooshed and barked into motion, raising a cloud of starlings from a nearby tree. The beat of the exhaust echoed across the land long after it had steamed into the distance, whilst Vignoles and Trinder walked towards the two figures beside the track.

One was a uniformed railway policeman and the other was from the permanent way department. The latter held a red lamp and wore an armband marked 'Lookout'. Both were wrapped up in heavy overcoats, but looked pale, perhaps not just from the bitter cold.

The policeman stepped forward and saluted Vignoles, who returned it. 'Morning, sir.' Both detectives had already seen the blanket spread over a lump on the ground some little way beyond and the policeman stepped aside as Vignoles walked briskly past. The railwayman said nothing, but gave an almost imperceptible nod and then just stared at the ground. Two big crows started cawing in the bare branches of a nearby tree, setting off others in the surrounding fields, their creaking calls seesawing backwards and forwards across the railway tracks like an echo.

Trinder stood beside Vignoles and they took a few moments to take in what lay before them. Vignoles had drilled into his sergeant the importance of approaching a crime scene methodically and patiently, trying to absorb every little detail and careful to not disturb any tell-tale marks on the ground. Heavy footprints, presumably those of Stevenson, already disturbed the snow around the body, but these were thankfully few in number.

Vignoles was the first to speak. 'Tell me: the two of you approached the body to lay the blanket over her?'

'Yes, sir. She had a coat already lying over, but we thought the blanket was better. But we tried to step into the footprints already there and to not disturb the snow too much. The doctor did the same.'

Vignoles nodded, 'So, there were footprints here when you arrived?'

'Yes, but just the one set. We stayed as far away as was possible. It felt more decent, if you know what I mean?' The constable was nervous and shifted his weight from one booted foot to another, his pale face blotched pink around his nose, his eyes watery from the cold.

Trinder stood up after inspecting a few marks in the snow, 'It certainly looks like she was thrown or maybe pushed from a train. There is so little disturbance in the snow around and she looks nearly buried in the drift.'

'It's as if she fell from a height and at some speed. Ready? Let's lift the blanket.' Vignoles stepped forward, careful to place his feet in the deep depressions already formed by other feet. He noticed that both the constable and the lookout man cast apprehensive glances towards them, but then turned to look away down the line. Vignoles felt a knot in his stomach and, with a nod from Trinder, they lifted and pulled back the blanket, careful to loft it high over the body.

'Oh, dear God!'

Trinder spoke softly but with passion. Vignoles just sucked icy cold air in through his teeth, welcoming the fresh, stinging sensation into his body, drinking in its purifying coldness and hoping that by holding this inside he would somehow cauterise the effects of the sight before him.

Her skin was now of the palest alabaster and lightly veined with pale blue. She looked so very cold and dead and still that there could be no question of a flicker of life left within. She almost looked like a sculpture, a stone impression of a living being, and yet one that despite the best efforts of the brilliantly gifted sculptor, lacked life or vitality. The effects of the profound cold were only heightened by her shocking state of undress and her legs that splayed across the snowdrift.

'I fear that this poor girl has been raped. The post-mortem will confirm that, of course.'

Trinder nodded grimly, his jaw set firmly closed. The two men were momentarily taken aback by the brutal image that met their gaze, but this was soon overridden by another wave of revulsion as they looked at her face and the gag that cruelly blocked her mouth, and the two deep, bloody wells that once contained her eyes.

'What the hell? Oh, that's just horrible! Just awful...' Trinder was shaking his head slowly, visibly shocked.

'This is a terrible business.' Vignoles looked upwards for a few moments to compose himself, then turned back to look more closely. 'And very strange.' He approached the body with another step and bent forwards, looking at the snow around her head. His feelings of initial revulsion were now replaced by professional curiosity. As he did so, the crows suddenly launched themselves into the air in a loud commotion of flapping and cawing, sweeping across the empty cutting and wheeling around and behind. Vignoles turned and watched the sinister birds filling the air with their beating black wings. He then stood upright and addressed his sergeant.

'John, I think that the loss of her eyes has nothing to do with why she is lying here. She could have been gagged and raped and thrown here to die, or was raped and killed and then dumped from a moving train, yes?' He met Trinder's eyes, and he nodded in agreement. 'But after she hit the ground and lay dead — for there are no signs that she moved once here — then, and only then I believe, did she lose her eyes.'

'So someone came along afterwards and did that? This is even more sickening.' Trinder looked angry.

'Yes, but it was not a person and quite possibly not just the one, either.' Vignoles looked around and then fixed his gaze on four of the ragged black birds now staring intently down at them from a wooden fence at the top of the embankment.

'There you have your culprits. Hungry carrion crows.'

*   *   *   *

'Oh dear, is there nothing you can do? No one you could call?' Heather Spencer was trying to fight back a feeling of mounting panic and her eyes were starting to prick, threatening to stream tears at any moment. The young ticket clerk shook her head slowly and pulled an apologetic smile just as she had done at least twice before that morning. 'I'm sorry, I know I am making an awful nuisance of myself and you must be sick of the sight of me.'

'Not at all...'

'I just don't know what to do next. It's so unlike her to be late and to not find some way of getting a message through.' She extracted a small handkerchief from her handbag and dabbed the corners of her eyes, 'But as you say, the trains are so awfully delayed and then maybe she is at some station somewhere... but it just feels all wrong.'

The ticket clerk looked at her whilst she was speaking, furrowing her brow in thought whilst placing a forefinger to her lips for a moment. 'I'm also a bit concerned because actually, the trains are not that delayed — just an hour or so, certainly not all night. And you said it was yesterday evening that you were expecting her?'

'Yes, that's right. It's been simply hours and hours. I have even tried to call her fiancé, but he was out on business or something last night and was still away this morning. I keep leaving messages with his landlady. I'm even thinking to call her parents, but I'm reluctant to do so in case I alarm them. Her mother is not in the best of health, and anyway she would never have gone to their house instead of here — that would mean she never left Nottingham. Oh, gosh, sorry, I'm rambling.' Miss Spencer dabbed her eyes again.

'No need to apologise, dear. I quite understand. This is a bit odd. I shall go and speak to the stationmaster. Ordinarily I would not trouble him over a matter not directly concerning his own station, but I feel this needs his attention,' the clerk paused. 'I wonder if perhaps we should alert the police?'

'The police? You don't think that something very awful has happened?'

'Oh, goodness, no. I am sure your friend is all right, it's just...' she paused, looking for an explanation, '...that she's had an accident or something. Slipped in the snow and broken an arm — we've had a few of those recently — and we just need some help to track down her whereabouts.'

'Yes, that will be it.' Miss Spencer seized upon this suggestion eagerly. 'It makes so much sense now you say it. I don't mind betting that she's sitting in a hospital being a thorough bore with everyone. Vera is a terrible patient, the absolute limit.' She now managed a smile.

'My thoughts exactly. Come along, I shall take you to Mr Roberts, the stationmaster.'

Chapter Five

'BLUES IN THE NIGHT'
Woody Herman & the Band that plays the Blues

Edward Earnshaw walked briskly across the treacherous yard, the ground only dimly illuminated by the yard lamps, whose diet of poor town gas produced little more than a pale and flickering light, though they did pick out the silent fall of flakes of snow like bonfire ash kicked up in a wind. The snow already collected upon the ground reflected some of this weak light, but as it was now thoroughly stained black by filth and mire it offered but a slight enhancement.

He carefully placed each booted foot in the prints of those who had walked before him but still felt for any hidden obstacles, of which there were many, and was careful to avoid the raised running rails and the deep inspection pits sunk between them. He had seen too many colleagues break a leg or twist an ankle to make the foolish mistake of trying to cross this terrain at anything more than a quick walking pace, despite the urgent call to arms from the shedmaster.

Five minutes earlier he had been seated on a battered, metal-framed chair inside the indescribably filthy bothy used by the loco crews at Leicester South shed. It was not a place for the faint-hearted. The air inside this poor little building was thick with cigarette smoke and the odour of unwashed bodies, laced with the tang of sulphurous coal smoke and the heavy taste of engine and machine oils. The only relief was an ancient radio blackened by many dirty hands, which sat on a shelf in the corner tuned into *Variety Bandbox* and a melody by Bert Ambrose and his Orchestra brought a much-needed cheer to the miserable little room. A wooden table stained with layers of tea and milk, smears of grease and yet more of the universally prevalent black filth was littered with enamelled tea cans, milk bottles — some furred with mould — a huge, aluminium tea pot, various cracked mugs and cups, newspapers and a jumble of grease-topped caps. Eddie's own cap had joined the collection, as had a big mug of tea freshly poured from the massive pot. He had been looking forward with anticipation to swigging this whilst he ate his cheese sandwiches, because his stomach ached with hunger after a long shift on the footplate.

The bread in his snap tin was an odd, greyish colour and smeared with the very thinnest glaze of equally grey margarine, encasing a shaving of cheddar cheese. It was colourless fare, but he was grateful for it. The fact that the bread came from his father's bakery only added to his sense of anticipation, as he knew it would taste good. However, he was only one bite into his sandwich when he and the odd assortment of other men seated around the room were roused by the arrival of the shedmaster intruding upon their well-earned break. The man was looking for a volunteer crew to take the snowplough and a group of gangers and signal and telegraph men down line towards Nottingham.

There had been jeers of dismay around the table coming, Eddie reckoned, from the local lads, judging by the contemptuous looks that they gave the harassed shedmaster. One driver even muttered something about 'the union' and 'agreed rest breaks', which had caused another ripple of dissatisfaction around the table. Eddie, still relatively new to the railways, was not yet completely accustomed to the cynicism that seemed to colour the conversation when his fellow railwaymen gathered together. The shedmaster held up a placatory hand but continued speaking. Despite the grumbles, Eddie noticed that the man held the attention of all in the room. He explained that there were reports of a build-up of snow along the line with more forecast for the early hours of the morning. He wanted to avoid a full-scale blockage and felt that it was best to give the line a run-over with the plough, just to be safe. And then there were reports of an incident near Clifton colliery, possibly a broken signal, and he had been telephoned to send some of the signals and telegraph men down to assist.

Well, it was all experience, and as Eddie's wage as an engine cleaner was meagre he jumped at the chance to earn a few bob more. He noticed that some of the older hands seemed less enthusiastic, despite the potential extra earnings. However, as they had already done a full day's slog on the footplate and on long-haul trips at that, he guessed most were looking forward to their return working or the cycle ride home, a good wash and an all-too short kip before tomorrow's shift. So Eddie was grateful for the chance to volunteer and the shedmaster didn't seem to care one jot that Eddie was probably the least experienced in the room. He wasn't even a passed fireman. The shedmaster just needed someone prepared to get the plough and the men down the line as fast as possible.

Leicester South was not Eddie's shed. He was a Woodford man, but he had been rostered all day on short-trip goods' workings away from the huge marshalling yards that dominated the tiny, rural community of Woodford Halse. A number of runs up to one or other of the Leicester yards and back to Woodford; typical work for a young cleaner just starting the climb up the rungs to eventually becoming a fireman. He could expect a few years on these shorter workings, avoiding the high earning rosters until he had more miles on the footplate. So, to work a snowplough run at night on overtime was really something. He knew he had only got the roster because the situation was desperate and no one else seemed willing, so he had better not mess up. Thankfully the driver he had been with all day had also volunteered, and Eddie was grateful for that as they were at least used to working together and got along pretty well.

Driver Hance was in his late fifties and still trim and fit through a combination of hard work and the enforced cut in food consumption of recent years. He had a face deeply lined and creased with years of exposure to all weathers upon the footplate. A quiet man not much given to idle chat or gossip, or indeed any real conversation, he would often communicate with only a slight grunt or just a nod of the head and the occasional 'aye' or 'nay', though he would occasionally pass the time of day with some of the other drivers. Eddie suspected that Hance held the opinion that drivers were the elite and everyone below was strictly second-class. At first Eddie had found this disconcerting, but he soon realised that it was just his way and Hance was never unpleasant towards him. Eddie also noticed that the crow's-foot creases around the corners of Driver Hance's eyes were there because he had a broad smile and when the mood took him he could laugh like the best of them. It was just that when on the footplate he seemed to prefer to keep his own counsel and his eye on the job.

Eddie was surprised to discover that he was crewing one of two engines that were coupled back to back, sandwiched between two guards' vans and the massive bulk of the snowploughs at each end of the short train. It was a mighty and powerful combination and he wondered what lay ahead. His engine was an old Robinson G2. This was a heavy goods' type with eight driving wheels, and if maintained properly they had plenty of power. It could shift some snow if it had to. This particular example was a typically filthy beast, having seen no attention from a cleaner in months or years and had an ominous, rusty scorch mark at the base of the smokebox door. It was also leaking steam from just about everywhere an engine could possibly leak. At some point the engine had taken a hefty bash at the front, as there was a distinct downward dip to the frames, damage possibly sustained working behind the snow plough, and this made Eddie realise that if they did encounter a serious drift it would be dangerous work ramming this plough into snow that often proved as unyielding and as hard as concrete.

Eddie decided he should get a measure of what they were going to propel down the line and so had a quick look at one of the ploughs. At the front end it presented two smoothly curving blades reaching from just an inch above the tops of the rails to about the height of an engine's boiler, welded together down the centre line into a surprisingly sharp edge that ended in a point extending someway forwards between the rails to cut through the snow and push it high and wide on either side of the train. The blades were attached to a small, but robustly-constructed, wooden cabin, where tools and ropes were stored and where the crew could brew up tea after their duties were done. The whole vehicle ran on eight small wheels in a set of massively strong and heavy frames. It was built to take a hammering.

On the other freight engine coupled to his machine he could hear the fireman busying himself with the fire, and four railway workers were having a smoke standing near a brazier burning beside a water column. Eddie nodded a greeting towards them and received a 'How do' in return from one of the men, and as he was hauling himself into the cab another called across, hoping that he would 'Give 'em a warning before 'e rammed the bugger into a drift.'

They all laughed and Eddie smiled back.

''Ere, ain't you a bit young for this sort of lark?'

'Well, I've done about six months on the footplate.'

'Six month? That's nowt, that is. They're getting younger by the blummin' day. Fresh out of school 'e is!'

'You ever took this 'un out before?' Another of the gangers joined in.

'No.' Eddie felt his confidence draining away.

'You'll wish you hadn't by the time you've finished: she's a right pig!' The man looked at the others conspiratorially. 'That's why it's kept for rubbish jobs like this. It's a flipping heap a' junk.'

'Leave him alone. How'd you know, any road? You could no more as fire this as fly a rocket to the blummin' moon! If 'e reckons as 'e can manage, then good luck to 'im.' The ganger speaking then looked up at Eddie and called out, 'Though you mind you don't run out of steam and leave us stuck, eh? I want to get 'ome an' join the wife before she gets out of our nice warm bed!'

They all laughed, including Eddie, who was getting used to the joshing that railwaymen seemed to give out in an almost constant stream. At that point he saw his driver approach, accompanied by two other railwaymen, one of whom was talking quickly and earnestly whilst gesticulating with his hands. Eddie didn't wait to see more as he had still to check his fire and get the feel for the layout of the engine.

After opening the blower and throwing a couple of rounds of coal on the fire he tried the injector and watched in consternation as it repeatedly jetted steam in angry bursts onto the snow whilst he struggled with the lever that opened the water valve; he just couldn't get the steam to engage with the water flow and force it into the boiler. He started over again and after another furious tussle heard the soft gurgle as he finally got it to work. With dismay he also heard a couple of the men applaud his efforts with ironic handclaps and was grateful for the darkness that hid his now-burning cheeks. This was to be a long night if the injector was going to play up like this. As if he had read Eddie's thoughts, Driver Hance, who was now on the footplate, added: 'We'll be out all night — it's not just snow and ice — they've confirmed a signal failure and we've got to take the engineers up to fix it. We'll be parked up for a fair time whilst they do their bit.' The driver was also familiarising himself with the engine as he was speaking. 'She's gonna run rough.' He shook his head in dismay. 'You won't have propelled one of these before, will you?'

'No.'

'Thought as not.' Driver Hance winked, then having received the right away from the guard he made a quick crow on the whistle, received the same in reply from the other engine, and eased open the regulator a touch. The engine slowly breathed into life, issuing a slow, deep exhaust beat as it pushed against the dead weight of the plough. The train was short but surprisingly weighty. Driver Hance jiggled the regulator expertly as he felt the wheels about to slip and they started to trundle forwards with a solid, metallic grating sound and much squealing of wheels as the plough eased over some points.

As they gathered momentum and headed for the open line, Eddie felt a curious sensation: as the engine pushed the heavy plough forward it eased away from the engine with its momentum, exerting a strong jolt as it was caught by the coupling chains, followed by the engine in turn catching up with the plough and shoving it forwards, all in a rapidly accelerating series of buffeting tugs and pulls that made Eddie feel like someone was repeatedly nudging him in the small of his back. This sensation was unpleasant and made him unsteady on his feet, particularly when he tried to swing the shovel. If that was not bad enough the engine and plough behind were exerting their own influence upon the motion of the odd train, and he struggled to get a feel for the motion of the footplate, repeatedly banging his shovel against the firedoor opening as if it were his first time. It was a severe test of what skill he possessed. As if that was not bad enough, the plough kicked up a fine spray of powdery snow like talcum powder and flung it down each side of the engine, reducing visibility to almost nothing and forcing Eddie to lean out into the scything wind and take eyefuls of sharp snow flakes as he helped the driver see the route ahead.

Progress was slow, as they could not exceed twenty miles an hour propelling the cumbersome plough, though apart from an occasional buffeting from a small build up they thankfully encountered no significant drifting along the way and eventually and without incident reached the junction where the coal line from Clifton Colliery joined the main running lines. They were travelling along the slow relief line and just managed to see the signal that routed them into one of the holding sidings, where coal trains would wait for a clear path out onto the main lines.

They could see that a long line of wagons was already occupying one of the sidings and Eddie thought he could detect a pale plume of smoke rising at the far end, suggesting that a locomotive was still coupled up. The signalman was standing on the veranda of his box, signalling with a hand lamp for them to pull up alongside. As they did so, Eddie realised that it was actually a woman who was hailing them and she called across to Eddie, who was nearest.

'Am I glad to see you. We've got a right situation here.' The signalwoman leant over the wooden rail the better for the two crewmen to hear her above the hissing sound of the leaky engine.

'I thought a signal wire had failed, so I wrote out a ticket and released that coal train onto the siding here. We could sort out the signal in the morning. But you'll never guess what?' Her eyes were wide and full of expression, 'I held them here whilst I tried to find them a route, which was proving a real struggle, and then after twenty minutes the guard came along the trackside to ask me how things were looking. As he did so, that's when he noticed it: There was coal all down the middle of the line!' She spoke the words distinctly and with emphasis. 'Someone's only gone and opened up a few of the hoppers and dumped the stuff on the track, mostly back down on the colliery line.'

'Get away!'

'On purpose, like?' Driver Hance squinted up at the signalwoman, then exchanged a puzzled look with his fireman.

'Certainly. One hopper door might open by accident, three is too much of a coincidence, and then there's the broken signal wire that held them on the branch long enough to release the hopper doors.'

'Well, I'll be blowed — the cheeky devils!' Driver Hance made a rare outburst.

'There was nothing much we could do until now, with just the three of them with the train and myself here, but now you've arrived and there's some more lads due down from Annesley any time, we can get the line cleared.'

'Shovelling coal? Tons of it, I wouldn't mind guessing?' Driver Hance shook his head. 'It's going to be a long night for some.'

'I've informed the railway police, but I doubt there's much they can do here in the dark so we best get the line clear ready for tomorrow.'

'I wonder if they got much?' Eddie was shaking his head in amazement.

Driver Hance pulled a face as he made a mental calculation. 'Half hour or so shovelling, with a gang of 'em working at it? Twenty sacks or more? But I've heard you can get ten bob a sack on the black. A nice little earner. The spivs will be laughing all the way to the bank.'

'You're right enough there, driver. It's an absolute disgrace. Pure selfishness and greed.'

'Or a wish to be warm?' added Eddie.

'They should flog the lot of them. Blinkin' scandal, that is.' It was one of the signal engineers who had walked forwards to listen in. Other heads could be seen nodding in agreement. A cigarette was flicked onto the snow, an act that somehow communicated disapproval.

'I just hope the police catch them.' The signalwoman looked along the line for a brief moment, her brow furrowed in thought. 'Right then, driver, draw your train into the number two siding and the S and T can start fixing up the signal wire. The colliery is sending down three empty wagons and I'll hold them on the branch whilst the men start to fill them.'

'Right you are, m'duck.' Driver Hance gave a short blast on the whistle, got a nod from the driver behind and eased forward onto the siding beside the waiting coal train, pulling up alongside the engine already parked there.

Eddie was at first surprised and then delighted to see that the fireman on the other locomotive was his best friend, Simon Howerth, and they exchanged warm greetings. Driver Hance, after applying the brake and picking up his tea can, stepped across into the other cab to while away the time with the other driver whilst Eddie and Simon just leant across the divide between the engines and talked excitedly of their respective adventures.

Chapter Six

'RUN RABBIT RUN'
Harry Roy & His Orchestra

Woodford Halse was gleaming bright as a new penny in the morning air. The rooftops were cushioned with snow and, except for the roads, which had been largely swept clear, every surface was smoothed and undulating as if covered with royal icing; the sharp angles had been chamfered off and all was softened and rounded. The rolling fields beyond the boundaries of the small town — really no more than a village — were also a brilliant white, edged with a black filigree of trees and hedges. The far hills blended into a sky that was a washed out paleness with just a tint of lemon towards the east.

Violet McIntyre had her arm linked through John Trinder's as they walked gingerly down the steep incline of Station Road. They were picking their way along the icy pavement and stepping around the larger mounds of snow that frequently blocked their path.

They had just come from the early morning service at St Mary's, and were now thoroughly chilled to the bone after an hour that had felt like three within the frozen walls of the church, and they had decided to try and walk some life back into their limbs before seeking the comparative warmth of the desultory fire burning in the back kitchen of Violet's dressmaking shop at the bottom of the hill. And so they walked past her shop, continued on beneath the twin arches that carried Woodford station overhead and strolled along the gently curving road set down between two long hedges and wide snow fields, over a small bridge across the meandering Cherwell and into the tiny hamlet of Hinton. There was another slight hill to climb as they came out from the gloom, and this was negotiated with some sliding and slipping that had both Violet and Trinder laughing and providing each with a welcome cause to repeatedly hold the other until they arrived at the white expanse of snow that was the Hinton village green. The twin pillars of the scarlet telephone box and brick-built post box stood out boldly against the white, whilst to their right a clutch of pollarded limes formed a loose and disorderly row, their fine branches like the upturned bristles of a stiff brush.

John Trinder was enjoying the morning despite the fierce cold, gratefully drinking up the moments of pleasure and escape that he had with Violet. The murder case that he had been called to yesterday had sickened and appalled him, and he needed this time to cleanse his mind before he returned to the office later that afternoon. Vignoles had suggested that both of them might benefit from a morning away from the case before tackling the next steps in the investigation. They were waiting on a full post-mortem report and, since that might not arrive for a day or two, they could afford to steal a few hours that morning. Yet, despite the distraction, and almost without being conscious that it was happening, his mind was drifting away into much darker and unattractive places, his eyes losing their joy and his body stiffening slightly.

Trinder shook his head and tried to push the image of the dead and mutilated woman out of his mind. He fell silent for a few moments. Violet sensed the change in mood and stopped.

'Are you all right, John?' Her eyes looked intently into his, her expression ready to fluctuate between worried concern and a warm smile in an instant.

'Me? Oh, don't worry. It's just this case. I can't seem to be able to get it out of my head. In a way, I suppose I shouldn't get her out of my mind: that poor woman deserves justice and we have to catch the beast that did it and as soon as we damned well can, if you will pardon my language.'

'Was it really dreadful?'

'Worse than you can imagine, Vi. But I won't say any more — you really don't need to know the details. Just because I'm a detective, it doesn't mean you need to share everything I do and see.'

'But I can, John. You can tell me, if you think it will help'.

'It won't. No, don't be put out, it's kind of you to say that, but some things really are better left unsaid. Trust me.' He smiled and drew her close, hugging her through his thick overcoat.

A solitary bell struck repeatedly, ringing with the glassy clarity that only the snow can bring. Violet kept her arms around Trinder's body and rested her chin against his sleeve, enjoying the feeling of the woollen fabric studded with tiny crystals of snow against her cheek. She watched as groups of worshippers gathered outside the Methodist and nonconformist chapels that sat side-by-side along one edge of the green. Unlike the far older St Mary's, these places of worship had been built at the same time to provide spiritual comfort to the various denominations of workers brought in by the Great Central Railway.

Violet thought that most of the chapel-goers stomping their feet to shake off the snow were railwaymen's families, as some of the faces were familiar to her, and a few of them — though it was but a handful — even used her shop. St Joseph's Catholic church, which was an extremely modest building, to the point of being little more than an ironstone barn with gothic, pointed windows, lay to the other side of the road and had a steady stream of people walking towards it and its insistent bell. Violet observed that a distinctly different group were gathering in their Sunday best. They looked quieter and more reserved; they acted like visitors to the area, less confident about their place in the village and seemed eager to dally outside the church and to enter as a group. It was hard for Violet to say why she thought this; perhaps it was the sly half-glances they received from the chapel fraternity who were now filing into their respective buildings, or something about the way they clumped together and gave hurried, shy looks across the green that made her think they were not completely sure of themselves or worried that they were unwelcome guests.

She narrowed her eyes to improve her sight and then suddenly pulled away from Trinder.

'Oh look! It's the Walentynowiczes. They're just the sweetest people ever — you will love them.' And with that, she waved and called over to a group nearby.

'Hello! How nice to see you!'

Trinder looked mildly startled at Violet's sudden and enthusiastic reaction and found himself being steered towards the family before he had time to recall why the name Walentynowicz was familiar. Once he had, it was too late to avoid contact. He inwardly groaned and cursed his luck that, during these few precious hours away from his job, he was going to be reminded of it again.

Whilst Violet was making the introductions, Trinder was responding with a slight smile that he hoped would seem polite, but which he knew lacked any enthusiasm, his mind already troubled by this sudden collision between his working and private lives. He desperately hoped that they would not engage him in conversation. Violet was also sensing that something was suddenly going wrong and her face was losing its joyful vivacity and being slowly overtaken by a look of growing confusion.

Mr and Mrs Walentynowicz nodded their heads coolly in response to her effusive greeting and offered their hands without the customary kiss to each cheek that Violet found so disarmingly friendly. The young boy resorted to looking sulky, kicking his nicely-polished shoes in the snow and avoiding any contact. However, when it came to Kat Walentynowicz, Violet was left in no doubt that something was amiss; her face was flushed with anger and her dark brown eyes were wide with disbelief as Violet approached her with Trinder in tow. At first Miss Walentynowicz had looked away whilst her parents had gone through the polite show of shaking hands, but now she turned back and confronted Trinder, her eyes occasionally flicking across to Violet's — but it was clear to whom her anger was directed.

'So, even as we go to church you are checking on us? Making sure we don't take the collection, maybe? Or steal the wine?' She stood with a hand on her hip, resting her weight on that leg, the elegant lines of her long, green coat which Trinder noticed was surprisingly well-tailored and showed off her striking physique to perfection, lending her a presence far in excess of her age. Her dark hair was held in a tortoiseshell clip at the nape of her neck and tumbled in deep, black curls onto her shoulders, and with her hat set at a rakish angle she had something that struck Trinder as oddly piratical or revolutionary about her.

'Mr and Mrs Walentynowicz.' He blushed, 'Er, Miss Walentynowicz... good morning. I had not thought to see you here...' Trinder was treading water, unsure how to counter the sudden attack and unsettled by having Violet standing so close beside him and looking into his face in confusion.

'No? Well it's more surprise to us, I tell you — and not such a nice one. What you want with us, eh? Why you can't leave us alone?' Her voice was becoming raised and a few faces nearby were looking across at the confrontation. Her mother spoke a few hurried words with the same pleading voice that Trinder had heard before.

'Miss Walentynowicz, what on earth is this all about? John?' Violet looked taken aback, her eyes moving quickly from one to the other in confusion.

'Miss Violet, I am sorry but we not know that you are friends with this policeman. And he didn't tell you what he was doing last week? No? Well, that's nice. Checking on us, coming into our house, accusing us of stealing, looking through all our food like we are criminals — ha, what a joke, we have so little. Oh yes, and he doesn't like my father's cigarettes either! Thinks they are not right sort for Polish man.' She shot a glance at her father, who was lighting up even as she spoke. Jozef Walentynowicz was staring intently through the smoke at Trinder with a long and inscrutable look. He said something in Polish that might have been directed towards Kat, but just might have been a threat towards Trinder.

'Now look, really this is not on. This is just not the time and place...' Trinder kept his voice calm, but felt his face flushing despite the cold and was stung by the sudden assault from the young woman.

'No? Coming into our home and scaring us is?' Kat looked at Violet. 'I am sorry, but you keep wrong friends.' The church bell stopped its insistent ringing and the groups of people outside started to pull away from the confrontation with murmured comments and many a backward glance. Mrs Walentynowicz placed an arm on her daughter's and urged her to stop the tirade and join the others going in to worship. She shepherded the young boy ahead, but he still had time to spin around and make as if he were pointing a pistol at Trinder. He took aim and made a shooting sound, then raised the invisible barrel to his mouth to blow away the imaginary smoke. It occurred to Trinder that this was the second time the boy had done this. His father clipped him smartly behind the ear, accompanied this with a sharp comment, then took one last, long drag on his cigarette, nodded coolly towards Violet and turned to walk towards the church.

'What on earth was all that about, John?'

Trinder sighed. 'I am sorry, that was not what I wanted at all.'

'I should hope not! What is all this about you going into their home and accusing them of stealing?' It was Violet's turn to look flushed with pent-up anger.

'Vi, this is police business and should never have been raised in this manner. But I am sorry to say there is some truth in what she said. We did investigate — well, investigate is a bit strong. We paid them a brief visit last Friday. But to suggest that we threatened them or did something untoward is quite true. That was her own misinterpretation of events.'

'The Walentynowiczes, investigated for stealing? That is ludicrous. A lovelier, kinder family you could not hope to meet. I'm sorry, but you've clearly made some kind of mistake.'

'And I'm sorry to shatter your trust in them, but our investigation was based upon previous cases of being caught in the act of stealing coal. Kat and her brother were both caught red-handed.

'Adam? He's just a little boy!'

'And little boys can still shovel coal from a station yard into a baby carriage. I'm sorry, Violet. They are clearly friends of yours, so it is uncomfortable to talk like this and I would prefer to say nothing. But they are guilty of theft. However, we have repeatedly taken a lenient approach because we appreciate they are cold and coal is in short supply...' He opened his arms in a gesture that implied that he had little other option.

Violet fell silent and bit her lip for a few moments. 'Were they really caught stealing?'

'I'm afraid so. Three times. But we have left it — again — with just a stern warning. I must be frank, though: they could have been prosecuted.'

'I see.' Violet walked slowly, Trinder falling into step beside her. 'But surely you cannot think that they are up to anything else?'

Trinder exhaled slowly and measured his words carefully. 'There were some unfounded suspicions, more like rumours, kicking around the camp but we saw nothing to cause us any real concern.'

'Rumours? People are too suspicious. With everything so short these days it's bringing out the worst in people. There's so much envy and suspicion around. I don't know about all this "Dunkirk spirit" they keep harking on about.' Violet shook her head as she spoke. 'I've seen precious little of that at times. Most people look after themselves first and others second.'

'And that I fear might be the case with this family.'

Violet grimaced and nodded almost imperceptibly. 'But I am not surprised you found nothing.' She slipped her arm through Trinder's as they walked, her body visibly relaxing, 'They are a thoroughly decent family, really they are. Though I am a bit taken aback that they took some coal.'

'It was just a baby carriage full, to be fair.' Trinder sought to soften the mood. 'And, as you said, they are just kids, really.' Though Trinder was finding this description far from appropriate for the strikingly mature and confident Kat.

'Taking that coal was wrong. But I am sure it was just foolishness, not some sinister wish to profiteer. Mr Walentynowicz is no spiv.'

'I'm inclined to agree with that.' Trinder was careful with his words, hoping to preserve the still delicately balanced truce between them.

'But you really have to believe me. And they bring me plenty of work as well — and for that matter, so do many of the other Poles who live in that ghastly camp. You saw how they liked to dress well.'

'Ah, so you made Kat's green coat?'

'You noticed?' Violet suddenly flashed a warm smile, though her expression rapidly returned to looking pensive again. 'To be honest they've practically kept my business going. Maybe it's because I am still a bit of an outsider here, like they are. We seem to share a common bond. I'm like them in a strange way: always the last in the queue at the butcher's and the greengrocer's. No titbits, no nice cuts saved for me and always the smallest cauliflower or the weediest carrots. Unlike some I could name in the village. If you are shopping for Lord What's-his-name at Sulgrave Manor — well, you can get anything you want. And as for the doctor's wife...' She shook her head. 'We're all supposed to be having a fair share, what with the rationing and everything, but since when has life ever been truly fair? And then there are the comments I get. Oh, they don't say things to my face, but I hear them. About Jenny and how I am a — well, you can imagine the hurtful words — because she has no father.' Violet fell silent for a few moments as they crunched through the snow. 'And I can't really argue with them. And then our friendship, John.' She squeezed his arm. 'It does not exactly help. About us not being married. They say all manner of unkind things.'

'They'd better not say them near me — it's none of their damned business!' Trinder flared.

'I know, but people will talk. It's human nature, I suppose.' Violet looked sad. 'Really, they should try to look beyond their petty prejudices and see us for who we are, not what we seem to represent. But I fear people can be terribly stuck in their opinions.' There was a slight break in her voice. Trinder placed his arm around her shoulder and pulled her close beside him.

They had often spoken at length about this; about Violet's daughter Jennifer, whom the villagers had believed was actually her young sister until events the previous year had exposed the truth for all to see — and to judge. There was little he could add.

'I've tried to do my bit in the village; to ignore some of their whispers and ugly glances, and we manage of course; but then I met the Poles and we got along famously. And now I don't suppose I shall be seeing any of them again. Bang go my customers!'

'I'm really sorry. Truly I am. That should never have happened.'

Violet breathed in deeply and seemed to draw strength from so doing. 'Oh, I forgive you.' She exhaled in a long stream of white breath, as if purging herself of her frustration and anger, 'It's all part of being seen with a policeman, I suppose. It appears to carry a price with it.' She gave a sad, wan smile.

Trinder looked at her with a questioning glance. 'Yes, I am afraid it does. We're not best liked by some people and our work certainly doesn't always make us friends'. He hesitated a beat as the air was punctuated by a loud croak from a fat magpie perched on a wall. 'One for sorrow,' he remarked, and saluted the bird before continuing, 'Perhaps the price is too high to be worth you paying. If you understand me?'

'Don't be ridiculous!' A second magpie flew overhead. 'Two for joy! Come along, I have a rabbit at home waiting to be made into a stew for our lunch and then some half pay pudding for afters. And before you ask, the rabbit came from farmer Turvey, who shot it on his fields. And yes, he is one of the villagers who does look out for me. Bless him. Still, if I lose any more business, I might have to seriously consider taking up poaching.' She shot Trinder a winning smile and they both laughed.

Chapter Seven

'INTO EACH LIFE SOME RAIN MUST FALL'
Joe Loss & his Orchestra

Vignoles and Trinder were travelling back to their office located within the beautifully ornate — though smoke-blackened — building that was Leicester Central station. Their tram was lurching its way along tracks still partially blocked by compacted snow, making for an uncomfortable ride with the jolting and jarring of the undulating surface punishing their backs against the hard wooden slats of the tip-over seats.

'So, the pathologist confirmed asphyxiation through strangulation and has given us a time of death of anywhere between 5 p.m. and 10 p.m., when the body was found.'

'I wonder how many trains passed along the up line between those times?'

'A fair few, I reckon, sergeant, but it will be far from impossible to list them all.'

'I'll get P.C. Blencowe on to it as soon as we get back — that's just his cup of tea.'

'Good. Ouch!' Vignoles lurched sideways and had to put a hand out to stop himself colliding with the rattling window beside his face as the tram wobbled even more violently. 'This tram is in danger of coming off the rails. Luckily, we've just two more stops to go.'

'But we need to know who this poor girl is.' Trinder furrowed his brow beneath his trilby, which he wore at a rakish slant.

'Let's start with what we found on the body.'

'The cinema ticket in her coat pocket was for the Odeon in Nottingham.'

'Yes, so we can cautiously assume Nottingham to be where she lived. Though she could have been just visiting. Where is her handbag or luggage? With no purse, house keys, ration books, diary, we know so little.'

'But the handkerchief was intriguing,' said Trinder.

'Agreed. It was a ladies' one, so let us assume that it's hers. The initials "V. H." embroidered on the corner suggest her name.' Vignoles shook his head slowly in thought, 'But who are you, V. H? And who is missing you?'

'She looked the sort of person who would be missed.' Trinder left the sentence hanging and pulled on his cigarette; as he did so he looked across at Vignoles, who was framed against the tram window. The detective inspector was looking his normal, well-groomed self, despite the ravages of seven years of austerity living: an elegantly cut suit in navy blue, matching hat with a slight curl to the brim, rectangular, silver-framed glasses, a silken tie and the heavy R.A.F. greatcoat that he almost invariably wore, whatever the weather, with the collar turned up high and the silver buttons gleaming. His new pipe was jutting from the corner of his mouth, unlit but ever-present.

Vignoles nodded in agreement, his eyes betraying a trace of sadness. 'She was a fine looking woman and she met a dreadful end.' Vignoles smeared a hole in the condensation on the window, peered out for a moment to get his bearings then commenced inspecting his pipe, turning it slowly in his hand, considering whether to fire it up or not. 'We have a lot of work to do. The man that did that is clearly crazed.'

'Do you think he could strike again?'

There was a crack of electricity as the power arm momentarily lost contact with the wires looping along the road.

'If he can do such a thing once, then why not again? But that suggests a serial killer, and despite what you read in American pulp fiction novels, they are, thankfully, rare. I suspect it will prove to be someone she knew and a sorry tale of jealousy and too much alcohol. Though the gag disturbs me.' They both fell silent, listening to the rattling of the tram and the jingling bell calling it to stop.

'We need to get the artist's impression of her distributed up and down the line. The artist promised it would be ready from the printer's by now. The Nottingham Constabulary can post it around their patch and we can try to get the Met to start doing the same in London; likewise with the Leicester civvies, and let's see if anyone remembers her. She's a missing person for God's sake — someone must have noticed that she never arrived.'

'Maybe they've already reported her missing, but some distance away?'

'Good point, so get Lansdowne or Benson chasing any missing persons' reports — right across the land, if needs be.'

'Everywhere?' asked Trinder.

'As we have no idea where she was heading, we'd be better

cast the net wide. However, London is the obvious choice, so that can be the first place to check.'

The tram stopped outside the station; the two detectives descended the steep, curving staircase from the top floor and dropped down into the dirty slush of the road, their heavy shoes taking another soaking, though this at least served to hide the pale tidelines of salt already blooming on the leather. Snow was now falling heavily and the station building was rendered only partially visible.

A few minutes later and they were back in their office, stamping the wetness from their shoes onto the polished linoleum, and Trinder was calling the others to gather around to discuss the case. However, as they had walked in, Vignoles's secretary, Mrs Green, handed him two small pieces of paper, each with a name and a telephone number upon it. He now looked briefly at the first, but shook his head slightly and frowned. Mrs Green replied to his silent question.

'I don't know, sir. He just said to call him when you had a moment.'

'Who is he?'

'The new stationmaster at Woodford and Hinton. He didn't say much, just that he was keen to talk with you.'

'All right.' Vignoles tucked it under the second slip, which also bore a name and number but with the addition of a comment: 'Coal train robbery'.

Vignoles groaned. 'Oh no, not another? We really don't need this now...'

'Problem, sir?' Trinder looked across at Vignoles.

'Another blessed coal train has been done over, by the looks of it. When did this come in?'

'An hour ago. But the man who reported it said it was Friday night that it was done.'

'Friday? Why wait so long to report it?' Vignoles pulled a face. 'Well, the coal'll be burning in someone's grate by now.' Vignoles unconsciously scrunched the notes into a ball in his hand and stuffed them into his trouser pocket. 'We're stretched to the limit with this murder case as it is, we could have done without this complication. It'll just have to wait a while longer.'

'But he said it was very urgent, sir. He wanted you to telephone as soon as you got in.' Mrs Green had to speak loudly as Vignoles was already walking into the larger back office to speak with the assembled officers. 'The Badger also said to phone him, to keep him informed on developments.'

Vignoles spun around on his heels. 'The chief super called? About the murder case?'

'No, about the coal robbery. He says — she adopted an imitation of the chief super's rather plummy voice, — 'it's to be a priority and wants an immediate stop to their activities.' She cringed even as she spoke the words, knowing what the reaction was likely to be.

'What? Is the man crazy? Doesn't he realise a young woman has been brutally murdered? He really is the absolute limit. Maybe he hasn't seen my report yet?' Vignoles reined his anger in a little. 'He'll soon change his priorities when he does.'

Mrs Green smiled sympathetically. 'I'm sure, but it might be an idea to send someone to look at the crime scene, at least?'

Vignoles gave her a stare.

'Just trying to help!' She raised her hands in a gesture of surrender and turned back to her Remington to fiddle with some foolscap and carbon paper under its rollers.

Vignoles shook his head and pushed all thoughts of Chief Superintendent Badger to the back of his mind whilst he, with a few additional observations from Trinder, ran through what they knew so far about 'V.H.' and pinned up some gruesome photographs of the body for all to see.

By the time he had finished the mood in the room was as dark and grim as the day outside, but there was little doubt that everyone was resolutely determined to start work on tracking down the man responsible. P.C. Blencowe, a large, rotund and habitually smiling fellow, had a rare scowl upon his face and was already making notes whilst Vignoles was speaking. An officer never, even by his own admission, likely to win a place on the Brains Trust, Blencowe was nonetheless a man who saw 'the Devil in the detail' and could be relied upon to undertake much of the routine checking and cross-checking that modern policing was founded upon. So, it was no surprise that Blencowe was eager to get to work on plotting every train movement past the spot where the body was discovered. Blencowe's desk was always piled with train timetables, additional working instructions and all manner of trade directories, telephone books and other useful reference material. Vignoles found himself feeling pleasantly reassured to see this able and affable man already leafing through a hefty volume, a candle burning beside him to alleviate the gloom cast by the poorly-burning gas lights above.

'We should have a reasonable idea of all trains she might have travelled on, thanks to Blencowe's work. Later today?' He threw a questioning look towards the P.C., who merely grunted by way of reply without looking up, his finger marking a place in one timetable whilst his other hand skimmed through another.

'With that list we can start to track backwards and see if the train guard can remember her. We need to get the picture of the victim's face in front of as many ticket clerks and porters as we can. Benson, Lansdowne...' he looked at the two young women officers seated close to the front of the room, '...get onto this — stop at every station back down the line from where she was found up to Nottingham. Get on to the northern section and enlist their help beyond Nottingham. I'll try and get the various civvy constabularies to do their share. Make sure anyone who just might have seen her, sees that picture.'

'Yes, sir!' The women answered in unison.

'Any questions?'

'Sir? I think finding her luggage could be useful. No woman travels without a handbag, and I would be surprised if she had not at least an overnight case. It's noticeable that she was found without either. We could contact all the left luggage offices in case they were handed in?'

'Good idea, Benson, get on to it. There's a lot of foot slog to get through. I want regular updates on progress. Make up a chart on the chalk board — I want every station checked off as it is covered, that way we can see where we are up to.'

'I'll do that.' It was Mrs Green who volunteered.

Vignoles nodded and stood up, putting his hands into his pockets as he looked for matches to light his pipe, and in so doing found the ball of paper he'd scrunched up and put there. 'Oh, blast it, the coal robbery.' He flattened out the paper ball and extracted the note, replacing the other in his pocket. 'Where is this anyway? I don't recognise the name. Do you, sergeant?'

Trinder took the note and shook his head. 'It's a Nottingham number, though. I can phone him if you like and see what the score is.'

'Please do.' Vignoles proceeded to light his pipe as Trinder crossed the room to his desk and started to dial. Vignoles sat on the corner of one of the heavy wooden tables that dominated the room and stared pensively at the photographs of the dead girl, as if by looking at her bloody image he could find an answer to the questions racing through his mind.

He had started the process of trying to identify the victim and tracing her movements, but had taken not one step towards finding her killer. It was a frustrating feeling. He had an over-eagerness to be getting on and doing something more than just giving out instructions, but Vignoles knew from long experience that patience was a basic requirement in policing. He'd started the process, and no matter how slowly, the investigation was now going to roll forwards. He just needed something to hang onto, some small clue to start them off on the hunt for this murderer.

On returning to his own office Vignoles noticed a cardboard box sitting on one of the chairs. It was securely wrapped and fastened with brown string and a wax seal, and he immediately recognised that it had been sent over by the pathologist. It would doubtless contain the clothes the young woman had been wearing. After cutting it open with a paperknife shaped like a Turkish scimitar — another curious artefact left behind on a train and unclaimed after many years — he looked down at an envelope resting upon the neatly-folded clothes inside. He placed the box on the floor, sat behind his desk, took a puff on his pipe and opened the envelope.

It contained the ladies' handkerchief found in a pocket of her coat. This was a chance to examine it properly. There were two letters embroidered in red thread in one corner: 'V. H.' It was clean and neatly pressed. Feeling the cloth, Vignoles could tell that it had been frequently but carefully laundered, as the cloth was extremely soft and supple. He sensed that the handkerchief had been important to the victim.

This was all he knew about V. H. apart from her choice of clothes. This gave him an idea. He decided to draw up a list of each item in the hope it might offer a clue to identifying her. Opening the top drawer of his desk he selected a clean but used envelope from the odd collection of similar he had assembled there as a supply for his note-making. With paper being in such short supply, it was necessary to reuse everything.

The first item from the box was her coat. He could appreciate that it had been expertly made, but had no manufacturer's label. Had she made it? Vignoles thought of Trinder's girlfriend, Miss McIntyre, who did this kind of work. Was it was worth asking her to take a look and run her expert eye over it. But why? It proved the victim had good taste and an eye for 'make do and mend', but how was it going to identify her and help him catch her killer? He laid it to one side.

The tiger lily brooch pinned to the coat looked home-crafted. Perhaps she had also done it herself, though such designs could be picked up at all kinds of fund-raising events on stalls run by the likes of the Housewives' League and the Women's Institute. It was distinctive and so someone might just remember seeing her wear it.

Her dress was made from what was certainly going to be utility-marked fabric and to a design currently fashionable throughout the land. His wife had a dress in a similar pattern. Again no maker's label — but Vignoles was already forming the opinion that the young woman was more than capable of running this up herself.

Her slip was of silk. Vignoles knew that there would be no maker's labels and sure enough it looked to have been fashioned at home or by a dressmaker from material cut in all probability from a parachute. There were no knickers. He lifted out a pair of shoes and noted that they were from a Northampton factory. They were green, wooden soled and had been re-coloured fairly recently, as he could see slight traces of another colour underneath, close to a seam on one shoe. They were presentable but well worn, typical of everyone but the most fortunate these days. Vignoles knew that they would have been purchased at least a couple of years previously and there was no chance of anyone remembering her buying them, even if he knew where to ask.

Vignoles looked into the box to see if he had missed anything, but it was empty. He was sure that he remembered she had been wearing stockings. The shocking image of her ravaged body had looked all the more potent because of the contrast between her pale thighs and darker legs. He picked up the large envelope on his desk that contained more crime scene photographs, and double-checked. Sure enough, she appeared to be wearing these most desirable of items, but there were none in the box. He nodded and turned the photographs face down on his desk. So she had not been able to source real stockings — what woman could these days? Anna was continually bemoaning the scarcity of nylons and placed their non-existence pretty close to the top of her list of things that 'made Britain truly awful right now'. Snow and ice, the lack of coal, sugar, a nice cut of beef and the much-hated bread ration all ranking far lower in Mrs Vignoles's eyes. Vignoles deduced that V. H. spent her money wisely by avoiding the extortionate spivs and black-marketeers and had chosen instead to use carefully-applied gravy browning and eyeliner pencil to achieve the look.

So, she was thrifty, in her early twenties and nicely dressed. And dead. Not much of a haul. There must be something he had missed? He replaced everything in the box and looked up as Trinder knocked and entered his office.

'This coal robbery is the biggest one yet. I can see why the Badger is baiting you about it.' Trinder risked a fleeting grin. 'Looks like a few of them this time and well organised with it. Up at Clifton Colliery.'

'Remind me, where is that?'

'There's a branch line off the mainline, between Ruddington and Nottingham.' Vignoles nodded and Trinder continued. 'They rigged the signals to stop the train and then opened up three of the hopper wagons. Once the train had restarted — the signalwoman called them past the danger on a ticket — it strewed tons of the stuff on the track. As it was dark they probably calculated that the guard wouldn't notice until the train was well away. The guard did in fact spot the problem because they got held at the junction awaiting a path, but not until a good half-hour or so later. Worth good money on the black market, so we might have real pros at work here.'

'Damn!' Vignoles flung his pen onto the blotter in frustration, a spatter of ink marking the place where it impacted. Trinder knew not to speak. Vignoles pulled a pained expression, perhaps because of his foolish action, then drew upon his pipe in a more measured manner. That was sign that he was reining in his emotions and considering his next response.

'So we've got to throw good men at this. But it will seriously slow us down on the other case.' He spread his hands wide. 'Nothing to do about that.' Vignoles looked around the room as if seeking an answer somewhere within its utilitarian walls and made a quick decision. 'Sergeant, I need you full time on the murder case. Benson! Lansdowne!' he called loudly, knowing that his voice would carry through into the adjacent office. They soon appeared at the open doorway. 'I have something else for you.'

The two women officers, aware that something was brewing, were filled with eager anticipation as they approached his desk and they were not disappointed when he spelt out his initial directions in the coal train robbery case, placing both women, with Benson as senior investigating officer, on to it. Both W.P.C.s were deeply surprised to be given such a high-profile case.

'It will mean some very long days and quite possibly nights — and surveillance springs to mind. Are you both up to it?'

'Gosh, yes, sir!'

'No question!'

'Good. Get me a result — I need to keep the super happy on this one.'

Trinder looked discomfited. 'Sir, with respect, won't this cause some problems?' He chewed his lip and gave the two women officers a guilty look.

'Problems? You mean with the stupid oafs in uniform?' Vignoles looked at the two women in their black police uniforms, 'Correction, the stupid *male* oafs in uniform won't much like it?'

'Yes. It's all a bit... unconventional.'

'Well, it's about flipping time it became a convention then! Excuse my language. Thank goodness we don't have a union calling the odds. It's either a couple of capable women in charge, or nothing. Hardly a choice is it? Benson? Think you can step up to the mark in the face of unconventionality?'

'Of course, sir.' She blushed though, and shot Trinder a nervous glance.

'Good. The sergeant's right. They'll give you some stick, I'm

afraid. Some of these uniformed officers can be idiots, to be honest. But I'm giving you the case, so don't be afraid to show them who's boss. Right, you'd better get on.'

'Yes, sir.' Benson saluted, turned and marched out, followed by Lansdowne, who did the same.

Trinder gave Vignoles a curious look, one that seemed to say, 'It's your funeral'.

'Dammit, what else are we going to do? They're both good detectives, you know that.'

'Agreed, but...'

'And I need you on the murder hunt.' Vignoles picked up his pen and inspected it, puffing at his pipe. Trinder knew when to bide his time.

'But keep a discreet eye on the girls. Look out for them, will you? If any of the lads cause problems, lean on them — and hard. I'm not in the mood to be indulgent with their prejudices. We've got a killer to catch.'

٭   ٭   ٭   ٭

The detective department was not going to be alone in the hunt for the coal train robbers. Edward Earnshaw and Simon Howerth were both in agreement that this was a case for their detective skills, such as they were.

The two were sitting in the cab of one of the attractive, Robinson-designed Atlantics that were still to seen at Woodford shed. These beautifully proportioned engines had once been top express locomotives back in the days of the Great Central Railway. But now they were largely replaced by more modern and powerful machines and so, like ageing racehorses, were put out to pasture, eking out their final years in service trundling about on less-demanding local passenger trains. Simon and Eddie both liked these engines and so took every opportunity to look one over when they came on shed.

Eddie was minding the fire on number 6264 in readiness for a passenger turn to Marylebone later that afternoon, whilst Simon was doing the same on 2909, stabled close alongside. The engines were placed on lines running between the engine and carriage sheds that offered a slight relief from the bitter wind that was bringing ever more snow upon them. It was not ideal weather to be huddled in the inadequately-small half-cab of an Atlantic, but Eddie's locomotive had a tarpaulin lashed to the rear edge of the narrow roof, secured to a rather jerry-built metal frame constructed of old boiler tubes that had been fitted to the front edge of the tender. This now-sagging roof afforded some welcome extra protection and, with the fire doors cracked open, they could warm themselves whilst they sipped tea and ate their sandwiches. Every so often one would take turns to stand up and thump the tarpaulin to send a shower of the snow collecting there tumbling to the ground. Outside, smoke, steam and the hypnotic fall of snowflakes combined to render the vast locomotive yard virtually invisible. White on white on grey, it was a monochromatic world in which even the many sounds were muffled and hushed.

The lads had been discussing the weekend's abandoned football fixtures but had now turned to the extraordinary coal train robbery. Simon was reliving the experience yet again.

'...so, after stopping the train by cutting the signal wire, they sneaked up to the wagons, unpinned the doors and when it moved off we dumped coal all over the track.'

'And who would see them in this weather and at night?' Eddie sipped some tea.

'The barefaced cheek, eh? To think it was my train as copped it as well.' Simon grinned, finding a vicarious enjoyment from the notoriety. 'Not that I could have done much about it, of course.'

'It's not good though, Si. The police'll be down on them like a ton of bricks if they get caught. It's not the first time it's happened, either.'

'It's the third attack.'

'And we seem to be working that turn to Clifton quite often. You know, joking apart, if one of our trains gets it again, it might start to look bad on us.'

'On me, more like. I've already been done!' Simon suddenly looked concerned.

'I heard some of the lads around the shed are saying that it has to be an inside job and that any crews on that run have to be odds-on favourites to be in on it.'

'Blinkin' 'eck. That's a bit rough.'

Eddie looked thoughtful. 'It makes you think, though. What about your driver?'

'Nah. Doubt it. He looked like he was going to kill them if he ever has a chance. Still, I suppose you can see why people are talking like that?'

'And rumours can be hard to shake off. It could bugger our chances to make passed fireman.'

'Damn.' Simon sipped some tea and looked gloomily at the falling snow.

'Then we need to get serious: find out who's behind it all. Stop them before they do us any harm.' Eddie looked at Simon intently, his friend nodding in agreement from across the cab. 'If we sniff out these robbers it will do us all a favour. We might even get a bonus!'

'Fat chance of that. But since we're dab hands at spotting a Soviet spy or a Quisling and German parachutists, why not a Nottinghamshire coal thief?' Simon laughed and, visibly cheered up at his irreverent remark, took this as a cue to light up a cigarette, tossing the spent match between the firedoors. 'Except that we don't live in the same county, Eddie. A small detail, I know.'

'Accentuate the positive, Si! It's a problem, yeah, I agree. But we travel up there most days now and I reckon as that someone in the pit or on the railway up there's behind all this, and if we keep our ears to the ground we'll get wind of them soon enough.'

'Or get cold ears.'

'Yeah, yeah, you're a card, very funny.'

Eddie stood up, knocked the blower open, flung the firedoors wide and peered into the firebox. Having assessed the situation, he took the shovel and threw on a couple of rounds of coal. Satisfied that it was as he wanted it, he part closed the doors again and pulled the long lever near the cab side that opened the water valve and then turned a small wheel that opened the steam valve of the injector. After fiddling with the water lever for a few moments, nudging it backwards and forwards a touch to balance the flow of water with that of the jet of steam, he nodded to himself as he heard the gentle gurgle of the injector filling the boiler and then sat back down on the small wooden plank that served as a seat.

'Injector's cold. Playing up a bit.'

'I'm having the same problem on that one over there.'

'So what d'you reckon, Si?'

'I reckon as I'm up for it.'

'All in favour say aye!' They both saluted in an exaggerated manner and laughed.

'So where do we start?' Eddie was pouring some more tea into the lid of his tea can.

'Who do we know who work the turns up to the coal mine? Those who work it regularly are going to know when they're running and could tip off the gangs.'

'Sounds good. Likewise the signalmen: perfect position to hold train at a red whilst they strike. Maybe your dad will know who's working that patch?'

Simon nodded. His father had been a signalman at Woodford Halse for the past twenty years. 'He might at that, though he won't take kindly to us "casting nasturtiums" on his loyal comrades. They're a funny lot, signalmen and don't take kindly to having people asking questions about what they do. The can get right sensitive and ratty about it.' Simon winced in anticipation of the conversation and the sharp rebuke he would probably get for asking.

Eddie laughed. 'Who would? You best not be quite so obvious why you're asking him then. I think we might have to take the chance of a layover up Nottingham way to sniff around the place — someone must be hawking the coal on the side.' He turned away and looked out across Woodford shed as two large goods' engines slowly clanked past in Indian file, both moving towards the concrete coaling tower that resembled the Cenotaph. Oddly, it had been the scene of a gruesome death only the year before and this gave the tower something creepy, even menacing about it, especially when glimpsed through the veil of snow. One of the crew on the trailing locomotive caught sight of Eddie and raised a hand in greeting; he did the same in reply.

'It's funny. I've not been here all that long and already it feels like I'm part of this place.'

'Yeah, they're a decent bunch of lads, on the whole.' said Simon.

'Some are right pigs, though.'

'True.' Simon threw his fag end onto the fire as if to emphasise the point.

Eddie leant out of the cab of the Atlantic and watched a group of three women approach, all dressed in baggy overalls tightly cinched at the waist by leather belts, their hair hidden by headscarves tied in knots above their foreheads and each carrying a metal bucket filled with rags and metal scrapers for carving away the layers of grime from the wheels and motion of the locomotives. Two also had long-handled brushes in their other hands and all three were smoking and chatting loudly as they walked, heads bent down to stop the snow getting in their eyes.

'But I'm glad the girls stayed on. I like them around the place, though I think I'm the only one who does.' Eddie fell silent for a few moments. 'It was a dirty rotten trick to get rid of them without even a proper thank you, so it jolly well serves the railway right that they had to take some back double-quick time, when they got short.'

'I think you've got a soft spot for that Mary. You're always hanging around her.'

'I'm not hanging around. I'm just being friendly.'

'Not half as friendly as you wish, eh?'

'Get away! She's just good fun and sort of easy to talk to.' But Eddie, despite his protestations, looked back at the women cleaners who were now walking past the cab of the locomotive and he smiled as they looked up and caught sight of him.

'Halloo! Eddie!' The aforementioned Mary waved ostentatiously and blew an exaggerated kiss in his direction. By way of return, Eddie gave her what he hoped was his warmest of smiles. He was blushing, despite the fierce cold. One of the other two women nudged her in the ribs and all three laughed, though Eddie could not hear what was said.

'Aye aye! Your luck's in, Eddie, lad. She's soft on you.' Simon had stood up and watched the exchange over his friend's shoulder.

'Get off, she's married.'

'Yeah, well it didn't stop her winking at you.' Simon sat back down and was still laughing at his friend's embarrassment. Eddie threw a small piece of coal at Simon, which bounced harmlessly off his shoulder, but inwardly Eddie was glowing with pleasure.

Chapter Eight

'CHASING SHADOWS'
Bert Ambrose & his Orchestra

Vignoles and his wife were breakfasting at their new dining table. This was Anna's pride and joy, having only recently been delivered following a frustrating wait of many weeks owing to supply problems with the raw materials. It was made of a light-coloured wood in a simple but elegant design by Hardy Eames, which had found favour under the present austerity restrictions. Anna considered it to be *vero moda* and, taken together with the four matching chairs, it helped lend a much-needed lightness to their small dining room.

Vignoles, however, was not thinking about the table or even about the tired-looking floral wallpaper that added to the room's still-persistent tendency towards gloominess. No, he was concentrating on making the most of his solitary poached egg on toast. A real shell egg, a rare treat that he had heavily spiced with unrationed salt and black pepper. As he spooned the last morsel into his mouth he looked across at his wife and caught her running a hand over the new wood of the table, a slight smile on her face. Her egg was, as yet, untouched. As he began to wonder if she would be content to just admire a piece of furniture and forget the culinary privations of the time, she closed her eyes for a moment and inhaled in a slow and languid manner all the better to savour the heady aroma rising from a pot of freshly ground coffee brewing on the table between them.

She caught his eye and smiled. 'Caffè latte?'

'Anyway you please!'

They both grinned like children on Christmas morning. Anna had obtained the coffee after hearing a rumour from her father of some becoming available on the far side of town. Bepe Carelli had telephoned her at the office one morning to alert her of this vital intelligence and she needed little encouragement. Using her charm to concoct a plausible reason to abandon her post a few minutes prior to her lunch hour, so as to steal a march upon all the other office girls, who would be similarly alerted by the bush telegraph, Anna had rushed out to hunt down and secure a small bag of the precious beans. So now they were both indulging in the dark and slightly bitter tang of its flavour, so far removed from Camp Coffee, that poor abomination which Vignoles continually tried to convince himself he actually enjoyed. For Anna there was no such dilemma; her Italian parentage rendered such a low pastiche of coffee undrinkable, preferring to just dream and pine for the real thing between its infrequent availability. It was fortunate that her father, a restaurateur, had so many useful contacts across the city, none of which were ever fully explained. Vignoles had long since realised that it was better for everyone if he didn't ask too many questions and to just enjoy any coffee, olive oil, small and piquant goats' cheeses, shell eggs, half salamis and other such delicacies that appeared at intervals.

The valves on the radiogram were glowing in the corner of the room as the velvet tones of the Home Service newsreader announced a catalogue of disruption across the country: trains marooned in snow drifts in Scotland and Northumberland; power lines down, causing blackouts; roads blocked across the land; and dire warnings that there was to be no let up in sight and fears that this weather could presage a period of yet more coal shortages. Moving on from the weather, the prime minister, Mr Atlee, expressed his concerns over the worsening financial outlook, whilst Mr Bevin declared that he was becoming completely frustrated by the obstinacy of Mr Molotov, and indeed with all Soviets.

Charles and Anna Vignoles were both glad when the newsreader ended his litany of woe and played a soothing number by the Bert Ambrose Orchestra. The mantle clock gently ticked, along with the embers of last night's fire, which clicked and sizzled once Vignoles had stirred them and thrown on a few coal sweepings and something that looked suspiciously like incombustible shale. It might just take the edge off the bitter cold within the room. They both wore their overcoats whilst they breakfasted, Anna also sporting fingerless gloves.

'So this case, it's very distressing?' Her breath formed clouds as she spoke, intermingling with the steam rising from the coffee cup in her hand.

'Awful, Anna. I fear she suffered.'

'How was she killed?'

'Not really breakfast material, to be frank. But it appears she was strangled — helped along by being gagged.'

'Ugh. Poor girl. And you said she was also... you know?' She avoided saying the word.

'I'm afraid so.'

'And then she was thrown off a train?'

'That's about the long and the short of it.'

She fell silent for a few moments. Vignoles would never normally discuss police matters outside of the office, but had long since learnt that his wife had the ability to rapidly and with surprising accuracy pinpoint key issues in a case, often ones that somehow escaped him. Her observations were always worth noting, and he waited patiently to hear what she would say.

'What motive?'

'It was a sexual assault, certainly. Probably not a robbery, though her possessions are missing, but it was also a violent murder and that puzzles me. There's something odd about the whole situation, but I don't have enough information to get an angle on what that this.'

'You think it was someone she knew?'

'In four-fifths of such cases, it turns out that way.'

Anna nodded, then fell silent for a moment. 'But this all takes time — the assault and murder. How long you think it took him to do all that he did to this poor girl and then strangle her?'

'A good point. It's not something I've timed.' He pulled a face. 'But I suppose we have to think of what? Five to eight minutes, maybe ten?'

'Exactly, Charles.'

Anna leant across the table, her eyes eager with interest. Vignoles returned her gaze, the cup of coffee half-raised to his mouth. 'You see?' Anna continued. 'The timing is everything — think about it. Let's say eight minutes for the act and then he must move the body, but it's not going to be easy, because she's dead?'

'We presume so, or at least unconscious.'

'Same thing. So it will be difficult to drag the body down the corridor. You know what the trains are like now, very crowded and with luggage all over the floor. And this takes more time. Then he opens a door, throws her out and then goes back to hide any evidence. You said you don't have her luggage or handbag?'

'No.'

'You see? So what is all that? At least ten minutes. So why did no one see anything?'

'He got lucky?'

Anna sat back in her chair and threw her arms wide dismissively. She was ever the one for the expansive gesture. 'More than lucky — almost impossible.'

'Anna, you're right.' Vignoles furrowed his brow in thought. 'It could be an unpremeditated attack on the spur of the moment. In which case...' Vignoles took a sip of coffee before continuing, '...how on earth did he think he could get away with it?'

'Exactly. So the first big question is what train was so empty, so quiet, that it was safe for him to make this attack? If a compartment is empty, the one next to it won't be and then there are always gangs of soldiers having a smoke in the corridors.'

'Good point.' Vignoles nodded in agreement. When were the corridors not full of people smoking and blocking the way? 'It was Friday night by the time we think she died and that is usually a busy time. There's something more to all this, I'm sure of it.' Vignoles was still holding his cup aloft as he thought aloud. 'Oh, we must go for our train.'

'Quick, one other thing — what did he use to gag the girl's mouth?' Anna was gathering together the dirty plates and tossed this question over her shoulder as she walked into the little kitchen.

'The gag? Why it was... oh, but yes, of course. How stupid am I?' Vignoles banged his cup back down on the saucer with more force than he intended. 'I just can't believe I overlooked this. It was a neckerchief. A blue-and-white, spotted square, like workmen and railwaymen often wear to stop the dirt going down their shirts. It was not a woman's.'

'So it was the killer's?'

'Must be. And it was right in front of my face all the time. We have the first clue to his identity. And maybe his first mistake.

Chapter Nine

I WONDER WHO'S MISSING HER NOW?
Oscar Rabin & his band, with Harry Davis

John Beeby walked with a studied calmness and a measured tread, his boots crunching in the deep snow underfoot. His coat was buttoned tight up to the muffler around his neck and his hat had the brim pulled low over his eyes, which were further protected from the swirls of snow by the thick, round lenses of his glasses, which also reflected the dim lights of the gas lamps. In one gloved hand he swung a canvas bag filled with the tools of his trade whilst a rolled-up copy of the *Daily Sketch* was tucked under his arm.

It was early, and the shops were still being readied for the day ahead; their soft light spilling onto the snowy street and illuminating the constant fall of silvery flakes, pushing back the inky darkness when a door was opened or the window blinds rolled up to reveal the same meagre display of near-empty shelves and strident public information posters. A few hardy and pragmatic souls were already forming queues outside the food shops, the snow accumulating on hats and coats and around their feet, their mouths swathed in clouds of breath.

As he passed, Beeby glanced in an empty butcher's shop window and saw a young man, kitted out in a blue-and-white striped apron and a straw boater, place a rectangular blackboard in the window, angled to best attract attention.

WANTED

for next week's ration

MAGICIAN OR ILLUSIONIST

Beeby unconsciously gave a slight smile and in so doing caught the eye of the young man, who shrugged melodramatically with a broad but ironic grin. Beeby quickly averted his eyes and walked on. He passed a greengrocer's, which had a similar sign proclaiming, 'If we don't have it — grow it yourself!' But this time Beeby kept his eyes on the ground and hurried past. He had no garden and so thought it a stupid and unhelpful sign, and besides, these shopkeepers didn't like him. They never looked out for him, never showed him any favours or held back something 'a bit special', like they seemed to do for all the housewives in front. The shopkeepers all treated him like he was nobody. He always seemed to be at the end of the queue for the rotten leftovers and the cracked eggs. Even then, these jumped-up little shopkeepers, these self-appointed little Hitlers, handed over their pathetic scraps fit only for the pig trough with a supercilious look that suggested it was even wasted on someone like him.

He continued to walk along the street, his annoyance subsiding as the shops became progressively poorer. Many were closed, and Beeby thought that it would need more than a magician for these to reopen. Their signs were faded and peeling, the windows opaque with dirt and fire smoke, some with rotting blinds pulled down to mask the looted interiors. The tinkle of the doorbell had not welcomed customers inside these places since the bombing raids of the early forties. This area of Nottingham had been badly blitzed, many rows of shops had lost their roofs and the insides were burnt and shattered wrecks. Often, there were long gaps now filled only with great mounds of snow revealing angular lumps of masonry and brickwork, tall fingers of burnt timber and patches of scrubby bushes. The snow had softened everything, but could not wholly transform the harsh and ugly brutality of these skeletal buildings, now so empty and devoid of life.

And this was why Beeby considered this area to be the perfect place for him to dispose of the handbag stowed in the canvas holdall swinging in his hand. He knew the area well and had long since found the perfect spot. This was the closest he was going to get to a garden and it was not quite what the greengrocer had in mind, either. It was a corner plot, with tall, wooden hoardings on two sides erected by the corporation, where the shops' outer walls had collapsed. There was an access gate in the fence that had been forced ajar by the gangs of destructive kids who liked to enter this hidden world in order to set fires in the rubble and to smash and destroy anything that had been left unscathed by the Luftwaffe.

These bombsite kids were a menace and Beeby knew to pick a time to avoid them. Late afternoons and early evenings were rarely an option. Beeby had made that mistake before and had no wish to do so again. The kids were wild, almost feral, and they sensed something about him they didn't like or understand. It was the way dogs instinctively seem to know whom they should respect and who to attack. In a similar way, these awful children had turned upon him, calling him names: 'Mister Four-eyes! Mister Fatty four-eyes!' they had shouted and thrown stones that struck his back and legs, but whenever he turned to challenge them they would just stare back with stupid looks of exaggerated innocence and declare, 'It weren't me, mister! It must've bin sum-on else, mister.' He wanted to slap their grubby, insolent faces. But there were always too many of them and so he had had to retreat, humiliated and sore. As a consequence, he preferred to visit when he could be sure to be alone and early morning in a snowstorm was a safe bet.

Not that he ever had much to dispose of; just a small item or two lifted from each girl. He liked to discard these amongst the detritus of destroyed lives that lay intermingled with the blasted remains of the dwellings. These unremarkable objects instantly became just a part of the other shattered personal belongings embedded in the layers of soot, brick dust, plaster and splintered wood. The handbag was going to be one of the larger items he had dumped there. He'd like to keep it, but it was too large to risk retaining in his room. He could not risk that nosy Mrs Tipping discovering it. The smaller things were different and the few he had stashed away could even be explained away, but not the handbag. Anyway, he had messed things up so he needed to take a little extra care and be rid of it. Here, the crazy kids would soon scavenge anything flammable and cremate it on one of their bonfires and in so doing destroy the evidence for him. It was strangely satisfying to make these odious brats his unwitting accomplices. Yes, he liked that.

Beeby chuckled to himself as he looked around at the bombsite. He'd read up about the air raid and discovered that no lives had been lost in these streets. The Anderson shelters in the back yards and the big communal shelter under the primary school playground had saved everyone. Despite the devastation it was not really a place of death, so it was strange that it was to be the last resting place of that young woman. Of course she was not physically lying there in the rubble — what a dreadful thought — but once he had scattered her possessions across the jumbled ground this would be his own — what was the word — monument? No. Epitaph? No, that was not quite right either. Whatever the word, it would be there for all to see — if they only knew what to look for and where.

He thought about the others: about the broken comb that he knew was lying close to the half-open gate he had just squeezed through; the smashed hand-mirror that probably still lay on the floor beneath the snow so recently fallen. He grinned, threw the handbag in a long, looping flight high into the air and watched it tumble onto the pile of snow, scattering its contents along the way.

Bye-bye, Miss Harding. It was nice knowing you. As he turned to walk away, he carefully placed within his inside pocket one small item he had at the last moment rescued from the handbag.

※   ※   ※   ※

At about the same time that Beeby was standing in the bombsite, Vignoles was saying goodbye to his wife under the big clock suspended from the train shed roof in Leicester Central. They then walked their separate ways across the concourse: Vignoles to the operational headquarters of the London & North Eastern Railway police (southern division); Anna towards the goods' despatching department building, which stood like a mock-Tudor island surrounded by a sea of platforms, rails and canopies in the centre of the station complex.

Vignoles headed up the detective department, tasked with solving the more difficult and serious cases, and in so doing often liaised with the neighbouring railway companies, the various city and county constabularies and even, on occasion, with Interpol. Not that this more interesting work meant that those in the detective branch were completely absolved from rounding up stray sheep and cattle from the line, rescuing drunken demob-happy servicemen, arresting pickpockets and dealing with the many other daily problems and irritations encountered on a busy railway. It was, however, a job that Vignoles enjoyed, though it also carried with it some unpleasant aspects, such as discovering the remains of a young woman. However, Vignoles accepted that it was all part of the lot of the detective and he was at least familiar, if never quite inured to, the sight of death and the darker sides of man's nature.

His was an occupation that provided much mental stimulation and he enjoyed the problem-solving that was often part of a crime investigation. Rather like tackling *The Times* cryptic crossword, he was often to remark. One had to grapple to find the truth hidden beneath the immediate facts presented and decode and unscramble the often misleading or deceitful stories offered by defendants.

His job had another aspect that he considered to be strongly in its favour: he had to travel frequently along the railway and was, therefore, in close proximity to the steam locomotives that he so admired. And he was famous — notorious perhaps — for taking a great interest in the identity of the locomotive hauling any train. It was not for nothing that he had developed a close working relationship with a number of shedmasters who looked after the steam sheds along the line, and Vignoles never left home without a small, slim pocket book that listed all the locomotives in service, and in spare moments he would carefully underline those he had seen during the day. It was a well-filled book.

He was far from alone in this passion; in steadily-increasing numbers, at weekends and weekdays after the school bells had rung and regardless of the weather, the platform ends at Leicester Central and other stations would be filled by boys in school uniform eagerly anticipating the next arrival. They would often rush in noisy herds from one end of the station to the other, chasing an elusive 'cop', and attracting the reproachful looks and sometimes a sharp rebuke, from the top-hatted stationmaster. Nor was this solely the preserve of noisy school children, as the observant might also see gentlemen in smart overcoats, pinstriped trousers and bowler hats making subversive notes of engine numbers in small books with expensive fountain pens and even young chaps in demob suits with Brylcreemed hair loitering on the platform ends, fags hanging from the corners of their mouths, with a penny notebook, a pencil stub and an Ian Allan *ABC* spotter's book stuffed into a back pocket.

So, all in all, Vignoles considered himself lucky to have a satisfactory occupation that rubbed shoulders with his hobby. But, as with most things, his job had one major negative point — if the long and inconvenient hours and the not excessive remuneration were excluded — and that thorn in his side was Chief Superintendent James Badger.

The Badger was a small, compact man with an impressively military bearing. His ramrod-straight back, sharp, gannet-grey eyes, hair clipped in a 'number two' and fulsome grey moustache, all came packaged in a uniform clearly sourced from one of the very best suppliers in London — ration coupons and cost be hanged. Pressed, starched and polished, James Badger was the very model of immaculate but prissy presentation, quite able to be taken for someone far more important than his actual rank and standing. The quickest way to his heart was simple; fawn over him and offer him and Mrs Badger an invitation to a civic dinner.

Badger's northern accent was carefully concealed by a precise use of Received Pronunciation and all the affectations and mannerisms of the officer class. Vignoles suspected that the original Jimmy Badger from Huddersfield had been voice-coached at some point in his career. If so, then it had certainly convinced his superiors that he was cut out for leadership. However, there were clues to the real man lurking beneath the glossy veneer, because at times of acute stress or after one too many pink gins, his true accent would sometimes slip out and betray him with a trace of Yorkshire colouration. There had been one famous occasion late in the evening of V.E. Day, when Chief Superintendent Badger, like Eliza Doolittle, had completely lost his carefully manicured image and affectations and switched to pints of foaming ale. As he downed the beer in a steadily more drunken celebration, he joined the men of the lower ranks and suddenly lurched back into the beery, leery lad he once had been, his arm thrown around the shoulders of any unsuspecting victim he could find. He had even startled the women officers by dancing with them, rather finely as it turned out, Mrs Badger being nowhere to be seen. It was as if the hops and malt had stripped back the layers of gloss, revealing a man yearning to drop his defences and jump and jive and tell blue jokes like the rest of them. That night as his vowels became burred by a folk-memory of a Yorkshire accent, he had become almost likeable.

But this had been an aberration, and Badger had made it abundantly clear through an excessive punctiliousness and coldness in the days that followed, that V.E. night was a subject strictly off-limits for discussion. Badger courted minor politicians, small town mayors, railway company board members, bank managers, the senior ranks in the county constabularies and the secretaries of two (not exceedingly well-appointed) golf clubs, with unending zeal and consummate care. He never missed an anniversary or an event that might reinforce his not wholly robust sense of self-importance. Badger's great triumph, in his mind anyway, was a slight acquaintance with a permanent under-secretary of state; a man now suffering the pain of working for Atlee's dynamically reformist Labour government, and who had found a sympathetic ear with whom to unburden his frustrations and disapproval of this administration. Sir Anthony Prazen-Beagle's whinging bored Vignoles, but his chief superintendent insisted upon passing on this litany of complaints in slavish detail in the misguided belief that Vignoles might agree.

And so, as Vignoles walked towards the railway police head office, all his thoughts about how to progress the case, that he had been mulling over during the train journey to work, evaporated instantly as soon as Vignoles spied the chief super's driver, Mr Pedder, leaning against the wall outside the entrance to his office, smoking a cigarette.

'Oh, blast it, that's all I need.'

Vignoles muttered the comments under his breath as he approached the driver, who seemed to be obsessively preoccupied by the legs of a young WAAF standing nearby. Drawing close, but unobserved, Vignoles spoke out clearly as he passed Pedder, adopting his most Badger-like voice, 'Don't slouch man, and get that cap straight!' He gave a wicked smile as the young man hurriedly stood upright, fumbling to pull his cap forwards from the back of his head, whilst trying and failing to conceal his cigarette. As soon as Pedder realised that it was Vignoles and not Badger he slumped back and gave a sour look.

'Working hard this morning, Pedder?' With that, Vignoles entered the lobby and looked for his visitor.

As expected, the chief superintendent had taken over Vignoles's office and was awaiting his arrival, no doubt casting irritated glances at the clock on the wall. Vignoles made yet another mental note, which he would invariably forget, to call in the clock repairer to adjust this ancient timepiece so that it was not permanently five minutes fast. The clock was doing him no favours. He knew he could expect the silent admonishment of Badger's eyes glancing up at its face and the implication that he was late.

'Good morning, sir. Bright and early today?' Vignoles tried to put some warmth in his voice.

'Morning, Vignoles. It's hardly bright, and the country is practically at a standstill with the snow, and I have never considered eight, correction, eight-oh-five...' his eyes flicking across at the clock, '...early. One's military background instils an appreciation of the benefits of rising at five. I can get a lot done before most others start work. But I take your sentiment in the spirit it is offered. Do sit down.' Badger pushed his upturned cap a fraction to one side on Vignoles's desk, with one extended forefinger. 'I was working on my forthcoming presentation at next month's Railway Police Officers'

Annual Conference. It's an important paper, y'know?' He sniffed to re-enforce the point and checked the lie of one of his perfectly tailored cuffs.

Vignoles said nothing; his mind still thinking about the case. He was impatient to get to work. Badger, however, was wittering on in his curt, clipped voice, 'I was also able to take advantage of a pretty decent breakfast at the Midland Hotel. Not a patch on pre-war days, of course, but despite this bloody government nearly starving us to the bone the chef did a sterling job. All things considered, it was a pretty reasonable mixed grill.'

'Glad to hear it, sir.' Vignoles had enjoyed his solitary egg, but it was his first in two days and the last he was likely to taste until next week's ration, unless he braved the horrors of the dried variety. He already felt his stomach rumble enviously at the thought of a mixed grill. Vignoles wondered if it was an arrestable offence to brag about such plenty. He moved the subject on. 'But surely you did not drive down from London this morning, with all this snow?'

'No, thank Heaven. We travelled up yesterday. I had an engagement in the evening at my club. Pedder took the car by rail in one of those odd little wagons specially made for 'em.' Badger was proud of his comprehensive ignorance of any detail about railway operations and equipment, but was a vociferous champion of the motor car. 'I had hoped to try out the dining car on the way up, but can you believe this, there was no dining car. The whole damn way here without so much as a glass of wine. And we were three hours late. It's a disgrace.'

'We've not had dining cars since 1940, sir.'

'No? Well the blasted war's over now, and it's high time they got themselves sorted out.' Having got this off his chest, Badger allowed himself to slightly relax back into the chair, and he idly flopped the fine kid gloves into his upturned cap. Vignoles waited. 'Still, the hotel rallied around and looked after us royally. Despite everything, the British really know how to pull together in the face of a crisis and keep their chins up, makes one proud.'

'I rather think they are being tested by harder things than just knocking up a meal in a hotel — with respect.'

Badger gave Vignoles a hard look before replying. 'Hmm. But it's the principle, you see? Standards being maintained and business as usual. Sets a good example to everyone. Starts from the top, of course: we must be seen to be setting an example, despite everything. Gives the workers something to look up to, and that way, they can see that we're getting the country back on its feet. Well, we would if it wasn't for that blasted Atlee.' He flung down his gloves in disgust.

'Ah.'

'All of which brings me to why I am here.'

'It does?' Vignoles sat up, fearing that the prime minister was about to pay a visit.

'I trust you received my directions on the matter of the colliery train robbery? I left them with your typist.'

'That would be my *secretary*, Mrs Green.' He allowed himself to stand down from high alert.

'Indeed. I left them with her, since you were not in the office. I trust she did pass them on?'

Vignoles recalled her hurried message and wondered if that constituted 'directions', or if there had been something more, which he had managed to ignore. He decided to wing it. 'Of course. Though I was out investigating another case — an important one...'

'...And this is important, Charles, make no mistake about it. We are suffering an acute fuel shortage at present — as well you know — and whilst I might suggest that the damned minister of fuel and power pulled his finger out and found a solution to the problem, the facts are as they are. We cannot have vagabonds and black-marketeers acting like... like bloody pirates, robbing and selling coal. We need to stamp this out — and hard. I need you to set an example. If we're not careful it'll become an epidemic. There could be anarchy near every coal mine in the country.'

'You really think so?' Vignoles tried make his voice sound sufficiently convinced.

'Mark my words. We've already had those mutinous meat drivers go on strike and it took the army to sort out those shameful renegades. A bloody disgrace! Now with the coal mines going all socialist on us — as if they needed any further encouragement — it could be just the spark needed to light the fuse for all-out revolution. Do you want to hear something shocking?' Vignoles made a small movement with a hand. He was going to hear it anyway. 'Sir Anthony advised me that the country has coal stocks sufficient to last only three weeks, and now with this snowfall! Do the arithmetic yourself.' Badger gave Vignoles a long stare. 'So I need a quick result on this. Do whatever it takes.'

'I have two of my officers onto it already.'

'And why in heaven's name are you not heading it up?'

'Because of the rape and murder of a young woman. Your typist did pass my report on?'

Badger darted a sharp look at Vignoles. 'Of course.' He cleared his throat, 'Terrible business. Terrible. But look, we really cannot allow this one-off incident to divert our attention away from what could turn into a crisis right across the land.'

'Nor can we allow a cold-blooded killer to walk freely. Surely you are not suggesting that we don't find this man?'

'Of course not, don't be absurd, man!' But Badger fell silent for a moment considering his words, which were then spoken more quietly. 'This murder is on our patch?'

'Yes. She was beside the track, thrown off a passing train.'

'Do we know where she got on?'

'Somewhere north of Rugby.'

'Hmm. We won't get much interest from the constabularies then. The investigation might cross too many boundaries. Never the easiest thing to get neighbouring constabularies to co-operate. But still, I'm pretty sure a couple of your chaps can get that ghastly matter sorted out in no time.'

'I'm not so sure it will be that straightforward'.

'Why? They're not up to the job?'

'That's not what I meant, it's a complex situation.'

'Yes? In my experience, most cases like this turn out to be family affairs. Call the boyfriend in and grill him. He'll soon confess.'

Vignoles sighed deeply then proceeded to speak, choosing his words with care. 'It's very early to say, as we are still trying to identify her. The killer has done a surprisingly good job of making it hard for us to do so, deliberately removing any obvious identifying material, although he missed something, a handkerchief embroidered with her initials. It was also a brutal attack.'

'Too much alcohol, I expect.'

'I am inclined to say no. This was not...' Vignoles risked pushing the meagre facts beyond anything he actually possessed, '... this was not some argument that went horribly wrong, and was far too premeditated to be a drunken assault. Those options would be tragic, but at least would be the isolated case you suggest. No. I think this was a deliberate, cold-blooded murder with a rather sickening intent.'

'Good Lord. Are you sure?'

'Just my initial observations, sir, but I have reason to think so. He gagged, raped and strangled her, then took care to dump the body in a place where it took a stroke of chance to find her. If it had snowed that night like it is now, we might not have discovered her for days, perhaps weeks. Worse still, I fear he might strike again.'

'You know what you are saying? We've got a serial killer on the loose?'

'Possibly. His modus operandi suggests he has a method, a "style", for want of a better word. Can we afford to take the risk that he won't strike again?'

'Put like that, I can see your point of view.'

Badger looked out of the window towards the billows of smoke and steam swirling from a big express engine opposite, the slamming of doors and bustling of passengers suggesting that it was soon to depart. A young woman was standing alone on the platform, a suitcase beside her feet. She appeared apprehensive and was frequently looking around with a slightly bewildered look and nervously checking her wristwatch, her lower lip gently pressed between her teeth, an action that had already started to remove some of the glossy red lipstick. Vignoles followed Badger's glance, and perhaps the two of them shared the same thought; that this innocent young traveller could be the next victim. A train whistle screamed shrilly and broke the short reverie.

Badger seemed to make up his mind and looked back at Vignoles. 'Catch this man. And make it snappy. But I want you to keep the two officers on the coal robberies. Draft in as many uniforms as you need. Try to liaise with the constabularies and see what help they can offer. Both crimes are on our railway, so try to keep them ours. Getting a good result would do our service no harm. And I want a daily update on both cases. Well, it looks like you have a lot on your plate.'

'More than I had for breakfast', thought Vignoles. 'Indeed, sir. I have a couple of lines of enquiry to follow up today. I shall put them in today's report'.

'Good. I'll leave you to it, then.' With that the chief superintendent stood up, swept up his cap and gloves and, with the very slightest of nods towards Vignoles, left the office.

Mercifully free of the super's presence, Vignoles wasted no time in calling Sergeant Trinder to join him to discuss the neckerchief.

'So, we already have something probably worn by the killer.'

'And this gives us a clue to how he might dress, and his occupation. Some kind of tradesman?' Trinder shared Vignoles's excitement that they had at last something to follow through.

'Or a factory worker. Perhaps a warehouseman?'

'Or footplate crew?' said Trinder.

'Again, it's a possibility — he could have been "riding the cushions" back from a long turn away. This does give us an angle. We need to get the neckerchief analysed — maybe there will be some other clue — an oil stain or something caught in the fabric.'

'I seem to recall it looked very clean, but I'll get it over to the lab right away,' answered Trinder, 'It's a bit of luck that the Leicester civvies are prepared to play ball and share their facilities.'

'Yes, it's decent of them. We'd be well and truly scuppered without the help of their boys in the backroom.' Vignoles gave a rueful grin. 'There is another matter for us to think about. The time that it took the killer to do all that he did and then cover his tracks without being spotted. Thoughts?'

'You've hit the nail on the head. I've been worrying about that as well,' said Trinder. Vignoles nodded in approval, pleased that his sergeant had an enquiring brain. 'It's oddly unlucky for the poor girl that no one stumbled upon him during what must have been a lengthy assault.'

'It is puzzling, but I've an idea.' Vignoles stood up and thrust his head around his office door and called to Mavis, 'Is either Benson or Lansdowne in?'

'I'm here, sir.' W.P.C. Benson was buttoning up her long, navy overcoat and adjusting her scarf as she hurried into the office, closely followed by W.P.C. Lansdowne, who was adjusting her hat. 'We were on our way to Clifton Colliery, if we can get through the snow.'

'Good. But hang fire and follow me — there's something I want to try.' Vignoles ducked back inside and grabbed his coat and hat from the peg behind the door, 'Come along, we need to find ourselves a railway carriage.'

Ten minutes later, Vignoles was causing accidental hilarity amongst his officers as he tried to manhandle W.P.C. Lansdowne out of a carriage compartment and down the narrow corridor to an outside door in the end vestibule by variously lifting, dragging and generally pulling and bumping the poor woman.

The carriage was one of some empty stock awaiting removal from the station, and having gained the permission of the guard and enlisted the unsuspecting assistance of Lansdowne, he had instructed her to 'play dead,' as she was similar to the victim in height and build, whilst Trinder and Benson watched and timed his efforts. Vignoles hoped that his experiment might throw up some answers to a nagging doubt in his mind that the whole scenario was flawed.

The task was proving to be far harder than Vignoles could have imagined. His clumsy attempts to move the W.P.C. had reduced them to fits of laughter, despite the grim reasons for acting out this pantomime. Lansdowne was a lithe woman, trim and athletic in build and yet Vignoles still struggled to manhandle her with any grace and only succeeding in causing some damage to Lansdowne's knees and ankles, though she tried gamely to not complain, merely wincing in agony as he tried to drag her by her arms, and then in embarrassment, felt by both, as he tried a more intimate hold around her chest. The W.P.C. was not as gregarious as Benson, being a far quieter and more private individual and, although she tried to not show her feelings, and appreciated that there was a perverse necessity to the inspector's actions, she had rosy blushes upon her cheeks and averted her eyes from the laughing audience, clearly feeling embarrassed by the situation.

'OK. I've proved my point. Enough!' Vignoles paused to regain his breath, gulping in air and realising that he was not as fit as he had hoped. 'This is darned hard work. Or I'm especially unfit.'

'Thank you, sir!' Lansdowne was making as if brushing dust off her uniform but was actually nursing a bruised hip, and she allowed a quick flash of a look in his direction.

'Sorry, Lansdowne, that sounded rather awful; it's no reflection upon yourself, but upon my lamentable fitness.' He panted hard. 'The killer must have been a reasonably strong man, perhaps even practised in the curiously skilled art of moving the dead weight of a body, because it's a tricky task in a cramped space. It took me... how long?'

'Three minutes.' Sergeant Trinder was still trying to recover from laughing.

'A long time on a busy train.' Vignoles took another deep breath and looked at the W.P.C. 'Thanks for putting up with all that.'

'All in the line of duty.' She leant against the carriage wall and slowly rubbed one of her ankles. 'But I feel that it would preferable to be at least unconscious when being lugged around a railway compartment. Or to be hefted around by someone more practised.'

Vignoles watched her massage her ankle and felt the gentle sting of her rebuke. 'But all this Laurel and Hardy stuff has actually got a serious point. I find it increasingly hard to believe that our killer *did* do this. Yes, he could be strong and practised — a fireman, perhaps — but I'm not convinced. The point you made about being at least unconscious supports what we already suspect: that she was killed or knocked out prior to being moved and dumped.'

Sergeant Trinder agreed: 'It just takes far too long.' He was speaking seriously now, 'I can't see how he could unless he had help?'

'Or... but wait a minute though!' Vignoles was staring out of the carriage window at a short passenger train that had just pulled up in the adjacent platform. 'Look at that suburban stock on the train. It has no corridors — just doors that each open into a small compartment.'

A stunned silence fell as this revelation sank home.

'Lord, yes. It all seems rather obvious now — they must have taken a local train.' Lansdowne spoke eagerly, her bashed ankle and hip forgotten.

'It would be easy to throw the body out of one of those and no danger of the guard or passengers seeing him do it. If he and the girl were the only two occupants then they would be locked together in dreadful privacy.' Vignoles was speaking quietly.

'Why did we assume she was travelling long distance?' Trinder was looking annoyed with himself for having been complicit in such an obvious oversight. 'I'll get Blencowe to narrow down his search. This will considerably reduce the options, and better still, local trains are just that — local. A smaller area to search,' said Trinder.

'Get him straight on to it.' Vignoles shook his head slowly, also wondering how he had taken so long spot the obvious explanation. However, he was lifted by the sense that the case was starting to move forward.

As the officers walked away from the empty train, Vignoles stepped down, stood on the busy platform and looked around him. He was in a pensive mood. He needed a few moments to clear his head and order his thoughts. Sergeant Trinder glanced over his shoulder and made as if to speak, but decided to leave his boss to his thoughts and so walked away with the two women officers.

Leicester Central was busy with people moving in every direction: porters rumbled by with small-wheeled trolleys stacked with luggage, shouting and calling as they went. A guard blew a whistle and waved his green flag as he rested one foot on the open doorway of the last carriage of his train. A gang of women in blue overalls and heavy coats was sweeping and shovelling snow from the platforms. N.A.A.F.I. women were serving tea from a mobile stand that was swathed in steam like a miniature locomotive, whilst groups of travellers cupped their hands around steaming mugs. Beside the W.H. Smith stall, a few men were surveying the meagre collection of emaciated daily newspapers, now shrunken to just four pages. Vignoles could hear the clop-clop of iron-shod horses hauling wagons over the cobbled surface of the goods depot. Others did what passengers spent so much time doing; standing, transferring their weight from one leg to another, blowing on their gloved hands, glancing repeatedly at wristwatches and the big station clock as if this repetition would hurry along time and their invariably late-running train.

A group of W.A.A.F.s stood shivering and giggling nearby, their uniforms neat and attractive amidst the drab and tired utilitarian clothes that dominated the scene. One was the same young woman that Pedder's gaze had been drawn to, and she and her friends were obviously a source of attraction to two young, shaven-headed Americans who were now giving them the eye, and offering cigarettes accompanied with broad smiles and witty banter that caused little peals of laughter. One W.A.A.F., now with a cigarette in her mouth, leant forward to take a light, her dark eyes looking intently into those of the serviceman, his hand briefly touching hers during the exchange.

Vignoles smiled at the easy way the two men were smooth-talking the W.A.A.F.s. He closed his eyes for a moment to shut out the scene and then looked at it afresh. He now saw an alternative version, one reflected in a kind of evil wonderland looking-glass; a world of dangerous men with evil intent in their hearts stalking young women. He watched the G.I.s throwing their heads back in exaggerated laughter, and how they edged closer to one or other of the women, moved their hands occasionally to touch an arm or shoulder, forging a bond, making contact. Could there be something more sinister behind all this? Or was he being too cynical and it was just the mating game in action?

An engine blew a short warning whistle, and Vignoles was glad to shake off these sour thoughts and turn his attention away from this innocent flirting. The snow had stopped, and for a moment a few precious bands of weak sunlight streaked through the latticework of the station canopy to form elongated pools across the platform and to undulate over the body of the approaching locomotive. Snow was heaped in mounds in the tender and on the cab roof. But where the engine's heat had thawed the snow, the paintwork was washed clean and the pale light now accentuated the luscious green, complemented by the rich and complex tones of the varnished teak coaches behind. Vignoles was struck by the riot of autumnal colours of the train amidst the drab surroundings, and he imagined that he could smell the sweetly musty scent of the boxes of apples in his father's loft and feel the last blush of autumn's heat on his face. It was just the warmth radiating from the engine's firebox, but it brought a momentary lump to his throat.

The last time he had helped pack and carry the apples in from his parents' garden had been in September 1939. They had kept the radio on all that day listening for news and looked anxiously to the skies for the air assault they knew was coming. Immersed in an unexpected surge of nostalgia, Vignoles looked at the hissing locomotive before him and was reminded of one particular afternoon in the July of the same year, when he had stood at the end of this same platform to watch the arrival of the railway's two most famous locomotives for an open day at the depot.

The Flying Scotsman had looked elegantly beautiful; burnished and polished like a sleek racehorse prepared for the Derby. The very poise and gait of the big Pacific had hinted at both power and speed, like the thoroughbred after which its sisters were named.

But it had been Mallard that had stolen the show for Vignoles. He had rarely seen examples of these elusive engines, for they always worked the East Coast mainline from King's Cross up to Leeds and Edinburgh, hardly venturing into his neck of the woods. The world's fastest locomotive had been resplendent in a rich garter blue and the glossiest of blacks, with a glimpse of big, red wheels beneath the air-smoothed valances like a flash of bloomers on a music hall dancer. There was something outrageously decadent about scarlet wheels on such a machine. It was a far cry from the all-over black that so many still carried today. On that cloudless day, Mallard's shiny chrome numbers had dazzled in the sun against the rich blue of the sky. He had been struck at the time by the way the curvaceous shapes of the locomotive were echoed by the equally attractive, but sinister, silver barrage balloons that bobbed languidly in the still air above Leicester. These silent balloons on their long retaining wires looked as if they had been lofted high for the weekend celebration of steam, and indeed many of children crowded around the engines had coloured balloons in their hands, which bounced and bobbed across the hot railway yard.

Back in the present, Vignoles walked closer to the engine. It had a brass nameplate bearing the name The Cottesmore. Vignoles reached into his coat pocket, extracted his *ABC*, turned to the page listing the engines of this type and ran his eyes down the names of the fox hunts they commemorated. He looked back at the locomotive, but already he was no longer thinking about it. 'I am on the hunt for a killer', he thought, 'and whilst I stand here daydreaming, that man could be on the hunt for his next victim. What am I doing? This isn't some game.'

Vignoles spun on his heels and marched rapidly back towards his office.

Chapter Ten

'NIGHT RIDE'

Nat Gonella & his Orchestra

It was not until the late afternoon that Vignoles remembered the other note that he had been handed by Mavis Green earlier that day. He had just finished listening to Benson and Lansdowne present their initial report on the Clifton Colliery coal train robbery and this jogged his memory. One of these still remained unanswered, so after agreeing that the two W.P.C.s should organise a rota of night-time observations and draft in some uniformed officers to assist in this unattractive and most freezing of tasks, he dismissed them and only then pulled out the crumpled piece of paper. Smoothing it out on the ink blotter on his desk, he peered at the message and dialled the number. The call went straight through without need of an operator, as it was routed along the company's own lines, and just a few rings later it was picked up.

'Woodford and Hinton.'

'Hello, may I speak with the stationmaster, Mr Markham, please?'

'Speaking. How may I be of help?'

'This is Detective Inspector Vignoles, returning your call. I believe it was you who left a message with my office?'

'Indeed it was. Thank you for taking the time to call back, inspector.' Markham's voice was rich and warm, with the soft burr of the local accent. 'I can't say I have ever had any dealings with your department, being newly-installed in this position, so forgive me if I am barking up the wrong tree and wasting your time.'

'I can be the best judge of that. So what was it you wished to tell me?'

Markham cleared his throat and proceeded to speak in a quiet and measured manner. 'It was something that happened this morning at… let me see… about seven-fifteen or thereabouts. Yes, it would be seven-fifteen as the Stratford local had just pulled out and I'd seen it pass the window when I had Pinky —that is, Mr Eric Pinkett — the stationmaster at Banbury, on the blower telling me all about the young lady who's managed to lose her girlfriend somewhere along the line. Seems like she's clean vanished into thin air. No one has seen her at all.'

'Go on...' Vignoles felt himself holding his breath, a tingle running down the nape of his neck.

'Yes, it's all a bit of a mystery. Apparently this young woman has been waiting around the station...'

'Banbury station?'

'Correct. Banbury G.W.R., not Midland, to be precise. She was there all Friday evening and most of the night as well, waiting and asking after her friend and then was back bright and early in time to meet the milk train. So Pinky got curious and started to make a few enquiries of his own.'

'Why did he call you?'

'One of his men down there asked the young lady from where her missing friend had travelled, and apparently she was supposed to have got out here at Woodford to catch the connection onwards to Banbury.'

'Where did she start her journey?'

'From around your neck of the woods — Nottingham Victoria.'

'When was she travelling?'

'Friday last, late afternoon. Look, I'm sorry, I realise that this is probably a wild goose chase and that this young lady is just getting in a lather about nothing, but you see, I then heard the news about the poor murdered girl. Ghastly business, I must say. And whilst I don't wish to jump to conclusions, I just wondered...'

'There could be a connection.' Vignoles quickly wiped his face with his free hand and drank in a gulp of fresh air. He then picked up a pencil and started to make notes. 'What is the name of the woman at Banbury?'

'I have it written down here — a Miss Heather Spencer.'

'And the name of her friend? The missing one.' Vignoles felt his stomach tense and his breath tighten.

'Harding. Miss Vera Harding...'

'V.H. — so that is who you are...'

'I'm sorry — do you know her?'

'Listen, this is very important. Is Miss Spencer still there? Oh, but I am being foolish, how can you know that? She's at Banbury.' Vignoles could feel the excitement building inside. 'Did your colleague give you Miss Spencer's address and phone number?'

'I took the precaution of doing so. Pinky is a bit of a stickler like that and I must admit to sharing this attribute. Detail is everything in this job — but then I am sure you would agree.' Vignoles grunted in reply and silently thanked the Lord for the inherent efficiency and love of such detail bred into all railwaymen.

Stationmaster Markham continued, 'I would imagine that she has returned home by now. At least I hope she has, poor girl. Do you think the friend is the one who was killed?'

'It is possible, but we must be very cautious at this stage. It is very important that you say nothing to anyone about this conversation. I cannot be certain without a full identification, which Miss Spencer may be able to offer. Once we are sure, I can then make a statement to the press. Under no circumstances must you, or anyone else, let this out before that time.'

'I understand.' The stationmaster fell silent for a few moments. 'I fear that this story will not have a happy ending.'

'I am afraid not. I must meet with Miss Spencer urgently. Did Stationmaster Pinkett say if she had a telephone?'

'She has not. But this is her address: 7 Cherwell Crescent, Banbury.'

'Thank you. This has been extremely useful and your quick thinking is commendable — I'm only sorry — very sorry — that it took me so long to reply. I hope I shall not regret my tardiness. I shall travel to Banbury by the very next train. May I ask that, in order to save time, you put a call through to Mr Pinkett and tell him this?'

'Of course.'

'And advise him that if Miss Spencer should return to his station, then ask that he detain her there, but he must not tell her anything other than that I need to speak with her urgently.'

'You can rely upon my discretion, detective inspector.'

'I know that I can. Thank you again.'

Vignoles replaced the receiver, sat back in his chair and started to fill his pipe whilst he quickly ran through the information he had just been given.

He was filled with that curious mixture of emotions that every policeman experienced — the thrilling elation of a major breakthrough in a case coursing through his veins like adrenaline, and yet tempered by a profound sense of sadness. With the revelation of her name, the dead girl was now rendered all the more real. It was the living he had to deal with now, and he felt a stomach-churning twinge at the thought of the heartbreak and devastation that was going to break like a tidal wave upon this Heather Spencer and the family of the murdered woman. Their worst nightmares were about to become real and he was to be the carrier of this bleak news.

Vignoles scribbled down a few notes about the conversation with Stationmaster Markham before putting on his hat, coat and scarf. Just before leaving his office, he stopped and looked at the cardboard box filled with what were now likely to be the clothes of Vera Harding. He lifted the envelope containing the monogrammed handkerchief, slid this into a deep inner pocket of his heavy R.A.F. overcoat then walked into the main office, calling for his sergeant as he did so.

* * * *

By the time Vignoles and Trinder arrived at Banbury that night it was already past ten o'clock, and both men were feeling acute pangs of hunger, having been unable to find any real sustenance along the way. The refreshment room at Woodford Halse had provided a friendly respite and they had received a warm welcome from the proprietress, Mrs Walsh, and especially from Jenny, Violet McIntyre's daughter. But, as it was early evening when they had arrived, the meagre ration of food on offer had long since sold out. Tea, and a couple of home-made flapjacks, that clearly lacked much in the way of fat, helped but did little to ease the deep, gnawing hunger in their stomachs. Vignoles remembered that there was a bakery in the little town and had even contemplated venturing up the hill and knocking them up to see if they could offer any additional food, but the driving wind and ever-increasing snowfall persuaded him to stay huddled close to the stove and to seek solace in warmth and tea alone until their connecting train arrived to take them on to Banbury.

Their train had struggled through rapidly mounting snow and a full-scale blizzard was in force when they stepped off the train at Banbury. The snow was driving across the platforms in streams of white lines that wavered, twisted and turned like skeins of wool in the eddies of the penetrating wind. A mournful howl was being raised around the eaves of the creaking train-shed, whilst various directional signs, suspended by chains from wooden beams across the roof space, were swinging noisily above their heads. One particularly annoying sign screeched like a hoarsely braying donkey, setting Vignoles's teeth on edge. The smoke from the locomotive that had hauled them to this Siberian outpost was being whipped viciously from the lip of the chimney and pulled hard down along one side of the engine until finally being ripped into shreds, the effect being to suggest that the stationary engine was travelling at an astonishingly high speed.

The fireman clanged and banged around on the footplate, bathed in a rich orange glow illuminating the streaming snow as it passed the cab, appearing to transform it into tongues of fire as the two detectives walked down the dark and desolate platform towards a door marked Stationmaster, their coats flapping and gloved hands holding their hats in place as the vicious wind tugged and buffeted them.

'Damn this blasted winter!' Trinder's words, though spoken with force, were almost lost in the wind and rendered weak and indistinct. 'I wouldn't mind so much if I wasn't so darned hungry.'

Vignoles, ignoring the complaint, rapped on the office door then stepped smartly inside, as the hee-hawing sign above made it impossible for him to hear any command to enter.

The room was quite small, with two mahogany desks set facing each other on either side of a polished, cast-iron fire surround enlivened by a roaring fire that was filling the room with a delicious warmth and the tang of coal smoke and cigars. The walls were largely bare, but clean, with just a well-framed print of a large Great Western express engine in photographic grey behind one desk and an elegant map showing the extent of the Great Western Railway behind the other. Vignoles's detective mind instinctively assessed the map and judged that it dated from the turn of the century because of its flamboyant and fussy lettering style and the liberal use of heraldic devices, all a far remove from the clean, modernist styles that had become popular just before the war. A number of certificates and diplomas took up a third wall, which was also punctuated by a door to an inner room or corridor. The floor was covered by polished linoleum with a small rug placed before the fire and two very upright armchairs that tentatively placed a leg each upon this small shred of comfort. A circular clock with the letters GWR above the number six ticked quietly in solid, measured strokes.

A tall man with extensive sideburns, matching moustache and a head topped with waves of salt-and-pepper hair was seated behind one of the desks, a pair of half-moon reading glasses perched upon the tip of his nose. He was wearing a neatly-pressed and rather formal black suit with long tails to the jacket that Vignoles could see were carefully flipped either side of the chair back. His waistcoat displayed a gold watch chain draped between two pockets and was worn over a brilliantly-white shirt with a high collar and a fulsome cravat held in place by a silver tie pin.

An inkstand, wooden desk calendar and a black Bakelite telephone were ranged upon the desk before him. A set of railway timetables and operating instructions were stacked neatly beside a wire tray holding a pile of paperwork.

Stationmaster Pinkett was very much a man of his time, and that time was a somewhere deep before the Great War, judging by his dress. He had certainly served the railway for some years, quite possibly beyond the official retirement age, and so would have learnt his profession in the days of the first incarnation of the Great Western Railway, a company still suffused with the style and character of Isambard Kingdom Brunel and Daniel Gooch, and which could still remember the time when it ran along wonderfully broad and smooth lines that were far too go-ahead and innovative to survive. Vignoles could not help but be reminded that Stationmaster Pinkett might just have seen one of Gooch's broad gauge engines bowling along over rails patented by his own namesake, Charles Vignoles. The Western was a proud railway that fiercely defended its traditions and still retained much of its own elegant, if slightly old-fashioned, charm. And old-fashioned or not, charm was something the elderly stationmaster had plenty of.

'Mr Pinkett?'

'The one and the same, my dear fellows. So you must be the two detectives I have been so eagerly expecting. And how very intriguing and thought-provoking your dash down to us has been. Something out of the ordinary indeed, and not without a touch of the Sherlock Holmes about it.' He stood up as he was speaking, then stopped, and his face flickered into a sterner set. 'Though I fear your arrival brings only bad news. Very sad news, particularly for a certain young lady.' He walked around the desk, hand extended in greeting. 'But do come in, come in gentlemen. Shut that blessed wind out of the room, shake the snow off your shoes and don't spare the floor polish.' He grinned, showing a set of fine teeth and causing his sideburns to lift upwards and outwards with an effect that reminded Vignoles of some kind of woodland creature.

'I shall not insult you by enquiring how your journey was, as I can safely assume it to have been nightmarish.' Another woodlandish grin. 'And I'm sorry to say that it is likely to be an enforced one-way journey to boot, for this storm is set to last for the duration. I fear that there is little chance of anything going north again until at least tomorrow morning, perhaps later even than that.'

The two detectives winced, but Vignoles gave the warmest grin he could summon and extended his hand to meet that of Stationmaster Pinkett. 'D.I. Charles Vignoles. Thank you for meeting us at such short notice and under such odd circumstances. This is Sergeant John Trinder.' Hands were shaken and Vignoles continued speaking whilst the effusive stationmaster ushered them towards the armchairs before the fire, though neither man sat, preferring instead to draw what heat they could by standing with their backs to the merrily burning coals.

'We appreciate your allowing us to come here onto Great Western territory to further our enquiries. The death took place within our jurisdiction, but has ramifications that will no doubt stretch far beyond.'

'I dare say it will, and it's not a problem for you to be here. We shall get down to business in a tick, but first things first — you need sustenance to keep the old grey-matter functioning. I'll get my assistant to find something hot. Mrs Pinkett cobbled up a pretty fine Woolton pie earlier today and I know there's enough left over for you both.' And before Vignoles had time to reply — much to the relief of Trinder, who was convinced that his boss would refuse the much needed food — Stationmaster Pinkett strutted through the internal door and into another part of the building.

'A warm welcome. But I wonder where Miss Spencer is waiting? I need to get this over and done with. I'm not looking forward to it one bit.'

'Maybe that's why he wants us to eat first? After all perhaps another twenty minutes won't hurt?'

'And another twenty minutes of prolonging Miss Spencer's wait. We owe it to her to get on with this.'

'Gentlemen, food is being prepared. But I regret, no offal!' He winked extravagantly as he voiced this line, which came from the ITMA comedy radio show. 'You shall eat after you have met Miss Spencer.' Vignoles nodded slightly. 'She's here at the station and I shall bring her in directly. I should perhaps mention that she has been here, on and off, for the best part of a day and a half and whilst I have told her almost nothing — and indeed know only the little that was passed onto me by yourself via my esteemed colleague at Woodford — she has, quite naturally, drawn her own rather grim conclusions as to why you have travelled here. This is all to say that she is in a bit of a state. It's been an awful trial for the poor young lady waiting here these long hours.' With that, he left the room again, returning almost immediately and ushering in a slim woman wearing a thick, wide-shouldered coat that was cinched around the waist by a matching belt and with the collar turned up, though whether as an escape from the cold or a defence against the stress and worry that Vignoles could see was coursing through her veins it was impossible to say.

Miss Spencer had pale blue eyes that would have been startling and perhaps even beautiful under normal circumstances, but now were ringed by red and slightly puffy. Her daintily-upturned nose was also tinged with red from frequent blowing and the drying effects of the cold, and this, together with her pale skin that highlighted the sprinkling of freckles, made her the very picture of someone gripped by deep apprehension and who was only just managing to hold her emotions together.

'Miss Spencer?'

The woman nodded and gave an almost inaudible reply in the affirmative. After Vignoles made the introductions he invited her to take a seat by the fire whilst Trinder moved to behind the stationmaster's desk. Vignoles was pleased to see that Pinkett had quietly retired from the room, closing the connecting door behind him without a further word.

'I believe that you are waiting for your friend, Miss Vera Harding?'

'Yes. Is she…? Have you found her? I mean, has something happened to Vera?'

'I need to take this a step at a time. I know it is hard for you, but I really need to be sure that we are talking about the same person and so I need to ask you a series of questions to help me establish if that is so. Please be patient and try to answer my questions as carefully and as accurately as you can.'

She nodded and dabbed her eyes with a handkerchief. Vignoles noticed this and it prompted him to reach inside his coat and extract the manila envelope and remove the handkerchief recovered from the body.

'Tell me, do you recognise this?' He handed the small square of white cotton to the young woman. Her eyes opened wide and she stared for a few moments, her mouth moving soundlessly. 'Have you seen this before?' Vignoles gently urged her.

'Yes. It was made by her mother.'

'Vera Harding's mother? You are quite sure?' Miss Spencer nodded in an exaggerated manner. 'You know from just two letters embroidered in a corner?'

She met his gaze, her eyes swimming. 'I do. I remember her showing it to me so very clearly. Her mother's eyesight is failing and so it was really special that she managed to embroider this on a set of handkerchiefs. Vera was thrilled.'

Vignoles felt a cold dart stab him in the chest. 'When was this?'

'Two years ago, maybe a little longer. Did she lose this somewhere?'

'How would you describe Vera — to look at?'

'What she looks like? Well, oh, she is about my height. In fact in many ways she looks quite like me. But she has brown eyes. Not like my miserable, red ones.' Miss Spencer tried to force a smile and wiped the corners of her eyes with her own handkerchief, now scrunched into a ball in one hand.

Vignoles couldn't help but glance towards Trinder over Miss Spencer's right shoulder, and the sergeant silently pulled a pained expression. He looked back at Heather Spencer. 'What about her hair?'

'Light brown, short and a bit wavy — but I have not seen her for at least five months, so she might have changed her style.'

'Are you aware of whether she has recently bought a new winter coat?'

'Oh gosh, yes! She has a new one; it's a lovely green colour, apparently. She told me all about it on the telephone.' Miss Spencer's voice lifted, glad to lose herself in recalling the excited conversation they'd had, 'I think she described it as fern green. She spent a small fortune on a hat and handbag to go with it, never mind how much she gave the spiv for the blanket the coat was made from.' Miss Spencer stopped and suddenly put the hand with the balled handkerchief to her mouth, 'Oh gosh. I hope I haven't got her into trouble saying that? About the spiv...'

Vignoles saw Trinder making notes and wondered about both the missing hat and handbag. 'No. Don't worry about that. And where does Vera live?'

'Nottingham. She rents a room not far from the centre of town. It was easier than the tram and bus journeys she had to make from her parents' place, which is quite someway out. I have the address and the name of her landlady if you would like it?'

'Yes, thank you.'

'But is she badly hurt? Why not ask her all this yourself?' Her eyes again flickered with doubt and Vignoles was struck by the startling image that she looked like a small, hunted rabbit.

'Does Vera have a boyfriend?'

'Yes, she's engaged to be married this spring to David, David Ferens. I only met him twice, but he seems a nice enough man, and she of course simply adores him. I tried calling him late on Friday night whilst I was waiting for Vera, but he was not at home and I got the same story the next morning. I rather hoped that perhaps he was with her. Has he any news?'

Vignoles took a deep breath and then, trying to keep his voice as soft and gentle as possible, set about ripping a massive hole in the life of the young woman sitting on the edge of the seat before him as he explained the circumstances of the murder and how her friend was found. Why was it always the people trying to uphold law and order who had to be the bearers of such terrible news? It was never the perpetrators who had to sit there and watch a poor woman's face crumple with shock and disbelief. Those who committed these crimes never faced the true enormity of their actions: the families and friends left wrecked and ruined; the long hours of loneliness, anger, frustration and loss that would follow. They didn't have to see innocent people struggle to comprehend how such evil could be visited upon one of their own in all its ugly cruelty. Hanging perhaps was, as many said in the newspapers, too good for those who did these terrible things, but he wondered if this didn't just give the killers a short-cut to hell, but a side-step past the real scale of their inhumanity. The survivors had a long and painful purgatory ahead on this earth.

After Miss Spencer's initial body-wracking sobs had eased, Vignoles started to broach the subject he was dreading almost more than the fact that her best friend had been raped and murdered.

'We will need the names and addresses of her family and other friends and work colleagues.' She nodded in an exaggerated manner, eager to try and help, eager to just do something practical in the face of this crisis, her handkerchief pressed to her mouth and eyes staring at the floor. 'You said that her parents are elderly?' He did not wait for a reply. 'We are now pretty certain that it was indeed Miss Harding who was killed, based upon what you have said, but the coroner will require a formal identification, as indeed we do. We need this as quickly as possible so I was wondering if you might make the identification? We can of course try to find Mr Ferens, but as you are here with us now...' Miss Spencer nodded her head in agreement, her eyes glazed. 'But... I must warn you that there is something else. It is rather disturbing and I fear will make this even more of a trial for you. It would be impossibly distressing for her parents and that is why I am reluctant ask them.'

The wind suddenly howled even harder and the updraught fanned the flames in the fire, making everyone glance across at the grate. 'There is no easy way to say this, but Miss Harding has been mutilated rather horribly whilst she lay beside the railway line — by hungry birds.'

Chapter Eleven

'I GET A KICK OUT OF YOU'
Henry Hall & the BBC Dance Orchestra

Katarzyna Walentynowicz loved it when the band practised. It provided one of the few splashes of vitality within the confines of the dreary camp and helped to break up the monotony of the short, winter days.

The band was normally twelve strong, though others sometimes swelled the ranks, and all were pulled from the various families living at Finmere. They gathered in the large, single-storey wooden mess hall located opposite the block where Major Duffy had his office. The hall was draped with the Union flag, a tattered and scarred Polish flag and some rather faded bunting, dating back to the celebrations that marked the end of the war. On the walls, cheap wooden picture frames held a colour print of the king, a photograph of the young Princesses Elizabeth and Margaret, and one of Churchill. The stage was normally only used for formal concerts and shows, so at these twice-weekly practice sessions the men just pulled chairs away from the lines of trestle tables and formed a ragged semicircle around the drum kit. But, whilst they considered the practice to be informal, these sessions were almost as popular as the advertised concerts, with the greater part of the camp gathering to listen, sometimes to sing, and certainly to gossip and set the world to rights whilst spreading what meagre provisions each family could muster onto the tables for all to share. And by so doing they turned the afternoon into an event. These sessions often drifted long into the evening, if they were in the mood to keep playing through the finger-numbing cold, and especially if fuelled by plenty of warming vodka or sliwowice.

The band was always well presented, preferring to wear white shirts and knitted waistcoats or tanktops, some of which were very colourful, a testament to their wives' or mothers' ingenuity in finding different coloured wools from whatever source. At these gatherings the women would trade odd balls of one colour or another with friends, or sit and unpick a worn-out cardigan or jumper. The more ambitious were known to resort to dyeing paler coloured wools into something richer. The results were often a riot of colour and pattern and not always in the most tasteful combinations, but they provided some much-needed warmth. Most of the band wore ties, though some of the younger members would have an open collar with a scarf knotted at the throat. Dark trousers and a jacket, or even tired uniforms from one of the armed forces, would complete the effect. One man, however, habitually wore his full R.A.F. dress uniform when he played. He was always immaculately presented, with peaked cap and shoes shined to a glossy black, and proudly displayed the medal he won serving with one of the Polish squadrons during the Battle of Britain. Only his walking stick and oddly stiff gait betrayed that beneath his uniform was a battered and scarred body and a leg amputated below the knee after his Hawker Hurricane was shot down over Kent.

Some of the soloists liked to keep their hats on, pushing them onto the back of their heads in a manner they felt caught something of the American jazz scene, whilst three of the men wore the little, tight-fitting skull caps that clearly identified them as Jews, proud also to wear this symbol freely and without the hateful yellow star sewn onto their clothes. Few spoke now of the stinging humiliations and terrors of that earlier life, and of the extraordinary journeys that brought them, somewhat incongruously, together on the edge of a tiny English village in Northamptonshire. Only at times would a face stare into the distance in a silent and haunted reverie until some distraction broke the spell. When the band started to play the music would often do just that, pulling them back from memories of such suffering or even transporting them further back into a time and place filled with happier memories.

The music they played was often deliciously bittersweet, tugging Kat's heart from joy to sadness and back again in the space of just a few moments. But that was the point, explained her father, who played lead violin. This music knew how to induce a kind of delicious yearning, heart-rending and yet satisfying to the soul. She never ceased to be amazed how, as the clarinet or oboe would hold a note on the air, the performer drawing it out to breaking point until you would swear that you could take no more and your heart was fit to burst, the whole band would suddenly fire back into action in a joyous gallop of rhythm and swirling melody and counter melody, unlocking a rush of emotions like a bursting dam.

Their repertoire was varied, encompassing folk melodies intermingled with popular tunes of the day, even making a stab at Glen Miller and some of the other popular British and American dance bands. However, this afternoon, as Kat sat beside her best friend Ewa and tried to stop her brother from fidgeting on her other flank in a manner that tempted her to give him a cuff around the ear, the band was playing a much-loved klezmer standard. The oboe and clarinet were duelling as the band maintained the strong, hypnotic rhythm, each soloist taking the melody and, after first playing it through unembellished, as if sizing it up to get a feel and a taste for its shape and form, they would then thrown it back, kinked and twisted, with trills and runs of notes weaving around the original core, challenging the other to appreciate the additions and touches of virtuosity informing his performance, inviting a response that would have to first perfectly mimic the fantastic invention that went before, and then add further embellishments. And so the sparring continued, with gasps of appreciation and the occasional handclaps marking each performer's contribution.

Kat was captivated. Her sense of time and place blurring as the music drew her back into shadowy memories of a former life in Warsaw. She gazed beyond the semicircle of players and through the windows of the hall, the pale-green-painted metal frames glowing against the already-ultramarine sky of encroaching dark. The curtains would soon be drawn, but at this magical moment of brief winter twilight the yellow mess hall lights picked out the mesmerising fall of the snow and, as she watched, she remembered sitting at the upstairs window of their now long-abandoned apartment. Was it still standing — or was it now just a pile of rubble?

She remembered watching the snow on just such a night as this as she knelt on the cushioned window seat. Candles had illuminated the room and the windowpane reflected the many points of light. She had asked her mother to refrain from drawing the curtains a while longer so that she could watch the blue shadows of nightfall encroach upon trams jilting and jingling their way down the centre of the wide street; she observed a man hurrying home with two huge loaves of bread tucked under his arms; a woman wheeling a bicycle draped with heavy sacks; a rabbi in a long black coat and a full beard walking sedately towards the synagogue.

Kat sighed. Would they ever know something of that life again? It had all seemed so safe and secure. She had been just a young girl; how little she had understood the horrors that were waiting around the corner. There had been rumours amongst her friends of something dangerous, but they had not understood exactly what;

there had been snatches of urgent conversation between her parents that ceased the moment her presence was observed, replaced by a comforting smile and calming words that, ultimately, did nothing to hold back the dark terrors nor help prepare her for the profound upheaval and loss that followed.

The moment passed, her eyes moved away from the hall window and she glanced across at a chubby man seated at an empty table some way behind the throng of camp inhabitants. She did not recognise him and felt sure that he was not one of them, though perhaps he was a new arrival. He sat very upright in his chair, a small canvas holdall on the floor beside his feet and his hands folded in the crease between his barrel chest and curving belly. Kat looked away, but for some oddly compelling reason glanced back again, sensing that he in turn was looking directly at her. Actually it was difficult to say where he was looking, as his thick-lensed glasses made it hard to see the dots of his eyes with any accuracy across that distance.

She turned back towards the band, the hairs on the nape of her neck standing on end in a ripple of tingling unease. She could feel his eyes fixed upon her back and tried to convince herself that he was not staring at her, but at the band. It was just that she was sitting in between and so he could not help but look towards her. Why would he be staring at her, anyway? 'Typical', she thought, 'I get some fat old man interested in me, whereas if it was Karol. Well, that would be different...'

She tried to forget the uncomfortable sensation and looked at the Karol in question: a tall and handsome oboist who at that moment was musically jousting with her father on a new tune. The young musician's eyes were locked onto those of Mr Walentynowicz in deep concentration. 'Why does he never look at me like that?' Kat looked down at the winter coat that Miss McIntyre had run up for her and admitted that all things considered, it was rather elegant and fitted well. Yes, Miss McIntyre knew how to tailor a coat, but this was wasted on Karol. He never seemed to notice.

But she was again feeling that curious sensation across her shoulders and neck, prompting her to surreptitiously glance back towards the unknown observer, and was again sure that just at the very same moment as she turned her head, his snapped away and transferred down to his wristwatch. Kat instinctively wrapped her arms around her chest and wriggled in her chair to face further away from him, leaning over to Ewa to ask — as casually as she could

— if she knew who this man was. She immediately closed her eyes in embarrassed despair, as Ewa span around in her seat to fix her eyes upon him in an exaggerated stare.

'What man? There's no one there.'

'Ssh!' Kat turned to look, as any attempt at subtlety had already been lost, but then frowned with confusion when she saw that his chair was empty and that the canvas holdall had also gone. She quickly scanned the room, but in vain. 'But there was a man. He was ugly and had those jam-jar glasses and was awfully fat...'

'Katy! That's a terrible thing to say.' Ewa's voice was hushed, but still forceful.

'Well, he was. I'm just describing him. And the way he stared at me...' She shivered.

Ewa shrugged and made a face. 'Oh dear, you really know how to choose them. You should stick to the Yanks, they're far better looking!' Ewa scanned the room and made a rueful face as she failed to see the object of her own particular interest.

'I didn't choose him, I'll have you know.' Kat's voice, though hushed, had an urgent tone that induced her mother to throw a reproachful glance at her. 'He was just staring at me.' She dropped her voice to barely a whisper, 'Quite gave me the creeps.' She moved her shoulders as if to shrug off the feeling.

'So who was he?'

'Well if I knew that I wouldn't have asked. And I might not be feeling so strange'. She pulled a face at Ewa. 'I don't know. He looked like a workman.'

'Just a figment of your vivid imagination, more like. There's no one there.' Ewa turned back to face the band, 'Rather like my American. I thought I saw him around the camp earlier'. Ewa then spoke in English with a well-mimicked accent drawled out of the side of her mouth: 'Hey doll, want to buy some stockings? How's about a few sticks a' gum, huh?' They both laughed. Switching back to Polish, she continued, 'I was hoping he'd stop to hear the band. I suppose he doesn't care for our kind of music.' Whilst she spoke she had allowed her fingertips to brush against the precious nylons where they were revealed below the hem of her skirt. They had been impossibly expensive, but she and her mother had finally agreed on a price for a pair each and now she was enjoying the feeling that she actually owned such a rare commodity, made even more so because purchased from such a dashing salesman.

'Actually, he might have been a plumber, because he had one of those funny tool bags.' Kat pulled a face and then seemed to dismiss him from her mind. It was of no matter now and she turned to her friend and looked directly at her, finally reacting to what she had been saying.

'*Your* American?' She emphasised the word with force and some contempt. 'Since when?'

Ewa raised an eyebrow coquettishly, 'Well, he's mine in my mind. It's just that he's not realised yet that we are destined to be together.'

'Holy Mother of God, dream away! He just gives us sticks of gum — like we're children.'

'And stockings. Don't forget that.'

'Oh, I haven't. I'm still mad that mama would not buy me some. But he didn't give you those — he made you pay — and right through the nose.'

'I don't mind. It was worth it. You really should get some. Maybe Karol would take more notice of you then!' She flashed a wicked glance at her friend.

'Oh, that was a low shot!' But for all her mock anger, Kat looked towards the young musician and sat a little more upright in her chair, more relaxed now the episode of the watcher was forgotten. She ran a hand through her raven-black hair, tumbling it afresh over her collar in deep, fulsome curls and set a warm smile on her lips on the off chance that the oboist might glance her way. Ewa caught her doing so, jabbed an elbow in her ribs and gave her another grin. She flashed her eyes back and mouthed her to 'stop it,' then giggled, placing her hand over her mouth. She quickly glanced across at her mother and drew another stern look in return.

❊   ❊   ❊   ❊

If W.P.C.s Jane Benson and Lucy Lansdowne had felt thrilled to be given a case of their own to investigate, then the depressing reality was now hitting them hard. This was an almost unheard-of opportunity: two women police officers in charge of an investigation. It was flying in the face of tradition and, despite two world wars in which women had started to make inroads into the male working environment, this was perhaps a step too far for some. Both were determined to use every ounce of their abilities to see it through and collar the coal thieves and, whilst they had faith in their own abilities, they knew that the inspector had given them the job only because he was forced into it by necessity. Sadly, Vignoles's faith in the women did not stretch as far as the three sour-faced uniformed officers assigned to them.

These unprepossessing specimens of railway policing had remained unmoved by any appreciation of the work women had taken on in recent years, and in their opinion — one that they were happy to offer at any opportunity — women were not fit to command any investigation. What they thought women were fit for was alluded to just as frequently, making the two W.P.C.s feel at times quite uneasy. Their heavy uniforms and overcoats provided at least some protection from the lingering looks and pointed observations about their physical presence, but offered no barrier to the frequent comments about their hair and makeup (such as it was), and inane questions about when they were 'hoping to start a family' and offers to assist them in the process as soon as they were ready.

The two women knew that it was all only to be expected, but how much the men held their abilities in contempt still rankled. Not only were they not supposed to have the job, but also they apparently added insult to injury by fancying themselves to be some kind of 'jumped-up detectives from a newfangled department' that 'thought it was better than everyone else'.

'A right pair of Miss Marpleses!' had been the first response that their presence had inspired, and it had not improved much since. Privately, the two women dubbed the uniformed men 'the Three Stooges' in an attempt to retain their sanity in the face of such stubborn hostility.

However, despite the lack of empathy, W.P.C. Benson had an outgoing personality that gave her the confidence to challenge these men, being perhaps even slightly pushy in comparison to the more introspective, and more slightly-built Lansdowne, and had by sheer force of will and determination ground out a plan for the surveillance of the colliery line and cajoled the P.C.s into a grudging co-operation of sorts.

So now she found herself with stooge number one: a spotty, inexperienced youth by the name of Wilson, cooped up in a tiny platelayers' hut adjacent to the signal that had been rigged in the previous robbery. There was a temporary telephone inside the hut — placed there with much complaining and yet more mindless comments about their 'pretty heads not understanding the complexities of the undertaking' — by the signal and telegraph department. This 'phone was connected to the signal box controlling the coal yards at Clifton Colliery, where stooge number two had placed himself, ensconced with the relative comfort of a warm stove and a pot of tea, whilst W.P.C. Lansdowne was in the larger signalbox that guarded the junction where the coal branchline joined the mainline. It had taken a lot of paperwork and form-filling, and the personal intervention of Vignoles himself to square these stakeouts with the necessary authorities, which had been sceptical and unsympathetic. All things considered, it had been a long and arduous struggle to get to where she was now, seated, frozen and wracked by nerves. And it might all prove an awful waste of time.

The third officer, P.C. Tunstall, who was the most awkward and perhaps the most stupid of the trio, was meanwhile working his way around the many drinking holes of the adjoining colliery village in an undercover operation to try to sniff out anyone offering cheap coal on the black market. Benson had serious doubts about the effectiveness of this plan, which had been forcefully presented to her by Tunstall, who argued — not without some validity, she had to admit — that the gang members were unlikely to strike again until they had shifted the batch of coal they had already lifted. He had also undermined her confidence by suggesting that the gang was more than likely to move to another location, having already struck twice at Clifton. 'Lightning don't strike twice...' he paused, 'and if it did strike twice, it sure don't strike three times, do it?'

'But we are not dealing with lightning, but coal robbers.'

'Righty-oh, Miss Marple, but you do see as what I'm saying? We'll be wasting our time freezing our bleedin' whatsits off, all for nowt, you mark my words. Meanwhile them blighters will be off hawking the stuff around the place. Stands to reason, don't it?'

The other two stooges had nodded appreciatively and murmured acquiescence. Benson had been momentarily wrong-footed because she could see his point. Vignoles, however, had been clear about what he wanted and that was surveillance. Where else to start? She had to make a stand and so, after some further discussion, which at times verged upon heated, they had agreed on a rolling roster of surveillance and undercover work over the next few evenings. It was a plan that saw the men get to enjoy the warmth of the pubs and clubs on at least one evening each, whilst the women were stuck at the trackside or in a signalbox, as their sex would make their presence in pubs as obvious as if they were to enter with a flag waving above their heads. The feeling of having been somehow outmanoeuvred by these ignorant men niggled at Benson, but now, as she sat on a hard, wooden bench close to the frozen window of the hut, she fought to contain her emotions and concentrate on the job in hand. She reminded herself that this was what real detecting involved and aimed to be as focussed as Sergeant Trinder always managed to be.

The bitter cold fogged the window with their breath, turning it into ice, whilst the layers of snow outside collected in little curves on the sill and window bars like an illustration from a Victorian Christmas card. Very pretty, but serving to further hamper her view. If this wasn't bad enough, P.C. Wilson insisted upon stating every ten minutes that they 'couldn't see owt' and that 'it was just a waste of time', accompanied by a series of deep sighs.

Benson's patience was being tested to the limit. Unfortunately, she also could see very little and it irritated her that he might be right, whilst her fingers and toes were painfully frozen and her limbs almost locked into position. But she was determined to set an example and not betray her own misgivings.

'Just concentrate, Wilson. Sounds are as important in these conditions as sight and your sighing and complaining isn't helping. So just keep mum.'

'I can hear a train coming.' He spoke the words in a deadpan manner laced with boredom.

'Full marks for observation, but from what direction? Remember, we're only interested in loaded trains out of the colliery.'

'Yeah. Of course.'

'Saints preserve us,' thought Benson, briefly closing her eyes in despair. She then concentrated on listening to the sound of the approaching train.

It was slow and laboured, with each explosive exhaust beat followed by an almost impossibly long delay. This was a very full train and the engine was struggling to find grip on the icy rails. There was a sharp incline out of the colliery and if the driver were to let her slip then the engine wheels could spin and he might not get the train restarted. The gradient eased a little towards the hut that Benson was concealed within, but was still unwelcome and so both signal boxes would try their best to give a clear road where possible to allow the driver the benefit from any momentum he could build up. However, if a stop was forced by the actions of the gang, the pyrotechnics and heavy sanding involved in restarting the train would be loud enough to mask the sound of the coal being released from the hopper wagons onto the track. So, if an attack were to come, it surely would be here.

Benson could see but a suggestion of the towering clouds of steam rising in the distance and very little else through the thick blackness of the night, and decided that, if the gang members were lying in wait, then they could see nothing much else, either. So she stood up, opened the door of the hut and peeped out.

'Come on, Wilson, if they are going to strike then there's a good chance it'll be on this train. Keep your head down, switch your torch off and follow me.'

The eight-coupled driving wheels of the heavy goods' engine spun briefly, then bit into the sand being jetted between them and the rail surface by the anxious driver, who was leaning out of the cab, watching clouds of steam swirl around the wheels. The fire doors were partly opened to give some extra draft, and this light painted the two men in shades of flickering orange and red and coloured the billows of smoke that periodically enveloped them until the bitter wind whipped it away across the snowy slagheaps behind. The engine was roaring like a volcano with flashes of red appearing at the rim of the chimney as each deep, resonant thump announced another beat of the exhaust. But the train was still rolling and the driver seemed to be an experienced hand, more than able to coax her up the incline. The fireman flung the firedoors wide and started to shovel coal with quick, deft movements, his young face occasionally illuminated by the incandescent heat of the hungry fire, perspiration already forming on his brow despite the arctic wind.

The driver pulled the metal chain that activated the whistle and made two angry blasts in frustration as he saw the signal light stay stubbornly at red. All their efforts so far were to no avail, as they would have to stop unless the board was pulled off in the next few moments to give them the road.

Benson, despite her achingly-cold hands and feet, stood and watched in awe at the sight of the locomotive fighting the incline. She could not help but be fascinated by the sheer, elemental power of the steam engine as it hammered its plume of almost phosphorescent smoke into the sky, the crew on the footplate like black, devilish figures from a medieval vision of hell. She looked back and willed the signal to stay red. This was as it should be. She had prearranged with the signalwoman to hold the train for a short while in an attempt to lure the gang to strike without recourse to actually snagging the signal wires. She felt a pang of sympathy with the engine crew though, as clearly they had struggled to get the overloaded train even that far on the icy rails. She guessed that the language on the footplate was probably flowing blue.

The train squealed to a halt as the long line of coal wagons clanged and rattled in a Mexican wave down the line and around the corner. The locomotive appeared to sigh, then hissed and sizzled, accompanied by the metallic clang of firedoors closing and the sound of a shovel being tossed onto the coal.

'Wilson. Cross to the other side of the train, keep low to the ground and you might just see if anyone darts across to the wagons.' Benson was crouched down, surveying the undulating blanket of pale snow.

'They must be mad messing around with these — it's a sure way to get themselves killed.' The young policeman finally seemed alert and interested, his voice urgent as he made a crouching run across the single track.

Benson strained her eyes, staring along the side of the train, but the visibility was poor and made worse by sudden waves of fine snow being flicked up and into her eyes by the wind. She waded slowly forwards through a particularly deep drift, feeling the sting of cold upon her legs and the dead chill of icy water in her boots, despite her thick, woollen socks. Her long skirt and greatcoat tails were being flapped heavily by the wicked wind. She winced, but ploughed forwards until she drew level with the cab of the locomotive. She was some yards away and, masked by the darkness, was unobserved. She debated whether to make her presence known to the crew.

A minute or so ticked by, though it felt like far longer and, as this period of inactivity stretched on, Benson was gripped by indecision. She could see too imperfectly to make out anything useful along the line of wagons, but dared not use her torch. But if she continued to make her way along the side of the coal wagons, having sent Wilson along the other side, what would she do, a lone female officer in the dark, if she did encounter a gang of robbers? She would be placing herself in extreme danger and to no obvious benefit, if she were overpowered. Benson strained her ears to listen for any sounds, but the locomotive's safety valve at that moment blew off in an ear-piercing roar that blotted out everything else.

'Bother, this is impossible! I really need more officers to do this properly,' she thought.

Benson stood tall and walked towards the engine cab, raising her hand in salutation and attempting to hail the crew above the roar of the escaping steam. After a few moments the young fireman caught sight of her and leant out of the cab, peering down with the soft, orange glow of the fire just picking out her face.

'Oh, you surprised me! Is there anything wrong, Miss?'

'I hope not. We're keeping an eye out for trouble. Coal robbers. Have you noticed anything unusual?' Benson had to lift her voice to be heard, and the fireman cupped a hand around his ear to amplify the sound of her voice.

He nodded in reply, 'I heard about them. But it's hard to know what's happening down the train in this weather. It all seems OK, I s'pose.' He stopped and leant slightly to one side to allow more of the glow of the fire to strike Benson's face, stared for a few moments, then suddenly spoke out in recognition: 'W.P.C. Benson?' and grinned.

'That's me.' She looked more carefully up at him. 'Simon Howerth? So, you've made it up to fireman.'

Simon continued to grin like a Cheshire cat, 'Yes, miss. Actually, I'm a passed cleaner, but I've had a few good turns recently.'

'Not that good, lad, you've still got plenty to learn'. The driver had moved to look over and wink at the policewoman.

'This is a bit of test.' Simon glanced back at the driver. 'And Eddie's doing just tickety. We both work out of Woodford. How's the inspector?'

'Oh, his usual self.'

'Mind your backs, we've got the road!'

'Send my regards. Me and Eddie are looking out for those robbers! We'll find them. Ta-ra.' The lad gave another wave as the driver gave a curt blast on the whistle and released two jets of steam from the drain cocks as the engine started to heave itself into motion.

Benson stepped back as it blasted its column of smoke into the sky, the wheels slipping. As she watched it creep forward, dragging the heavy train behind, Benson smiled as she remembered the time she had first met Simon Howerth and Edward Earnshaw. The two lads had, somewhat unwittingly, helped unravel a complex case she had been involved with the previous year. They had even received commendations for their assistance, but she had seen neither of them since. Simon had surely only been joking, but if he and Earnshaw wanted to help catch the coal robbers then, based upon their previous record, she for one would not complain provided they never exposed themselves to any danger.

Benson brought her thoughts back into the present, throwing caution to the wind and playing her torch along the side of each hopper wagon as it trundled past, watching as the rails dipped and rose under the weight of each passing wheel, trying to cast some light into the pitchy blackness beneath the wagons and detect a tell-tale stream of coal falling between the rails. She felt reasonably confident that nothing was amiss. She was staking her reputation on her judgement being correct and could not bear the thought of the taunts from 'the Three Stooges' if she missed a robbery right under her nose. As the guard's van crept past, the guard waved a hand to her in acknowledgement and called out, 'D'you see owt, m'duck?'

'Nothing.'

'That's grand.' And with that, he ducked back into the warmth of his van.

Once the train had passed, Benson saw on the other side of the tracks the shadowy figure of P.C. Wilson running in loping strides towards her, lifting his feet high out of the powdery snow to try to make some ground. His flashlight was waving in her direction, possibly as a signal or perhaps as a result of his ungainly progress. Benson pointed hers at him and flashed it on and off in acknowledgement and Wilson immediately stopped and repeated the signal. He then called across the line, motioning with his free arm for her to join him.

'What is it, Wilson?'

'There's something going on down the line! A vehicle stuck in the snow.'

Benson felt her stomach churn. She started to run as quickly as she could, and soon realised why Wilson had taken up his strange running motion, for the snow tugged at her boots and dragged

'You're not scared, are you, Wilson? Come on, let's have a look around. These prints seem to lead to the trackside and back again'.

Benson fought back her own mounting nervousness and, with just a slight fear of being coshed by a hidden observer, she stepped through the white, powdery snow.

Chapter Twelve

'ONE MEAT BALL'
The Andrews Sisters

Vignoles was seated behind his large wooden desk, his swivel chair turned so that his feet — now free from his wet shoes — were resting on the thick, hot pipes running beneath his office window. A slight drift of steam rose as he enjoyed the slightly masochistic sensation of his extremities feeling too hot for comfort.

'That's a good way to get chilblains.' Trinder was seated opposite Vignoles.

'Quite probably, but it's either that or frostbite. Ouch, but that's nice.' He grimaced and lifted his feet away from direct contact with the water pipe, then swung back to face Trinder. 'To be frank, after the last few days, scalding my feet is nothing to bear when I think of what we've witnessed.' He took a long and slow breath, as if cleansing his lungs, 'It's been a trying time.'

Trinder grunted in agreement, drew hard upon his lighted Black Cat and looked at the floor, running a hand through his brilliantined hair as he did so.

It certainly had been a trying time. After an uncomfortable night on emergency truckle beds — a hangover from the war — in the stationmaster's office at Banbury, they had accompanied Miss Spencer back to Leicester: a long and painfully-extended journey in which all three had tried to remain cheerful and talk about other matters, whilst the grisly truth of Miss Harding's murder sat between them like an unwelcome guest squeezed into their already-crowded compartment. The subsequent identification of Vera Harding's body as it lay in the grim surroundings of the morgue at Leicester had been an agonising, though mercifully brief, affair. The horror of her mutilation was somehow enhanced by the clinical white and green tiled walls and the stink of formaldehyde.

The effect on Miss Spencer had been devastating. The emotional pressure that had been building up inside her finally found release and she had collapsed into uncontrollable fits of sobbing. And there had been no let-up for Vignoles, who then had to travel that same day onwards to Nottingham and fight his way across a snowbound city to visit Vera Harding's elderly parents. A telephone call would have been heartless, though the extra travelling was arduous and left Vignoles exhausted by the time he had to confront her parents.

He now concentrated on the sensation of his hot feet and closed his eyes, as if he could clear away the recollection of the wreckage his unwelcome visit had left in that neat, comfortable, suburban house. He hoped that Miss Spencer and Miss Harding's parents could find some way to comfort each other. He exhaled, opened his eyes, placed his hands upon the surface of his desk and looked at Trinder.

'Okey-dokey, let's recap where we are in our investigations. The Badger will be demanding a report, as I quite failed to submit one yesterday. We'll start with the less draining one. What were Benson and Lansdowne so excited about?'

'They saw the coal robbers' vehicle as it fled the scene. Benson thinks that they might have foiled another attempt. Admittedly more by accident than design.' Trinder pulled a rueful expression.

'But no arrests or any I.D.s on the gang?' Vignoles reached for a mug of cocoa on his desk.

'No.'

'So, we're not a lot further down that line. And, if I understand the situation correctly, it was but a fleeting glance, so it is only an assumption that it was the fleeing gang?'

Trinder winced slightly, and nodded. 'At least they didn't get any more coal, so that's a result of sorts.' Vignoles sipped his cocoa whilst looking at Trinder through the rising steam.

'And unfortunately they'll move somewhere else now they've been rumbled. No point in continuing to stake out Clifton Colliery.' Trinder sounded gloomy.

'You could be right. Let's pray they move off our patch. I won't be too unhappy to forget all about this lot. So what about this vehicle?'

'They got just a fleeting glimpse in the dark, but it looks like a delivery van with a shiny paint job, and looks in good nick. Had a lot of words painted down the side.'

'Ah, I know the very one.' Vignoles raised his eyebrows and opened his hands. 'All right, it is a lead of sorts, I suppose.' He replaced his mug on the desk and started to fill his pipe. Trinder remained silent. 'So they were foiled prior to the act? Maybe our undercover operation was rumbled, or just bungled?'

'I have spoken to W.P.C. Benson about the operation and she feels sure it was discreet. Maybe they were frightened off or feared that as the snow was so deep they might never have made a get away if laden with coal.'

'Possibly. Or they were suspicious of our beer-drinking private investigator asking too many questions.'

'Speaking of P.C. Tunstall — this is his report of his undercover work in Clifton village'. Trinder raised his eyebrows and placed a sheet of foolscap on the desk in front of Vignoles, who could immediately see that it was poorly typed and dotted with corrections. It was mercifully brief.

'So he spent a long evening in about five pubs being "forced" to drink ale to help him "blend in with the locals". I'm sure he found the work most arduous.' Vignoles snorted and tossed the report back onto the desk. 'Tunstall is a slacker, but it's not completely foolish trying to sniff out the black-marketeers in this manner. I can't help feeling that his motivation was more about avoiding being outside than nabbing this gang.' Vignoles leant forward and looked at Trinder. 'But I think you're right about them not returning to Clifton. They had a narrow squeak the other night so I reckon they will lay low and concentrate on pushing the stuff they already have. Ask Benson and Lansdowne to come up with a strategy for trying to purchase some of this illicit coal and catch the thieves red-handed as they do the transaction.'

Trinder pulled a face. 'Couldn't that be considered entrapment, sir?'

'Maybe, but quite frankly I don't much care. As long as we get them out of circulation whilst the lawyers argue the point, that'll suit me fine. Choosing between murder and coal theft, I favour our resources being used to catch the killer.'

Trinder nodded, a slight smile forming on his face.

'Righty-oh, so back to poor Miss Harding.' Vignoles struck a Swan Vesta and held it to the bowl of his pipe until a curl of scented smoke rose into the air. He shook his hand until the match went out and then tossed it accurately into the large glass ashtray advertising Mazzawatee Tea that lay on the corner of the desk nearest Trinder. This had been the latest odd item of lost property recovered from a train, that had found its way, as so many such items had a habit of doing, into his office.

'We know who she is, from whence she was travelling and who she was intending to visit.' Vignoles tapped his forefinger gently upon the box of matches to punctuate each point. 'Miss Spencer can be taken out of the frame, and so can her parents. We know that she's a typist with a firm of solicitors.' We could take a look at her colleagues, perhaps. Might throw up something. We still have a generous timeframe for her death, but Blencowe's work on the timetables will narrow this. We know that she travelled in a suburban carriage, tragically trapped in the compartment with her killer.'

'Horrible thought.'

'Indeed. Has Blencowe had any luck tracing the carriages in question?'

'He's got it down to two possible sets and has their timetables identified. As you suspected, they drafted in these coaches to replace stock trapped elsewhere on the system by the snow.' Trinder opened his notebook and flipped a few pages over, 'Looking at them, my money is on the three-thirty-three out of Nottingham Victoria, which appears to have run approximately an hour late. The other was not out of Nottingham until after eight, and with the delays along the line it would have passed the murder scene far too late.'

'We know Miss Harding boarded the train at Nottingham. But crucially, at what point did the killer join her?'

'The train was timetabled as an express, though it ran slow and late. It would have stopped at only Leicester and Rugby prior to approaching Charwelton, where it was not due to stop.' answered Trinder.

'Three stations. But he could already have been on board. He might have seen the lack of corridors on the stock as the perfect opportunity and lain in wait.'

'The train started at Manchester Central.'

Vignoles nodded thoughtfully. 'And taking the connecting services into account, it's a huge area the killer could come from. We'll start closer to home. The refreshment room at Nottingham has to be worth a trawl. It's just possible she fell into conversation with her killer there. Most women, from my experience, like to arrive in good time before a train is due to depart and so, with the train then delayed, she would have been stuck there for an age.'

'And sex crimes seem to be committed by persons known by their victims,' added Trinder. 'Even if it is only a brief connection, it could be enough to cause her to lower her guard'.

'And on that note, I think it's more than time that we paid a visit to Mr David Ferens.' Vignoles puffed on his pipe.

'The fiancé?'

'Yes. Miss Spencer provided the number of his digs and I've tried to reach him there twice with no success. His landlady swears he was out all of the night when his dearly beloved was killed, and the following night. Looking back at the notes of the interview with Miss Spencer, I notice that she also tried calling Ferens the evening Vera Harding died and again the next morning — confirming that he was out both times.'

'So where was he?'

'Exactly. I'm getting an odd feeling about Mr Ferens.'

'When did he first realise that Miss Harding was missing?'

'Presumably after the second time I telephoned his landlady — I was less circumspect about my reasons for calling by then — and told her it was about the disappearance of Miss Harding and our fears for her safety.'

'He has not exactly bust a gut to get in touch with us, maybe because he already knew what happened?'

'That's what's going through my mind. His relationship to the victim certainly makes him our first suspect.'

'But what about the neckerchief?'

'It's a piece of work wear and quite probably owned by the killer. Mr Harding — the victim's father — told me that Ferens is a store keeper and driver for a wholesaler's. That's not a white-collar occupation, so could it be his?' Vignoles spread his hands wide. Hearing the sound of a train pulling up in the platform outside his office window, he glanced up at the big, round clock on his office wall, made the necessary mental adjustment to correct the time, and stood up.

'Come on, we can catch that train out there to Nottingham. Let's pay a visit to Mr Ferens.'

✻   ✻   ✻   ✻

Vignoles and Trinder stepped down off the open rear platform of the double-decker bus into dirty brown plough-lines of snow, unsure of where the road ended and the pavement started. Small mountains of snow shovelled into ragged heaps the length of the broad highway indicated the approximate location of the kerb, but the slow-moving snakes of vehicles on the busy road were all following deep tramlines worn clear somewhere close to the centre, leaving an unappealing expanse of filthy snow and icy water to cross. A few cars and a small van were buried up to their mudguard tops in drifts of grubby snow close to the road edge, their owners evidently having given up the daily struggle against the dual headaches of petrol rationing and adverse weather. A man, head bent low over the handlebars with the effort, pushed a bicycle laden with a large shopping bag past the two detectives, the thin wheels cutting through the snow and ice but repeatedly twitching to one side or another as a particularly immovable lump deflected its course.

Vignoles looked up from negotiating the icy moraine they were crossing, towards the row of shops they were approaching. They looked hunched against the wind, which had developed an edge like a freshly-stropped razor and was now merrily whipping eddies of sharp flakes into faces, piling new drifts against doors and windows and spraying the sides of the buildings with a sparkling frosting. The soft lights inside tried to throw a warming glow, but could not hide the faded paint, the cracked window glass stuffed with old newspapers and the faded awnings extended over the pavement, now weighed down by snow. One shop was boarded over, its guts long since burnt out and left to rot.

Rosedale's (Fruit & Vegetable) Wholesalers inhabited a double-fronted shop that would have been grand at the turn of the century, but now was as dowdy and sad as the rest of them. The twin, curving windows that framed the wide central front entrance were stylishly crafted, but the glass was now grimy and offered but a smeared and soot-streaked view of the interior. Inside, there were stacks of wooden crates illuminated by two bare light bulbs hanging from a bulging and badly-cracked ceiling that looked in danger of imminent collapse. It was to be hoped that the rooms upstairs were not being used for habitation.

Vignoles opened the shop door, noticing that the paint had worn away so that the bare wood beneath was exposed and polished by many hands repeatedly pushing upon it. A bell tinkled as they stepped into a confusion of vegetable crates and fruit boxes across a floor strewn with straw and crumpled dark blue tissue paper, twine and old newspapers. The air smelt heavily of loam, mice and potatoes, with a hint of stored apple. It was as icy inside as out, perhaps colder, though a smoky paraffin heater in the centre of the floor struggled to offer some heat and a lot of fumes. As the doorbell stopped swinging, the Andrews Sisters could be heard belting out *One meat ball* from an off-tune radio laced with crackling static. As the two detectives entered, a young, slim-built man with closely-cropped hair in a military style was hefting boxes from somewhere out the back into the main shop area.

'Mr Rosedale?'

'No. He's not here right now. Can I help?'

'Are you Mr David Ferens?'

'Yeah. Who wants to know?'

The man stood up and stretched stiffly, placing a hand on the small of his back for a few moments, and squinted at Vignoles. He then started wiping his hands on a square of cloth he had extracted from the brown shop coat he was wearing. His eyes flicked between the two men, taking in their long overcoats and hats. 'You the police? Here about my Vera, I suppose?' He then bit his lower lip and glanced at the floor. It looked as if the air had been suddenly sucked out of him.

'Yes. We must ask you some questions — just routine.' Vignoles made the introductions as Ferens nodded and briefly glanced back at Vignoles, but his eyes darted away again, appearing to hardly take in what was said. His hands were shaking slightly. 'You have heard about what happened, I presume? I have tried to contact you a number of times.'

'Yeah.' Ferens nodded, still looking at the floor.

'It must be a dreadful shock for you. Our condolences.'

'I just don't understand. It's not sunk in, like. Not hit me yet, I suppose.' He suddenly looked up and straight into Vignoles's eyes. 'I'll kill the man who did that to her. So help me God I will. You just find him, then let me at him.' His voice was aggressive but the clenching of the muscles around his jaw betrayed other emotions coursing through his body.

'I can understand the sentiment, but please leave it to us to deal with the killer — and we shall see that justice is done.'

'Make sure he hangs.'

Ferens flung the cloth onto the floor, took a few steps away, then swung back to face them. He pulled out a packet of cigarettes from the breast pocket of his coat and flipped it open, shaking the packet so a cigarette slid forwards, which he picked out with his lips. Trinder had already stuck a match and offered it, joining him in a smoke.

'Did you say you were railway police? I thought you just dealt with stuff that happened on, well, the railways.' Ferens continued to nervously flick his eyes between the two detectives and the floor.

'We are part of the detective department and as the crime was committed upon the railway, we are tasked to investigate it. It already appears that this crime spans a number of counties, so we can better liaise between the various police forces.'

Ferens pulled a face, looking either bored or unconvinced.

'So, Mr Ferens, how long have you known Miss Harding?'

'A year, maybe a year an' a bit. I'm not best with dates.' He shrugged by way of apology.

'How did you meet?'

'What's that to do with owt?' Ferens dragged heavily on his cigarette, hand still shaking.

'We like to build up a picture of the victim and all those associated with her. We need to understand the relationship...' Vignoles spread his hands.

'To see if I did it, you mean?' Ferens gave a furious look at Vignoles. 'You think I bloody did it? Jesus!'

'We must look at every angle, no matter how distressing it seems.' Sergeant Trinder spoke whilst exhaling cigarette smoke, trying to keep the mood level.

'You were engaged to be married?' Vignoles tried to pull the questioning back on track.

Ferens stared at Trinder, his eyes slowly losing their anger; he then looked at Vignoles and eventually replied. 'Yes. Next April.' His body seemed to lose its shape and he visibly sagged, his voice now soft and expressionless, 'I can't believe how it's all been taken away.'

'Did Miss Harding often go away for the weekend?'

'No. Almost never.'

'You saw her off at the station?' Trinder kept his voice conversational.

'No.' Ferens looked back at the floor, and scratched the edge of his nose with the hand holding the cigarette.

'Why not? It was a long journey in hard conditions. Would she not have appreciated it?'

'I was busy. Here.'

'She might have had a long wait at the station.'

'Did she? I wouldn't know. I couldn't get away from work, could I? Vera got half a day from her office, 'specially.'

'Was she sore about that? You know what women can be like, no proper goodbye on the platform?' Trinder eyed Ferens through his cigarette smoke.

Ferens managed a tiny flash of a smile, 'Aye. I think she was when I first told her. But she understood.'

'So you telephoned to check that she had arrived safely at Banbury?' Vignoles asked.

Ferens hesitated. 'No, I was out.' He swallowed and rubbed an ear lobe then dragged heavily upon the cigarette before he continued. 'And anyway her friend doesn't have a telephone.'

'Did she not leave a telephone number of a neighbour, or arrange a time when she could call you to confirm her arrival?' Vignoles pressed the point.

'No. Anyway, like I said, I was going out late that night. What is all this?'

'It was a bad night to be out late. Where were you?'

'I had a delivery to make.'

'At night?'

'Well, early evening, then. Some veg and stuff we had not been able to get out during the day had to be taken to a place a bit out of town. But look here: I've about had enough of these questions. I'm no bloody murderer, y'know?'

'And no one is accusing you, but we do need to establish the details about your movements.' Vignoles's voice was soothing. 'You said you had prearranged with Miss Harding that you wouldn't be home that night?'

'Yeah. That's what I said.'

'Then the evening delivery was also prearranged? Not something that just cropped up?' Trinder observed Ferens closely as he asked the question.

'Well — it's kind of a regular delivery. Not every day, just... some days.' He shrugged, and scratched the side of his nose again. 'That's why me and Vera agreed we couldn't talk that night.' Ferens looked uncomfortable, his words tumbling out quickly.

'You can give us the address of the place you went?'

'If you want.' Ferens moved over the table and half-heartedly started shuffling invoices and order forms and other scraps of paper around, squinting at one occasionally.

'And at what time did you drop off this delivery? You do have the consignment order?'

'That's what I'm looking for. It'll be here somewhere in this shambles. I dunno exactly when I was there, about seven, seven-thirty or so. And then it was a devil of a job getting back into town, what with the weather and all that. Took me ages.' He stood upright, wincing slightly as if his back hurt, and handed a delivery note to Vignoles.

'Hurt yourself?'

'It's nothing. Just moving these boxes all day.'

'So what time were you back here?' Vignoles glanced at it then handed it to Trinder, who commenced copying down the details.

'I didn't. Come back here, that is. Seeing as it was Friday night, I wanted a few beers with my chums and a game of darts, you know. So I parked the van up on my street and went to see them. Must've been near ten o' clock.'

'We would like the name of the pub and the names of your friends, please? Just to confirm the details.'

Ferens licked his lips, 'Yeah, sure... it was the Black Horse.'

Trinder handed the delivery note back to Ferens, and then asked him for the names of those who could confirm his whereabouts that evening. Whilst his colleague noted the names, Vignoles took time to step back and observe Ferens and also to look around the shop, his detective mind processing any apparently insignificant detail that might prove important later.

'What time did you leave the pub?' Vignoles was looking at the piles of bills and other paperwork littering the desk and did not look up as he fired the question.

'Closing time.'

'But you didn't go back to your digs, did you?'

'How do you know that?' Ferens looked surprised and stared at Vignoles, the muscles in his jaw working as he thought about this revelation.

'Your landlady said so.'

'Ah.'

'So...?' Trinder had his pencil poised over the notebook.

'What?'

'So where did you go?' Trinder spoke the words slowly and with exaggerated patience.

'We all went back to one of the lad's places to play cards and have a few bottles of beer: we sat up late. My landlady would never allow us to do that in my room, so we chose Geoff's place.'

'This would be...' Trinder checked the notes he had made, 'Geoff Gardiner? He will confirm that of course?' Trinder looked up at Ferens.

'Why wouldn't he? I gave you his address, so go and flipping well ask him yourself.'

'We shall. And the next morning you were here?' asked Vignoles.

'Yeah, at seven o'clock. I worked here all day. Mr Rosedale can back me up on that.'

'And when you got home that evening, were you not surprised or a bit disappointed that Miss Harding had not telephoned to say that she was all right?'

'Not really.'

'You were home all Saturday evening?' Trinder had his pencil poised over his notebook.

'Well, I went out.' Ferens shuffled one of his feet on the dusty floor, impatiently kicking a stray cabbage leaf out of the way.

'You go out a lot. To the Black Horse again?'

'What's it to you? It's my time off. I was here all hours so I wanted to enjoy m'self.'

'Perhaps I am old fashioned, but I find it a bit odd that rather than checking to see if your fiancée had arrived safely, you drank beer and played cards all Friday night, and it sounds like much the same the following night.' Vignoles stood at the far side of the room, hands in the pockets of his long greatcoat, inspecting a pile of potato sacks on the floor with the toe of his shoe so that he could read the name of the grower stamped in blurred ink on the rough surface. One particularly dirty sack was so blackened with grime that it stubbornly refused to give up its name.

'Oh, that's not fair! How was I to know? Jesus, I couldn't even imagine such a thing.' Ferens looked genuinely distressed and stepped forward. Was he going to raise a fist to Vignoles? He approached so quickly that the inspector took a step or two backwards. Ferens stood still, breathing hard, but then looked away.

'Can you think of anyone who might have done that to Miss Harding?'

'You think I'd be standing here now if I did?' He spat on the floor in contempt.

Vignoles made no reply but glanced quickly across at Trinder. 'I think that is all for now. Thank you for your time, though may want to speak to you again. Here is my card. If you can think of any information that might prove useful, please call me.'

Ferens looked disinclined to take the proffered rectangle, so Vignoles placed it carefully upon the edge of the untidy desk, then tipped his hat in the direction of the discomfited young man and turned to open the door. As Vignoles let it clatter shut, he saw Ferens take a last drag on his cigarette then drop it onto the messy floor, stubbing it out with his toe in an angry gesture, his eyes never once dropping from looking at the two detectives.

Vignoles and Trinder walked with heads bent down against the rawness of the air towards the bus stop that hopefully might summon up the means of returning to Nottingham Victoria, neither man speaking for a while as they assimilated all they had seen and heard.

It was Trinder who eventually broke the thoughtful silence.

'So what do you make of the fiancé, sir?'

'Is it just me, or is there something a bit fishy about Mr Ferens? I can't help but think that he's not telling the whole truth.'

'He was nervous, angry and upset — but then who wouldn't be under those circumstances?'

'Accepted. And I think he is genuinely upset about Miss Harding. But there was something else underlying those emotions.'

'I noticed he modified his story a few times — why did he do that, do you think?'

'I think that his alibi is a flexible and shifting thing. I can't quite see him on a train killing his fiancée, but we do we need to check out all the names he gave you and really test his story. We should take a visit to the Black Horse and see if someone who is not inside his circle of friends can corroborate the facts. Most of his evening and all the night was spent within the same small group — all presumably willing to say the same thing and therefore covering for him if he wasn't there.'

'Surely they wouldn't cover him so as he could commit murder?' Trinder frowned at the thought.

'I darned well hope not! But he might have told them he

needed an alibi for something else, something more acceptable to their sensibilities? Maybe he has another girl? Whatever, something isn't right. I can sense it.'

'I agree. It could be coincidence, but did you notice the rag he had in his hand?' Trinder looked across at Vignoles whose face was faintly highlighted in the grubby chiaroscuro of a flickering gas lamp. 'It was filthy dirty but I'm pretty sure it was a spotted neckerchief, looking very like the same type as used to gag the victim.'

'Though it was red and white, rather than dark blue.'

'But it still makes you wonder.'

Chapter Thirteen

'BLACK MARKET'
Marlene Dietrich

Vignoles turned the brown Bakelite heating control knob one more time from 'hot' to 'cold' and then back again, but he knew it was a pointless action. Over an hour ago, when he had boarded the train at Leicester Central, he had discovered with dismay but little surprise that the carriage heating was malfunctioning. It offered little more than a faint breath of warm air into his compartment and he knew that it would not have suddenly and miraculously repaired itself. But, despite the futility of this action, Vignoles felt the overwhelming desire to at least fool himself into thinking that he was doing something to relieve the cold that was penetrating ever deeper inside. Unfortunately, he knew enough about trains to have already ascertained that the problem lay in a leaking steam-heating pipe connection between his carriage and the one in front. The roar and hiss of the escaping steam was easily audible and he could see a cloud of white vapour drifting past his window.

As he flopped back into the sagging moquette of his seat, his well-thumbed copy of John Clare's *Collected Poems* bounced on the seat beside him and clouds of dust rose into the air, making him sneeze. He snuggled deeper into his overcoat, tried to ignore the aching cold and looked out across the open, rolling fields. The gentle undulations of the land rose and fell in harmony with the hypnotic rhythms of the looping telegraph wires and clacking rails; whilst occasional, solitary trees appeared to stride across the concrete-hard land. A ploughed field of ferruginous earth slowly came into view, its furrows filled with snow and the ridges whipped clean by the fierce winds of recent days, but still tipped by hoarfrost. It was a bleak and unforgiving sight, and yet the colours rendered it strangely beautiful. The low sun, making a rare appearance, raked its surface and formed indigo pools of shadow across the snow. The sky was a misty yellow. Vignoles reminded himself to enjoy the sight of the sun and to savour the slight heat its weak rays cast upon the left side of his face as he looked out of the slow-moving carriage.

Earlier that morning the Home Service announcer, in clipped and precise tones had, yet again, predicted a further worsening of the weather with ever more ominous warnings that the cold front was not set to lift for the foreseeable future. The coal stocks were now down to just a week's supply, though Manny Shinwell was still trying to argue that all was fine underground in the nation's newly acquired coalmines. The dark storm clouds, just starting to form a narrow band across the horizon like a bruise in the sky, suggested to Vignoles that they were indeed soon to get another wave of snow dumped upon them.

He watched as a flock of lapwings rose up from a field and wheeled into the sky, their striking white-and-black feathers flashing with glints of emerald and deep sapphire as they caught the sun. Vignoles picked up his book and glanced back at the open page and to the nature poet's description of these birds in flight:

> Whizz goes the peewit o'er the ploughman's team,
> With many a whew and whirl and sudden scream.

Returning his gaze to the birds, he furrowed his brow and tried to remember the collective noun for lapwings, or peewits as Clare called them. It wasn't a flock, but a what? A *deceit*. Yes, 'a deceit of lapwings'. What a name to bestow upon such birds. Why were they deemed deceitful?

The lapwings passed from his view, but he continued to ponder the question, trying to imagine why these charming birds, with their jaunty feathers extending from the backs of their heads like those worn in the caps of Robin Hood's merry men, had induced such mistrust. He had no answer, but found himself thinking about the legendary character in green with the faintly ludicrous hat, who was supposed to have stalked the very county through which he was now travelling. Robin Hood, in Vignoles's eyes, was just an armed robber who flouted the law. It was strange, but Hood was romantically called an 'outlaw', dressed up in camouflage gear and in so doing was loved and celebrated in books, film and on the radio. But armed robbery was a crime, however you tried to justify the reason for committing it and no matter how odious the robbed may be. Vignoles smiled to himself. He wondered how his fellow passengers would feel if they had their money and valuables taken from them at gunpoint, even if the fellow was dressed in a green pantomime outfit with a hat like a lapwing's head, and promised to give the proceeds away to the homeless who shivered in the bomb sites of Britain. It was all a matter of perception really. And perhaps whether you were the 'doer', or the 'done to'.

Vignoles shook his head clear of these rambling thoughts, but they served to remind him that they had unfinished work to pursue with Mr Ferens. The fruit-and-vegetable deliveryman was, on the surface, the victim of a terrible tragedy and deserving of their sympathy and consideration — and yet there was also something about him that hinted at deception, at something not quite right. Ferens could well turn out to be a monster. Until they could be completely sure of his innocence, Ferens might just be every woman's worst nightmare and, if so, was still free to do his worst. It was the task of Vignoles to try and tease out the truth, no matter how unsympathetic and callous the act of so doing might seem.

He hoped that his journey that morning to Nottingham, and the work that Trinder and Lansdowne were already pursuing in the same city, would help answer his questions about Ferens. His two officers were visiting the Black Horse pub to see if his alibi stood up to scrutiny, and were also tasked with trying to cajole the Nottingham Constabulary into helping them track down the other five men in the group with whom Ferens claimed to have spent the night carousing and playing cards.

Whilst Trinder and Lansdowne tackled this strand of the investigation, Vignoles was following up a telephone call that his secretary had put through to him shortly after his officers had departed. The caller had the potential to offer a significant breakthrough in the murder investigation.

The woman on the line was a porter at Nottingham Victoria and felt sure that she had seen both the victim and a man enter the same suburban carriage compartment. Her vivid description and absolute certainty about the time and date were enough to make Vignoles take the next train north. He urgently wanted to quiz the porter and satisfy himself about the veracity of her sighting. He could have got the Nottingham civvies to do this for him and it would certainly have saved time and a freezing journey, not to mention the fact that he could have completed the mound of reports and other paperwork on his desk that he had promised he would address that morning, but Vignoles knew that there was no substitute for eye-to-eye contact when questioning a potential witness.

Vignoles felt a frisson of excitement, tempered by frustration at the painfully slow progress the train was making. The nagging cold meant that he found he could no longer concentrate on reading, whilst his fingers had long since refused to allow him to write anything but the briefest of notes. He had tried to underline a couple of new sightings in his Ian Allan *ABC* but had only succeeded in making a complete hash of it because of his unbending fingers, leaving him feeling annoyed at spoiling a page with an ugly blot of ink.

He left the compartment, stomping into the corridor to get some circulation back into his legs. He walked a few steps to the sliding door that closed off his carriage with the one in front. Pulling this to one side he was buffeted by a sudden roar of sound and by a huge puff ball of steam that had collected in the narrow concertina of black fabric and metal struts that formed the flexible connection between the swaying vehicles. The leaking steam pipe roared fiercely and filled the tiny space with a hot dampness that looked impenetrable but which was as insubstantial as a cloud, parting and enveloping Vignoles with its soft embrace. He stood there, blinded by the cotton wool whiteness and deafened by the noise of steam, the clatter of wheels over the rail joints and the bark of the engine.

Suddenly, a thin shaft of low winter sunlight pierced a narrow slit between the connecting plates and this light illuminated a narrow slice of the swirling steam to form a curiously beautiful, eddying curtain of moving white-and-grey vapour that spanned the passageway. Vignoles looked in wonderment at the constantly swirling whorls of steam moving like disturbed currents in a heavily silted river. He marvelled at the beauty revealed by the slicing action of the light, which was far more intense than the similar effect of when cigarette smoke was caught in a cinema projector's beam. He also felt a slight lessening of the cold, through being enveloped in the hot steam as if he were immersed in a Turkish bath. Vignoles pulled out his pipe and started to add to the effect by puffing a cloud of pale blue smoke into the raking light.

His enjoyment was soon broken by the door to the far carriage being slid open with a crash and the sight of a tall, wide-shouldered man ploughing through the steam and smoke, scattering it in spinning wheels and rushing torrents around his body.

'Excuse me, sir.' The man stopped as soon as he encountered Vignoles, who was blocking the narrow passageway. The man instinctively made a fleeting salute, whilst his soft American burr had an attractively rich resonance to it.

'My fault. Sorry. Was trying to warm myself in the steam...' Vignoles wondered what an odd figure he must appear to the stranger.

'No way? You should duck into my compartment — it's full to bursting, but real toasty, too.' He grinned companionably.

'Perhaps I should. But I had been trying to do some work and the lack of heating meant I had a compartment to myself — a rare treat.' Vignoles felt he needed to explain why he was standing in a fog of steam.

'And a mighty cold one, too, if it means you end up standing here.'

'True enough.' Vignoles laughed, and took a puff on his pipe, stepping backwards to allow the man to pass.

'No. It's all right, I'm getting off at Notting-ham,' he pronounced the city as two distinct words, 'and if it is OK with you, sir, could I just spend the last few minutes here in the steam room?' He grinned and pulled out a cigarette from a pack wedged in a breast pocket beneath his sandy green U.S. Army overcoat.

'I'm getting off there as well.' They stood saying nothing for a while, the rush and clatter of the train filling the space. 'You're a long way from home. You're still here on service?'

'Well, y'know, I kind of found I like this place. Let's get to the point,' the tall American leant forward conspiratorially, 'I like the women here — a lot!'

'I see.' Vignoles offered a slight smile. 'So you found yourself a nice English girl?'

'Not so sure about just the one.' He gave a wolfish grin and then drew upon his cigarette.

'Ah. But compared with the States, isn't it a bit... grey and cold here, and lacking in everything? I sometimes think that Britain feels like a place that has had all the colour and fun drained out of it. The rationing alone is driving many of us to dream about emigrating. So why not choose one of our delightfully appealing women, marry her and go back home?'

'Listen up, not all of America is sunshine and oranges y'know? Where I come from I promise you, this weather would be considered almost warm. Heck, we got snow ten, fifteen, twenty feet deep and for five months at a stretch. And the land is as flat and bleak and empty as — as, well I don't know what, but it sure ain't pretty after a while. So the food here — forgive me, sir — tastes of cardboard — and that's on a good day! But thankfully there ain't too much of it, and I reckon it can only get better, and so it all balances out. In my mind, anyway.'

Vignoles laughed.

'Say, could you do with something a little sweeter to smoke in that pipe of yours?' The tall stranger nodded towards Vignoles. 'I could let you have some really good Virginian. Got a few spare packs right here.'

Vignoles noticed the brown leather suitcase resting beside the man's feet and understood what was being offered.

'I don't think so.'

'It's good stuff. Better'n than that corn-stubble you're burning right now. It's from the P.X. store back at base.' He was already opening the case.

'I thought you said you were no longer stationed here?'

'I don't recall — but what's with all the questions? I can give you a good deal, no fuss. I'm just being companionable.'

'And turning a nice profit, too', Vignoles thought, looking at the spiv and wondering whether to collar him for illegal trading. He knew he should, but if he did so, it would lock him into a lot of tedious paperwork as soon as he got off the train, severely delaying the real object of his visit. It would be futile anyway: the man would have no address that could ever be pinned down, would never get the court summons and would slip away as effectively as the steam evaporating around them now. And if Vignoles was honest with himself, the American was a lot less oily and irritating than the cockney wide boys they normally collared on the stations. They were usually greasy, creepy little men in flashy suits with shoulders over forty inches apart and an attitude that made him want to spit. Besides, a nagging, devilish voice inside his head reminded Vignoles that his tobacco tin was nearly empty.

'So what d'you think? Look here, this is prime Golden Virginia. No kidding. I can do you two packs for seven shillings. You got to admit that's one helluv'a fair price!'

Vignoles stared at the two pristine packs of tobacco lying in the man's hand, unopened and colourfully branded in bright yellow, green and gold. He found that his free hand was in his coat pocket jangling a clutch of coins with his fingers, almost subconsciously testing the size and weight of each, mentally adding up what he had to hand. All he needed to do was extract some coins, hand them over, and that was that.

'Say, call it twenty, and these three pairs of nylons are added to the deal, and don't tell me your woman wouldn't just *love* you for those? She'll be just crazy with delight.'

Vignoles gripped his pipe between his teeth and pulled a face. Anna had been desperately trying to find a pair for weeks. She'd trailed across Leicester on endless wild goose chases after these apparently most precious and essential of items, and she'd even convinced Vignoles to make a fruitless stop at Rugby one morning to follow up a rumour of a supply in a tiny shop there. He suddenly pulled out his wallet, shook out two ten bob notes and then rapidly made the exchange, thrusting the tobacco packs and cellophane-wrapped stockings into his voluminous coat pockets just as the train started to slow for the station. He could hear the sounds of compartment doors sliding open, voices calling, feet shuffling and luggage being hefted into the narrow passageways all heralding the imminent stop.

'Thank you, sir, I hope we can do business again.'

'Hop it. I never saw nor spoke with you.' Vignoles glared at the man and was already feeling a sinking sensation in the pit of his stomach and still wondered if he should now arrest him, the evidence of the black marketeering secure in his pockets.

'As you wish!' And with a cheeky salute the American dropped the window of the nearest carriage door, swung it open, stepped from the still-moving train with an easy nonchalance and was gone. Vignoles soon followed, conscious of the bulges showing in his coat and fearful that they would betray his illicit dealing. He felt angry and disgusted with himself, feelings then replaced by annoyance as he realised he had left his poetry book in the compartment and had to step back onto the rapidly-refilling train to retrieve it.

By the time he was striding across the wide platform towards the porters' room he had regained his equilibrium. No terrible shame and ignominy had apparently befallen him and he had secured a wonderful haul for a modest outlay.

The smooth-talking Yankee was irritatingly right: Anna would be utterly delighted.

As the inspector reconciled his conscience, John Beeby was wrestling with a dilemma. He had seen the many posters pinned or pasted up at the railway and he had immediately recognised the artist's impression of the young woman, though he felt that the artist had rendered her slightly less striking than in real life. But then the artist had not had the benefit of sitting opposite her in a small railway compartment whilst she was alive.

So, what should he do now?

His heart was beating fast, and he could feel his mouth going dry and a nasty fit of collywobbles was upsetting his stomach. Beeby had taken down one of the posters from a waiting room wall and was standing at a tram stop in the centre of Nottingham looking at her image with his oddly blank expression.

'It's terrible that. An awful business.'

The woman speaking was leaning almost over his shoulder and clutching a wicker basket with both hands, her frayed overcoat buttoned up tightly to her neck and a pink, flowery headscarf bumpy over her hair that was clearly still set in curlers.

'Yes. You just can't understand it, can you?' Beeby glanced at the woman, stepping slightly away from her as he did so.

'What's that, Doris?' Another woman waiting for a tram craned her neck to better see the poster in Beeby's hand.

'The young girl who was murdered last Friday, the one as got thrown out'a train. You must have heard about it on the radio? He's got a picture of her.'

'Oh, deary me, yes.' The other shook her head and tutted.

'But ladies...' There was something in his carefully-weighted words grabbing and holding their attention, '... it's even worse than that. Well, of course nothing is worse than what actually happened to that poor young girl, but what I mean is, for myself it is most, ah, hum, disturbing.' He transferred his gaze from the one called Doris to her friend. 'You see, I actually travelled part of the way with her on that same train. On the same day.' He spoke the last two words with great emphasis and left them hanging in the air whilst nodding slowly at the two women.

'Saints preserve us, you never did!'

'On the actual day she were killed?'

'The same.'

'Never.'

'Oh, you poor duck. You saw her shortly before she was killed? How simply dreadful.'

'Yes, I confess I'm rather shaken up by it.' Beeby looked back down at the poster. 'I am absolutely sure it was her, as the likeness is so good.' He shook his head slowly and licked his dry lips. 'Quite a looker, too.'

'To think, if you had not left the train when you did?'

'I know. I know. The murderer would never have struck

and she would be still alive now. I feel so guilty, somehow.' His face radiated innocent distress.

'But you can't feel responsible! Gosh, but it makes you think, doesn't it, Doris?'

'Did you see the killer?' asked Doris.

'Well... you see, I'm not sure, perhaps I caught a quick glance.' He made a nervous giggle that sounded odd and incongruous.

After a sharp intake of breath Doris asked, 'What did he look like?'

'I think I should keep that for the police, don't you? It would never do to go telling you, and then he was the wrong man — imagine that.'

'You're quite right. So what'll you do?'

'I rather think I should go the police,' Beeby hesitated, and appeared confused, allowing his hands to fall at his sides, 'I've never done such a thing before. I don't really know the proper procedure. One must do such things properly, mustn't one?' He looked earnestly at the two women. 'It would never do to make a mistake over such an important matter.'

'Oh, yes, but I think if you just go to the nearest police station, or stop a policeman in the street and tell him what you have just told us, they will know what to do.' Both women nodded emphatically.

'They'll have forms and things for you to fill in.' Doris's friend continued to nod her head.

'They'll have a talk with you...'

'An interview and all that.'

'Yes, and write it all down, I expect. They'll know the proper way to do it.'

Beeby nodded, 'It's quite alarming, in a way' He surprised them with a strange smile, but his face turned again in a flash to one of utmost gravity. 'I think I had better go right along and do it now. I shall get into awful trouble with my boss, though.'

'He can't hold that against you, duck. Not with you helping solve such a terrible crime. If you help them catch that murderer, you'll be a hero.'

The two women nodded again, in unison.

'Gosh, it's a bit thrilling really!' He giggled. The women just stared at him. 'I mean, having to meet the police and be interviewed.' He tipped his hat, then thrusting his hands and the poster into his coat pockets stepped across the tramlines just in front of a delivery van being hauled by a scrawny horse which had to pull back to prevent striking him.

'Poor man, imagine that?'

'He must feel terrible. I pray he can help them catch that beast.'

'He was a bit odd, though. He began to make me feel a bit unsettled, like.'

'Oh, Doris, he's had a shock, poor love. I wouldn't fancy having seen a murderer.'

'True enough. I suddenly feel a bit strange. It makes that murder seem a bit more real. He could be anywhere right now.'

'I know, I feel the same.' She sniffed. 'Can you smell soap?"

✳   ✳   ✳   ✳

The Black Horse was a pub of a type that preferred to be known as a 'road house' and, when new, had probably aspired to placing advertisements in newspapers and the motoring magazines promoting its splendid Sunday lunches in the extensive dining rooms that lay towards the rear of the building. Wartime petrol rationing and the discouragement of travelling contributed to its failure to become an essential stopping point for motor-coaches and car owners, but this could also be blamed upon the fact of its lying at the side of a ugly and unremarkable arterial road in on the outer edge of an equally ugly and unremarkable suburb of Nottingham; all long lines of identical, semi-detached houses interspersed by ribbons of low factory buildings or faintly modernist blocks of shops in brick and concrete. The equally uninspiring appearance of the Black Horse would have done it no favours, though it could be argued that at least it blended in with the surroundings.

Built sometime shortly before the outbreak of war, it was a massive construction in red brick that conceded just the tiniest of architectural details to the then prevailing style of art deco by offering long, slim, metal-framed windows that ran in white-painted, horizontal bands across the frontage and which were now steamed with condensation. A stylised carving of a winged Pegasus was set in the wall above the concrete porch of the front door, illuminated by a vast lantern that looked quaintly Edwardian. To then further confuse the hotchpotch design, the building supported a Dutch-barn roof of red tiles with wide, overhanging eaves and tall chimneys, both issuing at each end plumes of dark smoke, like a factory. The whole ensemble was set in a bleak car park devoid of the Austin Rubys and Sevens, Morris Oxfords and touring coaches it had planned for. All in all, it presented a dispiriting appearance.

Sergeant Trinder, who liked a pub and a pint as much as any man, immediately sensed that this was not going to be a the sort of place he would wish to frequent and guessed that it would serve beer as unremarkable as the building's outward appearance. This was probably a good thing, as it was only half past eleven in the morning and he must not be tempted to extend their visit into opening hours.

He and W.P.C. Lansdowne walked through a dark-wood door that held a stained-glass window panel that depicted a horse's head of a more earthly and robust appearance than Pegasus, and were confronted by the sight of a large room that clearly had seen better days. It had a nicotine-browned ceiling and yellowing hunting prints in ill-matching but consistently cheap frames dotted around the walls. There was a loud Wilton carpet that had been subdued in places by staining and a long bar that had been designed with a regrettably twee mock-rural style that included black-painted wooden beams, a ridiculous fake thatched roof affair, and a scattering of horse-brasses that studded the construction with a randomness that defied logic.

'Still closed, love, come back in half an hour.' A woman, presumably the barmaid, was rubbing a damp cloth over the surface of the bar, a cigarette in her mouth.

'Actually, we were rather hoping to catch you before you opened. We wanted to ask a few questions.' Sergeant Trinder was showing his warrant badge, as was W.P.C. Lansdowne, and kept his voice light, hoping to win her confidence.

'Police? What's up? I don't know anything 'as 'appened?'

'We're just gathering a bit of information to help with one of our enquiries.'

'Oh, aye? Well, if it's about 'ere, you'd better wait until the landlord gets back.'

'We would like to speak to him, but you might be able to help just as well,' said Lansdowne.

'How?' The woman came out from behind the bar, still carrying her cleaning cloth and cigarette, and walked boldly towards the two officers. Her eyes were suspicious but she also showed little fear, clearly used to standing her ground. 'Can't see as I can help. Where are you from?'

'Railway. London and North Eastern, working out of Leicester Central. We're collecting a bit of background about a matter that took place away from here. On the railway.' Trinder gave a slight smile.

She looked at them a moment, considering their words. 'You'd better take a seat then, but make it quick as I've got to open soon. The regulars won't take kindly to the police being here.' She waved them towards one of the many tables close to a brightly burning fire that gave off a welcome heat.

The table was small, and a large ceramic ashtray advertising Ballantines Whisky occupied the greater proportion of it. The barmaid placed the grey ball of damp cloth on one corner of the table, where it exuded faint traces of steam from the hot water it had recently been plunged into, but the many interlocking rings left by beer glasses still remained unwiped from the surface and both officers were careful to not lean upon it for fear of coming into contact with the stickiness. Trinder found that he was not enjoying the sour smell of the Black Horse. It reeked of sweat, un-emptied ashtrays and spilt beer, all underpinned by a trace of boiled cabbage. Even the damp cleaning cloth was giving off an unhealthy aroma that suggested that it was just transferring dirt from one place to another.

Not that Elsie Jones seemed to care. Once they had seated themselves and made their formal introductions, she seemed more at ease and happy to light up a fresh cigarette and start to talk. She was a thin woman, with etched lines to her face that were imperfectly covered by too much make-up. Her hands looked dry and cracked and her voice seemed always on the edge of breaking into a deep smoker's cough. It was hard to say how old she was, but Trinder suspected that she was younger than she looked. Despite the bitter winter weather, Mrs Jones was not one to wrap up warm, and Trinder exchanged a glance with Lansdowne, who was clearly wishing that the barmaid would do up at least one more button on her floral print dress, which was revealing far too much, though mercifully slight, cleavage.

'So what is it you want? I mean, maybe it's better you do wait for Mr Tanner.' She inhaled and talked, little puffs of smoke punctuating her words, 'He'll be back here any mo'. He's just gone out for the paper. He'll be back to tap another barrel, not that we get so many in of a lunchtime, but a few cycle down from Mercer's — that's the electrics factory up the road...' Her monologue was suddenly cut short as she coughed into her hand, smoke again puffing out as if mimicking a steam locomotive, but the moment her coughing subsided she immediately took another long drag, narrowing her watering eyes as she did so.

'Do you know a Mr David Ferens?'

'Davey? Yeah, of course, he's one of the regulars. What about him? Eh, but wait on, of course, his missus she got murdered. Bleedin' Norah! You never think that he done it?' Her eyes widened.

'We cannot discuss an investigation, Mrs Jones. We just need to check a few facts.'

'Well I'll be blowed. Surely not 'im?'

'Mrs Jones...' Trinder spoke with some steel in his voice, '... we are not suggesting anything, and you must not go telling others that we are. We're just verifying some details. Is that understood?'

The barmaid nodded in an exaggerated manner that suggested that she was impatient to dash out the moment they left to tell everyone she knew.

'It's just that when such a terrible thing happens we need to check every detail, every possibility, no matter how unlikely. And so, we need to know if David Ferens was here last Friday night. And was he with his group of friends?'

'Oh yeah, he's always with them.' She hesitated a beat, and seemed to look past Trinder into the flames of the roaring fire, but just as quickly inhaled and continued. 'They're all right really, though they drink a bit too much and get a bit rowdy, but they're decent enough lads.'

'So, last Friday night?' W.P.C. Lansdowne spoke softly and smiled, but her question was ignored.

'It's war as made them a bit crazy. They lost one of the gang. Just the one wasn't bad, I s'pose. He — the lad as was killed — he was the kind of leader of their group. He was the brightest of the bunch really, that's why he became a pilot — the others were all squaddies and whatever, nothing special, if you know what I mean? Not that I mean any disrespect to the Tommies, y'understand. But this lad got shot down in Egypt. Awful really, when you really think about it. But we lost so many in so many ways, that I suppose we don't really notice anymore. I lost my Bert as well. Air raid. He was on the railways, a goods' guard. Hit by the blast.' She filled her lungs with smoke again, and sighed deeply. 'Yes, well. As I was saying — they've been a bit hot headed since, but I don't mind 'em.'

Trinder tried to pull her back on track whilst mentally sorting out the jumbled stream of information. 'So you can confirm that Ferens and his friends were here?'

'Most nights. I don't know where they get the money from, I can tell you. These young men must spend all their money on drink. But then again maybe they deserve to enjoy life a bit, eh? The war wasn't exactly a lot of fun. Not just Davey and his pals, the other regulars are all the same.'

'They have money to spend?' Lansdowne tried another approach.

'Plenty. They don't earn that kind of money working behind a bar, that I can tell you.'

'Recently? Or has this been the case for a while?'

'Now you ask that, I'm not so sure. They often come here and drink a bit, but maybe the last few weeks they've been splashing out a bit more then usual. One got a nice new wristwatch, and they were bragging about trying to get themselves those suits with the wide shoulders. You know, like as what the dodgy car dealers wear. Horrible. But of course they can't find anyone to make them.' She began to laugh but ended up coughing.

Trinder eagerly picked up the thread. 'All of them in Ferens's group? They all seem to have a few bob more in their pockets, or just Ferens? I have their names here...' He placed his notebook in front of Jones and let her read off the page.

'Eh, you're putting words in me mouth now. I don't know; I just serve 'em pints. Why, have they been up t'no good?' She suddenly pulled back and looked suspicious.

'So, they were all here on Friday?' Lansdowne smiled.

'Y' know, the funny thing is, now I think on, I'm not so sure as I remember 'em 'ere that night.'

'Who, and what night? What the blinkin' 'eck's going on here?'

The questions boomed out across the room, startling all three seated around the table into turning to see who was speaking. The landlord was a short, stocky man with a belly that betrayed a fondness for sampling the ales he sold and a neck so wide that it seemed to continue in a line perpendicular to his little ears stuck on either side of what could be seen of his close shaved head beneath a flat cap. He was holding a rolled up newspaper in one hand, the other, perhaps subconsciously, was balled into a fist.

Trinder and Lansdowne immediately stood up and started to approach, whilst Mrs Jones grabbed her cloth and made a half-hearted attempt to wipe the surface of the table.

'Sergeant Trinder, L.N.E.R. police, detective department.' He held out his hand. 'We are making a few background enquiries and Mrs Jones was kind enough to answer a few questions.'

The landlord ignored Trinder's offered hand but glanced at the warrant badges being shown. 'If you want to know anything about my place, you ask me, OK? I don't pay 'er to sit around talking all flipping day. He glared at Mrs Jones. 'And any road, what you sniffing around for? Someone got a complaint, or what?'

'Nothing to do with you, nor your public house, sir. We just wanted to establish if a certain Mr David Ferens and his circle of friends were drinking here last Friday night.'

'I got a lot of customers, especially on a Friday night. How'm I supposed to remember 'em all?'

'You don't know the man in question?'

'I think I've heard the name. Sounds a bit familiar.' the landlord stopped and looked as if he were weighing up options in his mind. 'But like I say, there's a lot of people as use this place.' His voice was tight and wheezy as if his lungs would not take in enough air; his nose red and cheeks blotched by tiny veins.

'Mrs Jones advised us that he and his friends are regulars and are well known here,' said Lansdowne with a smile.

'Did she now?' He paused, as if considering his reply; 'Well of course with 'er serving behind the bar and that, she would know them better than myself.' Mrs Jones made a sound, as if she were about to speak and then thought better of it. The landlord busied himself lighting a cigarette, then puffed at it in a bullish and confident manner, holding the cigarette in his hand, still making a fist, puffing the smoke contemptuously towards the two officers with a deliberately half-hearted attempt to waft the smoke away. 'Why d'you want to know? He in some kind of trouble?' He flicked his eyes around the room, then fixed them intently upon Elsie Jones, who was now standing beside the fireplace. He shifted his weight from one foot to another.

'So, you do know Mr Ferens?'

'Is he in trouble?' The question was asked, Trinder thought, with a hint of caution.

'That somewhat depends on the outcome of our enquiries.'

A brief silence fell. 'Yeah. He was here — all evening. Definitely. Was with 'is mates. Left at closing time.'

'You are sure? It's just that a moment ago you seemed unsure of his identity.' Lansdowne smiled sweetly again as she asked the question.

'Yeah. Now I think about it, I can put a face to the name. And he was here.'

'I don't remember them being here when we closed up. Not so sure I served them all evening.'

'Who flippin' asked you? Get on with sorting this place out, woman!' He snarled at the barmaid, who turned and walked back towards the bar, 'You need to get your blinkin' brains sorted out — if you've got any. She's got a memory like a flipping sieve.' He turned towards Trinder, shaking his head in exaggerated disbelief, and added sotto voce, 'Probably too busy doing her nails to notice,' and grinned as if he had made a joke. 'So, that's answered your questions and now, if it is all the same to you, love', he looked pointedly at Lansdowne, 'I've got to open up and my lunchtime regulars aren't the sort that are going to like a police*woman* being here. They're a bit old fashioned like that.' He grinned mirthlessly whilst staring at her chest. 'You'll be bad for business, despite your bonny looks, miss'.

'Thank you, that was most instructive.' Trinder extended his hand again and this time it was returned. 'I hope we shall have no need to ever return.'

As they walked out of the pub, W.P.C. Lansdowne half turned as she stepped through the door being held open for her by Trinder and caught, but perhaps just sensed more than actually observed, a flicker of confusion on the face of Mrs Jones, who was now repeatedly pulling a pump handle behind the bar to flush out the pipes. The barmaid was staring straight ahead and then gave her head a quick shake. It was just the slightest movement, but the look of confusion, though momentary, was enough to confirm the suspicion Lansdowne held, that Jones had been prevented from telling them what she had really seen — or not — that evening.

Chapter Fourteen

'STORMY WEATHER'
Lena Horne

The mantle clock struck ten and Vignoles and his wife were only recently back in their home following a nightmarish journey that had seen them take nearly three hours to travel just the short distance from Leicester Central to their station at Belgrave and Birstall.

The fire in their sitting room was now only just starting to flicker alight and Anna declared it too late to cook anything hot, so now the two were huddled in front of the fireplace, each wrapped in a dressing gown and a blanket, shivering with that deeply-imbedded chill that is so hard to shake off. They sipped mugs of cocoa, made with just a trace of milk and half a teaspoonful of precious sugar, savouring its warmth as they sought to thaw their bones. Vignoles silently willed the pathetic flames in the hearth to catch hold of the small heap of broken coal and dust that he had scraped from the floor of their coalbunker.

In addition to his physical discomfort, Vignoles was also feeling thoroughly guilty. The nearly empty bunker reminded him that he was supposed to have ordered more coal at least a week ago and now they were in a fix. On top of that, earlier that same afternoon he had persuaded Anna to wait on at Leicester Central until he was finished with his day's work so that they might travel home together. Anna had suggested that, as the weather was worsening, she should rather try to get home as quickly as possible to get the fire lit and some hot food ready in advance of whenever he might return. Unfortunately, Vignoles had been the more persuasive, and in so doing had hopelessly misjudged just how bad the weather had become.

The snow had started to fall at four in the afternoon and was still showing no signs of abating. The disruption to the rail services had followed soon after and it had taken them so long to get home because their suburban train became marooned waiting for a snow plough to clear a path, and then there was a further wait as the signalmen held them to allow a delayed express to pass. Once finally at their station they still had a miserable trudge through snow up to their knees, which had tested their patience and nerves to the limit.

Vignoles's stomach rumbled loudly and Anna glared at him. She was frustrated by the tedious journey home and the unbearable coldness of the house and some of this pent-up annoyance was being directed towards her husband. She wanted to eat, but now it would have to be just a few slices of the dark bread she had queued her whole lunch hour for, a sliver of the thinnest and wettest of ham and a precious piece of the mercifully tasty cheese a friend had been able to find for her. But right now her hands and feet were almost blue and she was at times shivering uncontrollably. Making the cocoa had been enough of a test and she needed some of its reviving warmth inside her before re-entering the arctic waste of the larder and tiny kitchen.

'We're pretty much out of coal. Two or three buckets left at best.' Vignoles made a sheepish grin at Anna.

She sighed and briefly closed her eyes before answering. 'I noticed you'd forgotten.'

Vignoles momentarily felt his spirits lift, thinking that his well organised and efficient wife was about to tell him that she had already placed the order on his behalf and saved the situation. But he was to be disappointed.

'Oh yes, I tried to get some more — but there's none to be had, it seems.' Anna sighed heavily. 'So now we have a problem, eh?' She pulled a face that admonished Vignoles for his forgetfulness. 'I was even a bit cheeky and asked a couple of the coal merchants I was dealing with through work, but nothing to be found.' She looked away.

'Oh dear. A'hem. Well, if there's none to be had, then that is that.' Vignoles felt glum. 'That is a problem. But thank you for trying. It's my fault. I should have thought about this a long time ago, before the coal shortages got so bad. As soon as they nationalised the coal, they predicted a crisis and, well...' He let the sentence tail off.

She pulled a face as if to say 'I told you so', but answered him with a softer tone to her voice: 'Sorry, I'm letting this weather and the cold get to me. That awful journey did nothing to help. But why didn't you listen to me, and let me get back and try to warm this place up? Though what with, I'm not sure,' she added, *sotto voce*.

Vignoles winced. 'I couldn't know it was going to be this bad.'

'You didn't hear the forecast this morning?'

'Yes, but...'

'But you ignored it?' Anna gave a slight smile that drew the sting from her words.

'After all the snow these last days, I couldn't quite believe it would continue. I mean, this is Britain! It always turns to rain after a day or so. I thought they were just crying wolf.'

'I see.' Anna gave a resigned nod of her head. She fell silent for a while. 'You're probably right, though. It will be just one big snowstorm and a couple of days of disruption, which will clear the air for a spell of nice weather. Or rain. We'll have forgotten all about it in a day or so. Though with no coal it will be pretty miserable.' Anna sipped some more cocoa and they sat contemplating the reality of a house without heat. The radio murmured with softly-spoken voices in the background. 'I'll make us a sandwich in a minute. Just let me drink this. It's a bit odd having cocoa before food, but you can forgive me, just this once?' She threw an arch look at Vignoles, who smiled sheepishly in response.

A howl of wind moaned around the eaves and pulled a draught up the chimney, brightening the sputtering fire. Vignoles leant forwards and threw another scoop of precious coal onto the flames; the dust flared up sulphur yellow and blue and gave out a little more heat.

'We have a few logs outside. About two dozen. I've been keeping them for just such an emergency as this. I'll put one on when this coal really gets going. There's something comforting about a log fire, don't you think? We can last with those for at least a week and let's hope we can find some more coal in the meantime.' Vignoles paused in thought for a moment, 'You know what? I'm beginning to understand just how serious these coal train robberies are. Perhaps I was not taking Badger seriously enough.'

'You're about to admit that The Badger was right?' Anna opened her eyes wide with surprise.

'Steady on, I wouldn't go that far. But I suppose I am appreciating the effect it could have on us all. Badger suggested there could be public unrest, and whilst he is far too eager to see public disorder in almost anything out of the ordinary, I can see that things could get pretty agitated if the coal runs out. Maybe just a selfish reaction, as Heaven knows what we will do if we can't get fresh supplies.' Vignoles pulled a face.

'Are you going to cause civil unrest, my dear?' Anna grinned at him.

'Hardly! No, seriously, what I didn't like was that he seemed prepared to push the murder investigation onto a back-burner in favour of the coal.'

'So how are the investigations going?' Anna snuggled deeper under her blanket, and deeper into the heavy armchair with its big, wide curving arms. Her face softened as some warmth finally seeped through her body.

Vignoles took this as a positive signal. 'Frankly, not a lot to report about the coal robberies. There have been three in total so far, though one was foiled, or at least aborted. With regard to the murder; we now know who she is, where she was going, and are starting to build up a picture of her life, all of which may prove useful. She was engaged, and we have spoken — informally for now — with her fiancé.'

'And?'

'Not sure what I think at this stage, but despite his giving us what on the surface looks like a cast-iron alibi, it seems to be founded upon sand.'

'So he's guilty?'

Vignoles paused before answering. 'A suspect. But, oddly, perhaps not for the murder.' Anna looked puzzled. 'It is most peculiar. There are some intriguing aspects to his alibi. Let me explain: The fiancé is a young man by the name of Ferens, and he gave us a story for the late afternoon and all of the night in which Miss Harding was killed. He claims he was delivering goods and then later went to a crowded pub — it was a Friday night — with a group of friends, later spending the very late night at one of their houses playing cards. Sounds good? But when I telephoned the recipients of his delivery, the rather dull assistant who answered seemed to think the delivery was much earlier than Ferens claims: more like late afternoon. However, I also got the impression that this rather lifeless specimen of shopkeeping had taken no great interest in the transaction and had just let the man drop the crates of produce off at the back of the shop and get away. The only thing he could say with confidence was that Ferens was eager to leave. He might not prove to be the best of witnesses, but it is still intriguing.'

'Is it surprising that he wanted to get away quickly, with these dark nights and treacherous roads? He would surely rather go to a warm pub with his friends.'

'True; however, he claims he joined up with a group of friends in the Black Horse. But Trinder and Lansdowne visited the pub today and reported that, whilst the landlord confirmed Ferens and his chums were there, they have doubts about the credibility of this witness. You see, the landlord had at first been vague about knowing Ferens and his group, but later seemed to change his tack and became very insistent that he did remember them that evening. They had also started to question a barmaid and, significantly, she could not remember seeing them that particular night.'

'And as Ferens was part of a group, they are all going to give the same story if you question them,' added Anna.

'Exactly. The Notts Constabulary are helping Trinder trace the other members of the group as I want to see if any does give a different version or slip up. I want to put pressure on Ferens over the early to mid-evening period, before he went to the pub.'

'But it's surely impossible to imagine that all these people would defend him against such a vile crime?' Anna looked perplexed. 'I mean rape and murder, Charles! That's pushing friendship to impossible limits'.

'That's exactly what Trinder said, and I agree.'

'So, assuming that your hunch is still correct and Ferens is up to something, it's not murdering his bride-to-be?'

'No. And I cannot place him on the same train as Miss Harding.'

'Putting aside the twin points of why the others would cover for him and how he joined her train going south, is there any reason why Ferens might want to do that to his fiancée?' Anna was speaking rhetorically.

'Not that I can fathom, and he seemed pretty cut up about it. I think I believe him. But I shall call him in for a proper interview and see if anything cracks.'

'It's just a thought, but is it possible that Miss Harding's death was made to look like a frenzied sexual assault in order to cover some other motive?'

'Hmm. Interesting idea. A kind of hit-man killing? But by whom, and why?'

Anna shrugged. 'Maybe she was mixed up in something fishy?'

'But it would be a very risky strategy and one fraught with the possibility of detection. Surely it would be easier to just stage a motoring accident? On these roads and in the dark it would raise few suspicions.' Vignoles reached for his pipe and started to turn it slowly in his hands whilst he pondered Anna's suggestion. The radio, which had been quietly murmuring with a reading of a play in the background, suddenly burst into a lively piece of dance music with accidentally dramatic effect.

'Miss Harding was a typist for a firm of solicitors, so she won't have been killed for her life savings...' Vignoles was thinking aloud.

'Perhaps she was privy to something she discovered through her work?'

'It's an angle. Did she stumble upon some kind of fraud or blackmail plot, perhaps? I perhaps do need to talk to her work colleagues. However, this afternoon there was another development, and a very significant one. There has been a sighting at Nottingham Victoria of a man, who bears no resemblance to Ferens, getting into what might just be the very same compartment as Vera Harding.'

'Now that is interesting. Who saw him?'

'A young porterwoman at the station. She saw the posters asking for information, recognised the woman and telephoned me this morning. I went to meet her; she does seem a credible witness and is prepared to give evidence if so needed. She gave me a very good description of the victim and could even recall the brief conversation that they had had about the coaching stock. Apparently, she apologised to Miss Harding for its lack of toilets. That in itself is a tremendous step forward. We now have the time and place of departure and can plot her progress close to the point where she was thrown off. And then there is the man. He rushed for the train just as it was departing and this observant young woman could tell that he was a big man — 'rotund' was the word she used — and she remembered being quite surprised at the turn of speed he found in order to jump aboard. She was also furious with him for doing so, and that probably accounted for why he stuck in her mind.'

'Could she describe him?'

'Not well enough for a definite I.D., but it's something to build on.' Vignoles placed his empty pipe between his teeth, opened his tobacco tin, but then closed it again as he remembered that it was empty. 'He had glasses and carried a holdall of some kind. He was wearing a long dark coat and matching trilby.'

'A bit like everyone else then?'

'Admittedly, it is not a tremendous amount to go on. But his proximity to the victim makes him a suspect, so I need to find him.' Vignoles was gesturing with his pipe whilst speaking. 'I started making enquiries around the station but have so far drawn a blank. If we can get an artist's impression using our helpful porteress, it might jog a memory.'

A jaunty tune by the Glenn Miller Band struck up on the radio and Vignoles took this as a cue to switch the conversation away from work. He jumped up and surprised Anna in doing so, then gave her an arch look. 'Before any further discussion, I need to fill my pipe and I've just remembered that I struck lucky today and managed to buy some rather fine tobacco.' He paused for dramatic effect to ensure he had his wife's attention. 'And I found something else, of far greater interest to you, my dear. I think you will be rather pleased. It might even make amends for the coal.'

Vignoles walked briskly into the hallway, leaving Anna frowning and wondering what had suddenly possessed him.

'Ta-ra! Three, yes you heard me correctly, *three* pairs of — nylons!' He held the flat packets like playing cards fanned out in his hand. 'I have no idea if the price was good or bad, but I consider it well worth paying.'

Anna's smile warmed the room more effectively than any fire in the grate and she stood up, her blanket tossed to one side, the cold momentarily forgotten, and stood open-mouthed, her eyes shining brightly with pleasurable surprise, whilst Vignoles quickly hushed the little devilish voice in his head that reminded him that these were items of questionable legitimacy.

Chapter Fifteen

'LET IT SNOW, LET IT SNOW, LET IT SNOW'
Connie Francis

It continued to snow. Falling rapidly all throughout the night in huge flakes blown across open ground in low, snaking eddies that tumbled and twisted like skeins of white wool until its helter-skelter dash was stopped by a fence post or bank of frozen grass to form wind-sculpted slopes that increased in size by the hour. Senses were confused by this cold and tasteless substance, as the normal and safe smells of damp earth, leaf mould and grass, of creosoted wood and oily metal were replaced by a deadening blanket of impenetrable whiteness. Those close to the ground might detect the tiny sound of millions of frozen particles rustling and rolling beneath the low moan of the wind in the eaves and the cruel, whip-lashing whine of the telegraph wires. Eerie locomotive whistles drifted long on the snowy air. Enginemen squinted into the stinging wind as they struggled to haul their trains across the snow-clad land, seeking the lifesaving pinpricks of coloured light that signalled their safe passage through a night of impenetrable steam snow and smoke.

A tiny shrew crouched beneath the mass of a steel rail. Hunkered down, her nose twitching constantly as she tried to interpret and understand the disorienting changes to her environment. The tiny creature was cold and pitifully hungry. Unless she could find a beetle or a worm or some morsel to give her energy, she would not survive the night. As each minute passed and the shrew scrabbled uselessly at the iron-hard ground, her life-giving heat was being sapped away and her fluttering heart was consuming what energy it still held within her tiny body.

The shrew lifted her nose, sniffed at the raw air and flinched as the driven snowflakes stung her eyes. It was unsafe to hunt in these conditions as she was losing the ability to hear or smell a predator lurking nearby. She looked anxiously around and then darted away, driven by desperate hunger, weaving a path through the narrow fissures and gorges created by the wind sculpted snow, her tiny body able to keep low and squeeze between the narrowest of gaps.

A red signal light winked as the snow sleeted past its warning light. A tiny bell sounded in the signal box. Metal squealed in protest and wires twitched and hummed, pulley wheels turned and spilled fresh snow onto the ground. The massive metal canopy above the shrew swung across the night sky and clunked heavily into place making the ground quiver as it came to rest. The shrew stopped, sat upon her haunches and sniffed. The noise of the railway was familiar and curiously comforting, but there was something else, something causing her to momentarily cease the desperate search for food. Perhaps it was intuition or a kind of sixth-sense, but the shrew felt, rather than saw, heard or smelt, the danger. She hunkered down between one of the massive blocks of wood carrying the rail and a mound of snow and waited.

The stoat had seen his prey and was now flowing like a rope of silken thread in a silent ripple across the undulating terrain. He seemed to mould his long, thin body to the exact contours of each obstacle and to glide like flowing water beneath even the lowest of obstructions, slipping between narrow gaps with the confounding impossibility of a conjuror's trick. His eyes were focussed upon the tiny ball of fur with hungry intent. The stoat bared his teeth; a row of tiny incisors as sharp as the morning frost, licked the snow from his nose, then darted forwards. But the shrew, sensing the unseen danger, suddenly vanished by scurrying deeper into the darkness. Her hunter delayed the attack and stood on the top of one of the rails, assessing the situation. He then rapidly trotted forwards in a crouching, low-slung run, his long fingers and toes gaining an easy purchase upon the shiny surface. The stoat stopped and flattened himself to the rail, now spotted with snowflakes, and peered down into the darkness, sniffing and scanning the pools of inky black for any movement. The polished steel beneath his body started to hum and vibrate. The stoat lifted his head to look along the line. He had hunted this patch all his life and knew when to avoid the massive creatures that rolled across these smooth, polished surfaces, and sure enough, one was now approaching with its twin white eyes advancing towards the stoat, a rich resonant thunder in a steady beat filling the night. A long mournful wail, as haunting as the curlew's over a high moor, streamed from the locomotive.

The shrew made a move by scampering out from the cover of a hollow in the snow and revealing, for just a fateful second, her location. The stoat flowed in one beautifully deadly movement down on to the neck of the tiny marsupial. With a swift bite she lay limp in his jaws and was carried away easily in waves of white ermine across the mounds and dips of the snowy track as the massive locomotive, towering above the hunted and the hunter, pounded by.

✻   ✻   ✻   ✻

As the stoat seized his prey, a man was sitting in the corner of a crowded compartment in one of the carriages passing overhead, smoking a cigarette and adding to the thick fug of blue that already filled the air. Condensation poured down the windows in miserable rivulets. The ripped and stained blackout curtains were partially drawn, and the air smelt strongly of the doggy odour of wet woollen coats; of sweat and unwashed bodies; cheap perfume and beery breath — the last contributed by two intoxicated young men, slumped opposite. None of his travelling companions were talking, and most were sleeping, or at least trying to do so: their heads lolling and nodding uncomfortably as the rhythmic clicks of the wheels over the rail joints lulled them to a state of partial awareness.

He liked this arrangement. He could sit alert and awake, in close proximity to others fooled by the apparent safety of sleep or dulled by its encroaching influence. He was free to recline in the corner and slowly savour his contraband cigarette, whilst his eyes studied each of the seven others, squeezed uncomfortably close into the rattling and rolling compartment. He enjoyed looking at their faces with an intensity denied him when they were awake, and if in so doing, his own face was to betray dislike for each or any of them through a twitch and a turn of his mouth, he could enjoy giving face to his feelings, safe in the knowledge that the object of his contempt was blissfully ignorant. And then of course, if he found a travelling companion that met his approval, and she was sleeping, he could stare for many minutes, and run his eyes over her sleeping face, over her body — always tantalisingly swathed in layers of winter clothing in this weather — and try to imagine what might lie beneath.

He had already selected a possible candidate, and was trying to imagine how it might feel. Would she struggle and fight? Would she acquiesce after the first shock? Would he need to gag her first? In his pocket he felt his newly ironed handkerchief. It was too small. He would need to find something bigger, like the spotted one he had used last time. That had worked well. He was running through a sequence of events and possibilities, trying to perfect his method and refine the process so that he might better remain undetected.

~ 167 ~

He looked at the woman's mouth, perfectly formed and shiny with bright lipstick, at her hair expertly set in waves and curves around her delicately-shaped head. He sighed regretfully. She was an impossible dream with so many others in the compartment and crowded into the corridor outside, and besides, the strapping lad in a naval uniform accompanying her looked like he could handle himself. No, she would have to remain just a fantasy, but it was still pleasurable to imagine how he might approach the challenge. He chuckled to himself as if recalling a joke, a sinister smile forming on his face.

Anyway, he had his eye on someone. Yes, she was to be the next. But she was really going to be a challenge. He needed to think through the many problems he would need to solve to ensure that he got what he wanted. Patience was going to be needed, and a brilliant strategy.

He finished his cigarette, stubbing it forcefully into the overflowing metal dish attached to the miniscule table below the window and allowed his mind to drift back to the last girl. Had he covered his tracks sufficiently? That was an unpleasant surprise. There was someone very much up to the mark on the case. He'd better keep on his toes and at least one step ahead. Had he overlooked anything? He felt sure that he had done enough to seriously delay the police in identifying her, but had been disturbed to see the victim's face plastered across every station booking hall so soon after.

He was pulled back from his reverie by the woman's blue eyes staring straight into his. She had opened them after being jolted by some sudden movement of the train and the jerking motion of the brakes. She was disorientated, and her eyes were unfocussed, unseeing and yet fixed on his. It was only for a second or two, but seemed longer. He felt a thrill. The train juddered as the brakes bit deeper. He smiled, and deliberately averted his eyes for a moment in a subtle play of embarrassment, and when he spoke, his voice was quiet and reassuring.

'Trains are deadly for sending you to sleep, aren't they? I've slept right through my station doing that.'

She looked down at her lap then back at him, both carefully performing the polite ritual of companion travellers accidentally meeting each other's eyes.

'Gosh. I was well away there!' She giggled. 'Where are we, please?'

'Approaching Nottingham.'

He smeared the condensation on the window, turned to press his nose against the window and peered into the night. 'Snowing so bad, I can hardly see a thing.'

His voice had stirred the other occupants and the train was perceptibly slowing. The woman nudged her sailor awake and the others started to move, some standing and stretching, others reaching for suitcases and kit bags in an awkward stumble of bodies and limbs in the cramped space. The train brakes squealed again as lights illuminated the streaming snow and glowed warmly on the wintry platforms that sparkled in a fresh coat of white.

The moment had passed. She was leaving, though not without just one last quick, half smile as she left the compartment. He stayed where he was, allowing the others, except one youth who remained huddled under a coat in the far corner, to shuffle out of the compartment. He wondered if he should also get off and call it a day, or if he should take the train further north. There was no question that he would do anything that night, but it was still good to see what the possibilities might be.

With that in mind, he opened his bag, which was lying near his feet, extracted a train timetable, opened it at a well-thumbed page and settled back to study, his index finger tracing patterns and connections, whilst around him the bangs and clatters of the station and the plummy tones of the announcer's voice were given a strange new quality by the snow altering the acoustics of the station.

Chapter Sixteen

'TUXEDO JUNCTION'
Glenn Miller & his Orchestra

Eddie was reminding himself that he should be careful what he wished for. He recalled suggesting to Simon that if they had an overnight layover at Nottingham then they could sniff around the colliery to try and find out something more about the coal robberies. Now, following the heavy snowfall of the night before, he was on an enforced stop for goodness knows how long, right outside that very colliery branch. And it looked like he was going to be stuck there for some considerable time. It was a miserable and lonely spot, and for the past two hours he had been marooned on a small tank locomotive stuck up a siding buried beneath feet of snow. Water was getting low in the tanks, as was tea in their cans, and both he and the driver were hungry.

The day had started with Eddie feeling both excited and optimistic. He liked snow and, as he trudged to work, the shed had been transformed by a thick layer of newly laundered white, rendering all the locomotives and lines of coal wagons black, as if drawn in charcoal against a startlingly white background. The engines were frosted over and had snow piled high on their tenders of coal. As the boilers gained heat, lumps of snow would slide down the sides in small avalanches, leaving the paintwork glossy and the colours deeper and richer because of the wetness. Steam and smoke mingled with a layer of damp air that hung like curtains of mist, allowing only the palest of light to filter through.

Beyond the etched outline of the saw-toothed roof of the shed and workshops, the undulating, sugar-dredged fields of Northamptonshire were a faded and indistinct series of fences, hedgerows and filigrees of trees, filled with the scrawking and cackling racket of crows. The relentless thunder of the coaling tower was strangely muffled, and yet other sounds seemed amplified; there was a steely clarity to every clang and scrape of many shovels clearing snow and a penetrating sharpness to each whistle. Voices carried far across the many parallel lines of the rails whilst the hammer-blows of a train pulling away from the station, elevated upon its long embankment, echoed far across the land.

Eddie was rostered on a freight trip, and despite being paired with a taciturn and apparently almost mute driver, he looked forward to a gentle day of stopping at all stations north to Nottingham to collect or drop off a wagon or two, and of taking in the magical, wintry landscape that surrounded them. With a bit of luck they might get the offer of a cup of tea from the shunter or a porter at most of their stops, have a quick natter about the abandoned football fixtures and then be home by early evening. A perfect day.

But as Eddie was now discovering, snow and a penetrating wind make for a less than enjoyable experience on a railway. The stillness and calm of the early morning was soon replaced by an ever-darkening sky and a vicious wind that flung needles of snow into his face. One side of his body was numb with cold, the other was warmed by the fire and his face hurt from constantly leaning out to see the way ahead.

As they had pulled into Charwelton, the first of the day's many irritations made itself known. Their wagons lay on a goods' line buried under nearly two feet of drifted snow. They inched the locomotive along the line, then Eddie had to help two shunters shovel the worst of the heavy powder from around the wagons. Whilst doing so, the wind was sliding icy fingers up his back, inside his overalls and down his neck. Despite this, he sweated heavily with the exertion and then the wind froze this moisture and chilled him unpleasantly. Eddie tied his scarf over his nose and mouth, but soon this was frosted white by his breath.

Eventually they coupled up and pulled the wagons free, but he was exhausted by the time these had been shunted into order. Now, over an hour late, they had missed their path and, whilst they could take much-needed respite with a roaring fire on the footplate, his driver offered no companionship that might have made the wait bearable. He just muttered and grumbled and sank into staring morosely into the distance for increasingly long periods.

The day continued in much this form, though repeated in ever-worsening conditions as they advanced from one bleak station to the next. The driver, after a morning of this tiresome cold, finally abandoned his silence and seemed to take a perverse pleasure in declaring at frequent intervals, 'It's getting worse, you know,' and 'We'll be stuck. Mark my words we will,' adding rather unnecessarily, 'and you won't like that.'

They were eventually pulled over into the holding sidings near Clifton. It was rapidly growing dark and the snow looked set to continue. The small signal cabin controlling the reception sidings and the branch to the colliery was an oasis of yellow light in a drear landscape of wind-sculpted drifts and whistling telegraph wires. The cabin's smoking chimney and cheery light offered little comfort though, after a long wait, the young signalwoman pulled a window open and informed them in a series of shouted exchanges that had to be often repeated because their words were whipped away by the wind, that the line was now blocked ahead by a deep drift and that 'nothing would be passing for heaven knows how many hours'.

With water now running low in their engine, decisive action needed to be taken. The grumpy driver repeatedly glanced at the water gauge glass, as if that action alone would solve their problems. He then cursed under his breath, glared at Eddie as if it were his fault, dropped down off the cab and stomped towards the guard's van. Eddie's spirits were low as he stood on the footplate, feeling useless and lacking in confidence. He heard some bells ring and the sound of the signalwoman pulling levers inside the cabin, and was then surprised to see a locomotive approach with a fully laden coal train from along the colliery line. It stormed around the bend in a volcano of steam and a bow wave of powdery snow. Two surprisingly cheery young men on the footplate grinned at Eddie as they drew alongside.

'How do. You all right? You look a bit in the dumps.'

'Hullo. Bit low on water, that's all.' Eddie replied.

'Yer bin 'ere long?' The driver was poking his head out of the open side window.

'Hour or so. Can't get any further as there's snow blocking the line.'

'That's us buggered, then.' The driver grinned, not appearing to be much distressed by the information. There was something about the scrawny fellow that reminded Eddie of an underfed alley cat. 'No problem lad, we can tek you back up line. They've got all as you need up at pit. Water, coal and best still, there's a pub quite 'andy like, with a great pint of ale!' As the driver was speaking, the fireman was already looking to drop down off the engine in readiness to uncouple the wagons. They were not ones for wasting time. 'Reckon as we'd best hook up to you and we'll get off.'

'Well... it's not for me to say...'

~ 172 ~

'Damn right it's not! And the snow's too deep. I'm not sure it's safe.' It was Grumpy, together with an anxious-looking goods' guard, who was nodding in agreement. They had both walked back to the engine and had overheard the last part of the conversation.

'Eh? We've just come down the line. And have yer not noticed this big bastard we're drivin'? It'll take more than a bit o' snow to stop us. Haha!' The young driver patted the cab side of his engine. Eddie had to agree that it was a massively splendid beast, with its six coupled wheels and four smaller ones on a bogie at the front and two beneath the commodious cab.

'That's a Gresley A5 isn't it?' asked Eddie.

'Correct. We nicked it off Whitemoor shed. The foreman didn't take much persuading. She's a pacific tanker from down Marylebone way. Should be doing passenger work but got marooned up our place somehow and we fancied it. Lovely, eh? Nowt much'll stop her.'

Eddie laughed, as much at the look of disapproval on the face of Grumpy, as at the obvious enthusiasm and gung-ho attitude of the younger man.

'Right then, what if we lose our wagons here, you marshal the guards' vans on yer back, and we'll couple on at front? We know the road and can lead an' you push. Give it plenty of shove. We don't hang around.'

After a few more hesitant exchanges, in which it was obvious that the two young Turks in the A5 were afraid of nothing, and also seemed to be offering the only solution to the predicament, the plan was agreed with the signalwoman. Soon the looming bulk of the squat tank engine was smoking busily at what was now the front of their train, the fireman visibly stoking the fire and turning the smoke pouring from the chimney jet black. Eddie did the same, building up a deep fire and taking the chance to top up the boiler in anticipation for what might be an entertaining ride, and the promise of replenishing the tanks at the colliery. Finally he was beginning to enjoy himself, even if his driver was looking to be in a right fug.

After an exchange of short blasts on their whistles and the green light of the signal winking through the falling snow, the massive tank engine issued a terrific bark followed by a long silence, then another eruption that sent smoke towering into the sky. They jerked into motion, forcing Grumpy to quickly push the regulator further open to match the pulling power of the leading engine. They were now gathering speed, with their loud exhaust beats slightly out of synchronisation so one sounded like the echo of the other. As the train accelerated away the flames were being rhythmically sucked inwards by the tremendous draft through the fire tubes. Eddie threw a round on to fill a hole forming in the centre of his fire, but then the pulling effort slackened as the train started to descend an incline and he could relax.

The train rattled and banged and the twin exhausts ricocheted across the undulating land, the leading crew adopting the approach that high speed was the best cure for drifting snow. What Eddie could see of the landscape around them was starting to become more ugly and distressed. Conical piles of slag passed on either side, with squat, ugly buildings of utilitarian red brick and concrete huddled between. Rails snaked through dark valleys of waste, occasionally illuminated by pale blue lamps. Mean terraces of houses dipped and rose beside undulating roads punctuated by tall chimneys streaming sickly smoke, each speaking of some filthy industry. Soon the vast spinning wheels of the pit winding engines illuminated by arc lights came into view surrounded by an untidy sprawl of more buildings of even greater ugliness, and the dark suggestion of long rakes of coal wagons, convoluted pipe work, telegraph poles and tall yard lamps.

It was a bleak place, yet it offered their best hope of sanctuary for the night.

※　　※　　※　　※

Vignoles was also cursing the weather that day. After battling his way into work he had been met by a scene of near total confusion: the office telephones were constantly ringing with callers demanding help on just about every conceivable problem that could be caused by ice and snow and many that were not. Most of these problems were not the concern of his department, least of all, the freezing over of the station toilets. Nonetheless they had been passed on to detective department, which was taken to be the source of solutions to all problems.

But the jangling phone was not the only interruption; Mavis Green was also taking calls and then handing Vignoles notes that were steadily forming a small mountain upon his desk, whilst his officers were coming and going and leaning around his door, seeking instruction. The station announcer was also working non-stop, squawking out futile messages about cancelled or delayed trains, and this endless stream of words just outside his office window only added to the headache that Vignoles was developing. Her broadcast was only silenced when the power failed, a kind of blessing in Vignoles's frazzled mind, as they were plunged into a filthy gloom and even worse tempers.

By early afternoon, with a candle burning on his desk, Vignoles had finally seen all his officers trudge away wrapped in their warmest coats and armed with shovels to assist in clearing the worst of the drifts. The volume of physical noise and bustle diminished slightly, aided by taking the receiver off the cradle of his telephone. There was little point in answering it as he had no one left to offer assistance, and he was tired of telling the callers to 'just do the best they could, and get on with it.'

And besides, he had other pressing business to attend to: the hunt for the killer of Miss Harding. The days were passing and Vignoles still wanted to formally interview David Ferens. He thought he had a chance to do so that afternoon as the line to Nottingham had just been reopened — he'd watched the massive snow ploughs thunder through the station with two Robinson O2 freight engines coupled together, and he calculated that he had a chance of making it up north before the snow got the better of them all again. Whether he would return that night was highly debatable, but duty called.

A telephone call had found Ferens at the fruit and vegetable wholesaler. Vignoles asked him to make his way to Nottingham Victoria, where he had a small interview room in the railway police offices — and to be sure to bring the delivery note for the evening of Friday the nineteenth with him. Ferens just grunted but Vignoles took this as consent. Sergeant Trinder would join them, assuming he had finished marshalling some army squaddies in their snow-clearing duties at Whitemoor Yard.

Vignoles telephoned his wife in the goods' despatching office. She sounded as harassed as everyone else that day. He could hear a similar cacophony of telephones, raised voices and general confusion in the background. Advising her that he would be late home, he suggested that she try and head back as soon as she was released from work. Anna, somewhat tersely, told him that she had every intention of so doing and did not really need his opinion on the bad weather and travel conditions. Vignoles winced, and then risked adding that he had so far not found a fresh supply of coal

— which was only partially correct — as he had found no time to even consider this problem.

'Then it's a log fire tonight. There'll be no deliveries for days. It's complete confusion here: nothing's getting through. There will be no milk tomorrow.'

'Oh dear; well, must dash and don't wait up. I've no idea when I'll be back.'

Anna's voice suddenly softened. 'I do hope you won't get stuck in the snow. Wrap up warm!'

The journey to Nottingham, whilst slow, was at least uneventful, and Vignoles arrived to find Ferens sitting on a hard, wooden bench just inside the police office reception area, the floor of which was wet with dirty water. Three recently-used snow shovels resting against the opposite wall were partially responsible, dripping rivulets of melt water that pooled on the linoleum. Vignoles could hear Trinder's voice in the back office and decided to leave the young man to stew a little longer, passing him with just a cursory tip of his hat. Ferens glared up at Vignoles, saying nothing, but his breath formed a long cloud, betraying a deep sigh.

Sergeant Trinder was seated at a small wooden table, his cap pushed back upon his slicked hair, his greatcoat buttoned tight around his neck and booted feet resting on the wooden cross brace between the legs of the chair opposite him. A pool of water was also forming beneath this chair, and Trinder was exuding a pungent aroma of wet wool. A cigarette dangled from his mouth and this bobbed up and down as he spoke to the uniformed policeman who was sitting across from him and looking at an article in a slim magazine opened upon the table.

Trinder was in full flow: '...fair point. Crosby is a mighty fine singer — I'll give you that, and his voice is terrific — but it's what he does with the voice. He's just so soft.' He gesticulated with his hands, 'It's like being pummelled by balls of cotton wool.'

'It's horses for courses, old chap. I like his mellowness; it makes me feel comfortable and cosy...'

'Like a shot of morphine does?' Trinder spread his arms wide and pulled a face.

'Debating the finer points of the law, I hope?' Vignoles had entered unobserved and both men were surprised by his interjection. Trinder dropped his feet to the ground, extracted his cigarette and stood up in one deft move. The policeman also stood to attention and saluted, the sound of chair legs scraping along the floor was harsh and ugly, making Vignoles involuntarily wince.

'Sir!'

'Relax.' Vignoles acknowledged their reaction and then with one finger spun the magazine around to glance at the contents. '*The British Songwriter and Dance Band Journal.* Hmm? Less gloomy reading than the *Financial Times,* that's for sure. So what was the big debate?' Vignoles raised an eyebrow at the two men.

'Sinatra verses Crosby. I think Sinatra has more edge.' Trinder gave a sheepish grin.

'You may be right.' Vignoles looked serious and nodded slowly, then started to walk towards the interview room, 'Bring the Ferens lad in and let's get to work on him. But... he paused, half turning, 'I thought Crosby did a cracking job on *Swinging on a star,*' and he winked at the uniformed officer.

※　※　※　※

Half an hour later and Vignoles was just as puzzled by Ferens as he had been before they had started questioning him.

'So tell me again: what did you deliver that evening?'

'Like I said: two dozen caulis, three sacks of spuds, three of onions and two of carrots. A couple of marrows and a half a sack of turnips. Oh, and a partridge in a flippin' pear tree. Only joking, *inspector.*' The young man spoke with a lazy insolence that was starting to grate. Vignoles also had the feeling that Ferens had swotted up on his story, as his spoken list always matched the written delivery note with an exactitude that surely could not be accidental.

'So where did you park the van when you returned to Nottingham?' Vignoles asked the question for the third or fourth time, with studied patience.

'As I said, outside my digs.'

'Right outside?'

'Thereabouts. Close, or as makes no difference.'

'So someone will have seen it parked there?'

'Suppose so. I dunno.'

'And when did you drive the van away?'

'Next morning — at six thirty.'

'You didn't move it before then?'

'No. Why should I?'

'It's just that the constabulary have yet to find anyone who remembers seeing the van there that night.'

Ferens made no reply.

'Did Mr Rosedale know you were not returning the van that night?' Sergeant Trinder reached for his second cigarette since they had started the interview.

'Yes. He didn't mind. Ask him if you like.' Trinder gave a look indicating that they would. Ferens continued; 'It were late, and it was back the next morning in time for us to open.'

'You often borrow the van for this kind of arrangement?' Vignoles continued the questioning.

'What of it?'

'What did you do with the money you took for the order you dropped off?' Trinder fired the question off quickly.

'Eh? I put it in my jacket pocket. I put it in the till when I got to work. What's that got to do with anything?'

'Mr Rosedale trusted you with it overnight, playing cards?'

'Of course. I didn't gamble it!'

Vignoles leaned back in his hard angular chair in an attempt to relieve a nagging pain that was starting to develop. 'You did not see Miss Harding off at the station?' Ferens shook his head angrily at Vignoles by way of a response.

'So you didn't suddenly change your mind and join her at the last minute?'

'No! I've told you this again and again.'

'Or perhaps drive on to the next station, maybe feeling regretful that you had not wished her a good weekend?'

'How the heck could I do that? I was working. You've got the note. And even if I did, what would that signify? She's my... she was my fiancée.'

'What did you drink when you were at the Black Horse?' Trinder changed tack.

'Eh? Beer, like I always do.'

'Who served you?'

'I dunno. A few of the barmaids, I suppose.'

'It was busy? They have a lot of staff on?'

'It can be. Friday night and all.' Ferens licked his lips and moved in his chair.

'But you don't know their names?'

Ferens was silent a moment. 'Some of them, I s'pose.'

'So you would know if it was Elsie Jones who served you?' Trinder narrowed his eyes as he looked at Ferens.

'Dunno. She might have done.' Ferens rubbed his nose and sniffed, his eyes twitched when Jones's name was mentioned.

'Can you explain why Mrs Jones can't remember seeing you there that night?' Vignoles watched Ferens carefully.

'Maybe the pub was full.'

'Well, was it?'

'Yeah, it was actually. Mad busy. I remember now.' Ferens was again sarcastic in his reply.

'She also cannot remember any of your friends being there that night. Does that not strike you as a bit odd?'

'Dunno. Look why d'you keep asking me the same flippin' questions? What's this got to do with anything? You're supposed to be catching a bloody murderer, not pissing about with asking me how many beers I had and if the barmaid knows me!'

'Did you and your chums perhaps leave the Black Horse before closing time?' Vignoles kept his voice calm and level.

'Why would we?'

'You tell me.'

'Tell you what?'

'Why did you leave? Because, Mr Ferens, we know that you did leave.' It was Trinder speaking, his voice gentle, but edged with a quiet menace.

Ferens looked momentarily flustered, stroking an ear lobe and looking as if he were chewing on something. 'How the...?' He shook his head. 'I never done nothing. We stayed put all night.'

'The sergeant did not suggest you were 'doing anything', he just asked if you left before closing time — so what do you mean by that?'

'Nothing.'

'It does not look that way to us.' Silence fell. 'Look, you can tell us. It'll be better in the long run, you know. Were you in fact up to something that you would prefer remained secret?' Vignoles smiled, 'something you'd rather not mention? Especially now, with the awful death of your fiancée...?' He sensed they were close to something.

Ferens stayed silent.

'Another woman?' Trinder raised an eyebrow, hoping to coax a reply, but Ferens just pulled a face in disgust.

'Got plenty of money, have you? We've been told you and your mates have been splashing it about a bit.' Trinder tried a different tack. 'We learnt quite a lot from Mrs Jones. She's the one you seem not to remember. Well, she knew all about you and your lot. She seemed almost like a friend'.

'This is stupid. You're just playing stupid games. Arrest me for killing my own girl, or just let me go home.' Ferens glanced at his wristwatch. 'I can't be doing with this anymore. If you think I killed her, then you just tell me how I flipping well did it!'

'It would help if you told us where you really were that night. Because I don't think you're telling us the whole story. And that makes it very hard for us to do our job and catch the killer. Don't forget that.' Vignoles paused a beat. 'We shall be asking each of your friends about this, and from my experience, one of them will slip up and let the cat out of the bag. So it would look far better if you just told us now.' Vignoles again kept his voice reassuring.

A stubborn silence fell. Vignoles allowed it to continue. He looked at the little room they were seated in; the bare walls were painted in a glossy cream, though now grubby and stained by damp and salts leeching from the bricks that were growing like fungus. There was a deep, chocolate-brown border that acted like a painted dado on the lower third of the brickwork. The ceiling was high and had a single bulb that flickered as the emergency generator struggled to maintain power, capped by an enamelled, blue-and-white shade hanging from a cord above the table around which they were seated. He noticed that this cord had become sticky with age and had attracted some dead flies. The ceiling was stained by nicotine, a testament to long hours of nervous questioning.

'Do you earn a lot in your job?' Trinder added a note of steel to his voice.

'Phaa. What do you think?'

'Exactly. So where'd you get the extra, eh? A bit of buying and selling on the side? Is that it?'

Vignoles thought Ferens took a sharp intake of breath, but also did a pretty good job of trying to conceal it. Silence fell again for a few moments, punctuated by the distant sound of a dripping tap.

'Do you ever wear a neckerchief?'

'What?'

'Like this? They're pretty common. I just wondered if you ever did.' Vignoles held up the very one that had been used to gag Miss Harding.

Ferens looked genuinely puzzled.

'What? The only scarf I wear is this one. Vera made it for me.' He pointed to the brown crocheted example around his neck.

Vignoles nodded.

'And, like I said.' Ferens spoke slowly and clearly, stressing each word, 'I was in the pub all night.' He looked again at his wristwatch. 'Can I leave now, please?'

※ ※ ※ ※

Two hours after Ferens had stomped away from Nottingham Victoria, Edward Earnshaw was contemplating the fact that he was now, somewhat unexpectedly, right inside the very place that he and Simon had wanted to explore in their attempt get to the bottom of the robbery business. Here he was at Clifton Colliery, the heart of where the criminals were supposed to be working. He looked around and felt a wave of mild disappointment now that he was here, and was stumped as to what to do. The very idea of collaring one of the robbers was beginning to sound faintly ludicrous. He was pleased that he had told no one else about his plan.

He was seated in yet another squalid mess room, surrounded by a bunch of unhappy, moaning miners who were finding that their cycle rides home were being prevented by the snow that had accumulated. Tea was being drunk by men tired by their exertions willing themselves to make the long, slow and bitterly cold walk to home and the waiting tin bath. And even by comparison with the 'hell hole' at Woodford Halse shed, the room was unpleasantly dirty and decrepit. The only warmth seemed to emanate from these groups of wiry miners perched on rough wooden benches and an ill assortment of battered and broken chairs that edged the black-stained walls. All were smoking to a man, and those not staring at the floor with looks of dogged tiredness were whingeing loudly and raucously about money and their meagre pay packets or cursing the snow, whilst others sounded off about the nationalisation that had been inflicted upon them — for many seemed to feel it like an affliction — just weeks earlier.

Eddie was puzzled by their rowdy arguments and mutterings. He made no pretence that he fully understood what nationalisation meant, but from the talk in the loco shed, and from things his father had told him, it was supposed to be a good thing. It was a chance for the working people of Britain to take ownership of the big industries. It was supposed to bring investment and better conditions. He looked around. Well, it had only started on January the first, so he guessed it would take some time before things improved. But the atmosphere was far from convivial and, judging by the bitter arguments breaking out, there seemed to be little excitement for this new system amongst those gathered there.

Eddie found the men faintly threatening, a sensation perhaps induced by their grimy faces, which made their eyes startlingly white, like those of startled horses or maddened dogs. It was stupid, because he probably looked not much different and the men seemed either uninterested in his unexpected presence, or offered just a cursory nod in his direction and then carried on as if he were not there. Nonetheless, their cursing and muttering and the awful surroundings made him wish to leave.

His locomotive was stabled in front of a two-road shed that housed the colliery engines. He had already replenished the tanks with water, though there had been a scare when the water crane had started to freeze, but a burning brazier soon freed it up and he left the fire low in his engine but in pretty good order. His driver had suggested that Eddie sleep on the cab floor on some sacking, 'to keep an eye on things', and Eddie was not too unhappy about this arrangement for the cab at least offered some warmth throughout the night and coal was in plentiful supply. There did not appear to be many other alternatives, and the cold mess room was not an option in Eddie's mind. His driver had subsequently disappeared in search of the local pub, along with the alley cat driver.

Eddie felt a pang of loneliness. These men were not of his world, and he felt like he was an intruder, an uninvited guest. Not scorned, but of no interest either. He could either endure a long evening listening to the miners' complaints or do something more constructive. Common sense told him to stay put and see if he couldn't at least pick up some clue to the robberies from amongst these men. But he chose instead to wrap himself up in his muffler and reefer jacket and to pull his grease-top cap down more firmly on his head, and — not knowing quite why or where he was going — opened the door and walked out into the colliery yard, head bent low against the wind and hands plunged deep into his pockets. The snow at least had ceased to fall and the night air did not seem quite so uninviting.

He walked past the locomotives, noting the wisp of smoke being dragged by the wind from the chimney of his engine like a thin strip of pale cloth, then continued past the curving lines of coal wagons, each topped with snow that made them look like a row of the small iced cakes his father sometimes made. The snow was illuminated by tall yard lamps that cast pale bands of light and created deep pools of shadow over the undulating ground, rendering the ugly landscape strangely magical. The pithead buildings lay behind him, and Eddie chose to walk away from these and the bustle and noise of the machinery that whirred and hummed and clanked within. For some reason he felt drawn towards the desolate landscape of the towering slag heaps, each one snow capped and conical.

The railway line he had travelled up an hour or so earlier was beside him, with just the rails now visible through the blanketing snow and in some places drifts were already starting to hide even these. He walked past a large wooden signboard placed at the entrance to the colliery. It was constructed from freshly-sawn timber and he could even smell the wood. Eddie turned to read the words painted in white upon the pale blue background, proudly declaring that 'Clifton Colliery is now Nationalised for the People of Great Britain'. The still-unfamiliar owner, British Coal, had its name in large letters across the top. Eddie stared at it and wondered at the hope and expectation it carried, and the stark contrast with the tired and argumentative miners he had just left. He wondered what nationalisation would bring him and the railways when it was their turn, next January. Eddie made a mental note to really try and find out what words like nationalisation, socialism and all those other 'isms' meant. That they didn't seem to make people any happier he already knew.

A narrow service road ran parallel to the track and the snow was deeply rutted with wide tyre tracks. It was along one of these twin channels that Eddie made his solitary way, eyes darting from left to right as he looked for he knew not what. Maybe he was just drawn towards the small pool of light he could see ahead in the distance? This was as good a destination as any. He decided that he would walk up close and see what it was, then turn back and turn in for the night. It was illogical, perhaps, but Eddie had always been inquisitive and was rarely bored. He could keep his mind alert by observing and wondering about almost anything, most especially if it concerned railways. He was always finding things that intrigued and puzzled, often prompting a note to be made in one of the little penny notebooks that he always carried and which were invariably full of locomotive numbers, odd jottings and unanswered questions.

As Eddie drew nearer, he was intrigued to see the outline of a delivery van that was parked in front of what appeared to be a very small signal box. This was a ground frame, and it lacked the elevation of a brick base. It controlled the junction where the railway line started to curve behind the steep slope of a waste tip and a fan of sidings that branched off in the opposite direction. The road crossed these tracks just in front of the cabin, and this was where the van was parked. Eddie could see that its engine was turning over, because the light spilling out of the cabin caught the drift of the exhaust. The headlights, however, were off.

It was a little cameo that should really have attracted no special interest. But Eddie was not like most people, and so, as he looked on, the scene raised questions in his mind. Why was the engine running while the lights were off? Why was the van even there?

Eddie sensed that he should remain unobserved, though he was unsure why. As he approached, he fished his notebook out from a pocket in his overalls and licked the stub of a pencil in readiness. The van was a little Morris J type, branded with the name of a Nottingham fruit and vegetable wholesaler, and this struck Eddie as particularly odd. The coalmine hardly looked the place to take a delivery of fresh fruit, and even more improbably at a building that just housed a set of levers controlling the points for the sidings.

There was a dim bulb burning inside the cabin and he could just make out the shapes of three figures crowded within, all seated around a small table. Why on earth were they there? No more trains would run that night, a fact that had been confirmed in no uncertain terms by the Coal Board's despatching officer after they had made their unexpected appearance at the colliery. This ground frame would not be manned tonight — and certainly not by a vegetable wholesaler.

Eddie felt safe in the knowledge that he was virtually invisible in his dark jacket on this black night, though he kept the van between him and the cabin, and then risked flashing on his hand lamp for a few moments and playing it across the driving seat and dashboard. Finding little of interest, he walked around to the rear, wiped one of the small windows clear of snow and peered inside. He could just discern a number of shovels and rows of dark sacks, each bulging full of something dark and of a shape and size that suggested potatoes. Maybe. He tried the rear door and it opened, so he reached in and lifted a lump from the nearest sack. It was coal. He closed the door again and looked around, receiving for his efforts an eyeful of snow flicked in his eyes from off the van roof.

He approached the cabin in a kind of stooping run, whilst keeping out of the way of the large, white-framed windows that formed the whole of the front and part of the two sides. He was now standing right outside the door into the cabin and pressed his ear close to the frosted wood, straining to hear what the voices were saying above the sound of the wind whipping the telegraph wires that looped overhead. But their conversation always remained on the edge of understanding with the wind pulling the words away from his ear, despite its being pressed hard to the jamb.

He tried cupping his hand around his ear to improve the acoustics, but then, just as he thought he caught a snatch of conversation about 'dropping some off in town', he felt a strong, vice-like grip on his shoulder, whilst another large and gloved hand slid over his mouth and pulled his head away from the door in a sudden and sharp movement.

'Keep it shut, or I'll break your bleedin' neck!'

Eddie moved backwards, powerless to do anything but follow the directions of the strong hands and the powerful bulk of the man holding him in his grasp. He tried rolling his eyes to get a glimpse of who had him, and a strangely illogical and irrelevant thought filled his mind that it was now he, rather than the miners, who probably looked like a startled horse.

'Now, I'm going to let go of your mouth and you won't make the mistake of crying out.' The voice was low and hard, and the words came from a mouth pressed to his ear. A wrench of the hand upon his mouth punctuated the sentence.

Eddie nodded. He saw the swarthy features of a big man wrapped in a long overcoat with a balaclava pulled over his head. His face was framed by the woollen opening, giving it a strangely childlike aspect, despite his evident five o'clock shadow and stern jaw line.

'So what are your mates planning, eh?' The voice was harsh in Eddie's ear.

Eddie shook his head.

'Come on, lad, what's going on?' He thrust his face closer, a sour smell of beer and tobacco filled Eddie's nostrils.

'I don't know, they're not my mates.'

'Don't mess me around. I could break yer arm and no one'll think owt other than you fell in the snow.'

'But I don't know... really!' Eddie, despite the shock of being accosted, was beginning to realise what he had stumbled into.

Suddenly, the sound of loud laughter and the scraping of chairs on a wooden floor came from inside the cabin. The surly man shoved Eddie away from the door and into the thick darkness toward the back of the cabin. Eddie stumbled and fell onto his front into a deep cushion of snow, followed by the hard jolt of the man's knee in the small of his back.

'Don't breathe a bloody word.' Eddie's right arm was twisted back and up towards his shoulders, causing a burning sensation that brought flashes of light behind his eyes.

The occupants of the cabin came out of the door and were walking towards the Morris, but the light had been extinguished and no one was using a torch, so Eddie and his captor remained unseen, though they in turn could distinguish little other than dark shapes moving across the pale grey backdrop of snow. There was the sound of the engine being revved hard, followed by that of the wheels slipping and spinning wildly. A few shouts were carried in the wind, then the sound of a hand slapping upon the metal side of the van as a signal to move whilst the others pushed it through the snow. There was a short racing of the engine and churning of the wheels until the engine settled down as it pulled away.

'Hey! Hold on, wait for me...'

A door slammed and it eased away.

'Bloody hell, they've left you behind.' The man leapt off Eddie, allowing him to roll over onto his back and nurse his aching arm. 'Why'd they do that then?'

'I don't know what you're on about.' Eddie yelled at the dark figure looming over him, whose attention, however, was now focussed completely upon the little vehicle slipping and sliding away into the distance. A shrill whistle blew, and Eddie was startled to realise that his assailant was responsible and that he was now trying to run down the road, the whistle peeping frantically.

'Get after them. Come on!'

'Couldn't you have warned us?' A woman's voice shouted across the wind.

'They surprised me... oh, bugger, we've bloody well lost them!'

'Mind your language, constable!' She signed deeply. 'But they were right in front of you. Did you identify them?' Torches were now playing across the snow, and Eddie from his position on he ground could see two other figures approaching from the direction of a small wooden hut the other side of the tracks from the cabin.

'But I got one of 'em.' The big, balaclavaed man was now walking back.

'What?'

'I got one.' The balaclava loomed over Eddie. 'Hey, lad! Get up — or I'll arrest you.'

Eddie slowly got to his feet, looking at the figures assembling, their breath panting in pale clouds whilst torchlight played continually across the ground. He noticed that two were dressed in police uniforms, both of whom were women.

'And who are you?' A young woman walked towards him, shining her torch in his face.

'Edward Earnshaw, miss.'

'And why are you here?'

'I'm with the railway. I'm loco crew.'

The policewoman made an exaggerated point of looking around her. 'So where's your engine?'

'In the depot at the colliery.'

'And the proper place for it. So why are you here?'

'I caught him snooping around. He had his head to the bloody door. Caught him at it.' The balaclava's voice boomed out triumphantly.

The woman looked across at the speaker and frowned, then turned back to Eddie. 'Are you part of this set-up, young man? And I had better warn you that we can arrest you and take you back to the station, so don't even think about lying.'

'No. Of course not. I was just taking a walk.'

She pulled a face at him, more in bewilderment than anger. 'Funny night to take a walk.' A sharp gust of bitter wind flung icy snow at their faces, illustrating her point perfectly. Eddie shrugged, though he might have been reacting to fresh snow spilling down his collar. 'Were you listening in on them?'

'Er... yes.'

'Told you, ma'am. Got him bang to rights.'

Again the policewoman glared briefly at the looming bulk of a man standing beside them.

'Let me get this straight, Mr Earnshaw; you were standing outside, listening to those inside?'

'Yes.'

'Why were you doing that?'

'It just seemed a bit odd to me, what with the van being parked there, and the men all in the cabin on a night like this.'

'A likely story! Come on, ma'am, he's pulling our legs.'

The policewoman turned yet again to the man in the mask, who was now grinning with a smug look of satisfaction on his face. 'P.C. Tunstall, explain why a member of the gang would choose to stand outside in the snow listening at the door to a conversation between his friends, and then get left behind by the very same people when they drove off?'

The policeman's face fell instantly.

'Think about it. Oh, go and do something useful!' She muttered loudly enough for him to hear, 'Dressed up like a commando but about as useful as a chocolate fireguard.'

The sound of a racing engine and wheels spinning on the snow could be heard for the second time in a few minutes and bright headlight beams appeared from an even narrower track that dipped down from the road and railway, the incline of which was causing the car considerable problems, often sliding to a halt, its underbelly clogged with ploughed-up snow.

'We've got no chance of pursuing them.' The policewoman made a gesture of frustration with the hand holding the torch. 'Okey-dokey. Mr Earnshaw, we shall have to take a statement from you.'

Eddie shrugged his shoulders in response to what was said and stared over her shoulder towards the man who had nearly broken his arm, wondering if he should make a complaint. He watched the man lean against the rear of the black police car and attempt to push it over the brow of the hill, making a promise to himself that he would certainly not bother to assist them extricate their car if they asked. That seemed a fair deal, under the circumstances.

But, in truth, Eddie had already pushed the rough treatment he had received to one side, and was enjoying the adrenaline rush of realising that he had surely walked right into the very heart of the coal robbers' gang. He had been just a foot or two away from them, and had seen what he now knew for sure were sacks of illicit coal in their van. Just wait until he told Simon about that!

He knew that they drove a van owned by Rosedale's; though this was something the police were also surely aware of. But what he did not feel inclined to share with them was that, as he had rolled over onto his back, his hand had felt something lying on top of the snow. It was a leather wallet, and it was still slightly warm from having been close to someone's body only moments before. It must have fallen out of a pocket as the men left the cabin. He had instinctively snatched it into his hand and shoved it into his fireman's reefer jacket. And that is where it still lay.

Chapter Seventeen

'You Got Me Crying Again'
Bert Ambrose and his orchestra

'It's all a bit of a shambles, Benson. In fact I'd say it's a blooming cock-up.'

'Yes, sir.' Her cheeks started to colour.

'And you failed to make a single identification?'

'No — I mean, yes, sir.'

Vignoles looked at the discomfited officer for a few moments and shook his head. He had chosen to speak to Benson alone: it was, after all, she who was leading the investigation, rather than the more reserved Lansdowne, and so she was going to have to take the flak. 'So, what did you gain from this debacle?'

'We ascertained the identity and registration of the van we believe they are using to deliver the coal. It was almost certainly the same one we saw the other night.'

Vignoles nodded slowly, flipping over the two pages of foolscap of her typewritten report. 'That's something, at least. But without being able to identify the men using the vehicle, it's no more than a just a lead.'

'But surely the Rosedale's van ties Ferens down as part of the gang?'

'It implies that he is, but it's not enough to convict him. Maybe Mr Rosedale himself was at the wheel.'

'Do you think that's possible?'

'Hardly. I was just making the point that anyone could have been driving it.'

'Yes, I see.' Benson looked momentarily crestfallen, but then spoke up with an eagerness in her voice that made Vignoles look up. 'I was thinking that the landlord of the Black Horse might be in on all this.' Vignoles waited for Benson to continue. 'Lucy — I mean, W.P.C. Lansdowne — — advised me that when she and the sergeant visited, they noticed that the pub was awfully warm. A rare experience these days. And the reason was, they had a roaring fire burning buring in there.' Benson anticipated her theory would be shot down in flames.

'Go on.' Vignoles looked at her with one eyebrow lifted, he was intrigued to see where this was leading.

'Well, coal is terribly scarce. How could he afford to be so profligate? And both she and the sergeant noticed that the landlord was edgy and defensive about our questioning the barmaid over Mr Ferens. I think he could be covering for them.'

'It's plausible, and a decent angle to pursue.'

The sound of typing could be heard from behind the matchboard dividing wall down one side of Vignoles's office. His eye caught a reference to the police Rover in Benson's report and he changed the subject. 'I knew allowing use of the car was a mistake.' Vignoles was already counting the cost both in precious petrol coupons and in the roasting he would get from Badger. He was not quite sure why he had agreed in the first place. He recalled that he had been (almost literally) snowed under with too much work because of the terrible weather and so, when Benson had approached him about using the vehicle, she had caught him feeling tired and distracted and her charming and ebullient nature had rather sandbagged him into submission. He seemed to remember that she had assured him that they had got a strong tip-off about a delivery van providing more than just a few pounds of spuds on its rounds. She had wanted to follow, observe the gang in action, then swoop down and catch them red-handed. Or was that black-handed? He had allowed Benson a free rein, and was now wondering if he would regret this action.

Vignoles exhaled slowly, puffing out his cheeks as he did so, as much in dismay at his own failings as that of Benson's. 'So, how did P.C. Tunstall get the tip off?' Vignoles was half reading the report, but preferred to hear his investigating officer's spoken account.

'He had been frequenting some of the local pubs. I'm not sure what he told the locals, but clearly he won someone's confidence and succeeded in purchasing a bag of coal. It was illicit, of course.'

'And then?'

'I believe that he made further contact with this source, and gave them to understand that he might be willing to take much more off their hands. Hinting at some kind of deal, he succeeded in obtaining an indication of when and where the gang were to next meet. And this proved correct.'

'Indeed. And what of the bag of coal? Where is that now?'

'I'm not exactly certain. With P.C. Tunstall, I presume'.

'Benson, I shouldn't need to remind you that this is government property, obtained by illegal means from one of our newly-nationalised mines. It might even be needed as material evidence when we bring these felons to court. Tell P.C. Tunstall to bring it here — to my office — immediately.' Vignoles looked back at the page before him. 'And advise him that he won't be seeing a farthing of his expense claim for the ten shillings he paid for that coal unless he gets it here by tomorrow morning. Ten shillings? It's daylight robbery!' Vignoles suddenly stopped and met the eyes of Benson, and they both laughed. The tension in the room dissipated noticeably. In laughing, Vignoles had also banished the evil little voice in his head that was telling him that this sack of coal could help solve his own coal supply predicament.

He continued. 'But then you conspired to arrest a young railwayman who, it seems, has nothing whatsoever to do with the gang. What was that all about?'

'A misunderstanding, sir.'

Vignoles looked down again at her neatly-typed report, which lay at the top of a deep pile of paperwork that was threatening to swamp his desk, and read a few more lines. 'Was this the same Edward Earnshaw we've met before? The baker's son from Woodford, involved in that rum do with the bag of counterfeit money?'

'Yes, sir. The same.'

'Good Lord. We gave him a commendation last year, and now that blundering oaf Tunstall nearly knocked his block off!' Vignoles sat back in his chair, removed his glasses and sighed. But his faced softened as he did so. 'Why was the lad there, for goodness' sake?'

'Apparently, he was trying to find the same gang as we were.' Benson took a deep breath in anticipation of the reaction she was going to receive.

'And a pretty decent job he did, too. Perhaps we should put him on the case.' He looked at Benson, whose cheeks were colouring. 'Just tell him to jolly well keep his nose out of our affairs from now on.'

Vignoles had a feeling, from his previous meeting with this particular young man, that this was a warning he was liable to ignore. He laid his glasses gently on his desk and looked up at the young woman standing bolt upright before him.

Her black police uniform had been carefully tailored to fit her perfectly and the effect was flattering; she was a good looking girl and he was sure that she didn't lack admirers, though he did not recall her ever mentioning a beau. He appreciated that she had in all probability made these alterations to the uniform herself, at home, in an attempt to make the poor offering they supplied look more elegant and professional. The silver buttons and insignia of her uniform were gleaming admirably and even her heavy shoes had recently been buffed and polished, despite the ravages of the snow outside. It all spoke of pride in her job and position. W.P.C. Benson's hair was tied into a tight ponytail held within a snood, a style that Vignoles recognised as one that Anna adopted when she had been unable to shampoo it for a few days. He then noticed her eyes and how they showed a trace of darkness around them: the poor girl was clearly exhausted. She probably had not more than a few hours' sleep in a week, nor eaten even her normal daily ration of food, working, as she had, such odd hours. When was she ever going have the time and energy to meet someone and form a relationship? Vignoles felt a pang of compassion flow through him.

'All right, so we lost the gang and they're free to hawk their coal for another evening. But the good news is that this Ferens lad is, by implication at least, likely to be one of them, together with at least two of his mates — we just need to prove it.' Vignoles started to fill his pipe whilst Benson allowed herself to breathe slightly more easily. It was a sign that the worst of the storm was over.

'Is the Rover safely back here?'

'Yes, sir. Lansdowne is giving it a bit of a clean.'

Vignoles nodded approvingly and took a few long puffs on his pipe. The clock ticked in a solid and measured manner upon the wall. 'They don't strike me as the brightest bunch. Ferens couldn't wait to get away from us when the sergeant and I questioned him; not because of our questions about his murdered fiancée, but because he had a rendezvous with his drinking mates to flog some knocked-off coal in a marked van. That really takes the biscuit. He's almost beyond belief. We suspected that he was up to something that night, and I think we now know what it might be. Though it's perhaps not what I exactly anticipated. Right, I want you and Lansdowne to tail this Ferens lad and get me some cast-iron proof that he really is in on this coal swindle. Hard evidence. Maybe hold fire on talking to the other fellows in the gang. We don't want them to go to ground. Tunstall could even work up another meeting, and then make sure that you do catch them in the act. You've got two days, no longer.'

'Right away, sir.'

'Get this nailed. Lure them in, tail them, arrest them: do whatever you want. Use all the skills I know you have. I need something to give the super.' Vignoles swivelled in his chair to stare out of his office window across the station platforms and took a long pull upon his pipe, enjoying the Virginia tobacco he had recently acquired, though he still felt the odd twinge of guilt about the circumstances.

'Dismissed.'

'Sir!' Benson saluted, then turned smartly and made to leave his office.

Vignoles suddenly spun the chair around, making a sharp squeak as it did so. 'Benson!'

'Sir?'

'This Earnshaw lad, he's not going to make a complaint, is he?'

'I don't think so.'

'Good. Then this is the deal: leave the car in perfect order, and don't go near it again. Do whatever else you need to catch these little bug... er, blighters,' Vignoles corrected himself swiftly: no respectable man swore when there were ladies present. 'When you've done that, rewrite this report and don't mention either the car or Earnshaw. Understood?'

'Yes, sir!' And Benson saluted and left with a spring in her step and a smile forming on her lips.

Vignoles closed his eyes and tipped his chair backwards, placing his hands behind his head, and held this position for a few moments, processing the information contained within Benson's report. Despite the failings of her operation she had made one startling leap forward, in that he could probably take Ferens out of the picture with regard to the murder of Miss Harding. His natural police instincts told him to remain cautious about completely discounting him, but the facts were starting to add up. His involvement with coal theft explained why Ferens and his gang wanted them to believe that they were in the pub that night, but also why no one remembered seeing them there, and why Ferens had borrowed the van, ostensibly for a late delivery, and kept it overnight. There was work still to be done, but Vignoles felt sure that they were not far away from pinning the robberies onto his shoulders. In which case, Vignoles had no further interest in Ferens and his gang of likely lads. He would leave them to Benson and Lansdowne.

No, what was occupying Vignoles's thoughts now was a far more chilling matter: if Ferens was not guilty of raping and killing Miss Harding, who was? It was too late to help Miss Harding, but if she had been killed in a fit of enraged jealousy at the hands of her own lover, then at least he could rest easy that no one else was liable to be at risk whilst he proved this. But events had taken a far more worrying turn, because without Ferens as the prime suspect the spectre of a crazed killer who preyed upon women started to slink around his mind. He had raised that idea with Badger a few days ago, primarily for effect, to ensure that the super gave the investigation the proper consideration it deserved. But now he feared it really might be true.

※　※　※　※

Vignoles closed his eyes, as if by doing so he could shut out the chilling image of women being stalked along the railway, right at this very moment, perhaps. He was fighting to subdue a sense of frustration welling up inside, a feeling that screamed at him to take some kind of action. He had to consciously suppress an idiotic desire to run out onto the station platform, confront every man there and shake him until he confessed. These ridiculous feelings were both foolish and dangerous. Vignoles needed to think calmly and logically.

He leant forwards, making to lean his elbows on the desk, but instead made contact with the deep stack of arrest reports, overtime claims, additional working notices, new directives, duty rosters and other pieces of tedious office administration on his desk, and the whole tottering paper mountain slid from under his weight and cascaded onto the linoleum floor.

'Oh, for crying out loud!'

He stared at the jumbled confusion for a few moments and sighed heavily, before opening the copious bottom drawer of his desk, that he knew to be almost empty save for his old gas mask in its cardboard case. This he lifted out and put to one side near his chair before scooping the papers inside, finally slamming the drawer shut.

He looked at his desktop, now fleshly clear of clutter. That was better. Now he could concentrate on the really urgent matter in hand. He needed space and time free from the unstoppable tide of paper and forms needing to be filled out in triplicate that seemed to block the pathways of his thoughts, just as the snow outside was blocking the railway. Now that it had been pushed aside — albeit temporarily — like the ploughs were moving the snow, he felt his mind already feeling soothed by this cathartic action.

And it was fortunate that he was feeling so refreshed, for when he responded a few minutes later to the telephone jangling at him he was presented with an interesting turn of events in the Vera Harding case.

Chapter Eighteen

'THE YOUNG MAN WITH A HORN'
Harry James & June Allyson

Katarzyna Walentynowicz was frowning. She alternated between sitting still and suddenly both moving and speaking at the same time, actions brought on by the heady combination of frustration and nervous excitement in about equal doses.

'Sit still! You drive me crazy. How can I make a good job with you wriggling around like a bag of ferrets?' Ewa Grabowicz was holding a small paintbrush in one hand and an upturned tube in the other. Kat was sitting on a hard wooden chair, her head thrown back as she let Ewa attempt to repair a smudge she had made to her precious lipstick.

'Get on with it, then. We need to get back. I'll do it myself if you don't hurry up. I thought you said you were good at this?'

'I am, but keep quiet. You know I do it better than you. I have a steadier hand.' Ewa had the brush poised close to Kat's lips, but waited for her to stop talking. 'And you need to sit still.' She rolled her eyes.

'I am.' Kat folded her arms in an exaggerated manner, that made her shoulders and head move again.

'St-ay st-ill. That's it. All done.' Ewa stood upright and admired her handiwork. 'You look perfect. Just don't go ruining it again, as there's not a drop left.' She breathed an exaggerated sigh of relief in a long white stream of breath that emphasised the perishing cold.

'Are you sure it's all right?' Kat was squinting to see her face in the small compact mirror she was now holding up, an action not helped by the dim lighting and the mirror beading over with condensation.

'Don't smudge it.' Ewa looked at the lipstick, 'I think this has frozen. Can you believe that?' Ewa was fiddling with the brush, stirring it around inside the plastic tube. She had been trying to eke out the last traces of lipstick colour using the paintbrush and warming the tube by holding the base of it in her tea to soften the colour. 'I only dipped it in a few minutes ago and now it's gone like ice.' She shook her head in disbelief. 'Do you want this? It's all used up.'

'Are you joking? "Everglades" is my best colour and I simply can't find it anywhere. I need every last smudge.' Kat smiled, her equilibrium regained.

'Can we go back in now? This tea's gone cold. Ugh.' Ewa pulled a face and emptied the china cup into the sink.

'Of course, what are you waiting for? The main feature will start soon.' The sound of talking and interlude music played on an organ could be heard coming through the door to the ladies' toilets. 'And I want to be in our seats whilst the lights are still up. That way I can get a better look.' Kat gave a mischievous glance towards her friend.

'You mean you want to make an entrance.'

'And why not? Anyway, I can't see you complaining.' Kat looked at Ewa, who was patting her hair and tweaking the belt on her thick, woollen overcoat.

She blushed. 'They're all right, I suppose. But just don't be so obvious. And be careful that our "protecting angels" don't notice.'

'They've had plenty of brandy, or whatever it is in that bottle your uncle bought, so they're not noticing much. And don't be so coy; those lads can't understand a word we say. Anyway, wrapped up like we are they're more likely to think we are a pair of polar bears than beautiful girls.' Kat's voice had an edge of bitterness to it, but the deep cold of the night allowed for no compromise, and so like everyone else in the audience, they were wearing layer upon layer of clothing in an attempt to stay warm.

A visit to the Savoy cinema in Woodford Halse was a rare treat for the two girls, and it had taken almost two weeks of pleading, nagging and being extra attentive with the daily chores for them to be allowed to make the short trip down the line from Finmere to the comparative delights of the railway town. The ever-worsening snow had not helped their cause but, since the railway lines had for the last few days remained clear, their pleas had finally been listened to. In fact, the snow had perversely rather ended up swinging the balance in their favour, because after two weeks almost permanently cooped up in their respective huts, and with tempers fraying and nerves straining in the claustrophobic confines of their inhospitable surroundings, it was a good excuse for at least some of the inmates to leave for a few hours.

And so, chaperoned by Ewa's uncle Piotr and his friend Mr Paleta, they had set off for Woodford in the early afternoon, tasked with trying to purchase a long list of items and suitably armed with carefully-clipped coupons and a raft of identification papers and ration cards. Their chaperones were in a cheerful mood as they had managed to pick up some cigarettes and a small bottle of something strong from their local spiv: a smooth-talking American who was often to be found loitering around the camp. He never seemed to do any service duties but he had a respectful manner that made him a cut above the usual fly-by-nights lurking near pub doors with their wide-shouldered coats, pencil moustaches and loud hatbands; and so, within the camp, the Yankee was their dealer of choice. He was Ewa's favourite too, though she would never dare let him know it.

Once at Woodford Halse the girls had thoroughly enjoyed themselves, walking the length of Station Road at least twice, despite the slippery slush underfoot and having to side-step the heaps of shovelled snow. They enjoyed seeking out, haggling and pleading for all manner of items with varying success. It had not gone unnoticed that, if the shopkeeper was a man, their winning smiles and youthful good looks worked wonders in finding hidden packets of pins, hair grips, or an extra onion or two and a sly tin of sardines slipped into the brown paper bag; whereas the older women who held the fort in some of the shops stood their ground with a fearsome manner whilst tiresomely repeating the exact rules of rationing, and reminding them both of the hardships of these austere times and stressing that it was 'fair shares for all', which, in the eyes of the two Polish girls, seemed to mean, 'none for you, as you're not from around here.'

However, upon arrival at Woodford Uncle Piotr and Mr Paleta had immediately declared that the two girls were far better cut out for this kind of work than they were, and that they would only be a hindrance to the expedition. They promptly repaired to the White Hart Hotel, which lay invitingly at the bottom of the slip road running down from the station yard. And it was here, after leaving their baskets of shopping with a helpful porter at the station, that Kat and Ewa had later met up with their now slightly merry and more gregarious chaperones for a warming cup of tea at six o'clock. They whiled away the time contentedly, sitting as close as they could to the smouldering fire in the saloon until it was time to walk back up Station Road towards the Savoy Cinema.

The cinema was only a modest construction in comparison with its counterparts in a city, but set as it was bang in the centre of a small Northamptonshire town — a village, some might say — it made quite an imposing sight; certainly so to the eyes of the two girls, whose life was largely dominated and coloured by life in a dilapidated ex-R.A.F. base. Its art deco styling in cream-painted stucco and the entrance portico with small electric lamps and illuminated sign above lent it all the glamour that the two girls were craving. It stood out with all the presence normally reserved for a church amidst the lines of two-storey, red-brick railwaymen's houses and the row of shops that it faced. It was even more incongruous when viewed against the delightfully higgledy-piggledy maze of ironstone cottages that backed up against the rear elevation.

The cinema had two wooden boards propped against the wall bearing a poster for Blithe Spirit, the main feature for the night. The two girls were little concerned about what was showing: any film was a treat and a chance to escape their own world and enter into another. Even life in modest Woodford appeared to them both slightly alien and intriguing; it was a place whose life and rhythm was largely orchestrated by the whistles and bells and many comings and goings of the railway, elevated as it was on a long plateau level with the Savoy.

So now, as they awaited the start of Noël Coward's latest film, the adrenaline was pulsing through their veins, helping them to almost forget the cold, flushing their cheeks and making their eyes sparkle with enjoyment. Perhaps it was this excitement that had prompted Kat to be immediately fascinated by one of the two young men seated two rows in front. Both men were either in the services or recently demobbed, as they wore their hair in standard short back and sides and had heavy army overcoats that had seen much wear. One sported a narrow moustache that she thought looked dashing and slightly rakish. Their profiles were enough to get Kat nudging and whispering to Ewa who, whilst more reticent, was in cautious agreement that based upon the backs of their necks alone — for they had little else to go on in the dim, flickering light cast by the projected film — they had potential.

Of course this had to be circumspect speculation as Uncle Piotr and Mr Paleta were seated close by, though thankfully not right beside them; the usherette having placed them wherever she could find pairs of empty seats. Both men were under the influence of one too many beers, which might have induced them to fall asleep but instead prompted both to give full vent to their chaperoning skills by smiling and occasionally waving a hand at either of the girls when they caught their eye, much to their intense embarrassment.

'Don't encourage them! Why does he have to wave like that?' Kat was whispering into her friend's ear.

'I know. Everyone can see. And they are both grinning like cats that have got the cream. If I didn't know better, I'd find them creepy.' They giggled.

'But those two, on the other hand.' Kat looked towards the two men she had been admiring.

'Have not even looked around once, let alone smiled.' Ewa was being pragmatic.

'We can still hope. There's time. Maybe they'll get up and stretch their legs at the interval.'

'And then?' Ewa glanced at Kat, whose face was illuminated in flashes of blue and grey from the film image on the screen.

Kat shrugged by way of reply and gestured with her hands, then looked back at the film. 'I'm not sure I know what's happening here.'

'No. I find it a bit hard with the way they speak. I need to concentrate.'

'I think the main man has just seen a ghost of his wife. His first wife, who's now dead' Kat was turning to whisper in Ewa's ear, looking along the line of seats filled with coat and scarf-swaddled cinema-goers as she did so.

'The man in the film, not the one you've been looking at?'

'Of course, silly.' As Kat replied, her roving eye caught the sight of glasses glinting in the pale and shifting half-light. They were turned, not towards Rex Harrison and Margaret Rutherford, but straight towards Kat. She started in her seat as if stung by a jolt of electricity. Ewa glanced at her to see what was up. Keeping her eyes focussed on a spot somewhere to Ewa's left, Kat grabbed her friend's arm. 'It's him again! What's he doing here?' she hissed.

'Who? What's up?' Ewa was startled and spoke aloud.

A woman sitting behind the two girls made a shushing noise followed by a theatrically loud sigh.

'Don't look. I'll tell you where he is, and you just glance over. Don't attract his attention.'

Ewa slowly turned her head, trying to look nonchalant as she did so.

'With the glasses. About ten seats away,' added Kat.

'Shush! Keep it down, will you.' The annoyed woman tapped Kat on the shoulder, prompting a guilty look in return.

'Honestly, these foreigners come here and think they own the place!'

'No manners at all. I don't know why they bother: they can't possible understand what's being said.' The woman and her husband spoke clearly enough to be easily audible over the soundtrack that was building to a crescendo.

Kat fell silent, worried that any further disturbance might attract more attention their way. Was the creepy man really looking at her? Or had it just been chance?

'He is a bit strange.' Ewa pressed her mouth close to Kat's and spoke almost inaudibly. Kat wriggled her shoulders in disgust. 'He's the plumber, I think. The one at the camp.'

'Shush!'

'Why's he here? He was the one staring at me the other day.' Kat stole another surreptitious sideways glance, but now the man was in profile and appeared to be watching the film, a mist of pale breath curling around his face like a phantom. She turned away and stared at the screen, forcing herself to keep looking forwards even though a nagging voice in her head kept telling her to look towards the man again.

'Thank goodness they've shut up at last,' hissed the woman behind.

They could feel the irritated stares of the couple behind boring into the back of their heads and so with a force of willpower both girls focussed upon the film, hoping that by ignoring the ugly plumber he would go away. And then, to their astonishment and mutual relief, when the lights were raised for the interval he had done just that. His empty seat could be seen just beyond the waving and grinning of their chaperones. A sense of relief flooded through Kat and the whole episode suddenly seemed silly and foolish, though she still retained an odd feeling that this was now the second time that he had vanished after observing her. She was not sure what to think about this.

'I'm sure he's the plumber or gasman or something. That's why we've seen him before. We don't need to get in a flap.' Ewa was speaking Polish so that the grumpy couple behind them could not overhear.

'I just don't like the way he stares at me.'

'Let's be fair: those glasses don't help. They just make him look like he's staring. Anyway, I suppose you can't blame him for looking.' Ewa was trying to reassure herself, as much as her friend.

'Ugh! Please yourself.' Kat looked horrified.

'You know what I'm saying. You wouldn't complain if it was either of those lads, but when it happens to be someone you don't like, it's a crime. I don't think we should be so hard. Anyway, he's got bored and gone.'

They both looked again, and his seat was undeniably empty. 'And good riddance.' Kat gave one last reassuring look, and then settled back in her seat for the second half.

The film passed without further incident and was given a pleasing coda at the close when one of the young men stopped to allow the girls out of their row, smiling as he did so. It meant nothing, but they giggled about it later as they walked down the hill towards the railway station. The few street lights were dim and sickly as the town gas was too low for them to burn brightly, but the snow seemed to glow all around and they made their way with little difficulty, the snow sparkling like millions of tiny diamonds under their feet. Uncle Piotr and Mr Paleta found the White Hart Hotel again, as if guided by radar, and insisted upon one last little beer for the road. Kat thought she caught a fleeting glance of their friendly Yankee, the supplier of all that was normally unobtainable, walking into the public bar, but she might have been mistaken. After a long day and the debilitating cold, which was now really gnawing away inside her, and the curious and stressful moments in the cinema, she was no longer inclined to very much care, though the thought that this was the chance to finally procure some precious nylons whilst her mother was not about, did flash through her mind.

After some cajoling, the men were coaxed away from the bar and up the steep access road onto the draughty station, where the girls collected their shopping from the porter's office. They were soon rewarded by the cheery sight of a train chugging its way out of the gloom, steam billowing from around its wheels and a yellow glow flickering in the cab. The coaches were close to being warm, but also gloomy, and they smelt of stale smoke and damp bodies, though this mattered little as they collectively flopped down into the soft and spongy seats with creaking springs.

Kat had, however, taken one last glance along the platform before stepping aboard, searching the clusters of people waiting for the train. Surely he would not be travelling to Finmere at this time? The plumber probably lived in Woodford, and was at home by now. This thought relaxed her, and she dismissed him from her mind. She, too, was eager to be home, and as she leant against the moquette her eyes suddenly felt heavy with sleep. Her head started to nod forwards. The two chaperones were already snoring within minutes of sitting down opposite her, and soon the whole train fell silent of voices. Just the gentle rumble of wheels, the clicking of the rail joints and the muffled huffing of the locomotive filled the dark shadows and the dim corridors.

As each traveller slumped into sleep a lone man watched, struck a match and smoked in silence, only stepping away from his vantage point when the train slowed for a station and stirred the object of his special interest.

'Finmere! This is Finmere!' The guard walked along the corridor, slid the compartment doors open and thrust his head into each as he went along. Bleary and confused heads lifted up to look back at him or jumped up, startled into action. Feet shuffled, doors opened and then clunked shut and the whistle blew, carried forwards towards the locomotive by the wind that scoured the exposed platform and whipped eddies of fallen snow into the eyes and down the necks of those who descended from the train.

'Let me get this fixed.' Kat put her shopping bags and handbag down on a wooden bench beside the small rectangular station block, re-wrapped her crocheted scarf in thick coils, then turned up the collar of her smart green coat and readjusted her hat tighter upon her head. Whilst she did this, Uncle Piotr cupped his hands and lit cigarettes for himself and Mr Paleta, then seeing that Kat was ready they turned and descended the steps onto the Buckingham to Bicester road, their hands thrust deep into their pockets.

Walking in pairs, with the two men in front, they passed beneath the railway overbridge, soon turning off the main road to make their way down the snowy lane that led to the camp. The wind howled and fresh snow started to fall in scattered flakes. The pitch darkness of the open country made it hard to see their way, although the two girls and Mr Paleta had pocket torches, which they played across the ground. The two men trudged onwards, arms gesticulating as they argued about something, whilst making better time with their heavily booted feet on the snow, and soon were just indistinct shapes, marked only by a wavering torch beam.

'Oh, my handbag! It's at the station. I just don't believe it.' Kat stopped in her tracks and looked at Ewa, her eyes wide with alarm.

'Are you sure?'

'Yes. I put everything down on a bench. How could I be so stupid?' Kat then cursed under her breath in Polish. 'I'll go back, you carry on.'

'Surely a porter will find it and we can just come back tomorrow?' Ewa's words were spoken without much conviction.

'The place looked almost deserted. Anyway, I can't risk it: all our documents are there, all the coupons for our families. Can you imagine if we lost those?'

'Oh Mother Maria! That's true. I'll come with you.'

'No; you catch them up and say that I'll be just a few minutes late. Don't say what an idiot I've been or they'll get angry with me. I'll only be ten minutes.' Kat pulled a face, despite her optimistic words. 'But can you take these bags? Sorry to load you up, but I can go faster without.'

'Kat, I'm not sure. It's better I come with you.' Ewa looked worried, but inside she was also dreading the extra effort involved in walking back again. Her feet were so cold that she was desperate to be home. She accepted the two bags of shopping from her friend with a very worried look on her face, but did not offer any further resistance.

'Go on. Just tell your uncle that my ankle hurts or something and I'm following behind.' And with that, Kat turned and half walked, half stumbled towards the station; after a short interval she turned to flash and wave her torch towards Ewa, and received the faintest gleam by way of return.

Kat made good progress now that she was free of the bags, which had been swinging repeatedly against her shins and had pulled her arms towards the ground. Soon she was trotting up the steps of the entrance hall and, as the platform fell away before her, she could see the handbag sitting in splendid isolation upon the slatted wooden bench. Kat thanked God silently that no harm had been done and admonished herself for her forgetfulness.

Picking up her now snowflake-studded handbag, she stopped for a moment to survey the scene around her. She was in the lee of the rapidly-increasing wind, protected from its full force by the small, rectangular station building with its overhanging canopy, and this blessed relief induced her to stay a moment and watch the now-gathering fall of snow as it was caught in the pale blue gaslights. The island platform was occupied by just three small buildings, each of red brick, but only the largest had the benefit of a canopy, which reached as far as the steps that descended to the road below. A large wooden name-board was planted in the ground close by. The elevated and exposed position of the station showed just what a lonely place it was, with only a few individual house lights studding the coal-black night. An ugly pub, the stationmaster's house, a few isolated farms and the tiny points of light in the far distance that represented her home were all that seemed to exist, as far as she could see.

A distance away across the railway line a low building sat hunched and closed up, surrounded by goods wagons laden with tarpaulins weighted down by snow. Behind her a pale light glowed behind the narrow window of the booking office, but there was no sign of life inside, or indeed anywhere else on the exposed station. Where was everyone? It was a quiet and empty place, but the attractive buildings stopped it from feeling desolate or threatening. Kat knew she must get going immediately, as it was going to be a difficult walk back to camp, but the gathering snowstorm was uninviting and by backing against a doorway she found some welcome shelter.

'It's no night to be out.'

The voice startled her and she took a sharp intake of breath as someone stepped in front of her. The tip of a cigarette glowed. Kat looked at the dark figure, thinking that it might be the stationmaster, but it was not and she quickly mumbled 'Oh, it's you,' being unable to think of any other response, and then turned her face away. She didn't know what she ought to say and instantly felt uncomfortable standing there alone with him. If Ewa had there then it would have been all right, but now she hoped he would just step aside and let her hurry back to the camp. The man, however, appeared reluctant to move and seemed to want to engage her in conversation.

'I wondered whose that was, and if I should hand it in, or should I just leave it there for its owner. Was having a smoke whilst I chewed the idea over. Glad I did now.'

She glanced at her handbag and there was another pause, with just the glow of the cigarette between them. 'The station's empty at this time,' he added, 'just a night porter, and he's fast asleep with a western novel on his nose. Can't have been much of a book, eh? '

Kat's mind was turning over and over. Why was he telling her all this? She wanted to leave but was nervous that he would follow. Was it better to stay upon the station? The lane to the camp was long and dark and Ewa and others would now be far ahead. Should she say she was expecting someone to meet her? Or pretend that she was waiting for a train? Her thoughts were swirling in a disorganised manner like the ever-increasing snowflakes in the night sky.

'The stationmaster is on duty.' Maybe just saying this would make him appear.

'Nope. Think he's clearing snow down by the signal cabin. Saw him head off that way just a while back.'

Kat's heart sank. Why is he telling me this?

'No point to stand here in the cold; there's a blizzard coming. It's warmer in here.'

'No! I mean, thank you, I'm quite all right. My friends wait for me. I have to be going.' She moved to pass the man.

He flicked his cigarette into a red metal bucket hanging on the wall, where it continued to burn and smoke upon the sand and rapidly collecting snow. He moved slightly, not so as to quite block her passage, but enough to cause her to stop. 'And they are a long way down the lane. It's no night to be out there walking alone.'

Kat licked her lips, which were very dry, but said nothing. How did he know they had walked ahead?

'Sorry, I'm being very impolite. You want one of these?' He proffered a pack of cigarettes. 'Go on, take one!'

Kat made no response so he deftly eased the last two out of the pack, which he then crumpled and tossed carelessly to join the cigarette butt already lying on the sand bucket. Kat found herself oddly annoyed by this action. The man cupped his hands and lit a cigarette; just like her uncle had done in almost the same place only half an hour or so before.

'Don't tell me you've never had a smoke.'

She stared at his hand holding the cigarette. It was encased in a brown leather glove that reflected the gaslight. Kat was filled with a fluttering mixture of fear and a nervous temptation that disturbed her. She had no idea what was the correct thing to do. She wanted to be home, but was now scared to just walk alone into the night. Should she turn away and refuse to have anything to do with him? Perhaps it would be better to run and seek help from the sleeping porter. But did he even exist? The station really did look deserted. And she needed the porter's help from what, exactly? The man was polite and courteous, so why be so rude and dismiss him off-hand?

Her mind was spinning with arguments and counter-arguments and so she remained standing, staring at the clean, white tube of tobacco glowing brightly in the wind. Why not? Tata would clout her for even trying one; Mama would be furious, but since both smoked like chimneys anyway, why not try one now?

Slowly she raised her gloved hand, which trembled slightly and took it with a fumbling and awkward manoeuvre. At no point could Kat bring herself to look at his face.

'That's my girl! Now you come along out of the cold: it's warm in here.'

He swung the door open to reveal the ladies' waiting room. As if in a dream, Kat cautiously stepped inside and was relieved to at least escape the now driving blizzard, but noticed that he glanced at his watch and then darted his eyes up and down the platform in a quick movement, before joining her and closing the door.

Chapter Nineteen

'OPEN THE DOOR, RICHARD'

Jack White & Sonny Rose

The telephone call Inspector Vignoles had taken was from the Nottinghamshire Constabulary. It was concerning a man who claimed that he had some important information about the murdered woman. The man had come forward in response to the posters placed around the railway station. The desk sergeant at Nottingham was not able to tell Vignoles very much specific detail, as he was merely passing on the message, but in answer to Vignoles's questions, he did offer a curious observation: 'Well he's a strange one that's for sure. We get all sorts — you'll know yourself what odd apologies for humanity we have to deal with. But even so, he stood out some, an' I only saw 'im, for what, ten minutes or so?'

'In what way do you say he was odd?'

'Well sir, he was so excited to be just waiting around at the station, happy as Larry he was. Well, that's right queer for starters as this place is as dreary as you could hope to avoid. Stinks of disinfectant and the smells it's trying to cover,' the desk sergeant had laughed with a rich, throaty sound, 'And no one's got the time to even give him a moment, but he just couldn't stop talking about how as he'd some important information, very important information that had to be listened to by someone in authority. It quite drove me mad. He just wittered on and on until I begged someone to see him, and get him off me back.'

Vignoles grunted down the phone. He could imagine the scene and it was quite familiar to him, including the Oddball, who loved to loiter around the place. Generally they were harmless, but irritating all the same.

'Ah, but the thing is, inspector, he kept telling me as how he'd been the last person to see that poor woman alive. Now, normally I'd dismiss this as just being a bit excitable, like. But to be honest,' and the desk sergeant at this point lowered his voice on the telephone, as if by doing so, he would protect himself from ridicule, 'I think he might just have done it. Killed her.'

'What? Do you think this was some kind of confession?' Vignoles was not convinced.

'Got it. Hit the nail on the head, sir. Of course, you're the expert and what do I know? But he made me feel a bit strange, uneasy, like. His manner was...' the desk sergeant paused to find the word, '...boastful. Yes that's the word. I hope I've not spoken out of turn. It's just I sometimes think it's good to give across one's impressions. It's another opinion, like.'

'Indeed, sergeant, that was useful. But you said he came in nearly a week ago? Why the inexcusable delay in letting me know? '

'Ah, apologies are in order there, sir. We've been in a bit of pickle up here, what with all the snow and everything. Everybody's been all over the place and working all hours and it's been quite a nightmare. We've been fully occupied with traffic accidents and injuries, and then when the water pipes burst in the gents', well, it really was a complete disaster...'

'Very well, I get the picture.'

'And then there was some, um, uncertainty as to who was leading this case — what with you being railway and all that...' Not the constabulary, but some two-penny outfit who play with trains. Vignoles silently filled in the unspoken slur. '...So somehow this matter did not get passed directly on to you with the alacrity that we would normally have...'

'This is a very serious matter to overlook. And I just hope it does not have dire consequences, particularly if your interpretation proves to be correct.' Vignoles let the admonishment hang in the air a few moments. 'Well, I think you had better give me his details then I can get on and call him in for an interview.'

As he waited for the informant to arrive on his inevitably delayed train, Vignoles chewed over the desk sergeant's comments, keeping his thoughts to himself, choosing not to share them with Sergeant Trinder, who was standing on the other side of the office. It would be beneficial to get Trinder's observations without any prior influence upon his thinking. Vignoles was conscious that he must curb the urge to believe that this man was anything more than someone with information that might lead to the killer. The desk sergeant may indeed have a lot of experience of life in all its curious forms, but it was far from rare for people to act a little oddly once they became close to the law, and acting oddly did not make them guilty of murder. Depressingly, this Mr Beeby was probably just going to be a bit of a fruitcake who liked the sound of his own voice.

'Sir? He's here.' W.P.C. Lansdowne had tapped lightly upon the door and poked her head around the jamb.

'Good. Show him into the interview room. Offer him a cup of tea.'

'Very good, sir.'

'Let's hope this gentleman can point us in the right direction. We could do with a breakthrough.' Sergeant Trinder was leaning against a tall set of shelves placed to one side of Vignoles's office, idly turning over in his hands a small statuette of an elegant female dancer scantily clad in little more than a bronze suggestion of a string of beads, a highly decorated skull cap and an artfully placed, though small, feather. She was frozen in the throes of some jazz-inspired dance.

It was another part of the odd collection of items inexplicably forgotten on the railway. Most of these made their way to join the forest of walking sticks and umbrellas in lost property at Marylebone, but some of the more intriguing items migrated to the inspector's office, although never by his own invitation, to form a acurious museum of unclaimed objects. Trinder carefully turned the beautiful figurine in his hands, but then perhaps something about her youthful figure and joyous, vital dance troubled him, and his jaw clenched. He carefully placed her back on the shelf and, with a dark and determined set to his face, followed Vignoles out of the office.

*   *   *   *

John Beeby stood up and shook hands with an expectant smile upon his face, a nervous chuckle accompanying his helloes. This over, Beeby immediately dropped his smile and cut through the attempted pleasantries by reprimanding Vignoles for taking so long to call him in to make a statement.

'I would have thought after making such a show of wanting the general public to come forward, you would not have left such a considerable delay. Is not time of the essence?' He sniffed. 'You surely cannot afford to risk that this monster will strike again?' Beeby gave a thin smile that was icily cold. His eyes seemed to be challenging Vignoles.

'We contacted you the moment the message reached us. Unfortunately there were delays within the Nottinghamshire Constabulary...'

'Most unfortunate, and I do so hope it won't prove, ah, um, costly.' Another half smile. Vignoles kept his face impassive, but was reminded that this had been his own reaction when the desk sergeant had tried to explain the delay.

He tried to elaborate to Beeby. 'In these difficult days it is unfortunately inevitable that not everything will run as smoothly as we might wish. However, you are here now, and I would like to thank you for coming forward to do your public duty and help us catch the perpetrator of this awful crime. We appreciate the time and trouble you have taken to make the difficult journey.' Vignoles was now pulling the interview back to where he wished it to start from.

Beeby was nodding slowly, with a serious expression on his face, though he seemed to be pacified by the inspector's words. After confirming Beeby's address and work details and other preliminaries, which Beeby was eager to answer with a boldness and an enthusiasm that chimed with the desk sergeant's observations, Vignoles was able to start the questioning.

'So what information do you have for us?'

'I feel sure you would like to speak to the man who travelled upon the very same train that the murdered woman took on that day — that fateful, final day, it would now seem.' He stressed the phrase with some melodrama.

'You are referring to Miss Harding?' Vignoles slid across the table a copy of the poster with a representation of her face. 'The woman in this picture?'

'Mmm. That is most certainly her. Though I must say that...' he made a great show of looking at the poster as though he had never seen it before, '...whilst the artist has done a decent job, she was far more beautiful in real life. Much bonnier. But then you will know that...' Beeby smiled and raised an eyebrow, '...having, to coin a phrase, seen her in the flesh.'

Vignoles was startled by both the words and the relish in Beeby's voice. It was surprising and more than a little distasteful. Was he talking to a witness or interviewing a suspect? He was also reminded of the grotesque image of Vera Harding's eyes gouged out by birds, and wondered at Beeby's words. Was this some kind of sick joke?

'You say that you travelled upon the same train as she?'

'Most certainly.'

'How can you be so sure that you did?'

'Because, inspector, we shared the same compartment. It was a very small compartment, and we were sitting close together. Can you imagine? And I can tell you, you don't forget such a pretty girl when you're so close that you can smell her perfume.' Again Beeby gave a smile and a chuckle, but worse than that, Vignoles was sure that he made the very slightest suggestion of licking his lips. It was just the tiniest of movements, but enough to send a jolt of revulsion through him. Vignoles was also becoming aware of a strong scent of soap permeating the air, blending with the slight memory of disinfectant used on the floor. Vignoles sensed Trinder's body tensing as he leant forward in his chair.

'Where did you board the train?'

'Nottingham Victoria.'

'And why were you taking this train?'

'I had a late call-out in Rugby — a hot water geyser on the blink — and knew that I might manage the four-oh-four ex-Nottingham, though, of course, this proved to be late. Really threw my plans into disarray, which I found most unsettling. It made a mockery of the timetable, everything was just chaotic. So, I made the rather unusual decision of taking a small glass of something in the station refreshment room whilst I waited and reworked my travel itinerary.'

'And then?' Trinder asked the question.

'Well, I pretty nearly messed up the whole thing by not noticing the train had arrived.' Beeby stopped and made an exaggerated shudder at the memory, 'I was really cursing and had to dash across the platform, and I'm not much of a runner as I'm sure you can tell.' Beeby laughed. Vignoles however, was watching Beeby's hands whilst he was talking; they were making slow washing movements as if he were hamming-up Lady Macbeth on stage. The smell of soap was, if anything, growing stronger.

'I had to jump aboard, which quite knocked the wind out of my sails. But then I found I'd landed myself a nice private compartment with that delightful young lady.' Vignoles looked at Beeby with an eyebrow raised, encouragingly, preferring to not speak but to let this odd man continue. 'Well, it was suburban stock. There was no corridor. Inexcusable really, to put such things on a London train, but I wasn't complaining. There was just me and her.'

'You are confirming that it was Miss Harding with you this compartment?' Trinder was careful in his note taking, a slight colour rising around his neck.

'Yes, as far as Rugby, where I got out. So that would make me the last person to see her alive.' Beeby spoke the last words with some drama to his voice.

'The last but one, I think you mean?' Trinder was looking at Beeby with a set expression and narrowed eyes.

'Of course! I meant that I was the last person to see her alive who had nothing to do with her death. Must get the facts straight, eh?' He laughed, but then stopped almost immediately and Vignoles noticed that Beeby swallowed and commenced rubbing one of his palms with the thumb of his other hand. A bead of sweat glistened on his temple, despite the deep chill within the room.

'So you left the train at Rugby, and Miss Harding stayed within the compartment?' Trinder was making notes as he spoke, though his jaw muscles were tensing and his voice was less relaxed.

'I've already said so. I had work to do.'

'And the name of the company you were called out to visit?' Trinder poised his pen above his notebook.

'Harrison's dairy. Look here, why all the questions about this? I'm the witness. Oh, but I suppose this is all part of the way you do things, isn't it?' Beeby paused, and then continued when neither officer answered. 'Yes, well. My company installed the heating and the pumps they use to handle the milk way back in thirty-eight. I can show you the full job spec, if you like. Fine equipment, but you just can't get the parts nowadays...' Vignoles shook his head and waved a hand to urge Beeby on. 'No, perhaps this is unnecessary detail?' Beeby looked mildly crestfallen, then continued. 'The contract has remained with us ever since. I was going to see Mr Harrison, the owner.'

'And he will be able to confirm this?' Trinder was still writing.

'Ah, you see now there's a very slight hitch. He was not actually at the dairy when I arrived. I waited and waited, but the place was all locked up and empty.'

A silence fell in the room, only broken by a sharp whistle from a locomotive.

'You must have been pretty annoyed about that?' Vignoles took a casual puff on his pipe.

'Damn right I was. It was infuriating. It appears that he called my company earlier in the day — as soon as our office opened — but with so much extra work on, what with frozen pipes and the like, I was the only one who offered to do the work. That didn't surprise me of course, as the others, quite frankly, are a bunch of lazy slackers and, between you and me, were not prepared to make the journey.' Beeby shook his head in disapproval. 'But, to get back to the point; I informed him that I couldn't get there until late afternoon and Mr Harrison knew that, and the arrangements were made. I do so dislike someone who cannot keep an appointment.' Beeby stopped fiddling with his hands to rub his brow. 'It seems a strange way to carry on. Why can't people do what they say they will? However, I was able to return the following afternoon and he was at least there then, and the boiler got repaired. It only needed a new... well, you can read these details for yourself, if you wish.' Beeby looked at each man in turn. He spread his clammy hands wide and gave an oddly inane grin. 'I have a log book: it lists all my work jobs, the faults, the repairs made, parts used, time taken and so on. And I record all the trams, buses, trolleys and trains that I take to all my jobs, and these are listed exactly. One must do this in order to claim expenses, and I am meticulous in my attention for detail, unlike some of the others, who frankly make a complete shambles of their records. I feel sure you will want to check the log book.' Beeby was rootling in his canvas bag on the floor as he was speaking, and then brandished a small, cardboard-covered notebook.

'So what did you do that Friday evening? You were standing outside a locked building in Rugby in the snow.' Vignoles was flipping through the notebook, taking in the entries that were written in a tidy and precise hand. The train times, with adjustments for lateness in a separate column were clearly laid out on a page for that Friday, and appeared to confirm Beeby's fruitless journey.

'After waiting half an hour, ringing the bell, and taking a walk around the back yard to have a look, I had no choice but to find a telephone kiosk and make a few calls.'

'To whom?' Vignoles placed the book on the table and leant back in his chair. He waved his pipe slightly, adopting a relaxed pose despite a curious nagging sensation growing in his stomach.

'To this Harrison chap. But...' Beeby made an attempt at a laugh, '...of course I only had the dairy number and realised I was calling an empty building. I felt pretty foolish.'

'Indeed. So then what?' Trinder was looking up from his notebook.

'I called head office. But it was now long after they had closed.'

'So no one took your call?'

'No. Well, they had all gone home. Look, shall we talk about the murdered girl? It's why I'm here.'

A silence fell again.

Vignoles cleared his throat. 'Mr Beeby. It is important for us to be able to confirm the statements that we take from all witnesses. We need everything to connect, to square up as it were. I am sure you can appreciate that?' Beeby nodded slowly. 'As it stands, despite your notebook, which is delightfully clear and helpful, I need you to actually prove to us that you got off that train at Rugby station.' Vignoles took a puff on his pipe.

'Prove? Why do I need to prove anything?' Beeby's eyes flicked from one man to the other. 'Oh! No, you cannot be serious. You think that *I'm* the murderer?' Beeby's eyes grew startlingly wide behind the thick lenses. 'But that's outrageous! A suspect? Here I am, being the good citizen, coming forward to offer my assistance and travelling all this way to Leicester, and now I end up being called a cold-blooded murderer. It's a damned outrage.' Beeby stood up, his chair scraping the floor with a sharp and ugly sound.

'Mr Beeby, I am not accusing you. Do please sit down. It's just that we need to get the facts straight and corroborate the timings, the details. I can see you like detail — and so do we.'

He stood looking down at them, biting his lip and nodding. 'Yes, well, I suppose I can understand that.'

'But, as it stands right now, your story...'

'...Is completely true. Look at my notes...'

'...Which may indeed prove to be so, but at the moment has no supporting evidence. And we need some, so that we can be sure.'

'We could always speak to Mr Harrison,' added Trinder, 'but if what you say is correct, it looks as though he will only be able to confirm that you were there the day after Miss Harding was killed.' Trinder placed his pencil beside his notepad on the table and then loosened two cigarettes from the pack he removed from his breast pocket, tossing one to Beeby in a gesture of conciliation and placing the other in his mouth.

Beeby slowly sat down, mollified, turning the cigarette around in his fingers as if he had not seen one before. 'I see. It's the correct procedure isn't it? I suppose you get lots of people coming in here and having to find alibis.' Beeby appeared to be considering the situation. 'Gosh. It suddenly looks as though I need one. It's rather like something from a film. How very dramatic.'

'Spot on. We just need you to find someone who can vouch for your whereabouts after you left the train at Rugby. However, if you cannot, then perhaps you might not find it quite such an entertaining prospect.' Vignoles gave Beeby a stern look.

'Oh, but it is. Because, inspector, I'm completely innocent.'

'Glad to hear it. Then it should be simple to prove that to us.' Trinder gave a grin through the smoke of his cigarette and reached forward with the match so that Beeby could light his own. 'So, did anyone see you or speak to you whilst you were waiting outside this dairy? Did you meet anyone when you returned to the railway station?'

'Gosh. Well I can't say that I spoke to anyone. And of course it was very dark and cold, so everywhere was deserted.'

'Ah.' Trinder shook the match until it was extinguished, a thin curl of acrid smoke rising for a moment from the blackened stick, and then he returned to his notebook.

Beeby watched Trinder's pen as it moved across the paper. He smoked for a few moments in silence. 'This suddenly feels a bit awkward. I came here to help you, not to get grilled.'

'And we've not forgotten that, Mr Beeby'. Vignoles shifted his weight in the chair, forced a smile and changed the direction of the interview. 'OK, we can come back to this matter. Let me ask you more about Miss Harding. You say you recognised her from this poster?'

'Yes. It was most certainly her.'

'She was travelling alone?'

'Yes.'

'Did anyone see Miss Harding off from Nottingham Victoria?'

'Well I jumped in at the last moment, so I couldn't say.'

Vignoles nodded. The story tied in with the testimony of the young porteress at the station. 'And how did she seem during the journey? Did you speak with her?'

'She read a newspaper much of the way. We only spoke a few words and that was about the snow. Pretty women like her rarely talk to the likes of me. More's the pity.' A sigh.

'So you wanted to talk to her?'

'Of course. Wouldn't you?' Beeby gave a sly grin, but then

his face fell into something deeper, sadder. Trinder put pen and notebook down and folded his arms. The action seemed to suggest that the sergeant was being careful to control his actions. He then spoke slowly and deliberately.

'Were you attracted to Miss Harding?'

'What a question!'

'Well, were you? It's a perfectly reasonable question. Look here, old chap, you've already mentioned a few times how nice she looked.'

Beeby glanced at the poster lying on the table between them and chuckled. He took a long drag upon his cigarette and met Trinder's eyes. 'Well, I wouldn't have said no.' He raised his eyebrows in a suggestive manner. The action was like a jolt of electricity through Trinder, who suddenly unfolded his hands, then with considerable self-control brought them slowly down upon the table, clutching the edge so that his knuckles showed white. Trinder leant forward so that his face was close to Beeby's and was about to say something, but stopped.

Vignoles made a slight restraining gesture with one hand, but never took his eyes off Beeby. 'Mr Beeby. You are aware that this woman was raped before being killed?' Vignoles tried to keep his voice level.

'Indeed, I read that in the paper. Most shocking. You really must catch that animal.'

'We will.' Vignoles paused a moment. 'Did you harbour any ... how shall I put it ... *ideas* towards her?'

Beeby grinned and then answered in mocking tone, 'I can't imagine what you mean.'

'Did you harbour any sexual thoughts towards her?'

'Oh, come off it inspector, what do you think? I mean, you couldn't blame me for that. But don't worry; pretty girls of her kind don't bother with the likes of me. No one bothers with the likes of me.'

'Are you admitting something to us? Is this your way of leading towards a confession?'

Beeby stared at Vignoles, beads of sweat now visibly trickling down his round, shiny face. The scent of soap was intensifying with a cloying and almost sickening smell. His eyes widened, magnified by the thick lenses. 'Haha. Oh, dear me, oh dear, no, inspector.' He continued to laugh, but despite the convincing depth of his guffaws, he never took his eyes from Vignoles. 'You really do think I did it.' He stopped suddenly, and his face became calm. 'I had rather hoped that you would be less slow and stupid than that. You can't really have expected to hit lucky first time? Your man just walks into your police station and confesses everything? Now that would indeed be a lucky strike. Oh dear, no, inspector. I'm not confessing to anything. You need me to help you, not to gift you the prize on a plate like Salome.'

Vignoles stayed silent. The interview was veering off into unexpected directions and he knew that he must stay focussed. He heard the desk sergeant's words in his head again. Beeby was a queer fish indeed, but he must remain objective in his assessment. Despite his workingman's trade, Beeby was demonstrating a wit and intelligence that Vignoles, somewhat ruefully, had to admit he had not expected. Beeby was clever, and Vignoles suspected he was playing some kind of game, but quite to what end he was unsure.

'So, what exactly is it that you want to tell us?'

'Thank goodness you are finally getting to the point! I was beginning to wonder if you had completely forgotten why I was here.' Beeby looked at Trinder who gave a cold stare in return. 'Do take notes, sergeant. You must get my moment in the limelight on record.'

'Don't worry, I shall.'

'I came here because I felt you would want to know about the other man.'

'What other man? I thought you said you were alone with Miss Harding?'

'I was, until we reached Rugby, and then, as I was stepping out of the carriage, a tall chap was waiting to enter the same compartment. Not that I stopped to take a close look at him. Why should I? But I think you will find that he's your man.' Beeby sat back in his chair and gave a satisfied smile and drew on his cigarette as he let the information sink in.

'What did he look like?'

'As I said, I took almost no notice.'

'You said he was tall?'

'Yes. But it depends on what you call "tall", I suppose. Youngish. Short hair. But beyond that...'

'What was he wearing?'

'Much the same as everyone else these days: a dark coat,

dark hat and dark shoes. Like we all do. But no, come to think of it, perhaps it was an army coat and a bit greenish in colour? Oh, but I really can't say for sure. No. It's quite gone clean out of my head.' Beeby grinned. 'You're the detectives. I'm just a poor, lonely plumber who is accused of murder because he fancies an attractive young lady.'

'Was he carrying anything?'

'Possibly a bag or a case, but I can't say for certain. I seem to remember he was carrying something. Maybe a bag of some kind.'

'You are certain that he definitely got into the same compartment as Miss Harding?'

'When the train stopped our compartment door was right bang opposite him. I got out, and the door was wide open. So I presume he did.'

Trinder tapped his pen against the pad lying on the table and looked at Beeby. A locomotive could be heard huffing and hissing into motion in the distance, the station announcer's voice echoing around the train shed. The three men sat silently for what were only a few moments and yet to each, consumed as they were by their own thoughts, it appeared longer. It was Vignoles who broke the stillness.

'That is very interesting, Mr Beeby. We shall get your statement typed up and you can sign it. In the meantime I shall get another cup of tea brought to you. The sergeant and I will see what we can do with the information you have been so kind to give us.'

'Am I free to go?'

'Of course. You are at liberty to do as you wish. Just wait until you can sign the statement, please. But Mr Beeby, I suggest that you give some thought as to how you might prove that you did actually get out at Rugby that evening. And most importantly of all, if you remember anything more about this mysterious man, we would be very grateful. Telephone me directly, if you need.'

Vignoles pushed his card across the table and then he and Trinder stood up. Beeby did the same and they shook hands. 'Thank you for taking the time today. Oh, and one other thing. We shall be contacting you again, so please don't take any unexpected holidays away from the area. Though in this weather, I imagine that is unlikely.' Vignoles gave a slight nod and they left the room, the odd gaze of Beeby following them out.

✢   ✢   ✢   ✢

'I need to do some thinking. Let me buy you a pint.' Vignoles buttoned his overcoat whilst he was speaking and then collected a thick, brown envelope from Mavis Green, who was flapping it around in the air above her typewriter to attract his attention.

'Don't mind if I do, sir. I know I could do with one.'

The two policemen walked along the platform and then cut through the goods' loading bay and out from beneath the elegant archway of carved brick that bore raised letters declaring 'Goods Entrance' and some fancy decoration, now highlighted by thin traces of snow.

It was already dark, though a trace of indigo light was still glowing behind the buildings to their left. The gas lamps were burning fitfully and more light was cast upon the snowy road by a tram that jangled beside them. They sidestepped out of the way of a heavily-laden dray pulled by two sturdy horses, their hooves slipping on the icy cobbles as they exited the station yard. Neither man said much until they had walked the short distance to the Great Central Hotel.

This was a double-fronted building built of brick and stucco, placed at a crossing point of two busy thoroughfares in the lee of the squat viaduct that carried the railway across the city. It was a popular drinking place, but only because of its location, otherwise it was noteworthy only for its unremarkable drabness. It had perhaps never been salubrious, but it served the purpose for a swift pint or two at the close of day and the large back room had even been the location of the necessarily low-key wedding reception for Anna and Charles Vignoles back in 1944.

Seated with a pint each, Vignoles placed his pipe and tobacco on the table and then started the conversation. 'So, what do you make of Mr Beeby?' Vignoles took a sip of ale and sat back, looking at his sergeant as he commenced to fill his pipe.

'Well, I don't much care for him. Correction, I dislike him. But I must be careful to not let that prejudice my thinking.' Vignoles nodded approvingly. 'However, there really is something very suspicious about him, do you not think?'

'He's not the most likeable of fellows, and his attitude seemed to verge on the mocking and was disrespectful to the memory of Miss Harding, but as far as I am aware these are not arrestable offences.'

'You might think I'm getting carried away, but could he not be the killer? Despite his claim to have seen that other man, his story does not ring true.' Trinder took a deep draught of beer and met Vignoles's eyes as he did so.

Vignoles gave the sergeant a long look before replying. 'Oddly, I've had the same feelings. It flies against logic, but I have to give the idea some credence. Realistically, what evidence do we have to support such a notion?'

'One: he admitted he was sexually attracted to her and he enjoyed letting us know that. Quite disgusting, really.' Vignoles nodded in reply. 'Two: he shared the compartment with her and seems to have a weak alibi for getting off the train prior to when and where she was killed. And three: he looked nervous as hell in the interview room. How do you sweat when it's so damned cold?'

'Fair comments. But being unpleasant, attracted to a pretty girl and unable to find witnesses to his movements still doesn't make him a killer. You said he got off the train before Harding was killed? That reminds me that we don't know exactly at what point she died along the line.'

'True. But what are you suggesting?'

'I'm not sure. But what if she was raped and murdered before Rugby station?'

'But she was thrown from the train a good fifteen, twenty minutes later, near Charwelton.'

'I know, I know. But is there a scenario that could see her body dumped where it was, and the killer get out two stations in advance? In other words, could Beeby have done it and still have an alibi? No, this is not helping at all. I am getting drawn into idle speculation.' Vignoles waved his pipe to dismiss the idea as he would a puff of smoke. 'He really could be telling us the truth, you know. After all, he volunteered to come forward to offer us his testimony.'

'It would be pretty darned strange to do that, I agree. But I don't trust him. It felt as if he was trying to confess something to us.'

'I have a curious feeling he's playing some kind of game. But why?'

'Bloody fool. This is a murder case, not some parlour game.' Trinder gulped some ale.

'Until we have a better reason to doubt him, we must play him a straight bat. So, what of the mysterious "other man"?'

'If he's real, then he's the killer.' Trinder shrugged.

'Tallish, youngish, dressed in dark clothes like everybody else. It could describe almost anyone. It's frustratingly vague.'

'But can we believe this joker? It's a pretty poor invention.'

'So what you're saying is that if you were Beeby and going to invent someone as a distraction, an alibi, in effect,' Vignoles was speaking slowly, trying to construct an hypotheses as he spoke aloud, 'might he not fit that rather woolly description? A vaguely plausible construction, but lacking in detail.'

'That's what I think. At first it sounded like a breakthrough, a glimpse of the killer, but thinking about it, what did he actually tell us? Nothing! Beeby was wearing almost the same clothes as he described.' Trinder ended by taking a deep sip of beer.

'So am I, for that matter: I have an ex-military coat, like he suggested. But I see your train of thought. This other man neatly deflects us away from Beeby's weak story of going to an empty dairy. This other man supposedly provides proof of Beeby's getting off the train.' Vignoles puffed at his pipe in thought for a few moments. 'So, the question is, do we believe Beeby and go looking for this tallish everyman, or do we turn the heat up on our good citizen? We're desperately short staffed and I know we cannot realistically do both at the same time. It's a Devil of a choice.'

'We can start by asking around Rugby station. See if someone remembers Beeby getting off or this other fellow getting on. That way we may get a clue to which way we should go.'

'Good thinking. There's this as well.' Vignoles picked up the envelope he had collected as he left the office. He carefully opened it up and peered inside, extracting a short note slipped down beside something wrapped in tissue paper, which he left inside. Unfolding the note, he read for a few moments and then passed it to Trinder. 'Traces of copper and steel filings were found in the fibres of that spotted neckerchief.'

'Don't plumbers work with copper and steel?'

'They do.'

'It's pointing towards Beeby, if we can prove it is his.'

'It is looking that way, but I wish to urge caution. Plenty of workers handle these metals and wear such scarves. We can't assume it's his on these traces alone.' Vignoles paused a moment. 'I shall, however, use it to argue the case for a warrant to give his room a going over. I would like to know some more about this Beeby. And since that means Nottingham, we could try to interview some of Miss Harding's work colleagues on the same trip.'

'And sniff around Rugby station on the way back?'

'It's an ambitious plan, John, and I like it. I'll call a friendly magistrate and hopefully twist his arm to get us the warrant for tomorrow.'

Vignoles drank some beer and leant back against the cushions of the settle, removing his glasses and rubbing the bridge of his nose for a few moments. 'It's good to have a quiet pint. This is the first I've had in weeks. I need this. We've had quite a time of it, all in all.'

'I'll drink to that!' Trinder drained his glass and walked to the bar, soon returning with two more pints.

'And how is the lovely Violet?' Vignoles felt the need to push work aside for a moment. Chewing over a case, as he had been doing almost constantly since that early morning call, did not always help him see things clearly. He needed time off to let things settle and give his mind time to find some order.

'Pretty good, all things considered. She's finding work a bit thin and the weather and the endless queuing gets her down.'

'Yes, Anna complains of the same. There seems no end to the daily grind of trying to find food and fuel.' He was reminded that he had still failed to secure any more coal. 'She's forever counting and calculating points and trying to work out what to do with those other odd bits of the ration book that I don't even understand. At the risk of sounding gloomy, I realise that it's all a bit of a cheerless and colourless existence in Britain right now.'

Trinder was nodding in agreement. 'The tough thing is, I might not have made things much easier for Vi, either.' He explained about the confrontation with the Walentynowiczes at Hinton. 'They were her most recent and reliable source of work. She won't quite admit it, but I'm not sure if she's making much of a living. I suppose there are only so many winter coats people need and can afford. In warmer weather she is a right little Mrs Sew and Sew, altering and fixing and running things up for people, but now all they care about is wrapping up in anything they can find and paying through the nose for coal. And then some of the villagers are being pretty rotten to her, what with her being...' Trinder paused, looking uncertain, '...

you know, unmarried and a mother. Hell, you'd think they'd have more important things to worry about.'

'I'm afraid society can take generations to alter its views, and even then some people remain entrenched in their beliefs. But surely not everyone is treating her badly?'

'No, not everyone. In fact, saying that, there are quite a few who stick up for her. Everyone at the station treats her well and a couple of the local farmers seem good sorts.'

'The duck?'

'Yes, the Christmas duck. And of course there are the Earnshaws at the bakery. But it only takes one or two to make things unpleasant. Pointed comments over a shop counter and whispers behind her back in a queue. You can imagine the sort of thing.'

Vignoles nodded. 'Do you mind me asking what future you see for the two of you?'

Trinder slowly drank some beer then carefully placed his glass on the table. He gazed across the room, apparently taking in the faded and stained seats, the odd assortment of horse brasses, the cheap hunting prints in thin frames illuminated by pairs of little lamps on the walls with pink conical shades set at odd angles. Finally, after appraising the decorative order of the Great Central Hotel, he answered.

'I've been doing a lot of thinking recently. Violet needs some stability and she deserves more support than she gets from me at present. I'm hardly ever there. Work demands are so intense, as you know.'

'I regret that.'

'No, sir, it's my job and my duty.' Trinder paused. 'I rather think she'd like to get married. Actually, I know she would like that very much. Of course a church wedding is out of the question,' Trinder sounded sad, 'but with me in Leicester and she there? It just does not seem to add up. My being around her is not helping silence the tongues that are wagging around Woodford, either. It feels like a circle I cannot make square with things as they are.' He fell silent, looking deep into his beer glass.

'John, what are you saying? Violet is one in a million. Look here, old chap, I know we're working all hours right now, but things will lighten up. Don't go making rash decisions that you will seriously regret...'

Trinder looked up and grinned at Vignoles, a glint in his eye. 'Well I know I can count on your blessing then.' He reached into his coat pocket and extracted a folded piece of newsprint. 'Don't worry, I'm not walking out on her. Heaven forbid.'

'Thank God for that. I was quite prepared to knock some sense into you. Really I was.' Vignoles looked relieved and puffed at his pipe, though now with a broad smile. 'Well, go on, what are you going to show me?'

'They're thinking of erecting some of those new prefab houses. Have you seen the designs?' Trinder passed the article over to Vignoles, who unfolded the paper and looked at the artist's line drawing. 'Twenty at first, and more to follow when materials get easier to come by. Now I know some people don't approve of them and they've been compared to animal houses; but inside they are really quite acceptable.'

Vignoles thought that they did indeed have something of the hen house about them, but this was perhaps more because they always came in regimented rows, and those he had seen from the train were so very new; they had no time for gardens and trees to develop between to soften the effect.

'I was thinking to put our names down for one. It's the only chance we'll have to get a house. You know what it's like around here? Everything's bombed out or overcrowded to the rafters. But whilst I admit these are no picture book, they are modern and have electricity and inside toilets, a bath and a geyser for hot water. Can you imagine? Far better than the rooms in that tumbledown shop she rents. And besides, that would never do as my work is based here.'

'Haha, John, I never thought I'd hear my hard-boiled sergeant, who likes to spend his money on beer and collecting records, talking about modern bathrooms.' Vignoles laughed in a kindly way. 'But, don't you have to be — ah hum, if I may broach the subject — married, to apply for one of these? I thought the corporation was quite strict on the matter.' Vignoles raised an eyebrow.

'That can be arranged.' Both men paused a beat. 'If Violet agrees, that is...'

'You've not asked her yet?'

'Oh, no! And I've not quite got around to mentioning the idea of the prefab either.' Trinder looked embarrassed, colour rising.

He took an urgent sip of beer. 'I mean, she might be one of those who think they look like pigsties.'

'What are you waiting for, John? I've got no idea about her opinion on prefabs, but she's never going to say no to marrying you. I'll eat my hat if she does.'

Chapter Twenty

'SMOKE! SMOKE!'
Paul Adam & his Mayfair Music

The following day Inspector Vignoles and Sergeant Trinder were in Nottingham, taking a look at Mr Beeby's rented room. His landlady, Mrs Tipping, had been torn between outrage and intense curiosity when they first knocked at her door. At first she appeared to gallantly protect the honour of one of her lodgers by blocking the doorway and speaking with a stern coldness that even out-performed the weather. However, once this formidable woman had seen their warrant cards and glanced — clearly without much comprehension — at the search warrant, like a true quisling she changed her tune in an instant, adopting a positively enthusiastic fervour in her damnation of Mr Beeby. Law and Order were going to be upheld by Mrs Tipping at all costs. A part of Vignoles secretly hoped that Beeby would be proved guilty, as he was unlikely to get anything but intense scorn from his landlady from this day onwards even if he were innocent.

'I knew it. I just knew it right from the start. I suspected he was up to no good. How I ever let him stay under my roof, I just don't know. I offer food and shelter to him, and all the time he's waiting to throw it right back in my face. Really, it's quite distressing. And the disgrace! What will the neighbours think?' Her eyes flashed with something more akin to interest than outrage.

'Mrs Tipping, if you could show us to his room, please?' Vignoles replaced his hat after making his introductions and then cast a reproving glance at Trinder, who was half-smiling behind the landlady's back.

'Of course, inspector, I shall get the spare key. Thank goodness I took the precaution of cutting one. I have them for all my guest rooms. Not that I pry, I'll have you know.' She shot a hard look at Vignoles and an even harder one at the sergeant's boots, which were slowly dripping melting snow, despite his best efforts with the sisal doormat that proclaimed 'welcome' in red letters upon its surface.

'Wait here, please.' She hurried off into a back room.

They duly waited a few moments in the hall, taking in the intermingled smells of laundry, violet-scented furniture polish and damp. The hall was bitterly cold, feeling almost worse than outside. A grandfather clock measured the time with a sullen and depressing clunk. Trinder stared at a small, wooden frame that was little more than an assemblage of sticks holding a rectangle of cream cloth embroidered with the statement that 'Cleanliness is next to Godliness'.

'So what has he done? I just knew that he was a suspicious type.' The landlady was back, her eyes eagerly scanning Vignoles's face for some clue.

'We are not at liberty to say, Mrs Tipping. This is merely a fact-finding visit. I would thank you for not challenging Mr Beeby about this, nor broadcasting that we have been here to all and sundry.'

'My lips are sealed! It's quite a disgrace to have to the police raid my establishment. I shall never live this down if the neighbours were to know.'

'This is not a police raid. Now, please — his room?' Vignoles gave a cool smile and as he followed Mrs Tipping up the heavily-carpeted stairs, he wondered how long it would take her to inform the whole street after they were gone. His money was on about ten minutes, depending on how many neighbours were back from queuing at the shops.

'We can manage now,' Vignoles held his hand out for the key to the bedroom. Reluctantly Mrs Tipping passed it over.

'Would it not be more — appropriate — if I was to be present? What with him being my lodger? I have responsibility for all that takes place under my roof.'

'No. It would not. The warrant only allows access for the sergeant and myself.'

Mrs Tipping hesitated, and then with great reluctance, turned and slowly walked back towards the stairs. She had a flash of inspiration. 'I shall make a pot of tea. Can I bring you a cup?'

'Thank you, but no, Mrs Tipping. Now, if you will please excuse us?'

Vignoles inserted the key and opened the door.

The first impression was of an overwhelming scent of coal tar soap, perhaps even oppressively so, but certainly preferable to the odorous combinations within the rest of the house. The room was quite large, though dominated by a massive, dark-oak wardrobe with an oval mirror inset into one of its doors. There was a matching dressing table of similar bulky proportions, and a single bed that appeared to sag in the middle. A small vanity sink was set against the wall beside the dressing table. A sash window encrusted with delicate white designs of ice like fronds of bracken overlooked a tiny, snow-filled yard with an outhouse and toilet, all surrounded by a brick wall.

Vignoles could see that beyond the backyard there was steep drop onto a series of railway sidings where a row of box vans was being propelled by a small shunting engine. At the far side of the railway there was an ugly backdrop of factories and tall chimneys in grimy brick and grubby concrete. It was a mess of saw-toothed rooflines and louvered ventilation stacks issuing steam. There were pipes and valves on elevated supports linking one building to another and spanning a series of sharply curving railway sidings occupied by oily tank wagons. The snow that coated every surface was a welcome relief to the unrelenting ugliness of this backside of British industry.

Turning away to look at the room, Vignoles saw Trinder close the door firmly and nod to indicate that he believed Mrs Tipping was lurking outside. They would keep their voices down, for she was liable to be more effective than a front-page headline in the *Daily Herald*.

There were four bookshelves along one wall and Beeby had lined these with neatly-ordered editions of timetables covering the railways and the local motor omnibus and tram companies. Vignoles could quickly see that Beeby appeared to have examples for all of the major companies in the Nottinghamshire, Leicestershire and Northamptonshire counties dating back many years. Did he harbour a secret desire to become a timetable compiler? And did he read anything else? There were no novels or other books or magazines immediately visible within the room.

Vignoles scanned the shelves and selected a slim booklet. As he examined it, he was surprised to feel a slight pang of nostalgia. It was a timetable for the Great Central Railway, dated January 1923. He knew that this had been last year of its existence before the G.C.R. had become part of the huge London & North Eastern Railway Company: the same railway line that he now policed. This pristine timetable rather unexpectedly transported Vignoles back to a very different time — long before the war — when the railway was dressed in a far more genteel and even flamboyant garb than the drab, grubby and clapped look it sported now. That had been an era of beautifully elegant locomotives painted in a rich green and deep reddish-brown, with copper and brass reflecting like mirrors in a sun that appeared to always shine on this most relaxed and elegant of lines. Each express engine was driven by a gentleman dressed in a smart suit and a perfectly white shirt, a company tie and a neat cap with the letters G.C.R. in yet more gleaming brass. These be-whiskered men would wink and lift their caps to a certain young schoolboy making his regular childhood train journey to boarding school. Sometimes they would deign to speak a few words to him before turning away to give yet another polish to the many copper and brass pipes, levers and wheels in the cab of their splendid locomotive. Most of these engines had survived until the present, perhaps one would even pass along the railway lines behind Beeby's rented room, but they were now more often than not coated in austere black, exhausted by the war and driven by crews often feeling the same way.

Vignoles closed the timetable and replaced it, shaking off the memories and pulling himself back into the reality of the task in hand. He selected a number of timetables and flicked through them, looking for any annotations and to see if there was anything slipped between the immaculate pages. Nothing. Beeby was not a man taken to writing in margins.

He started replacing them in the careful date order that Beeby used, but soon decided against it and simply piled them randomly upon the shelves as he hastily flipped the pages and inverted the books to see if anything dropped out. It might do no harm to unsettle and annoy the smug and obsessive Beeby.

Trinder was poking around in the wardrobe and opening two suitcases stacked on top. His expression suggested that there was nothing of interest. The room was Spartan and soulless, apparently devoid of personal effects. Was there anything to give them an insight into this man? Vignoles looked at the small pictures on the walls, each one a poor colour print extracted from a book or magazine, mainly of Constable landscapes and almost certainly the choice of Mrs Tipping.

Trinder's interest was now taken with a stack of about ten bars of Wright's Coal Tar soap, still in their wrappers, and the one that lay opened and used at the side of the washbasin. Vignoles noted some more wrapped bars of various other brands of soap.

'He likes to keep clean.'

'Excessively so, I remember he smelt strongly of soap. How long to collect the coupons for all that lot?' Trinder was shaking his head. 'Cleanliness is next to Godliness.'

Vignoles grunted, recalling the embroidered panel downstairs. 'When we talked to him, I was struck by the way he seemed to mime washing his hands.' Vignoles was inspecting the items laid out on the narrow glass shelf above the basin: There was a toothbrush, a Jif shaving stick and razor with a few spare blades, a jar of Brylcreem and one of Snowfire Hand Jelly and a cheap black plastic comb. Nothing unusual, and yet Vignoles looked thoughtful.

'What are you thinking?'

'It's not logical, but I keep hearing the line "All the perfumes of Arabia will not sweeten this little hand".'

'That's more Shakespeare, isn't it?'

'Yes. Lady Macbeth.'

'Hadn't she just killed someone?'

'Correct, and found that she could not wash away the stain of blood upon her hands, no matter how much she tried.'

He shook his head slowly and turned towards the dressing table and opened one of the small top drawers. Vignoles immediately attracted Trinder's attention.

'Ah. Now that *is* interesting.'

'I think so, too.'

They both looked down at an odd collection of items that, whilst fairly unremarkable in their own right, jumped out at both detectives within the context of the coldly impersonal room. There was a ladies' aluminium comb with a long, thin handle to one side; a silver compact; a tube of Outdoor Girl lipstick; a small glass jar of red nail varnish. A packet of Dubarry face powder was leaking slightly onto the paper lining of the drawer.

'Is he some kind of pervert? You know? Dressing up... and... all that.' Trinder looked outraged at the unnamed vices he hinted at. Vignoles just shrugged and pulled a face.

There were two documents in the drawer, a ration card issued to a Miss A. Haverthwaite and a driving licence belonging to a Miss L. Smith. Both men exchanged knowing glances. Vignoles picked up the comb and held it up to the light and they could both see a long blonde hair trapped in the tines.

'Does he use this stuff to impersonate a woman? I think maybe not, as that is probably a woman's hair. But there is something very twisted about all this.'

He pulled the drawer further out and in so doing revealed more. A handkerchief and a small metal badge made of a silver metal bearing the letters 'W.V.S. Civil Defence' in red enamel beneath a crown. Trinder examined the handkerchief. It was freshly laundered and neatly pressed. As he unfolded it he showed one corner to Vignoles. They both looked with grim fascination, but perhaps not in surprise, at the neatly embroidered letters, V.H.

A long and shrill warning whistle sounded outside the window from a passing steam engine. Thick balls of smoke and steam rose from the cutting below as it passed the house.

'Got the bastard. We were right.'

'Bag all this stuff up. I'm going to see if I can use Mrs Tipping's telephone and arrange for the Notts civvies to have Mr Beeby arrested immediately.'

※　※　※　※

With the call for the arrest of Beeby duly placed and the L.N.E.R. police watching the major stations, Vignoles was sure that it would only be a short time before he was in custody. They would then have him brought to Leicester for questioning. The plan was now to make a stop-off at Rugby on the way back to hopefully find information that would further dismantle Beeby's now flimsy alibi.

Vignoles was aware that Mrs Tipping had overheard his telephone call, and whilst this was annoying it was unavoidable as time was of the essence. Beeby had to be taken off the streets as quickly as possible. Trinder joined him in the hallway, a brown paper bag in one hand containing the evidence they had collected from Beeby's room. Mrs Tipping hovered around, visibly gripped by curiosity, her gaze repeatedly falling upon the evidence bag and she was clearly fighting down the urge to ask to see inside. However her curiosity was partially slaked when Vignoles started to question her about Beeby.

'Does Mr Beeby have visitors?'

'Goodness me, no. I discourage visitors at all times.' Her lips formed a thin line.

'So, no lady friends in his room?'

'Absolutely not. It is a strictly enforced house rule. I would never stand for such behaviour. This is a very respectable establishment, inspector.' Vignoles nodded his head slightly. 'Are you suggesting that he... that he has done so without my knowing?'

Vignoles didn't answer her question, 'Does he receive many letters, phone calls?'

'Rarely. His superior at work has on occasion called him, though quite why he needs to bother us here, I can never understand, but there you go. His infrequent letters all seem to be of the official kind.'

Vignoles was sure that Mrs Tipping was very reliable on this matter. 'So nothing that might suggest a lady-friend?'

'No.' Her tight-lipped face confirmed that it would be a brave woman who risked Mrs Tipping's disapproval.

'Does he keep regular hours?'

'No. He is in and out at all times. I appreciate that he appears to work long hours, but still, one never quite knows when he will be here.'

'You said, "appears to work" — why did you say that?'

'Well, inspector, it is quite obvious that he is up to no good and so I can only presume that he has not been "working" the whole time he is out.' She formed a tight-lipped face.

Vignoles nodded assent. 'And when he is at home, how is he?'

'Quiet. I never really see him nor hear him. He stays in his room. We only see him at meal times.' Mrs Tipping sniffed. 'I like my lodgers to be quiet, but perhaps he was too much so.'

'Did he get on well with the other residents.'

'Never said a word. I don't think they liked him very much. Exchanged greetings and that was about it.'

'Was he here on the evening of Friday the nineteenth of January?'

'I can't be expected to remember every movement of my guests, inspector. I am not their keeper.' Vignoles thought that she was underselling her observational powers. 'However... now that I come to think about it, I recall that he did not dine with us that Friday evening and I do remember that later that evening he was acting most oddly. He looked quite in a daydream, perhaps even ill. I suggested that he had been drinking. Why? Is that when he — *did* — whatever it is?'

Well done, I knew you had it you, thought Vignoles. He smiled, 'At what time was he home?'

'I think it was gone nine-thirty, perhaps later.'

Vignoles was already mentally calculating how this might fit in with the murder. He had a nagging feeling that Beeby was home too early to have killed Miss Harding, but also later than his alibi had suggested. He already sensed that this puzzle needed more time to fully resolve.

'That is very helpful. Thank you. If we need anything more then we shall be in touch.' He tipped his hat to her and moved towards the front door, eager to hurry to the station and onwards to Rugby.

✣   ✣   ✣   ✣

After a bus ride back to Nottingham Victoria, during which both men had chewed over the morning's revelations, they were feeling re-energised by the investigation. This was the breakthrough they needed and both felt certain that with just a few more hours of work unpicking Beeby's alibi they could secure a conviction. The evidence alone was compelling. It was a heady feeling. Their mutual tiredness was forgotten and the lack of food since early that morning was nothing but a nagging irritation now that the adrenaline had kicked in. So, as their bus pulled to a squealing halt in front of the massive smog-blackened tower of the imposing station building, Vignoles stepped down into the crunching snow and strode purposefully inside, eager to make a number of telephone calls before they caught their train.

Trinder was despatched to find some tea and get his hands on anything edible, whilst Vignoles surprised the duty sergeant as he banged the door open and hurried inside the railway police office. The sergeant was seated upon a tall stool behind the desk, a candle burning to one side, as evidently the power was off and the emergency generators on the blink. He was wearing a knitted black balaclava beneath his cap, a heavy overcoat buttoned up to his neck and fingerless gloves. He still looked cold.

Vignoles waved away his salute and hurried greeting, leant on the reception counter and, pulling the telephone towards him, commenced dialling. He soon established that Beeby was under arrest, having been traced to a factory only a few miles from the centre of Nottingham. He would soon be in custody at the central police station. Vignoles fought down the urge to cross the city and confront Beeby immediately: he knew that would be a mistake. He must first organise the evidence and look for any discrepancies; it would be awful to allow the case to fall on a technicality or some gaff induced by undue haste.

He replaced the receiver and fired up his pipe, feeling a little more satisfied now that things were on the move. With the pipe burning nicely and clenched between his teeth, he dialled his office to see if there was anything urgent awaiting his attention. As Mrs Green answered, he knew instantly that what he really wanted from the call was to be told that there was nothing pressing for his time, and so it was with a steadily-deepening feeling of gloom that he listened to her worrying message. There was a report of a missing person, a young woman, last seen at Finmere station.

Vignoles's heart sank. He simply had to give this his immediate attention, though it was, as the annoying little voice in his head said, a damned inconvenient time for her to go missing. Just as he was reminding himself that this was a shameful attitude, Trinder arrived with two steaming mugs in one hand and a china plate holding four sandwiches and what looked like two thin slices of some kind of fruit pie. Vignoles eyed these and raised an approving eyebrow, then indicated for Trinder to listen in to his conversation, repeating certain phrases aloud for the sergeant's benefit.

'So she vanished from Finmere station. Last seen at about 10.45 p.m.' Vignoles started to make a few notes. 'Who reported her missing? I see... have they searched the area? It was a bit haphazard. Just asked around and no one has seen her...I see. Just a local bobby?' Vignoles took a puff on his pipe, whilst Trinder took over the note taking. Vignoles nodded and then used his pipe to punctuate his speech. 'This is what I need you to do: Sergeant Trinder and I will travel there directly... yes, to Finmere. Nottingham Vic at the present moment. We'll be there, at...let me see... four o'clock or thereabouts. Get the family, friends, and whoever else was with her that night to rendezvous at the station. Yes, at about four. Depending on the snow and the timetable. I think they are still running... Let's hope so. We'll take statements and see what we can make of it. And what of Benson and Lansdowne? A steak house? Oh, I see, a stake-out. As in a gangster film, yes, the line is bad. Well let's just hope they get them this time.' He reached for a cup of tea and snatched a quick sip. 'Anything else? Badger? Ah. I see.' Trinder could hear Mrs Green's voice down the line, and though he could not decipher what she was saying her tone and Vignoles's expression said everything. 'Did he? Well, then he'll have to wait a while longer... Because I've arrested a man for the Harding case and I need to check his alibi, keep an eye on Benson and those dim-witted uniforms she's lumbered with and now I need to sort out a missing person's case! I just don't have the time. Yes, do that! Thank you.' Vignoles replaced the receiver, looked up at the ceiling, took a deep breath and held the air inside for a few moments before exhaling in a slow release. He looked at this pipe, found some kind of consolation within its burning bowl and made two small clouds of smoke in the air.

'In case your deductive skills were not up to speed, that is what one could call a change of plan, though right now it's a bloody annoyance. Blast it! What more can we have thrown at us?' He shook his head slowly, though it was already with resignation and Vignoles's brow was furrowing as he digested and processed the new information.

'So, straight through Rugby and onto Finmere?' Trinder swigged some tea, and wondered if now was an appropriate moment to start on the sandwiches.

'We must. She went missing on Tuesday, but apart from a local bobby taking a statement it seems little else has been done. There's been a haphazard search attempt by her family and friends, apparently. She's probably a runaway. Just vanished clean off the station platform with a handbag full of ration books, I.D. cards and some cash. We'll pin up some posters and appeal for her to return and see what happens.'

Vignoles then looked at the plate on the counter. 'We'd better eat those, don't you think? It's going to be an even longer day now.' He reached for a sandwich, and then stopped. 'But you know what is strange? Perhaps even a bit unsettling...' Trinder, mouth now filled, just looked at the inspector. 'She belongs to one of the Polish families we met at the D.P. Camp. The one called Kat. Remember her?'

Trinder made a grunting sound and his eyes widened, he stopped eating for a moment before munching on, but more slowly now. They both fell quiet, contemplating this fact. Vignoles looked disconsolately at his pipe, which had suddenly gone out. Drinking down the now already cooled tea in a few rapid gulps, he looked at the desk sergeant. 'Any chance of another?'

Chapter Twenty-One

'IT'S FOOLISH BUT IT'S FUN'
Terri Devon, The organ, The Dance Band & Me

As young engine cleaners went, Simon and Eddie seemed to approach life in a different way from their fellow workers. Not that their work was any less hard or dirty or poorly paid than anyone else's at the Woodford engine shed, and their daily tasks put them through the same extremes of cold and heat — made all the more so by the wintry weather — as any of the other men and women working there. At the end of each day their muscles were aching and there were cinders lodged in their hair, and their fingernails and the pores of their skin were etched black ready to be scrubbed each evening with icy Swarfega or stinking paraffin and scalding water that induced chilblains, whilst their clothes always reeked of the sharply sour taste of locomotive oil; a smell that would lodge in the back of their throats and never be washed away, no matter how much tea they drank.

It was a tough and unforgiving world; many saw it for what it was and stayed well away. The railway had been robbed of many men by the war, despite its being a reserved occupation and, whilst returning servicemen were refreshing the more senior grades, the junior positions were hardly proving an attraction. Perhaps when a young man had served along the coast of the Adriatic or camped out in a succession of sunny hill towns in Italy, he saw things a bit differently and discovered that there just might be more to this life than four a.m. starts in a freezing locomotive shed. Their horizons had been forcibly broadened; they had felt the burning sun on their backs, enjoyed the scent of the pines on a warm evening breeze and picked wild asparagus from the roadsides beside their trucks and tanks. And so many of their pals had not returned. So these survivors, demobbed and back home, found Britain a drear and depressing place, and it was hard to fit back into the reality of oiling a grimy engine in a Northamptonshire loco shed.

But to Eddie and Simon, who had grown up surrounded by the never-ending sights, sounds, smells and carefully-ordered pace of the railway, it offered all the romance they could imagine. There was the rugged beauty of walking between the tall aisles of stabled locos as they quietly simmered amidst wreathes of steam in the hazy morning sunlight and the intense excitement that came with riding an engine at speed in a heavy rainstorm. They knew how to enjoy the rhythmic beat of the pistons and the wild rocking of the engine as they belted along with a rattling freight in tow, or the awesome wonder of the incandescent heat of the fire that contrasted so harshly with the bitter sting of the wind on their faces as they leant out of the cab; a seesaw of temperatures and harsh conditions that will have ravaged their faces into creases as deep as that of the saltiest of sea dogs by the time they came to hang up their grease-top caps and retire to their rows of beans in a little back garden with a shed.

But Eddie and Simon shared with the demobbed something of the need to look beyond the four-foot way of the railway for other adventures. They were bitterly disappointed that the war had passed as uneventfully as it could when spent only in a small town nestling in the gentle hills of rural middle-England. Not for them the bombing raids of the Blitz and the hunt for shrapnel the following morning, or the rush to gaze at downed aircraft in a scorched field. The air raid shelters had rarely been used and had quickly just become damp repositories of junk. Their war had consisted of a few Home Guard patrols and then the initial excitement of the evacuees arriving, bewildered and belligerent, but later the forging of strained friendships and odd clashes of culture. And then the odder tension of the POWs: the enemy, so close at home in their barbed-wire camp, but after just a few months this feared enemy had changed into something rather normal and unassuming — and disappointingly polite — just men who would smile and wave as they worked in the fields and offered no threat at all.

So their vivid imaginations had been developed to compensate and they had found a taste for looking into that which they felt needed investigating, though more often than not it was a spurious matter that they both knew to be false. But the very act of imagining that it was real was enough to fire both up. Their heightened sense of adventure certainly separated them from their fellow cleaners; many of whom were — much to the acute embarrassment of the shedmaster — women who had been invited back just a year after being summarily dismissed (sometimes via the pages of the *L.N.E.R. Magazine*) from their wartime cleaning jobs, a move that had proved both callous and short-sighted.

Unlike the male cleaners, the women could never aspire to fire or drive a steamer — the bosses and the unions were unanimous on that — but they joined the lads in all other aspects of cleaning, oiling, watering and preparing, lighting up and disposing of the engines. They were great to have around and the lads saw them as enjoyably exotic and colourful in what was otherwise an almost colourless world, but the women had interests and concerns that were quite different from theirs, and whilst talk of the latest film at the Savoy was enjoyably engaging, Eddie and Simon still preferred to make their own adventures rather than watch celluloid ones.

The male cleaners were all local, and whilst on the whole were decent enough fellows, they were too unquestioning of the world. Their futures already seemed mapped out in a deliberately solid and uneventful manner. Happy to just read the back pages of the paper and discuss the football and cricket, place an occasional shilling bet on the horses and practise bemoaning their paltry pay. One dreamed of racing some pigeons; another liked to fish; another was saving for a motorbike. But none seemed remotely concerned by, or very much interested in, the coal robberies. Certainly none of them harboured a desire to try and catch these law-breakers.

But that was exactly what interested and motivated Eddie and Simon. Perhaps they could find intrigue amidst this harsh, austere world because they both had inquisitive minds, always looking and wondering and asking questions of each other (and often never finding answers). As eager trainspotters, both habitually carried notebooks that were small enough to tuck into a pocket along, with a short stub of pencil ready to be called into action at anytime. All manner of information could be logged in these little books, from the sighting of a heron beside a river, to a charm of greenfinches rising like a gay cloud of green and gold from the spiky framework of a winter hedgerow or a note to discover more about the men commemorated upon certain locomotive nameplates.

And sometimes they noted the registration plate of a fruit and vegetable wholesaler's delivery vehicle, such as the one that Eddie had inspected at the colliery. The van's number was alongside a note to identify 'Sir Sam Fay' who had a particularly splendid engine named in his honour. The registration number, when taken together with the name and address in the wallet that Eddie had fortuitously found lying in the snow that same night, had led the two of them to surmise that they had the identity of the driver of the van, or at least one of his chums. And as the van had been laden with coal, and a burly policeman had seen fit to nearly wrench Eddie's head off at the same time, it did not take a lot of Holmesian deduction for the pair to realise that they were on to something exciting. And so, with both Eddie and Simon having a rest day, they knew that there could only be one plan of action: to go looking for this driver and his van.

Their plan, however, had not been fully thought through. Having found both the address and the van with disarming ease, they now found themselves not only in a tight spot, but one that was rapidly tightening ever further into a potential disaster, and for this they had only themselves to blame. As the pair sat shivering against the cold metal sides inside the rear of the very same vehicle, they were both harbouring evil thoughts of whether to blame the other for the pickle in which they now found themselves. Which one had decided that the best way to escape almost certain detection was by leaping into the back of the Rosedale's delivery van? It had been a dumb idea. The thinking had been that, hiding at the very back of the rear compartment by crouching down low behind the sacks of coal, they would be safe — although quite how they were going to extricate themselves again was a bridge too far in their reasoning.

In their defence, they'd had only a split second to take decisive action, and there had been no time for discussion. It had been an almost instinctive reaction, possibly voiced by Simon, though he was denying it now. But, whoever was to blame, moments after climbing inside they realised too late that this was the kind of trick that worked only in films but cut no ice in the real world. They had escaped initial detection, but had been rumbled and were now locked inside and being driven away at high speed to Heaven knows where.

Not that they had been detected immediately, and perhaps this had lulled them into a false sense of security. They had heard voices and the tramp of booted feet along the narrow cut leading to the rear of the house and realised that some of the gang were perhaps approaching. That was when the decision to pile into the back of the van had been made — and not a moment too soon. The van had been driven away promptly to some new destination, where three men had got out of the cab. Someone had opened one of the rear doors and hefted out a sack, but had not seen the two lads crouched down at the far end. The man's action had been quick and smooth and he had probably not even looked into the dark. They heard footsteps crunch through snow and a few words were exchanged, but then silence fell.

It was at this point that things started to go wrong.

'What now? Do you think they're making a drop off?' Eddie whispered to Simon.

'Reckon so. Let's have a gander.' Simon clambered clumsily over the sacks and then ventured to poke his head out and take a cautious look around, closely followed by Eddie.

They appeared to be at the rear of a large building that was perhaps a hotel or pub. It was very ugly from the view they had. The rear wall was a forest of downpipes and plumbing festooned with long icicles, whilst a row of small windows with frosted glass gave off an unmistakable stink of urine and cheap disinfectant. Empty beer crates and a couple of broken chairs covered in snow were piled beside a tired and battered door that stood ajar and that, presumably, was where the men had entered.

There was nothing to indicate their whereabouts, nor even the identity of the building, but Eddie and Simon guessed that they were still somewhere on the outskirts of Nottingham. Simon stepped out of the van and stood upright for a few moments, flexing his back, a hand shielding his eyes from the blinding light of the perfectly clear and sunny day, hair shining like burnished copper where it was visible beneath his bobble hat. He squinted and blinked, and was assessing what their next move should be when they both heard angry voices and shouting coming from within the building. A glass broke in a bright tinkle and they heard the sound of feet running towards them. They both ducked back into the van. It was a mad scramble across the tightly-packed sacks of coal into the tiny space they had cleared at the far end and Eddie struggled to close the rear doors from the inside, banging them ineffectually once or twice before he drew them, only imperfectly, closed.

A whistle cut through the air and there were more shouts and some heavy cursing. The front cab doors opened on the other side of the thin bulkhead where the lads crouched and the ignition was impatiently turned, misfiring once or twice until the engine gunned into life. At the same moment a figure was silhouetted at one of the small windows at the rear of the van. With one hand upon the door handle he called over his shoulder to another.

'Oi! There's someone in the back! It's a bloody set up! Get out of here!'

The order was not addressed to Eddie and Simon. The man slammed the door closed and they heard the locking bar move into place. There followed more shouts in different voices, all characterised by alarm or fear and a whistle was repeatedly blown. The over-revved engine was now racing, sending noxious fumes up through holes in the floor of the van, poisoning the already heavily pungent air. The lads coughed and wheezed and were thrown from side to side as it slipped and swerved, the fear and apprehension of the driver being perfectly communicated through his driving and the knocks and bumps being endured by the two captives in the back.

'Bloody hell, Si, we're really in it now.'

'Yes, I had — ouch! — realised that!' Simon was jolted backwards and banged his head on the side.

'Crikey, they nearly lost her then. He's all over the show.' Eddie tried to steady himself as the vehicle careered to one side then swung dramatically the other. 'Remind me, was this your bright idea?'

'Don't look at me. You brought us here.'

'I meant getting us in this death trap. Blinking heck, they'll kill us, driving like this.'

'They certainly will when we stop, that is for sure. I reckon they think we're police. You heard that whistle. And can you see that car behind? It's following us.' Simon was leaning forward over the sacks of coal, trying to see through the rear windows, 'I reckon as they're police on our tail.' They bounced over something rough. 'Aagh, my blinkin' elbow.'

'Yeah? I want a better look.' Eddie craned his neck to observe the car. 'Only one in uniform, so the others must be plain clothes.'

'A real undercover operation.' Simon's excitement was getting the better of his apprehension.

At that moment the coal sacks started to shift along the floor towards them as the van descended a hill. A few hundredweight was slowly advancing towards the bulkhead, squashing their legs and placing immense pressure on their bodies. They both fought to push back the dead weight, struggling to wriggle and crawl out of the cramped and painful corners within which they were in danger of becoming trapped, and eventually eased themselves free, clambered over the sacks and hauled up against the rear doors, peering through the frosted windows.

The two lads could see that the smoking chimneys and grubby sprawl of the city was now just a jagged stain in the horizon, fleetingly glimpsed across pristine fields of white. The road was curving between deep corridors of snow formed into steep, perpendicular-sided walls, as if constructed from new concrete. When the road rose up to the crest of a hill they could see across a wintry landscape bathed in brilliant sunshine, but when they were between these towering snow cliffs their vision was restricted and the light took on a strange, blue quality. The sound of the racing engine was also amplified and this just added to the mounting sense of drama.

The van was barely keeping a grip upon the road surface and they repeatedly felt the heart-stopping sensation of the vehicle sliding sideways towards an almost certain crash. But the driver was skilful, and he expertly recovered control to bring the van back on course, though he clipped the walls and sent small explosions of snow behind them like fireworks, whilst the wheels kicked up clouds of powder-like smoke.

Despite their fears of what might lay in store, Eddie and Simon could feel their adrenaline racing and were almost enjoying the ride. It was exhilarating to watch the road unspooling behind and their fear was tempered by the realisation that they were being followed by the police, though curiously, the man in the front passenger seat appeared to be in his sixties and looked nothing like a policeman, sporting a fine white moustache and wearing a loud bow tie and a green chequered cap.

Adding to the intrigue was the fact that this car was being driven at high speed, and quite expertly, by a woman whose face was not only familiar, but was set into one of grim concentration beneath her police cap. If she could just control the high speed cornering that saw her car often take the bend sideways, then the lads knew that help was at hand when they finally stopped. Between the policewoman and the country gent they could glimpse a man and another woman crowded onto the back seat, their faces a comic gallery of expressions varying between something like determination and teeth-gritting nervousness.

The pursuing car closed in on them, only to fall behind as the road conditions worsened, sometimes disappearing completely from view behind a series of corners as the road twisted and turned. This continued for some time and, having now squeezed themselves into a position with a decent view out of the windows, the two lads turned their attention to forcing open the locking bar of the rear doors. The option of jumping from the van when it slowed, crashed or chose to finally come a halt seemed infinitely preferably to remaining trapped inside and awaiting whatever fate the gang had in mind — after all, the car following might also crash at any moment so this was at least an insurance policy — of sorts.

Eddie and Simon started to work on the metal bar that ran from roof to floor holding the van's doors shut. By easing gloved fingers behind this and pulling hard, they hoped to sufficiently bend the metal so that it would ease out of the retaining holes it slotted into when closed. But frozen fingers combined with their cramped position made this hard work.

'It's not budging at all.'

'Here, let — me — have — another — go!' Simon gritted his teeth and yanked the bar with all his might. It moved a fraction, but not enough. His naturally pale face was starting to glow pink. 'Uff!' And he heaved again. 'It's no use. We need something to lever it.'

Eddie hunted around the tiny area of van floor not occupied by sacks of coal, but apart from some wilted cabbage leaves and a rotten carrot there was little of promise. 'What's that behind you, under that newspaper?'

'Eh?' Simon twisted himself around into an uncomfortable knot and then scrabbled around with one hand, unable to see where he was reaching, but he succeeded in feeling for a yellowing copy of the *Daily Sketch* and then caught hold of the wooden handle of a screwdriver.

'That'll do the trick.'

They wedged the screwdriver under the metal bar, and with one pulling and the other pushing, gave all their energy to bending the metal. They were lucky that it was a hefty screwdriver, for it held out longer than the locking bar, which slowly bent out of shape and then with a sudden explosion of force came free of its securing holes, sending both lads off balance, a movement exaggerated by an even more dramatic series of swings left and right by the van. They could see clouds of white spray almost completely obscuring the now-receding image of the tailing car. The van driver was clearly going all out to get some distance between him and his pursuers and was pushing his driving to the very limit. The view was also changing: the tall corridors of snow had given way to a wider and brighter world, suddenly much flatter and open but still blanketed in snow. There were now wide stands of rushes and reeds lining the road to one side. The tips of wooden fence posts were just visible were they protruded from drifts of snow. The road was now just a thickly compacted bed of ice and offered no purchase for the tyres despite the heavy load, which until now, had probably worked to the drivers' advantage.

'We need to bale out.'

'At this speed? Have you got a screw loose, Eddie?'

'He's going to crash this thing any moment — it's our chance to jump ship. Better still, if he slows for a corner, we can... Whoa! Oh! We're spinning...'

Both lads reached out to steady themselves as they felt the vehicle twirl around, once, twice, maybe thrice, the centrifugal force pushing and pulling them as if on a fairground ride.

'He's lost control.' Eddie leant back onto the coal sacks, placed both his feet against the meeting point between the two van doors and kicked hard. They flew open and an icy wind bearing clouds of dusty snow engulfed them. The sound of the wheels sliding across the road could be heard clearly, and despite the whole move from the start of the spinning until the doors were flung open taking but a few seconds, it seemed that they had time to observe everything that was happening as if in slow motion. They saw the dark silhouettes of trees whirl past, a wide expanse of frozen lake and its stands of yellowing reed trapped in ice, the dipping and rising of mounds of snow and the glimpse of a big engine pulling a passenger train across a distant viaduct with the stream of white cotton wool from its chimney looking bright and cheerful against the brilliant blue of the sky. Everything was a whirl of startlingly fresh colour, magically unreal in its beauty and masking the very real danger of what was happening.

The van straightened up and raced forwards. For a few moments it appeared that the driver had regained control. But it was too late. Eddie and Simon had no forewarning of what was about to happen. There was a hefty thump and a vicious jolt that lifted lads and coal sacks up from the van floor, followed by a curiously stomach-turning sense of flying, and another sickening crash that flung the lads back against the coal sacks as everything slid forwards towards the bulkhead. Again they started to spin, but this time it was smoother and quicker than before; a dizzying whirl around and around, the complex curves and circles made by the wheels unfolding behind them on the surface of the ice. These arabesques slowed as they gently came to a halt. The engine had cut out.

A kind of silence fell. Actually it was more a dramatic reduction of sound, than a silence; a stripping away of the pounding roar of the racing motor and the rumble of tyres upon compacted snow, and what sounds could be heard were small and clear. The tick tick of the cooling engine; the distant chuff of the passing train; a few angry birds cawing in alarm as they circled in a disturbed flight above; an ominous cracking like the snapping of a pan of brittle toffee, and deeper noises, like the gentle creak of a great wooden galleon calmed upon an ocean groaning as it rocked in the water.

The occupants of the now stationary van remained silent, holding their breath as if the very act of breathing might upset the precarious and dangerous equilibrium that held them.

'Crikey, Si. I think we're in the middle of Ruddington bloody Water.'

✻   ✻   ✻   ✻

W.P.C. Benson had little idea that the operation she had planned was going to end in such a dramatic fashion. The idea of a high speed car chase along frozen roads had been the very last thing on her mind, especially as the inspector had specifically asked her to avoid using the police Rover — and she took that order to extend to not using anyone else's vehicle for the same purpose. Oh well, the ability to think quickly and make rapid decisions was an aptitude the inspector claimed to value and often stressed, so she was hoping that he would at least appreciate her ability to react to a developing situation.

Benson had been determined that this time they would get them bang to rights. It had become a matter of principle for her now and she found that she could draw upon a deep well of self-belief in order to see this through, and this despite feeling almost unbelievably tired. When had she last worked just an eight-hour day and then had a decent night's rest? She couldn't even remember. If lack of sleep was not bad enough, she had the continual strain of working with men who were stubbornly set against everything she wanted to do and who seemed to never tire of making stupid remarks about how she looked, counterpointing this with her failure to capture the gang

~ 247 ~

at the colliery stakeout. Why should her hairstyle be thought to have any bearing on her ability to make decisions?

When she was not fighting their waves of ignorance she was faced with a desk filled with outstanding paperwork, most of which seemed destined never to be completed; for no sooner would she sit down to make a start than the office would be called out for emergency snow-clearing: hard, physical work of shovelling and wheel-barrowing; or she was rescuing beasts trapped in snow-bound wagons or herding lost sheep wandering across the line; or, as on two occasions in the last week, tending to people with broken limbs sustained by slipping in the snow.

But, no matter how tired she felt, she really was not going to disappoint the inspector. He had given her a dressing-down over the last operation — and quite rightly so — though she would never have admitted this publicly. She had mishandled the whole affair and it had left them looking like prize chumps, not helped by that idiot P.C. Tunstall grabbing the first likely lad who came within his grasp and seeking to make two and two add up to six. She'd certainly made sure that Tunstall realised his mistake in the days that followed, and this gave her the narrowest of advantages over the uncooperative P.C. The important fact was that the inspector had given her a second chance and had even run with her hypothesis that Ferens, his drinking mates and the landlord of the Black Horse were somehow all linked together in this nice little earner of a business.

It was therefore with a sense of quiet satisfaction that she had approached the same Black Horse pub earlier that Thursday afternoon in the knowledge that this was to be the place where they nabbed the gang in the act of selling illicit coal. Not only would she get Ferens, but also that unfriendly landlord. W.P.C. Lansdowne had suspected the publican from the start, and Benson knew that if she delivered him up as well it was going to be an extra feather in her cap.

To that end, P.C. Tunstall (of course) and W.P.C. Lansdowne had gone undercover — drinking inside the pub, awaiting the close of the lunchtime service whilst acting out the role of would-be black-marketeer and his girlfriend. P.C. Tunstall might not be the brightest button on a railway police uniform, but Benson had to admit that he had the knack of infiltrating himself easily and comfortably into the shady world of the racketeer. She had long since pushed aside any thoughts that his knowledge and convincing role-playing might be based upon an understanding of this grim underbelly of society that went beyond the strictly professional. Whatever Tunstall was up to in his private life, Benson would have to leave that for another time. She needed what abilities he did possess — of which fraternising with crooks was one — to lure in the gang and effect a transaction, and at this he had been spectacularly successful so far. The gang members had apparently remained oblivious to their failed operation the other evening and Tunstall had managed to gain their confidence sufficiently to induce them meet him at what might be considered the centre of their operation.

However, the requirement to have another officer observing the transaction and to be on hand when the raid was made had resulted in Benson's suggestion that W.P.C. Lansdowne accompany Tunstall. The look on poor Lucy's face had been a picture. Whilst professionally thrilled to be tasked with such an important role, Lucy Lansdowne was mortified at the very thought of having to even role-play a personal relationship with that gorilla. Still, she had the last laugh: in order to quell any over-enthusiasm by the surly P.C. her parting shot before they trudged their way into the pub was to stress: 'We're a couple, but one that's just had a dreadful and unquestionably terminal row and is not getting along. That means absolutely no canoodling.' She glared at Tunstall, who just laughed and made as if to give her a squeeze around the waist, but this was expertly sidestepped, accompanied by a hard glare.

Benson and P.C. Wilson waited outside, along with two uniforms from the Nottinghamshire Constabulary. The latter were fresh recruits and had been spared, she suspected, because they were of little practical use for anything other than making tea. They were far too inexperienced to think for themselves, but at least Benson could tell them what to do and they seemed to follow her commands without complaint.

They were all squashed, with great discomfort and ever deepening coldness, into a tiny hut made of fabric stretched on a wire frame erected by the G.P.O. over a telephone relay box. The snow was bringing down telephone cables and damaging connections right across the county, and this handily-placed construction offered just the cover they needed, providing a great view of the front of the pub. Benson just hoped that the surreal sight of first one, then a second, followed by a third and fourth uniformed police officer walking along the street and then apparently vanishing as they drew level with the fabric hut had not been observed.

She crouched and peered through a slight gap in the door flaps and time crawled by. A few lunchtime drinkers came and went; all men in flat caps, long dark overcoats and heavy work boots tramping their way from the ugly factory buildings nearby. A hooter sounded and others followed suit across the city, calling the workers to return, and the pub emptied in a rush. A few late stragglers left the Black Horse in a hurry, risking a docking of their pay. Then nothing. The pub was probably all but empty now, except for Tunstall and Lansdowne.

It was then that two things happened in quick succession. A van came into view, slowed, turned into the large expanse of car park and drove around to the rear of the building. Benson could see that this was the Rosedale's vehicle, which they had been expecting. She felt a twitch of excitement and could hardly believe that it had arrived on cue. It was supposed to be loaded with coal, dropping some off for the landlord so that he could keep his fires burning brightly, and Tunstall was going to barter for the remainder.

Benson had agreed to wait a minute or two before she and the men swooped in and caught them in the act. However, she was momentarily put off by the unexpected arrival of a smart red roadster that was all shining paint and gleaming chrome work, driven by a mature gentleman with a splendid white moustache of generous proportions, a loudly chequered sports coat and tan leather driving gloves. The Riley pulled up outside the pub and the driver kept the engine running whilst he leant across the empty passenger seat, perhaps to try and ascertain if it were still open.

'Who on earth is that?' Benson exclaimed under her breath.

'Dunno, miss. He looks sort of important, if you know what I mean.'

'That's all we need: a posh nob in our blinkin' way. You seen his clothes?' One of the Nottingham lads was peering over their shoulders.

'Hell's bells. We'll just have to ignore him and wing it. Come along.'

Benson then stumbled, somewhat inelegantly, out of the tiny hut, the remainder following in what must have looked like a scene from the Keystone Cops, as more and more police crawled out of the unfeasibly small space. The expression on the face of the well-to-do gent in the Riley was one of profound surprise as he watched the four officers trotting towards the front door with warrant cards on display.

'Well, I'll be blowed. And I've not even had a drink yet.'

The gentleman stepped out of his vehicle and watched the curious procession with a smile playing across his face. 'Well, well, well, something interesting is going on here.'

Benson was now pushing through the entrance door, glimpsing the people within through the stained glass design of a horse that gave her an advance warning of where they were positioned. As the door swung open the faces of those gathered in the room turned towards her. She could see P.C. Tunstall leaning against the bar, a nearly full pint glass beside his arm, and two young men standing near him who were just receiving fresh pints from the landlord. One of them was Ferens. What looked like a bundle of money was lying close by. Another man had just placed a sack of coal on the floor beside the tellingly large and bright fire and was transferring some of the contents into a gaudy brass and copper coalscuttle using a small, decorative scoop. It was an oddly incongruous image. Lansdowne was sitting close to him with a small half-empty glass on a table beside her.

'We're closed...' The landlord reacted first.

'Police!'

The lad scooping the coal threw the implement down and immediately started to run towards the rear of the room. Benson blew her whistle. 'Stop! You're all under arrest.'

P.C. Tunstall turned to the lad in front of him. 'You're nabbed. Under arrest for dealing stolen...'

'Push off!' shouted the man, throwing the pint in Tunstall's face; he then turned and ran.

Things happened quickly. Benson attempted to grab Ferens as he sprinted away, but he succeeded in shrugging her off. Lansdowne confronted the man with the coalscuttle, but he threw this at her feet as he made his exit, and tipped a number of chairs and tables over, hindering the W.P.C.'s ability to give chase. Benson ran after the three younger men, who were racing towards the rear entrance, Tunstall was close behind, his heavy breathing audible, and he was growling like an angry bear in fury at being drenched. Benson blew her whistle again, hoping that they would realise that the game was up. However, the sound of an engine being started and someone shouting was all she received in return, and as she and Tunstall skidded into the bright and blinding white of the rear yard they saw the van manoeuvring away and Ferens clambering into the passenger side with a frightened look upon his face.

'Damn! Damn! Damn!' Benson allowed an uncharacteristic curse.

'The bloody little buggers!' Tunstall was shaking his fist at the van.

'Quick — to the front, I've an idea.' Benson grabbed Tunstall and pushed him forwards. 'Out the front! You two — arrest him for dealing!' She pointed to the landlord, who was trying to block their way back into the pub. Tunstall growled again and landed a solid punch on the man's chin that sent him reeling.

'Take that!' The P.C. smiled grimly as he saw the effect of his well-aimed punch. He looked at the two coppers. 'Well you heard her — arrest him!'

The two young officers at last reacted and approached the landlord, who was rubbing his jaw.

Benson was relieved to see the shiny, red car outside and to hear the engine ticking over. The gentlemanly motorist had been watching proceedings from the front porch, but was now looking at her with an expression that held more than a hint of admiration. His eyes were twinkling and he appeared to have already fully appraised the situation, glancing down the road towards the van, which was now speeding away, and so as soon as Benson's eyes met his he responded.

'Do you require her services? She's pretty fast and can hold her own against that underpowered old van any day.'

'Yes we do. Tunstall, Lansdowne, in the back. I'm driving...' Benson slid into the driving seat.

'You'll never handle these conditions, let me.' P.C. Tunstall was hesitating whilst standing on the road.

'It's an order, just get in.' She looked across at the owner. 'You'd better join us. But we need to commandeer your car. Police business.' Benson indicated the passenger seat.

'Delighted. Have a care, though. She packs some punch so go easy until you get the feel for her. Just been serviced, y'know. Been laid up over the war...' He was thrust back into his seat as Benson let out the clutch and accelerated down the road, following the clear and fresh tyre tracks of the van. 'You might want to double de-clutch; she responds jolly well to that... oh yes, I can see you've handled a car before, my dear.' Benson swung the Riley around a tight corner in a controlled skid and expertly regained control. 'Golly, a chance to give her a real blow out. Marvellous.' The car's owner chuckled and settled down in his seat apparently quite content to see his valuable vehicle being driven around the streets as if in a rally.

Tunstall was still chuntering in the back, but Lansdowne was leaning forwards, looking between the driver and passenger with an expression of exhilaration upon her face. 'Go on Jane, we can catch them. Look, there they are!'

'Got it. I wonder where they're heading.'

'Idiots. Just wait until I lay my hands on them. Just don't go and lose them, that's all.' Tunstall's face in the rear view mirror was a picture of bad humour. 'I'd get them all right, if you'd let me drive.'

'All under control, P.C. Tunstall. You just get ready to jump out and cuff them.' Benson met his eyes in the mirror whilst the car drifted around another bend then weaved between a milk delivery cart and two men pushing bicycles laden with sacks of something bulky.

'I say, you handle a motor car all right. Where d'you learn? War service, I expect?'

Benson just gave a slight grin in response the questions.

'I had heard that quite a few gals got behind the wheel and seemed to suit it. Our dear Princess Elizabeth included.' The moustachioed gent smiled and winked at the W.P.C.

'Yes, sir. We're London and North Eastern railway police — so trains are rather our main business.' The gentleman just raised his eyebrows at this odd revelation. 'But I did fair bit of motoring and had a few training courses in advanced driving.' Benson was again smoothly handling the sports car and they were rapidly gaining ground on the delivery van.

'Looks like we're heading out of town — West Bridgeford way,' observed Lansdowne.

'Where the flippin' heck are they going? They'll never shake us off now, not with this little beauty on their tail'. It was uncertain if the gentleman was referring to his car or to Benson. His eyes twinkled.

'Probably reckon they can lose us down a side road. You'd better stick like glue to 'em.'

'Wilco, P.C. Tunstall. All under control.'

'Look: there's two more in the back — I can see their faces at the window.' Lansdowne was pointing between Benson and the car's owner. 'We've probably got the whole gang on board that van.'

'I don't believe it — it's that stupid lad again.' Tunstall was now straining to identify the two faces pressed to the glass. 'I told you he was involved. Look, it's him as I nabbed up at Clifton!'

'Gosh, I do think you're right. It's that Earnshaw boy all right. How queer. I'd have sworn he was nothing to do with them.'

'Told you. My instincts rarely let me down. And you made me let him go.'

'And that ginger-haired one too. I've seen him before. What was his name? Simon something?' Lansdowne was straining to identify the features of the two faces at the windows of the van.

'Hey, steady on, were all over the shop...' P.C. Tunstall called out as the car lifted its wheels passing over a rise in the road then flew around a series of s bends in slithering sideways skids as a fine spray of snow from the van reduced visibility.

'I'll hang back. They'll not lose us here, whatever you might think. We'll just let them lead us to where they're going. Any ideas where we *are* heading? I'm too busy...' Benson stopped speaking as she fought to control the car, '...as I was saying, I'm too busy driving to read the signs.'

'South. Towards Ruddington, though it's hard to tell, as the land looks like something from a fairly tale.' Lansdowne gazed in wonder at the black trees dressed with white and the ever-deepening corridors of snow down which they were travelling.

It was only a matter of time before something went wrong and, when it did, Benson's decision to drop back a distance was proved to be sound, otherwise they, too, might well have met the same fate as the van. The twisting and treacherous road was virtually, but not completely, devoid of traffic and the first near miss was when the van had to swerve to avoid an ancient steam lorry that was approaching, completely enveloped in a hissing cloud. The tower of steam acted like a warning flag and no doubt sufficiently alerted the van's driver to the hazard, and they sidestepped it with just a few inches to spare. However, they were not to be so lucky the next time.

As the snow dropped away to reveal the huge frozen expanse of Ruddington Water to their left, Benson and her fellow travellers saw the van apply its brakes hard as it sought to miss the dual threat of a horse and cart laden with winter feed and a motorcycle combination with long ladders strapped to its sides, which was in the process of overtaking the cart. The van skidded first one way then the other and waltzed completely around in a number of circles. The driver stopped braking and accelerated whilst attempting to steer the van back on course, but it mounted a smooth lump of compacted snow on the edge of the road, lifted its wheels from the ground and flew straight up and over the bank and onto the lake. As Benson slowly drew the Riley to a halt, her companions watched in mute fascination as the delivery van made its graceful arc in the air and then in disbelief, as somehow the ice held when it landed and proceeded to describe a series of spins and loops like a bizarre ice skater.

Stepping put of the Riley, they all stood with hands shading their eyes and were joined by the telephone engineer, who had dismounted his motorbike and watched as the van quietly span to a halt. The harness of the horse jingled as the driver muttered calming sounds to the startled animal. The crows cawed. The distant train crossing the viaduct looked like a miniature made by Bassett-Lowke and they could see rows of faces pressed to the carriage windows, watching the curious scene below them.

'By heck, that was an impressive sight.' The gentleman readjusted his cap and extracted an intricately-carved pipe from a pocket.

'If nothing else, we can sting them for five pounds each.' W.P.C. Lansdowne nodded in the direction of a small construction formed of three short lengths of wood screwed into a wigwam shape, upon which a framed notice was hung by a length of twine over two of the protruding ends. This assemblage was placed upon the ice a short distance in from where the shoreline probably started. In neat and bold green letters it warned:

DANGER.
Any person going on this ice
is liable to a fine of FIVE POUNDS,
by order of the Town Clerk.

'Shame they didn't see the notice first.' P.C. Tunstall laughed.

'This is no joke. The ice is going to give way and if they go under they're really in a fix.' Benson understood the danger.

'Gosh, yes. We'd never get them out of the water. They

don't have much time.' W.P.C. Lansdowne was now biting her lip in consternation.

'Get out! Get away from the van!' P.C. Tunstall had apparently forgotten his petulance towards the gang and was gesticulating at the three men huddled on the front bench seat, each staring with wide eyes towards the bank. As they watched, two more figures tentatively stepped out of the rear and onto the ice and appeared on either side of the stranded vehicle. They walked slowly, placing each foot with great care. The ice cracked and complained as they did so.

'They need to lie flat. They must spread the load.' It was the telephone engineer speaking. 'My ladders might do the trick — help me off with them. We can reach out further and they'll reduce the weight on the ice.'

'Good thinking.' Tunstall immediately ran as best he could through the deep snow towards the motorcycle combination.

'That's definitely the Earnshaw lad. What the devil's going on?' Lansdowne was furrowing her brow as she observed them.

'Lie down! Lie flat. Spread your weight and get away from the van.' Benson was doing her best to shout across the icy lake, her voice carrying in the still air. The two lads squinted back at her with looks of confusion, but then as they saw her mime the actions of swimming they understood and both carefully dropped down onto their knees in movements that were frustratingly slow. Once lying on their bellies they attempted to push themselves forwards with their hands and feet, though they made little progress on the smooth ice. The men in the van were now also stepping gingerly from the cab. One of them losing his footing and waved his arms wildly until he managed to hold onto the edge of the open door.

Tunstall and the telephone engineer were now sliding the ladders across the lake towards Simon, who was the nearest. The engineer left Tunstall holding one end of the ladder and went back to the sidecar and pulled out a big wooden reel of telephone cable. The well-dressed gentleman went to help, and together they unwound fifty feet or more and slung this towards the unsteady man nearest the van. 'Lie down, hold on and we'll pull you ashore.'

'Move away from the van.' Benson was becoming increasingly concerned that the ice was going to give way at any moment. She could see that in the distance there lay an expanse of shimmering water with a few ducks bobbing about on the sun-dappled surface. The ice was not as extensive as it had first seemed. Anyone drenched by this icy water was going to be fortunate to survive the shock. Meanwhile the ice continued to groan and crack.

Simon was now hauling himself along the ladder but this was proving almost as hard as it was on the smooth ice. He could not get his fingers around the rungs and his feet kept slipping off the rounded wood. He was cursing and complaining to himself and then just stood upright, a few yards from safety and chose to make some hurried running steps to the snowy bank where P.C. Tunstall hauled him up.

'Thanks. That was getting pretty hairy...' Simon turned to watch Eddie as he was hauling himself along upon his belly. He was near a stand of reeds embedded in ice and, by grabbing the yellow stalks, was making adequate progress; though he was showering himself in tiny fragments of ice broken from the reeds that were scattering like shining jewels across the ice sheet and refracting the sunlight. Tunstall moved across and stood ready to offer a hand, which was gratefully accepted by Eddie.

'Get up there, stay where you are and I'll deal with you later,' and he shoved Eddie up the bank.

'It's not what you think...'

'Shut up. We've got all your dumb friends to rescue now.' Tunstall was moving off to help the driver haul in the cable with the unsteady man holding on to the other end.

'No, really, it's not how it looks...' Eddie's words were half-hearted and tailed off.

'Leave it, Eddie. We can explain later.' Simon turned away from his friend and watched the scene unfold. 'The van's going under, for sure.'

'Those two are too close to the van.' Eddie had forgotten his complaints for the present and was transfixed by the unfolding drama.

'Get up and run. We need to throw the cable out again!' Lansdowne was urging the man being hauled in on the cable to make more of an effort. He was now scrabbling around trying to clutch onto the ladder but, like Simon before him, he was finding it hard.

'Just hold on and we'll haul the ladder in.' The telephone engineer dug his heels into the snow and started to pull on the ladder, P.C. Tunstall assisting him. When the man was just a yard or so away from the edge he let go, stood up and lurched forwards in a series of shaky steps to Lansdowne's outstretched hand.

'You're under arrest.' The young man just shivered in response and looked at the W.P.C. with a crestfallen expression.

'Lash one end of the cable to my cart. We can pull the two of 'em at the same time.' It was the carter speaking. Whilst they had been making the first rescues, he had backed the cart down towards the lake's shore.

'Good thinking'. The engineer took a knife from a pocket in his oilskin coat and sliced through the cable close to the drum. 'I'll get a right ticking off for this, though.'

'Police business. We'll square it with the G.P.O.' Benson was nodding in approval, but privately was wondering what the consequences might be and if she really could square it.

With the cable hitched to the wagon, the elderly gentleman tossed the coiled cable with expert ease, so that it dropped in front of the two men still beside the van. He looked at Benson and winked. 'Sailing. Years of practice, don't y'know.'

The two men were attempting to gain a firm purchase upon the smooth telephone cable, which was not easy with hands already aching with cold. The first had wound the cable around his wrists and forearms, whilst the other passed the free end around his body and was fumbling to make a secure knot.

'Hurry up. You've got to get off now.' Tunstall bellowed across the lake. The fumbling man waved to signal he was ready and they both lay down upon the ice.

The carter made a clucking sound and the horse, with a gentle clink of metal and a soft noise of leather, pulled at the wagon, which creaked and then rolled forwards with a slow ease. The cable tautened and both men grimaced as their weight made it bite deep into their flesh. But they started to move, and not a moment too late. There was a snap like a pane of glass breaking, and two sheets of ice lifted on either side of the nose of the van, which dipped straight beneath the dark waters suddenly revealed. It slid effortlessly and peacefully into the lake, making almost no sound as it did so, leaving just a slow boiling and bubbling of trapped air on the surface that continued for some minutes afterwards.

The ice ripped asunder in great slashes and in pale crazy fractures that made the surface white with its patterns. The trailing man let out a cry of anguish as his legs were plunged into the water. The ice sheets were now starting to rock and thin washes of water spilled across the surface, soaking both men.

'Pull! Pull!' Tunstall was bellowing at the carter. Needing no further encouragement, he urged the horse forwards. With a steady and regular walk the horse found its footing through the snow and without appearing to notice the weight it was hauling, and the two men were swiftly dragged across the now-splintering ice and through a growing wave of water.

'Jesus! Aaagh...!' One of men, who Benson identified as Ferens, was screaming loudly with the shock of the cold, whilst the gentleman car owner and Tunstall freed the cable and tried to haul both to their feet. Their faces were already a pale bluish white and both were shivering uncontrollably.

'Cold. I'm so cold. Oh I'm fr-fr-fr-eezing...' Both men cursed repeatedly but, worryingly, they were visibly losing the energy to do even that.

'We need to get them somewhere warm.' Benson looked at the car owner.

'At your command, miss. Put them in the car and I shall be happy to oblige!' He saluted ostentatiously.

'There's a farm just a mile or so up the lane. I was mending their telephone so I know there's someone home,' the G.P.O. man chipped in. 'I'll lead the way on my motorcycle.'

'Righty-o. P.C. Tunstall? Go with them and call the office. Try to get these men dry and warm. We'll rendezvous at the farm as soon as possible and take stock.' Benson barked the orders. 'I don't suppose they'll try anything, but they are under arrest, so no funny business from either.'

'Come on, you.' Tunstall bundled the shivering Ferens into the back seat.

'As for you three...' Benson looked at Simon, Eddie and the third gang member, but then turned to address the carter. 'Maybe we could use your wagon?'

'Aye, reckon so. It's my master's farm you'll be going to, so I don't see how a trip back will make any odds. But first I've got to drop off this feed. The sheep're starving and they can't wait no longer. Sorry miss, but that's how t'is.'

'But how long will that take?' Benson was thinking to argue the point, but then realised that she had imposed enough upon other people that afternoon already. 'Okey-dokey, that is tickety-boo. Thank you.'

They could all hunker down on the bed of hay and make the best of it, and she could use the time to start asking some questions of the three young men in her charge.

Chapter Twenty-Two

'WE'LL MEET AGAIN'
Vera Lynn & Arthur Young on Novachord

A splendid locomotive, with the equally-splendid name of 'Butler-Henderson', pulled their local stopping train into Finmere station as the sinking sun was blinding the group gathered upon the snow-clad platform, awaiting its arrival with urgent anticipation. The sun raked its golden light across the small group of buildings on its elevated position above the rolling, hedge-bound fields. Telegraph poles and trees waist-deep in snow cast impossibly long shadows and helped trace the lines of buried roads, whilst small skeins of smoke floated upwards in the windless afternoon, each burnished by the last of the light and indicating a dwelling place. The overall impression was of one vast and gently-undulating wilderness.

The reception committee looked grim, their faces and tired eyes spoke of debilitating apprehension. These were not just the weary wartime faces that had become commonplace, but were strained by something profound and personal. As they stepped off the train, Vignoles and Trinder were immediately struck by a powerful wall of pain and worry emanating from those gathered beneath the short, overhanging station canopy. The women were all wearing headscarves and clutching handkerchiefs, their eyes were red and filled with a heart-wrenching look of silent pleading that made Vignoles flinch away. The men — of which there were at least twenty assembled — looked sullen and sulky, others angry. Some stared at the platform, hands thrust deep into overcoat pockets; others faced the detectives square on, watching as they advanced along the platform, their expressions a complex mixture of hope and anxiety, contempt and frustration. Many of the men held shovels, garden rakes and canes in gloved hands. If they had not known different, Vignoles and Trinder might have mistaken them for a lynch mob from an Alan Ladd Western film. All appeared to be smoking with short and hurried movements, drawing on their cigarettes with harsh inhalations, and their smoke was caught in the dying rays of the sun, as was their frosty breath, making clouds of golden light that was strangely beautiful.

Major Duffy stepped forward, a brown-leather gloved hand extended in greeting.

'Ah, inspector. It is a relief to see you here. And Sergeant Trinder.' He made a brief salute. 'We are all rather hoping that you might bring some professional expertise to this terrible situation. There is a feeling that we must start a proper search for poor Katarzyna. The camp committee and band have formed a search party...' He indicated the assembled men with their assorted tools.

'Major Duffy.' Vignoles and Trinder both tipped their hats. 'And Mr and Mrs Walentynowicz.' Vignoles extended a hand to the parents, who were standing immediately behind Duffy. They looked as pale and lifeless as a pair of ghosts. Mr Walentynowicz, however, slowly extended a hand and gave the coolest of handshakes. Mrs Walentynowicz just lowered her head forwards in a tiny movement of acknowledgement and then turned to look at her husband, placing upon his arm a hand that was still clutching a balled handkerchief. Two other men, unknown to Vignoles, started to talk at the same time in a confused mixture of English and Polish, one of the men pulling off his cap and wringing it in his hands, the other, his face flushed and florid, perhaps with the effects of drink and the cold, spoke at the same time so that Vignoles could only get a sense of what they were both trying to communicate. The confusion increased as other angry and emotionally-charged voices chimed in from amongst the crowd.

Something said amidst this confusion prompted Mr Walentynowicz out of his ghostlike shell and he turned, the colour now rising in his face, pointed a finger at the two men and hurled a torrent of bitter and scolding words towards them. They responded with increasingly apologetic or defensive voices until finally some of the women joined in, urging calm. Tempers were clearly at breaking point and the strain of the last few days was overspilling into recrimination and guilt, and loud expressions of frustrated emotion.

'Please! We must all try to stay calm. I need to speak only with those who last saw Miss Walentynowicz.' Vignoles held up both his hands to try to urge some order amongst the crowd. He looked around and saw the stationmaster standing close by, easily identifiable by his long black coat and top hat. 'Sir, if I may have the use of one of the waiting rooms?'

'Of course.' He doffed his hat and made a slight bow of his head. 'Edgar Thompson, stationmaster.'

Vignoles just nodded.

'I have taken the opportunity of making the provision of a good fire in the general waiting room to better facilitate your needs.' The stationmaster opened a door. 'Ladies and gentlemen, if you please...'

Vignoles followed the stationmaster a few steps into the nearby room and indicated that he would like him to remain, and then turned to face the crowd gathered at the door. 'I would just like to speak to those who were with Miss Walentynowicz that evening.'

The florid-faced man pushed forward, introduced himself as Tomas Paleta and encouraged the cap-wringing man to come forward. 'This Pan Piotr Grabowicz. We with her on this night. And Ewa, she is — sorry, I not know word...'

'His niece. I am Katy's best friend.' A young woman with eyes sore with crying walked forwards and the crowd respectfully parted to allow her to approach. She extended a hand, 'Ewa Grabowicz. Mr Grabowicz is my uncle.' An ominous silence settled upon those gathered around that was slightly unnerving.

'Come inside. Please close the door.' Vignoles glanced back at Major Duffy and was pleased to see him respond by gently ushering the gathering away from the door. 'It would be useful if you could, one at a time, tell me what happened that night.'

'We say all this before. The policeman, he ask us all. We need search, not talk!'

'I can understand your feelings. But I am from the L.N.E.R. detective department, a different police force. And I need to understand exactly what you think happened, before I can decide the best way to proceed.'

'Oh, you crazy? We know what to do! She had accident and now lying in snow. We must look for her.'

'No, we must answer his questions. It is better we tell him everything.' It was the young woman who spoke. Her voice was quiet but had a surprising assurance and calm to it, in stark contrast to her face, which betrayed an acute distress.

'Then perhaps I may start with you? Remind me again — you are?' Vignoles was mindful that his sergeant struggled with writing Polish names.

'Ewa. Ewa Grabowicz.'

'And you were with her that night?'

'All day. We went shopping together in Woodford, with Uncle Piotr and Mr Paleta.'

Vignoles questioned Ewa and, together with frequent interruptions from the two men, the story of that fateful day unfolded. Sergeant Trinder took notes. There was little about the story that caught Vignoles's scent for trouble and so he focussed upon the decision by Miss Walentynowicz to return alone to Finmere station, asking the three of them to repeat why they made the decisions that they did.

'So can you tell me exactly why you did not go back to the station with Kat?'

Ewa was dabbing her eyes with a handkerchief. 'She said I must go ahead and catch up with my uncle and tell him not to worry. I must tell them Kat was following behind. And I carry the heavy shopping bags so she could go quicker and catch us.' Her uncle shuffled his feet uncomfortably and looked at the floor whilst Ewa was speaking.

'Why did she say that? Why was it so important to her that you said this?'

'She said if they found out she nearly lost all documents, her father would never trust her to go out again. He'd be really angry.' The two men made protestations in Polish that seemed to suggest that this was an exaggeration. Vignoles hushed them with a wave of his hand. 'You believed her?'

'Of course I did. Why not?'

'Was it not a strange thing to do, leaving her on her own?'

'Why strange? What could else we could do?' Her eyes filled with fresh tears and her voice broke.

'I'm sorry. I do not mean to sound unkind. So was Mr Walentynowicz often hard on her? ' The two men made more angry protestations, but Vignoles silenced them. This was no time for niceties.

'No. But... he cared about her and sometimes he gets a bit crazy if he thinks she gets in trouble. It's normal, but this is not the problem....'

'How did Kat seem that day? Was she — different — in any way?'

She gave Vignoles a long look. 'No. She was always full of life and happy, maybe a bit annoying sometimes. We had perfect day... until...' Ewa dabbed her eyes with a handkerchief, her voice again on the verge of breaking.

'She didn't seem nervous, anxious, especially towards the end of the day?'

'No. If I understand you correct, then no.'

'So you do not believe that she was thinking to run away? I realise that this might be a hard thing admit, but we need to know if she confessed any such thing.'

'Run away? No!' The two men made protestations of disbelief in harmony with her words. 'She would never do that.' Ewa flashed an angry look at Vignoles. The two men started to remonstrate with Vignoles.

'Please! I have to ask these questions. We must look at the facts. She disappeared from a lonely country station platform. Apparently she has just vanished. What is the easiest way to do that? To get on a train and leave.'

The room fell silent.

'Miss Walentynowicz had some money, ration books and coupons for a number of families — worth good money on the black market. So it is a possibility that I regret, I must consider'. He left it unsaid, but he also knew that this was likely to be the better option for the girl's long-term safety.

'Never. She would never do this.' Ewa shook her head and folded her arms in stoic defiance. Vignoles was struck by her conviction. The two men also nodded assent and looked angrily at Vignoles.

'Mr Thompson?'

'Inspector?'

'After the 10.30, what further trains stopped here that night?'

'There were two more: one down at 11.03 and one up at 11.57. Then nothing until the milk train at 5.07 and then there was a pick-up goods that collected a hound van for the Grafton, at around 6.10 or thereabouts.'

'The Grafton. Is that a hunt?'

'Indeed it is.'

'Did you see Miss Walentynowicz and her party get out of the 10.30?'

'No, I cannot say that I did. I would, of course, normally greet each arrival and wait to see its safe departure, but as you will know, the snow has been causing havoc and I have been forced to adopt emergency measures to keep the station functioning. And so on that particular evening I was — accompanied by two porters and the goods' clerk — clearing snow and ice that had accumulated along the signal wires and excavating the points to the goods line and burning oiled cloth around the moving parts to free them. We were close to the signal box at the time the 10.30 pulled in. The signalman can confirm this, if you so require. I could see the train at the station, but could not discern passengers in any detail; nor, I confess, was my attention particularly directed towards the same. Our work was of a rather strenuous and backbreaking nature and observing the smaller details of station activity was not my primary concern at that moment, added to which a blizzard came on and we were soon forced to take shelter in the platelayer's hut alongside the cabin.'

Vignoles nodded, silently impressed by the thought of the impeccably turned-out Stationmaster Thompson shovelling snow and burning oily rags. 'So, you would not have seen if Miss Walentynowicz boarded either of the following trains?'

'I regret no. Visibility was much reduced.'

'The booking clerk would have still been at his post, though. I wonder if he saw anything?'

The stationmaster cleared his throat before replying. 'This matter was also raised by the constable who attended initially. The young man in question has been severely reprimanded, of that I can assure you, but to spare you unnecessary details...'

'We would prefer to understand the situation, exactly. Unnecessary or not.' Trinder butted in.

'Ah.' A look of annoyance flickered across the stationmaster's face but he quickly recovered his composure. 'It was a windy night, of course, what with the aforementioned blizzard, and the clerk saw fit to block the ticket office service window with a piece of cardboard to prevent undue ingress of snow. And then he promptly fell asleep. In mitigation, I should point out that he had been on duty since six a.m. and there was little or no ticket-buying traffic at that time.'

'Understandable, perhaps, but unfortunate.' Vignoles waved the issue away. It was of no consequence now. Turning back to Miss Grabowicz, he asked where she was when the blizzard commenced and what happened later in the night when Miss Walentynowicz did not appear.

'I was halfway home. I could see almost nothing, even with torch. It was terrible. When I got to camp, uncle was waiting with hurricane lamp to show me way to the gates. I was worried about Kat. We stood there for over half an hour.'

'And then you did what?'

'I went to fetch Mr Walentynowicz, and they all walked to station. They made me wait at camp.'

'We saw nothing. Too dark, very much snow,' added Mr Paleta.

'Terrible.' Mr Grabowicz was shaking his head in a regretful manner.

'We had big problems to walk. Snow was up here...' he held out a hand about two feet from the ground. Paleta shrugged and made a face.

'What route did you take to and from the camp?' Trinder asked the question.

'From Barton Hartshorn. The gate is near a farm'.

'That would be Home Farm,' added the stationmaster.

'Same road as we used, sir.' Trinder looked across at Vignoles, who gave a nod to his sergeant as he recalled the trudge they had made just to tick Kat off for filling a baby carriage with coal.

'At station was nothing. She not there. We ask at pub here...' Mr Paleta pointed over his shoulder roughly in the direction of the road below, 'and at stationmaster's house, but again nothing. I walked to next village but nobody see her.' Paleta looked at the floor, his shoulders sagging.

'What is the name of that village?'

'That would be Newton Purcell — it's just a small cluster of houses. It lies beyond my house and the public house along the road towards Bicester.' Stationmaster Thompson was eager to help.

'We wait here all night... ' Grabowicz's words tailed off. There was nothing else for him to add.

'I can vouch for their being here, inspector,' added Stationmaster Thompson, 'They asked my, ahem, no longer sleeping ticket clerk if he had seen her. And at about one in the morning I returned after finally giving up on our snow-clearing duties'.

'And you did what?' Vignoles looked at Thompson, who was standing very upright, in stark contrast to the two Polish men who looked weighed down by regret.

'What could I do? It was very late, pitch black outside and perishing cold. The snow was still falling and my men and I were pretty darned tired. I made a note of their concerns about Miss Valentina.'

'Walentynowicz.' Vignoles corrected him.

'My apologies.' He coughed, and twitched his mouth,

making his flamboyant moustache move in a most animated manner. 'It was I who contacted the local constabulary at about seven o' clock the next morning, after first confirming that Miss Valen..., er, after the young lady had not reappeared.'

'I see.' Vignoles stood up and walked to one of the windows.

Silence again fell as he stood, chin resting on one hand, his other supporting his elbow. Upon seeing his reflection in the glass, a foolish thought entered his mind that in adopting such a pose he probably looked a little like Napoleon. Well, the little Frenchman had been forced to contend with the forces of winter though, worryingly, he had lost.

Vignoles tried to look beyond his pensive reflection into the impenetrable dark outside. The gas mantles hissed and their pale blue light was reflected in ever-diminishing sizes in the glass close to his face and again in the window on the opposite side of the room, the little lights vanishing into ever-smaller pinpricks. It was so dark and cold outside. If she had fallen at the side of the lane she would surely have swiftly succumbed to the cold and could be lying there now, buried beneath mountains of snow. No wonder they had not yet found her. If that is indeed what had happened. Vignoles had his doubts. Had she just stepped on the next train and headed away to some other life?

Vignoles removed his glasses, pinched the bridge of his nose briefly, and then wiped the lenses with a clean handkerchief he had pulled from his trouser pocket. Replacing his glasses he turned to face those in the room. 'Could you ask Miss Walentynowicz's parents to join us?'

Trinder obliged and soon ushered the couple inside.

'I am sorry, but I need to ask you some questions that I fear you will not like; but if we are to have any idea of what happened to your daughter we need honest answers.' He turned to Ewa Grabowicz, whom he perceived as having the best command of English. 'Perhaps you could be good enough to translate, if needed?' She nodded, coloured and bit her lip.

'What you want ask?' Josef Walentynowicz stared back at Vignoles.

'Did Miss Walentynowicz have a beau, a boyfriend?' He glanced at Ewa. 'Did she mention anyone at all?'

There was no need for her to translate. As if to perfectly express the look of outrage that crossed the faces of the

Walentynowiczes as he asked the question, a freight locomotive issued a sudden whistle as it trundled through the station with a long line of noisy coal wagons. Stationmaster Thompson instinctively glanced at his silver fob watch, and then replaced it in his waistcoat pocket. Josef Walentynowicz made it abundantly clear that there was no possibility that his daughter had a boyfriend. Vignoles nodded that he accepted this observation as being true. Ewa looked at the floor, but said nothing.

'Then, indeed, we must assume that she attempted to return to the camp after collecting her handbag and sought shelter along the way — perhaps in one of the farm buildings. Or that she met with some accident. Sergeant: I need you and Major Duffy to organise search parties. Get a large scale map of the area.' Vignoles looked across at the stationmaster, who, pleased to be able to do something practical and inwardly smarting from the sleepiness and inattentiveness of his clerk, immediately took the hint, declared that he had just such an Ordnance Survey in his office and quickly left the room.

'Break down the area into sections, radiating away from the station. Starting with the road between here and the camp gates, take each side and with sticks, shovels and whatever else you can improvise, test every mound of snow, follow every track and indentation, clear the snow if needs be. If this is to be of any use it has to be thorough.'

Trinder looked at Vignoles. 'There's an awful lot of snow, sir.'

'Too much, but it's what we have to deal with. We'll need all the men from the camp and whoever can be spared from the station staff, and the major can perhaps summon up some squaddies? There must be Land Army in the area — so rustle them up. And get the local civvies involved.'

'Understood, sir.'

Without further prompting the Polish men immediately left the room with hurried shouts and urgent conversations amidst the huddle outside of the waiting room.

'It looks as though they won't need a lot of motivation to get cracking. And, sergeant, you had better make your base camp at Woodford. This might take some considerable time and facilities here are rather rudimentary. I think it might be wise for you to be based at a railway junction.'

'You have reservations about her lying in the snow here?'

'I do. But keep it under your hat for the time being, and stay alert to the possibility and ask around at Woodford for her. She might have changed trains there perhaps? Anyway, you have somewhere to stay at Woodford, at least — a nice bonus, John. Heaven knows I can't afford to lose you right now, but needs must.'

Trinder coloured slightly at the inspector's words. 'Understood... but,' he hesitated, 'I'm not sure what the neighbours will think about that. I mean, with me staying there, with Violet, that is, if you catch my drift?' He glanced around, but Mrs Walentynowicz had left the room and only young Ewa remained, silent and thoughtful and standing someway off. 'She has been somewhat feeling their disapproval in recent months, what with my visits, though these have been strictly within the boundaries of the, ahem, working timetable to Leicester.'

Vignoles stared back at Trinder and said nothing for a few moments.

'Yes, I take your point. I would never wish any harm to Miss McIntyre's good name.' He paused a beat. 'So I suggest, dear chap, that since we are somewhat over an operational barrel — if you will forgive the mangled metaphor — then you had better go and do what you really should have done months ago, and immediately announce your engagement to her! I defy the good people of Woodford to say a flipping word about impropriety then. And if they do, I'll arrest them — personally! Now, get on with organising that search.'

Trinder, scarlet in the face but with a twinkle in his eye nonetheless, saluted and promptly left the room.

It was then that Vignoles noticed that Ewa was still in the room. Something about her manner suggested that she was deliberately hanging back as if she were summoning up the courage to speak. Her gloved hands were intertwining in a washing motion that reminded Vignoles of the odious Beeby, though her actions looked wholly innocent. He tried to make a smile and kept his voice low and calm as he spoke to her. 'Ewa, is there anything you wanted to tell me? About Kat?'

A brief silence fell, but one that confirmed to Vignoles that he was on the right track.

'She did not run away. You must understand that.'

Vignoles nodded, and waited.

'She had no boyfriend. Of course we liked to talk and

daydream.' She forced a smile. 'She is quite fond of Karol. He plays in the band, at camp. He is outside now and has been searching all day like everyone. He is not involved. I don't think he even knows she likes him.'

Ewa's eyes, wide and limpid with approaching tears, looked at Vignoles and he felt a dart of pain stab his heart. She chewed her lower lip for a few seconds as Vignoles waited for her to continue once she had plucked up the courage. 'But...' she sighed deeply, 'I think it is nothing, but it is better to say everything, yes? To help find her?'

Vignoles nodded.

'A man was looking at her. Maybe he was following her. Twice I was with Kat and she told me about him and pointed him out. She got unhappy about it, though I teased her at the time.'

Vignoles narrowed his eyes and felt a tingle down the nape of his neck. 'Can you describe this man?'

Ewa did her best to do so, her description being surprisingly measured and perceptive and, to Vignoles horror, it was a perfect description of Mr Beeby.

'When was this? I need the exact dates and times, please?'

'On this night she went missing. We were in cinema — in Woodford. We went to see "Blithe Spirit". In one of the intervals Kat pointed him out: he was sitting a few rows away and looking our way.'

'He was looking at Kat?'

'She thought he was, but his *okulary* — how you say — oh, yes, *spectacles*, made it hard to be sure. But I think maybe yes.'

'Then what happened?'

'He left before end of film. We were very happy at this and I think we said no more about him.'

'And the other time?'

'At the camp. Oh, I don't remember when — about a week maybe. A Tuesday, yes, it was band practice day. We listen to the band and Kat say he is sitting behind her. He looks like maintenance man. I think I even said this to her.'

A plumber? Vignoles fell silent. His mind was racing as he tried to work out the dates and times in his head. He still had Beeby's little notebook on his office desk. He needed to refer to this before he questioned Beeby further. It was strange how things worked out, this visit to Finmere had been forced upon them by circumstance and had been an awkward intrusion upon the murder investigation, but now it looked as though it could be central to the whole case.

What if Beeby really was involved in the disappearance of this girl? Vignoles felt his stomach knot. Then the chances of feisty Kat, the cheeky stealer of baby carriages filled with coal, still remaining alive were slim. And she would not have died because of the cold and snow. Was this now a murder investigation? Should he cancel the search? No. Her body still needed finding and this could be anywhere and it would give those gathered on the platform, now busy lighting lanterns and blowing on frozen hands, something practical to do to fill the void.

'Did he speak with her?'

'No. He just looked.'

'Thank you, this is very interesting. I will need you to make a formal statement soon. But in the meantime if you remember anything, no matter how small, about this man or anything else, please tell the sergeant. Or you can telephone. Here is my card.'

Ewa took it, her eyes seeming to grow ever wider as she stared at it. 'Please, sir: Kat is all right, isn't she? Please, sir, tell me, nothing bad happen to her.'

Vignoles was reminded of Miss Spencer in Banbury, and of poor Mr and Mrs Harding in their neat little semi-detached house in Nottingham, with the slow tick of the mantle clock, their open and innocent faces as he was ushered inside and then the crushing blow. Oh, how the innocent always had to feel the most pain. He looked into Ewa's tearful and frightened eyes and suddenly found his mouth dry and his throat constricted. The words would not form. He swallowed.

'I must get on,' his voice was just a croak and he had to clear his throat. 'Go and join your uncle. He's waiting.' The anxious face of Mr Grabowicz could be seen peering in through one of the small panes of glass in the door; each still stained with diagonal strips of hardened glue residue from the anti-blast tape that had been applied for six years, now forming an opaque X across the man's face.

The station slowly fell silent as Major Duffy and Sergeant Trinder commenced the search by trooping down the covered stairway onto the Bicester Road below. Vignoles stood alone on the empty platform and looked around him. His head was filled with questions. Ewa's testimony about the watching man was compelling and he felt sure that this was somehow linked to Kat's disappearance, but how had Beeby managed this? If a strange and unattractive man who was already known to the victim — and disliked by her — wanted his evil way, what would he do? How could he take her away from the station without anyone hearing her protests? Surely she would not have gone quietly and freely with Beeby. Would the sleeping ticket clerk not have awakened if Kat had cried for help? And would Beeby have even run the risk? And what of the train guard? Even with a heavy snowfall, he must have seen them board. If Kat freely chose to step on a train, it was surely not with Beeby. And, if not with Beeby, then with whom?

Vignoles walked slowly along the island platform, his feet crunching on the thin layers of snow where the staff had tried to sweep the surface clear and great mounds of shovelled snow were banked up against the walls of the little station buildings in the centre. The stationmaster certainly tried his best to keep the place operating. Finding himself at the corner of one of the buildings below a rectangular, cast iron sign edged with a series of little circular designs bearing the legend 'Ladies Waiting Room', he stood and lit his pipe, then looked for somewhere to put his match. A row of red fire buckets was hanging on a series of metal hooks on the wall and each had but a thin layer of snow on top, having been only partially protected by the overhanging eaves. He cleared a small area of snow and dropped his match into the wet sand below. He had not been the first to do so, as three fresh-looking cigarette stubs lay there with a scrunched-up packet that once held Lucky Strike cigarettes. The butts matched the packet. It suggested that the smoker had been waiting some time. Vignoles puffed at his pipe and drifted into a kind of reverie whilst looking, for no particular reason, at the various enamelled signs screwed to the outside walls of the waiting room block: Colman's Starch, Virol — what was that stuff? It was forever being advertised along the railway — Bristol Cigarettes, Player's, Woodbine — 'the great little cigarette' — were all variously promoted. However, Lucky Strike was not there, reminding Vignoles that this was an uncommon brand. Now, where had he heard them mentioned recently? He could not remember, but his detective's mind niggled away at him and, without exactly knowing why he did so, he slipped off a glove and inspected each butt closely under the weak light of the sputtering gas lamp. One had traces of red lipstick and was only half smoked, the other two had burnt down almost to the heavily-stained filter. Vignoles reckoned that a man or two men had smoked these, and hard, whilst standing beside a woman, who had smoked the third. So two, or maybe three, people were waiting and smoking. What of it?

He shook his head: this was wasting precious time. He must find a train north and get to Leicester Central and see that his prisoner had been safely delivered and under lock and key. It was unfortunate that Trinder was not now going to help in the questioning of Beeby. This was a blow, but he would just have to manage. Suddenly Vignoles remembered that Trinder had brought a bag containing the items they had collected from Beeby's room: items apparently taken from women and quite possibly as grisly mementoes from his victims. Trinder had passed this into the office at Leicester Central on their way down to Finmere. There might be something of Miss Walentynowicz's within that very bag. What an awful thought! Vignoles needed to retrieve these items urgently and look at the contents, perhaps he would even show them to the Walentynowiczes or to Ewa, to see if anything was familiar.

A porter started to sweep more loose snow away from the platform, whistling *We'll meet again* as he worked. The choice of tune struck Vignoles as poignant, and so, with no further ado, he jammed his hands firmly into his coat pockets and, with pipe clenched between his teeth, strode towards the booking office to enquire about a suitable train so that he could meet with Mr Beeby again.

Chapter Twenty-Three

'THREE O'CLOCK IN THE MORNING'
Glenn Miller & the Andrews Sisters

Vignoles was impatient to commence interviewing Beeby, but there were some anomalies surrounding the exact timing of his movements on the evening Vera Harding was killed: Beeby's own logbook and statement told a story that Mrs Tipping appeared to corroborate, as she was sure she could place Beeby at home by no later than ten o'clock, which suggested that he could not be the killer. However, Beeby had a very weak alibi in Rugby, there was strong physical evidence of him at the crime scene and there were the chilling artefacts in his bedroom. Miss Grabowicz's observations also demanded serious consideration but, taken together, Vignoles just could not get a timeline drawn that worked for linking Beeby to the disappearance of Miss Walentynowicz, and he was now beginning to question whether her sighting of Beeby was not proving to be a red herring.

It was all most confusing, though he felt sure that he was close to untangling the threads and solving the mystery if he could concentrate solely on this one problem. But with just a candle burning upon his desk (the power was off again) he could barely see to make the notes that might have helped him order his thoughts. How he wished Trinder were there to bounce ideas off; but his sergeant was probably trudging around with a lantern and a long wooden stick, prodding ominous lumps under the snow.

Vignoles needed time to think matters through, preferably aided by a lighted pipe and a mug of cocoa. But even this modest requirement was proving impossible, because he now had W.P.C.s Benson and Lansdowne with him in the office, attempting to explain the bizarre circumstances that had led to the arrest of the gang of coal thieves. He was not really fully listening to their testimony, his mind still preoccupied with the Beeby case, but he was suddenly aware that they seemed to be requesting that a van be hauled from the bottom of a frozen lake, that they had expense claims for petrol used in a Riley owned by a certain Wing Commander Manton (retired) and, most curiously, for a replacement reel of G.P.O. telephone cable. It was all very muddling and not made any easier by the urgent ringing of his telephone.

'Yes?' Vignoles impatiently spoke into the handset. 'Ah, and good evening to you too, sir.' It was the Badger. Vignoles groaned silently. That was all he needed right now.

'How's the matter of these blasted coal robbers going? I heard on the bush telegraph that you've had some success, is that correct?'

'Indeed, yes. We have a number of fellows under arrest and the circumstances under which we apprehended them, lead me to feel sure that this will lead to a prosecution.' He was desperately looking at W.P.C. Benson whilst speaking, silently praying that, by interpreting his expression and words, she would nod assent or otherwise to the statements he made aloud. He was winging it.

'Good show. So I can tell the Minister for the Lack of Fuels that we have put an end to that matter?'

'Indeed.' An attempt at humour by the Badger, whatever next? 'Of course, there could be others doing the same con.'

'What others?'

'None that I know of, it was just a precautionary clause.'

'Well, you just make jolly sure it stays one. We cannot do with any further impediments to the distribution of fuel across the land, Vignoles. You'll have heard that the army have been called in to hack the damned stuff out of the wagons? Frozen solid like lumps of iron — well, I suppose that will help stop any other robbing blighters, at the very least.' Badger guffawed down the line. 'Though, apparently, they're meeting with mixed success as they just render the coal into piles of useless dust. And so the lights are still going out everywhere. D'you have electricity up there?'

'No, sir. We have candles, and precious few left. All our torch batteries are spent.'

'I tell you, it's worse than the bloody war, even my club is lit by oil lamps. It's like the blackout all over again but in reverse: no lights inside! It's a disgrace. Of course, I blame the government. I knew they spelled trouble with their idiotic, socialist ideals. What we need right now is a firm leader like Mr Churchill. He'd see us right. Anyway, how did you nab the little buggers?'

Vignoles bought some time by repeating the question and stared at Benson. She was miming, pulling a face and Vignoles was unsure how to interpret this. 'Well, sir, it's a fairly complex story and probably better that you read the full report.' He looked at Benson to enquire if they had commenced writing it. W.P.C. Lansdowne then mimed that she was about to start, by nodding rapidly and simulating the action of typing. 'I shall have it with you by tomorrow morning. Actually better make that the afternoon as the mail may not get through.'

Both W.P.C.s gave a pantomimed sign of mutual relief at the extra time allowed.

'Hmm. I hope I shall not be reading about any of your unorthodox policing methods.' Vignoles held his breath and wondered if commandeering a gentleman's Riley and rescuing persons from a van upon a frozen lake could be considered orthodox. Badger continued, 'I do keep reminding you that straightforward, "proper" policing will always get the best results.' Badger did not wait for Vignoles to answer but ploughed on to another matter. 'There has been a request, which has travelled through numerous offices before eventually landing upon my desk, asking for extra military resources to help undertake a search for a woman presumed missing in the snow. Your sergeant and a certain Major Duffy submitted it. Is that so?'

'Most probably. Sergeant Trinder is overseeing that particular operation. The girl has not been seen since Tuesday and appears to have vanished. We are most concerned for her safety.'

'I can understand that, but look here, there is one hell of a lot of paperwork to do before this request can be approved. We have to jump through hoops with the Ministry of... The Ministry of Snow and Bad Weather or some other damned foolish waste of time. Have you not read the latest ordinance on Snow Clearing and the Proper Resourcing of Personnel?'

'Not quite had the time, sir, though it is on my desk.' Vignoles added rather lamely, feeling sure that it was among a pile of papers he'd scooped into the bottom drawer.

'Better apprise yourself of it, then. But, look here, d'you think this search is vital?'

'Definitely. She has little chance of survival out there and I fear the worst.' Vignoles decided that this was not yet the time to bring Beeby into the equation. 'She is one of the D.P.s at Finmere Camp. A Polish girl.'

'Ah. I see. Then we must be seen to be fair to everyone. It might play out badly with the press otherwise. But is this really a railway matter? Can't we give it over to the Bucks Constabulary?'

'The girl might be beside the running tracks or within the

yard. And she did vanish from one of our stations,' Vignoles adlibbed. Perhaps he should have left the investigation to another agency, but he knew the girl and her family and there was a connection, no matter how tenuous, and deep inside he knew he owed them this, though he already feared that there might be an unhappy outcome.

'Hmm. Very well, I shall get my man Pedder onto it — just this once. But look up that ordinance and make sure you fill in the blasted forms yourself, if there is a next time. All this paperwork just takes us away from the real heart of policing. I await your report. That's all.'

Click.

'Lansdowne, get that report typed up immediately. And try to... to tone it down as much as you can.'

'In what way, sir?'

'Minimise the... unorthodox policing methods. Just write down what happened accurately, but very concisely. Don't dwell upon Wing Commander Manton's Riley, for example.'

'I see. Perhaps I should not mention the Earnshaw and Howerth lads, then?'

'What? Those two again? I hope you are not being serious.'

'I can explain...' Lansdowne started to speak.

'Not now, not now.' Vignoles waved his hand. 'Yes, do leave them out. But in my copy I want footnotes with every gory detail. Understood?'

'Very well, sir.' She saluted smartly and left the office, carrying her own candle in a metal holder.

'Come along, Benson. You can sit in as I interview this Beeby fellow. You've never had interrogation experience, have you?' Vignoles was speaking as he stood up and re-wrapped his scarf and adjusted his heavy overcoat.

'No, sir. Gosh, it's quite a responsibility. Are you quite sure I'm up to the job?'

'I've no idea, but I don't have time to worry about it. Just sit tight, keep mum and observe. Listen carefully to what he says and the way he says it. Make notes. And if you notice anything you think is significant and that you think I've missed, just give me the nod and we can consult outside the room.'

'I have a pencil and notebook at the ready. Perhaps we should fetch another candle.'

'If you can rustle one up.' Vignoles managed a wry smile. 'It'll be more than "unorthodox" to be interviewing a suspect by candlelight.'

✻   ✻   ✻   ✻

John Beeby was proving every bit as perplexing as he had been at the first interview. Vignoles was far from admitting that he had met his match, but Beeby was proving an oddly tough nut to crack, though not in quite the manner Vignoles had expected. In many ways, Beeby was anything but tough, but he was most definitely infuriating: one minute he was outraged and angry at being under arrest and being questioned — emotions that Vignoles could readily understand and which he knew how to play upon and use to his advantage — but there again, Beeby would suddenly react with almost childish excitement at some question posed to him, and seem to be thoroughly enjoying the experience of almost sparring with Vignoles. Beeby appeared to enjoy being the centre of attention and, even more maddeningly, he repeatedly interrupted Vignoles's line of enquiry with questions of his own about the minutiae of police procedure. Who was questioning whom? It was headache-inducing to remain calm and focussed upon the matter at hand.

It was no fault of Benson's, either, but having a pretty W.P.C. in the same room as a letch like Beeby was also proving to be a distraction. There was no doubt that Beeby lapped up every moment when she looked his way, and gave the most lingering of looks in return. Benson was forced to retreat to staring down at her pad and making notes — which she was doing diligently, despite the poor light — but her observational powers were now limited. Vignoles was sensing that the whole session was in danger of turning into a confusing muddle, not made any easier by tiredness, hunger, cold and working against the clock. Vignoles needed some strong grounds to extend the period he could hold Beeby, and a considerable amount of that time had already been lost in transferring him to Leicester.

Luckily, Vignoles still had some aces up his sleeve, and after a short break for a cup of tea he felt that now was the time to play them. He was growing tired of the chess game of niceties and so he decided to cut to the chase, and trump Mr Beeby.

'Let's be perfectly frank about this, shall we? From where I am sitting you will be hanging for the murder of Miss Harding, and possibly for the murder of a second victim. So either cut the games and give me a reason to believe you are not guilty, or confess.'

'Really, where do you get these ideas from? I can't help thinking that you might need to freshen up your detecting skills, *detective* inspector.' He emphasised the word with relish, 'I am most disappointed in your performance, and you're wide of the mark here.'

'I don't think so and I don't much care for your observations.'

'But you should. I can steer you out of this muddle into revelation.'

'We've talked about your train journey with Miss Harding, and you still insist that you got off the train at Rugby, leaving her to the mercy of some mysterious man that you cannot actually identify.'

'Correct on every point. But, look here, it's your job to find this man — not mine. I can't just hand him to you on a plate, as I have said before.' Beeby smiled his most saccharine smile and looked at Benson with something in his eyes that started to make Vignoles's blood boil.

'Do you wear a dark blue neckerchief with white polka dots? Or should I say, were you wearing such an item that afternoon?'

Beeby dropped his smile like he might drop a hot brick. 'I can't remember, old chap. I just grab what I can each morning and go to work. Too cold and dark to worry about how I look.' He made a forced laugh.

'Could this be your neckerchief? The one that you discovered that you were missing later that evening?'

Vignoles slid the square of material across the table, resting it upon the manila envelope in which it had been sent across from the laboratory. Beeby stared at it with a look of surprise that he struggled to mask. Vignoles finally felt a jolt, almost a thrill run through his veins. He'd touched a sensitive point. Time to slowly reel him in.

'It is yours. We know that for certain. No point in you denying it. We did tests, you see. If I had more time...' Vignoles adopted a casual, almost lazy tone of voice, '...we might discuss the techniques used in more detail. You'd enjoy that, as you seem to find the whole police process so fascinating. But I'm afraid that we — well, you, to be precise — don't have much time. So let's crack on, shall we?' He stared at Beeby, who licked his lips by way of response and said nothing. 'The right to remain silent? Always a good card to play when stuck. Of course, you will know how we came by this item.' Vignoles carefully pulled it back towards him, and with his leather-gloved hands slowly folded the cloth and twisted it into the thick gag that had blocked Miss Harding's mouth. He stretched it between his hands. Benson, who was watching from the corner of her eyes and visibly stiffening in her chair, risked looking up at Beeby, a hard and defiant set to her jaw. She watched him carefully.

Beeby slowly and deliberately shook his head and when he spoke it was quietly and with an assurance that Vignoles found unsettling. 'I am sorry to upset your little charade, inspector, but quite what all this is about, I really don't know. I simply have no idea what you are doing, though it is all very melodramatic.' He grinned. 'However, that does look a bit like my neckerchief, and yes I did indeed mislay it that afternoon in the carriage. I was hot — can you believe that? I had been running, as I think I told you before, and — remarkably — the train heating worked most effectively. A rare occurrence and so much so that I even noted the fact in my logbook later that evening. It's all there, if you care to check. Because I know you like detail, detective inspector.' He nodded at the small book that lay beside Vignoles's right arm. Vignoles did not move, but held Beeby's gaze. He remembered reading the reference and had not been sure what to make of it. 'I think I untied my neckerchief and placed it upon the seat. I suppose I must have left it there when I got out at Rugby.' He spread his hands in a gesture that seemed to say, 'Well, there you are, then.'

'And we are supposed to believe that?' Vignoles placed the neckerchief back upon the table, though it remained twisted and coiled.

'Of course. But how on earth did you come by it? Was it handed in at lost property? What a remarkable service they offer!' Beeby's face was a picture of innocent enquiry. The safety valves on a locomotive standing in the station lifted with a sudden and violent 'pop' and a huge roar echoed around the train shed. W.P.C. Benson made a choking noise in her throat and turned away, a hand pressed to her mouth. Vignoles turned and watched as she quickly gulped some air and then converted her involuntary reaction of anger and shock into a mild fit of coughing.

'Oh, my dear, you really must look after that. It might go to that pretty chest of yours and we really wouldn't want that now, would we? Though I could always rub some Vick upon it...'

'Shut up, Beeby! Mind your damned insolence!'

'Oh my, the inspector gets angry. I've been waiting for this bit.' Beeby chuckled, but continued to look at Benson and shook his head in a manner that suggested concern.

'Listen. You know very well how we got the neckerchief, and we know what you did with it. So now, Mr Clever, explain this.' Vignoles dipped into his pocket and produced the monogrammed ladies handkerchief. 'Look: "V.H." Shall I spell it out in full? Vera Harding. That's the woman you admit that you travelled with, the woman you admit to being sexually attracted to, and the woman you raped and strangled. This is her handkerchief and a perfect match for the one we found in her coat pocket. But we found this one in your bedroom. Explain that.'

Silence fell.

'Ah. Oh dear. This is all getting rather awkward, isn't it? But I do advise caution.' Beeby stared at the handkerchief for a few moments before continuing. 'Inspector, you know your Shakespeare? But of course: you are an educated man. I always feel one should have a working knowledge of the Bard, don't you? Surprises you, doesn't it? A plumber with a taste for literature. Haha, not all workingmen are stupid, you know. Well...' He waved this thought away. 'To get to my point. This is unfortunate and looks most incriminating, I admit that.' He paused, allowing both Vignoles and Benson to relax and breathe, both anticipating the confession that was surely to follow. 'But if you get this wrong then there could be very dangerous consequences — and not just for myself. Rather as a handkerchief did for Othello, then a handkerchief could do for both you and I — but in rather different ways, of course. A misreading of the facts could so easily lead to tragedy.'

'What sort of riddle is this? This isn't a game. Start talking sense. So, about the handkerchief? You admit that it is hers?'

'Of course.'

'So you took it from her and kept it in your room? Is this some kind of distasteful trophy you took after killing her?'

'This is hers, and yes, I did take it. But the very idea that I killed her is quite monstrous. Why would I want to take such a beautiful girl's life? You are reading too much into the matter.'

'Really? It looks pretty cut and dried. So how exactly did it get into your room if it was not as a consequence of rape and murder?' Vignoles glared at Beeby.

'May I ask, you a question, miss? Do you carry two handkerchiefs in your coat pocket at the same time?'

Benson coloured and looked at Beeby, startled by the odd question.

'What are you getting at?' interjected Vignoles.

'Think about it. You said yourself that you found a handkerchief in her coat pocket — patently not the one that I had possession of. This one is unused and neatly pressed. I know this as I've inspected it closely.' On a number of occasions. Benson clenched her hands so that the knuckles showed white, but regained her composure. 'So, how many handkerchiefs do you have in your pocket right now, my dear?'

'One.' Benson risked a reply, her voice slightly croaky and uncertain.

'So from where and when did I obtain the second?' Beeby smiled. 'Ladies do tend to carry handbags, do they not? I wonder, have you recovered her handbag?'

Vignoles fell silent for a moment. 'So you admit that you took her handbag after you killed her? And that is supposed to reassure us? That is not an alibi.'

'But I took the handbag whilst she was still very much alive. In Rugby station, just as I left the carriage.'

'A likely story. You're confessing to holding incriminating evidence. This handkerchief cannot give testimony as to what time of day it was taken, and your alibi for actually being in Rugby is so far uncorroborated. You'll hang, for sure.'

Beeby winced and looked nonplussed. The safety valves reset on the engine outside. A guard's whistle blew and a door slammed. 'But the handkerchief also cannot give testimony that it was taken after she died. It cuts both ways.'

'And we found other items. What about the women you took these from? Take Miss Lucinda Smith for example and her driving licence?' Vignoles placed the little red booklet upon the table.

Beeby wrung his hands together in an action that seemed at odds with his apparent confidence. A bead of sweat appeared upon his brow, a remarkable feat in the freezing interview room that was filled with a coldness only accentuated by the sound echoing along the corridor of someone attempting to break the ice in a nearby toilet.

'What about this badge? Who's was this?' Vignoles placed the W.V.S. badge upon the table. Beeby stared at it, his eyes widening. He looked increasingly uncomfortable. 'And when you lifted Miss Haverthwaite's ration book, what did you do to her? Did you gag her mouth first, like you did with Miss Harding? Did you use the same neck neckerchief to stop her screaming?'

Beeby looked up at Vignoles and furrowed his brow. 'Did I do *what*?'

'You heard well enough. Tie it as a gag around her mouth. Come on, the game's up.'

'Oh no, this is all wrong. A gag?' Beeby' eyes had a mixture of confusion and fear behind the bottle lenses. 'Look, I just don't understand.'

'You understand very well. This is a murder investigation, in case you've forgotten. You killed that young woman and threw her out of the train, and I dread to think what grimy, vile stories might lie behind these other items.' Vignoles banged his fist on the table, making the metal badge bounce and Beeby wince.

'No! I'm no killer. I came to you to offer help, old chap, remember?' Beeby was digging the nails of each hand into his palms making his fingers white with the pressure. 'Look here. I... I've done some things that others might not exactly understand.' He swallowed and his nails bit deeper. 'But I never hurt anyone. I just like to... to *take* things. I can't seem to help myself. From pretty girls, I admit that. There, I've said it now.' He exhaled slowly, as if releasing a great pressure from within. 'I don't suppose you will understand.' Vignoles snorted, but said nothing. Beeby stared at his hands. 'Young women are not interested in me. They never have been. No one really likes me. I get laughed at and mocked and people think I'm not as good as they are. I'm not like them. But I can tell you something, inspector, I'm a darn sight cleverer than most. Mark my words I am.'

Vignoles was almost holding his breath as the story unfolded. Now was not the time to interrupt. 'But I get lonely, like anyone else does.'

A tense silence fell for a moment. The ice in the toilet was still being assaulted.

Beeby started to wring his hands again, as if washing, and a scent of coal tar soap filled the air. 'So... I indulge in little games to entertain myself. There's no real harm in it! I don't hurt anyone.' He had the rapt attention of Vignoles and Benson. 'I discovered that

I am very adept at lifting things. I have the knack of being able to take things so easily from a handbag or a jacket pocket. I unpinned that badge there from a coat thrown over a chairback, right under the young lady's nose.' Beeby looked at Benson, but now his eyes were filled with a kind of boyish excitement. The W.P.C. was unsure how to react and almost preferred his salacious looks, for she at least understood what lay behind them. 'I just want to have some little thing to remember them by. To help me imagine things... I like to think that they visit me in my ugly little room and then leave something of theirs behind. After all, no one is likely to ever visit me otherwise.'

Beeby stopped and fell silent. The resilient ice in the toilet was finally cleared, judging by the sound of a distant flush. Vignoles realised that he was becoming nauseous with the smell of the soap and with Beeby's sorry little tale. He considered not washing for the next day so that he could avoid soap.

'Look, old chap, it's an inconvenience to them, yes; but it causes no hurt. I don't touch them. Good God. They don't know at the time I'm taking anything, I'm that good. So, she lost a handbag.' He spread his arms wide. 'She can get another.'

'She's dead.' Vignoles looked coldly into Beeby's eyes.

'Not because of me. I could no more hurt them than hurt myself.' He looked back down at the table. Vignoles watched Beeby's fingernails dig into his hands and questioned the last statement.

'Miss Harding was quite a beauty. She looked lovely in that coat and dress. Of course she did not want me in the same compartment that afternoon, I knew that instantly.' Beeby was speaking quietly, softly, with an intense sadness. 'I am not insensitive to the mannerisms and actions of others. I tried to say a few words of greeting, but I know the signs all too well. And I'm not good at saying the right things. I never do. So I dozed off. I removed my neckerchief at about the same time'. Beeby stopped and shook his head slowly. 'When I awoke I found that Miss Harding was looking more at ease, less nervous of me now. And yes, I liked her and I wanted something of hers. So when the train pulled into Rugby station I decided to be bolder than ever before. Seeing that another gentleman wished to enter the very same compartment, I used the confusion to take her handbag. And I made a pretty fine job of it. I was away and the train had left before she even realised.'

No one spoke.

'I feel very sorry about what happened to her later. But that was not of my doing. So you see, old chap, I advise you to proceed carefully and not create a further tragedy out of an already terrible story by hanging me, whilst the real killer remains at loose. The man who got into the compartment at Rugby is who you should be looking for.'

Vignoles was resting his chin upon one hand. He may even have closed his eyes for a few moments, appearing almost to be asleep. Benson stared at her pad of notes, pencil poised, but her mind racing and aching as she tried to process the information. Her emotions were swinging wildly between contempt, pity and confusion.

'What about Miss Walentynowicz? Tell me about her.'

'I'm sorry, I don't know anyone of that name.'

'A Polish girl, strikingly pretty, age seventeen or thereabouts. Lived at Finmere D.P. Camp. Ring any bells?'

'There are a few lookers there, I do know that...' Beeby stopped himself and coughed. 'Sorry, old chap; I don't know their names.'

'But you have been to the camp. Several times?'

'Why yes. It is all logged in my book. The last time was when the major's hot water geyser went on the blink. But why are you asking me this?'

Vignoles stared at Beeby. Was he a masterful liar? For, if he was lying, then he did so with confidence. Or was he speaking the truth? 'Last Tuesday night. Where were you?'

'That would be the night of the fifth? Ah, that is easy,' Beeby seemed to suddenly brighten up in that maddening manner that he had. 'I stopped off at Woodford Halse on my way back to Nottingham as they had an early evening showing of *Blithe spirit* and I rather fancied seeing it. Though actually I found it a rather dull film and left before the end, but I wanted the warmth of a small and crowded cinema to thaw out in, so it served a purpose.'

'Why see the film at Woodford and not in Nottingham? Seems rather an odd thing to do.'

'Have you tried to see a film recently, inspector? The queues are quite horrendous. You can wait an hour or longer outside, quite freezing to death and then still not get a seat. The Savoy, whilst busy, it is far less trouble and they can normally squeeze one in.'

'Why were you following Miss Walentynowicz?'

'I was not aware that I was. Oh... but I think I know whom

you might mean. One of those two young ladies in the cinema…
Ah, yes, she is pretty. Imagine my surprise when I saw her sitting a
few seats away.'

'You are saying that it was pure coincidence that you were
there?'

'But of course. I had no idea they would be there. How
could I, they live in Finmere?'

'When did you leave?'

'Before the end of the film; as I said, it was not to my taste.
And yes, my train to Nottingham is logged in the book there. I might
even still have the ticket. And, inspector, I am sorry to disappoint
you, but I distinctly recall talking at some length with a most
interesting ticket clerk at Woodford about the punctuality of the
train services that evening and I feel sure that he will confirm that
I boarded my train, as he even — rather ostentatiously I thought
— waved at me from behind his little glass window. I remember this,
as it is so rare that anyone ever so much as gives me the time of day.
I think you will also find that one of my co-lodgers at Mrs Tipping's
boarding house, the rather odious Mr Blenkinsop, bumped into
me as I returned home that night and was most ungracious as he
did so. You may wish to question him. And, if you will excuse the
impertinence, I think you should try to talk to the tall gent in the
military gear that was hanging around Woodford station approach
road that night. He really did look just like that man who climbed
aboard at Rugby.' Beeby let this information sink in. 'And since you
are so clearly in need for assistance, I can tell you that he was an
American — if I am not mistaking him for a Canadian, that is.'

'An American? Why is he of any relevance?'

'Because he was the very spit of the man who joined the
train at Rugby. The moment I saw him at Woodford I knew where I
had seen his face before. Jogged my memory.'

Vignoles looked long and hard at Beeby, his mind was racing
and he could feel a vein throbbing in his temple. He nodded very
slowly, with an action that said more about his inner thinking than
as a communication with either Beeby or Benson.

'I shall get someone to fetch you some tea. W.P.C. Benson
and I shall take a break now.' Vignoles stood up and briskly walked
out of the interview room with Benson close behind. He said
nothing until they entered his office, where he sat on the edge of his
desk. Benson held the candle to provide a tiny glimmer of light. The
inaccurate wall clock struck eleven.

'What d'you make of our Mr Beeby?'

Benson looked around and then placed her candleholder upon a bookshelf before answering. 'He confuses me. I started off feeling sure he was guilty and that the evidence is compelling. But you know what, sir? I am almost convinced that his story could be true — though I find him most objectionable.'

Vignoles nodded. 'He's pathetic and an odd mixture of childishness, cunning and creepiness. But there is something about his story, I agree. I just can't tell if he is a murderer and a clever liar, or just a dirty old man, though essentially harmless, and a potentially vital witness. Is he playing games with us?'

'I'm not sure. At one point I almost felt sorry for him. Is that strange?'

'No. Clever people like him can manipulate one's feelings. We must stand back and remove any emotion from our thinking.' Vignoles looked thoughtful and something in his face encouraged Benson to speak.

'I heard around the office that you knew the Polish girl who's gone missing.'

'Word spreads quickly. We recently had cause to speak with her. We met her parents as well.' Vignoles spoke in short sentences, almost as if he were afraid to risk speaking for too long in case his voice betrayed some weakness. 'It was a run-in over something that seems rather trivial now. We hardly knew her, but I confess that it does rather catch one off balance when someone one has met goes missing.'

Benson nodded. 'If Beeby is to be believed, then at least the girl will not be one of his victims. I'm rather hoping that he is telling the truth.'

'Safe from Beeby, but at risk from someone else, as yet unknown, who might be a killer? Not much of an alternative. And with this insufferable winter on top.' He blew air out of his cheeks in a long sigh. 'We need to check every angle. It's something I should have been doing before I interviewed Beeby. We need to speak to that booking clerk in Woodford.' Benson started to make notes. 'And again to Mrs Tipping and this "unpleasant Mr Blenkinsop" who lodges there'. Vignoles pulled a wry face.

'He didn't like Mr Blenkinsop, did he? The pot calling the kettle black?'

'Quite possibly.' Vignoles allowed a short laugh. 'Right, you're seeking to get the exact time that Beeby arrived home that

Tuesday. We need absolutes. We cannot allow any ambiguities in his alibi. Then there is the Savoy. See if anyone recalls his being there and can confirm when he arrived and left. See how this fits in with the Polish group. I'll try to get a detailed statement from them about their timings in and out of the cinema. I'll get Blencowe and Lansdowne to help with all this, though...' he looked at the clock, '...I cannot see you getting much joy until tomorrow. Write up the interview now whilst it's fresh in your mind, then go and get some sleep. I want to leave Beeby to stew for tonight whilst I think about our next move.'

'Righty-o, sir.' Benson left the room with her candle.

Vignoles lit his pipe and stared out of his misted up office window onto the dimly illuminated station, the town gas burning fitfully. At least they were still burning. It was perhaps a pity that the offices had been converted across to electric lighting before the war. Blast that generator. When would they get it restarted? His candle was burnt down to a stump.

The American. Was he a figment of Beeby's imagination or was he in fact the murderer? Vignoles had to make a choice: press home his case against Beeby and place him in custody where, even with a few loose ends, there was surely enough evidence to see him convicted. Beeby was unlikely to persuade a jury. But as Beeby said, he might then see the wrong man hang and the killer stay free to kill again. Or did he go back, cap in hand, and try to regain Beeby's confidence to work together to find this dangerous serviceman? Vignoles could hold Beeby until tomorrow and that would buy some time until he could decide on his action.

Chapter Twenty-four

'I'LL BE WITH YOU IN APPLE BLOSSOM TIME'
The Andrews Sisters

Sergeant Trinder felt exhausted, as were his gangs of searchers. But no one was willing to stop the urgent hunt for Miss Walentynowicz. Trinder had spent most of the night prodding and digging and stomping through snow that was often waist high, but now he was sitting in a waiting room at Finmere station and trying to reorganise the various search parties into relays so that one lot could rest, eat, perhaps even sleep, whilst the others took over. But such was the determination and sheer desperation amongst the camp residents that he was having only limited success and he feared that soon they would all reach a state of complete exhaustion. He could hardly criticise their commitment, though, and understood all too well that if there was to be any real chance of finding the girl alive then it had better be soon. Now was perhaps not the time for resting.

Major Duffy had finally arranged for a truckload of soldiers and was now awaiting their arrival from the barracks in Bicester. The soldiers' fresh energy and their heavy vehicle would prove invaluable. Trinder had also managed to muster up a gang of Land Army girls from the surrounding farms, and they had joined the search with gusto, their value considerably enhanced by having the use of two tractors with trailers and some barrels of diesel, plus assorted rakes, hoes, spades and sundry other farm implements that would aid delving through the snow. The Buckinghamshire Constabulary was bringing some men over that afternoon, but Trinder had already been forewarned that they were likely to be in no great shape, as they were presently helping clear drift-filled lanes elsewhere in the county to allow the bread and milk deliveries to get through. At least he had five uniformed L.N.E.R. police working alongside a gang of women platelayers and their foreman from Woodford, all searching around the station yard and alongside the running lines.

He had plenty of people to help and they were making what he supposed was good progress, though the missing woman had still not been found. If their efforts were to have any value, then they needed to be thorough; but with the roads, ditches and fields under anything between two and six feet of snow, it was an almost impossibly daunting task. One group was attempting to visit every dwelling house within a five-mile radius, encouraging the owners to look into their barns, outhouses, stables, garages and abandoned air raid shelters in the hope that Miss Walentynowicz had sought sanctuary within. But, although the area was thinly inhabited, this was still a monumental task as the roads were virtually impassable. To make matters even worse no one had any petrol. The major's ex-U.S. Army jeep had been proving well suited to the job until it had become marooned somewhere near Shelswell Park with the petrol tank empty and little chance of replenishment.

Never mind the thirsty jeep, all those searching needed feeding and Trinder and the major had spent some time worrying over this logistical nightmare until the Women's Voluntary Service, apparently summoned by unknown forces or a mysterious sixth sense, had set up a makeshift tea and soup kitchen inside the ladies' waiting room at Finmere station, which feat of brilliant organisation cheered everyone on a profoundly cheerless day.

This emergency catering was being efficiently organised by a small and terrier-like woman with a strident voice, whom Trinder had been reliably informed was Lady Farthinghoe, though she wasted no time on such niceties as introductions. She wore practical green tweeds underneath a stockman's overcoat that was battered, ankle-length, waxed and smelt of horses and straw, beneath which could be seen thick, woollen socks and sensibly stout shoes, all worn in a manner only those of a certain class could carry off and yet still command respect. She had appeared at the station, unannounced, on the 7.23 a.m. local, having travelled up from Calvert with the guard's van stocked with a large urn, something called a 'Multipot', that was for brewing tea, trays of cups and mugs of varying vintages and designs, a pair of trestle tables, folding chairs and various tins, packets and boxes of broken biscuits, tea, coffee, sugar cubes (some rather the worse for water damage), vegetables, tinned peaches and evaporated milk, dried egg, paring knives, milk jugs and goodness knows what else accompanied by two equally-able ladies, who strode into the waiting room and occupied it with a focussed determination that lifted the spirits of all.

Further reinforcements arrived from Woodford Halse in a form that brought especial cheer to Sergeant Trinder: Violet and her daughter Jennifer were accompanied by Mrs Walsh from the Woodford refreshment rooms, which she had left in the sole hands of her other waitress, Miss Jones. All three had come prepared with another guard's van of stores, this time containing a sack of potatoes, half a sack of swedes and turnips (apparently forced out of the iron-hard ground by mechanical road-drill) and a freshly shot brace of wild duck. The box containing cans of whalemeat was placed in a corner of the waiting room and used as a seat, and everyone silently agreed to avoid mentioning, let alone using, the unappetising flesh contained within. There was going to be trouble back at Woodford, however, because at least half of the daily production of Earnshaw's Bakery seemed to have been donated to the cause. When the village housewives found their precious rations had been offered to the search parties, trouble was likely to break out. Trinder did wonder at the legalities of this gesture, and felt that there were going to be all manner of bureaucratic wrangles to sort out the complexities and difficulties arising from this generous, but highly unofficial support. He feared that the men from the Ministry of Inadequate Rations and Ample Starvation were going to take a very dim view of the affair. Still, there would be time enough later to worry about the pencil-pushers in their bowler hats. For now, his spirits were lifted at having Violet join him.

Violet had immediately set about collating and clipping coupons from what ration books could be garnered from those assembled, and in particular she was on the lookout for any precious petrol coupons, issuing instructions to the leaders of each search party that they should call upon the generosity of every householder they encountered to beg them for any petrol they could spare. Jenny McIntyre, meanwhile, was hard at work in the soup kitchen peeling spuds over a pail of almost frozen water. Her hands were already porcelain white, her veins showing blue, but she still managed a smile every so often and cheered herself by singing *I'll be with you in apple blossom time* in a voice that was both attractive and slightly ironic in equal measure. And so, the ladies' waiting room was filling with the delicious smell of a hearty vegetable soup laced with pieces of duck, and clouds of steam condensing upon the walls and windows from the continually boiling tea urn.

Trinder was seated upon a sagging leather bench in one corner with the stationmaster's Ordnance Survey map, now covered in blue and red pencil marks indicating the scope of the search, before him on a small table. A rapidly-cooling mug of tea was placed on the map covering Bicester, and when he lifted the mug to take another sip, he noticed that it had left a brown ring that appeared to encircle the ancient roman town. Bother. Well, he had pretty much ruined the map with all his scribblings and the snow had so dampened the folds that they were starting to ease apart. It was in danger of disintegrating, so he made a mental note that he had better try and find a replacement when this was all over.

Trinder's hair was still neatly slicked down with Brylcreem, but a dark shadow around his jaw and a redness around his eyes betrayed his tiredness. His clothes were damp and he needed a bath. He had worked all through the night and it was now early afternoon, and he was feeling his energy wane. Offsetting this was the knowledge that Violet was seated beside him, busily and efficiently making lists and calculating points, and talking excitedly of the donation of two whole jerry cans of petrol from Barleyfields Barn Farm. Trinder closed his eyes and leant back, listening to Violet and nodding occasionally or giving a slight smile in acknowledgement to things she said.

Oh, but he was weary, and what made it worse was that he was fighting off a mounting feeling that the search was becoming futile. He had always shared the inspector's belief that the young woman had left the station by train. However, he recognised the slight possibility that she might have got lost in the blizzard and taken shelter, or met with some accident. He also recognised the desperate need to do something practical that was emanating from her family and friends; this huge operation was at least meeting that need, though he wondered if it was not just a mistaken use of resources. Trinder felt that he owed the Walentynowicz family his complete dedication to the task, not just because their daughter was missing, but because of what had happened between himself and Kat what seemed an age ago.

Lady Farthinghoe bustled out of the room with Mrs Walsh and Jenny McIntyre to fetch a fresh supply of vegetables the Land Army girls had hauled to the station using their tractor. As the room suddenly fell almost silent, Trinder and Violet were finally alone for a few precious moments. She rested her hand upon his arm.

'You look exhausted.'

'A little, I'll admit that. Nothing a quick forty winks wouldn't cure.' He turned his head and smiled at her. 'Or a nice pint of beer. I have drunk enough tea for one lifetime.'

'Would it be inappropriate to do so now?'

'What, drink tea?'

'No, silly, a beer!'

'I don't see why it would be wrong, but scant chance of that in a ladies' waiting room.' He laughed.

'Ah, but you are underselling Lady Farthinghoe. She's a remarkable woman and a tireless organiser of the W.V.S. soup kitchens, so I have heard. She really understands such matters, and so...' Violet produced a pint bottle of Hopcroft and Norris's Brackley Bitter from a crate tucked beneath the section of bench that she was sitting upon '...she sequestered part of his lordship's ale supply.'

'Good show. She is rather a remarkable woman — if perhaps a bit... fierce.'

Violet's eyes sparkled. 'Haha, she's all heart, really. But I do think you deserve a beer. And we have plenty more, so the others can have one when they come for soup, so don't feel guilty.' She was removing the cap even whilst she spoke. 'Excuse the lack of a glass, but I don't think you'll mind under the circumstances.'

'We shouldn't let standards drop, y'know.' They both laughed. 'This won't even touch the sides going down. Thank you.' He gave her his warmest of smiles and gratefully took a long draught, though it was more measured than he had suggested. 'Oh yes, that does the trick. Here, try some.'

Violet nodded and took a sip then handed the bottle back.

'It was good of you and Jenny, and Mrs Walsh of course, to lend a hand. I appreciate that.'

'Just try and stop us! Remember the Walentynowiczes and the others at the camp are my customers. I like them a lot. I cannot even bear to think that something has happened to poor Kat. There was never a moment's doubt that we would do what we could. I'll dig snow the moment you tell me to do so, and do it all night, if it comes to that.' As she was speaking Violet was slowly turning over in her hands an empty lipstick case that she had found on the floor beside the crate of Brackley Bitter.

'We have plenty of diggers, so helping feed them is exactly what's needed.'

Violet placed the used lipstick case into the ashtray on the table, took another sip from the bottle of beer and closed her eyes for a few seconds. 'She might be wearing that lovely coat I made for her; she looked so wonderful in it. She's a real beauty. She could be a mannequin in a fashion house in London or Paris. And so full of life...' Violet's voice was soft and hushed. 'Truthfully, John, is there any chance for her? It's just that it's so cold outside. It's like the Arctic and there's more snow on the way tonight.' She looked at the frosted-over windows and the bright whiteness on the fields that rolled towards the horizon, a backdrop of ominous grey clouds banking up behind.

Trinder considered his reply. 'If she's lying in a ditch and under snow, then I am afraid it will take a miracle for her to have survived.' Using the beer bottle as a pointer, he indicated the map with its annotations. 'And quite frankly, she's just not anywhere we have looked. It was not such a long walk back to the camp and we've found no trace of her along the way. The search is spreading wider, but I'm doing that more out of duty than because I really think she lost her sense of direction and headed off the wrong way.' He took a long draught of beer. 'The inspector feels that she did a runner and left here by train, of her own accord. I think he might be right and I even hope that she did, despite what her parents might think of that idea. At least that way, she could well be safe and sound, holed up somewhere with a boyfriend.'

'Maybe you're right, though I find it so hard to imagine her doing so. But I suppose people can surprise one.' Violet looked at the floor for a few moments, took a deep breath and then looked at Trinder with an odd, half-smile on her face. 'I do so want to stay hopeful and not get too gloomy about things.' She paused a beat. 'John?' Her voice had a lighter tone to it. 'Before they get back...' she alluded to the little band led by Lady Farthinghoe, whose voice boomed loudly and energetically outside the waiting room. 'Talking of being surprised, did you really mean what you said last night on the telephone?'

'Would you like it to be something that I really meant? In the cold light of day, so as to speak.' Trinder returned Violet's look and then took a hurried gulp of beer.

'Of course I do.' She placed an encouraging hand on his arm.

Trinder put down the bottle and turned to face Violet so that he could clasp both her hands. He grinned and the tiredness suddenly flowed away from his face. 'That's wonderful! Really wonderful. So, Miss Violet McIntyre, I would like to ask you again — and more formally this time — will you marry me?'

'Good heavens! We pop out to collect some more essential food reserves and by the time we're back, they're getting married.

And drinking his lordship's beer ration, to boot. There's no time for all this romantic silliness, the war's long over, now's the time for practicalities, as we've got hungry troops to feed. You'll quite put them off their soup...' Lady Farthinghoe was already bustling about whilst she was speaking, in contrast to Jenny McIntyre and Mrs Walsh, who were both squealing with delight and doing their best to rush towards Trinder and Violet in order to hug them, despite being laden with crates of vegetables and trying to find a way past the chairs, trestle tables and general clutter that had already accumulated on the floor of the small room. Lady Farthinghoe's two lady helpers then appeared at the door with buckets of water to replenish the boiling urn. Amidst the congratulations and hugging and handshaking Violet managed to say 'Yes!' at least twice in approximately the direction of Trinder before being swamped by her daughter kissing her, and Mrs Walsh talking rapidly at high volume and already asking when they were to be married and where, and what kind of a do they were thinking of, and that she would, of course, be proud — no, honoured — to help arrange the reception, in fact: consider it done, but then, of course, she did not want to presume, and maybe they might like to think the arrangements over.

A whistle sounded shrilly and added to the confusion and noise as a train pulled to a halt outside, steam rolling through the open door in huge balls of nothingness.

'Yes well, congratulations indeed. But can we now have some order and discipline in here? We need to get this already-late lunch underway.' Lady Farthinghoe's strident voice cut cleanly through the noise. The excited chatter subsided, but many smiles and exchanges of glances continued and Trinder got a sudden sensation of everyone looking rather like naughty schoolchildren being brought to order by a stern schoolmistress. This image, and his relief at Violet's response, made him grin. Feeling that he was in danger of being reprimanded again, he turned away and walked out of the door and onto the platform, where he immediately saw the figure of Vignoles approaching through the swirling steam, his long R.A.F. coat and stylish hat set at an angle were both unmistakable, despite the rapidly diminishing light.

'Some kind of party inside?'

'Sir!' Trinder gave a smart salute, hoping to restore some sense of propriety. 'Not exactly. A spontaneous reaction to some good news.'

'You found her?' Vignoles was wiping his spectacles of condensation and gave Trinder a very sceptical look.

'Sadly, no. It's a bit embarrassing really. It's just that Violet and I have become engaged. A few moments ago, actually. And we were rumbled so there has been some excitement about the news. Sorry, it's most inappropriate, under the circumstances.'

'Not a bit of it. God knows we need some cheering news. Good show, John. Though I do hope that I was not responsible for any of this?' Vignoles gave Trinder a guilty look as he replaced his glasses and extended his hand.

'Don't worry, you just encouraged me to do what I should have done months ago.' Trinder laughed, grasping Vignoles's hand, which he shook heartily.

'Then we'll agree to forget my meddling and have a proper celebration — with wine and a decent meal, if such a thing can be found — the moment we can grab a free evening. I'll give my good wishes to Violet in a while, but first we need a quiet spot and I shall bring you up to speed on Mr Beeby, and you can do likewise with how matters stand here.'

Seated a few minutes later in the general waiting room, which lacked a fire — the allotted coal ration had been sacrificed to keep the ladies' waiting room more habitable for the W.V.S. — Vignoles summarised the situation as he understood it.

'That idiot Ferens is going to court soon on black-marketeering charges and is out of the equation for Miss Harding's murder. I'll leave Benson and Lansdowne to tell you the full story of their adventures another time.' Vignoles shook his head slightly. 'I might even smile about them one day.

'Significantly, we can discount Beeby as having any direct part in the disappearance of Miss Walentynowicz. His alibi for the night of her disappearance turns out to be cast iron. Benson and Blencowe did some good work corroborating his story and it stacks up. He was back home in Nottingham before she even went missing. The odd thing is, I'm rather beginning to think he's also telling the truth about Miss Harding. He might well have got out at Rugby and left her to this mysterious "other man".'

'But Miss Grabowicz gave a very good description of Beeby in the cinema, and she told us how he had been stalking them and upsetting Kat at the camp. But is this irrelevant?'

'An unfortunate coincidence, it would seem. Though perhaps not really even that, because Beeby has admitted that he does prey upon pretty girls and he probably had his eye on her. He would have seen her at the camp whilst fixing the major's hot water geyser. But, odious though he may be, I don't think he is a threat; he just likes to steal personal items from them as souvenirs.'

'Ugh.' Trinder pondered this for a moment. 'So, if Beeby is creepy but harmless, then you are suggesting that he cannot have brutally raped and strangled Vera Harding?'

'It seems rather out of characte. If we take Beeby's confession about his odd, kleptomaniacal actions on face value, then he could never have done what was done to Miss Harding. It's just not how he is.'

'But can you be sure? I know he came to us as a witness, but he was acting really strangely and suspiciously. He could be a clever liar. I've been thinking about his alibi and studying the timetables and Blencowe's estimations of the actual running times; he could have murdered Miss Harding, dumped her near Catesby and then got out at the next scheduled stop, which was Brackley Central. He could easily have doubled back to Rugby in time to put that call into the office and then return to Nottingham on the train he said he did. His alibi then appears good, though it actually has an hour or so missing. And he had her handbag.'

'And there was no one in the office to take his call, which further weakens his alibi, and no one has come forward admitting seeing him at Rugby. I accept what you're saying and that's why he is still under arrest, and how I managed to gain permission to hold him a while longer. But I am inclined to believe he might just be telling the truth. I think he inadvertently chose exactly the wrong woman to steal from. There were two birds of prey circling around Miss Harding that day — but Beeby was not the one who did the killing.'

'That's worse than bad luck.' Trinder shook his head.

'But he gave us more detail about the mystery man.'

'Ah, his memory was jolted. That's more like it.'

'He's tall and slim with a military style hair cut and clothing, which Beeby thinks was a kind of olive green. American. Quite possibly U.S.A.F.'

'Very interesting. So it looks like we're going to need his help after all.' Trinder shook his head in quiet disbelief.

'Let me ask you this: do you believe that Miss Walentynowicz ran away from home? You've been around her family and friends. What have you picked up?'

'To leave of her own free will seems impossible, based upon their statements. And that includes Violet's assessment of the family. She knew the parents quite well, but especially Kat.'

'And yet...?'

'And yet her leaving by train does seem the most plausible explanation for her disappearance. It's a contradiction.'

'No rumours or mutterings about a secret liaison?'

'Nothing. Apart from her friend's testimony about a strange man — who surely must be Beeby — appearing to be following and watching her.'

'So, you don't really think she is under a snowdrift?'

'Ah. Actually I am less and less convinced. We've covered a pretty decent area now and I am feeling less hopeful as each hour passes.'

Vignoles nodded. 'So could her disappearance be linked to the murder of Miss Harding?'

'You think that she might have been killed? Lured somewhere else?'

'Now, don't say anything to the others yet. It's just a hunch. But I fear we must consider the possibility that there is a killer on the loose. And this tall, American air force man is one suspect.'

Both contemplated that thought for a few moments. A porter walked past, whistling a tuneless melody, whilst the sound of voices and booted feet could be heard ascending the steps to the platform. One of the search parties was returning to have some of Lady Farthinghoe's soup.

Vignoles continued. 'The killer stumbled upon Miss Harding by chance in a private compartment and took his opportunity. He could have done the same when Miss Walentynowicz returned alone to find her forgotten bag. But then what? How did he coax her away from the station?'

'Won her confidence and somehow urged her onto a train? She's awfully young, despite her feisty nature and mature look. She would have been out of her depth if she was dealing with a clever and manipulative man.' Trinder was lighting another cigarette.

Vignoles nodded. 'I think that's plausible. He could be a very dangerous customer indeed. Perhaps charming, persuasive and plausible. And this supports my theory about Beeby: Miss Walentynowicz had already spotted him and had formed the opinion — at least according to Miss Grabowicz — that she didn't like him, so she would surely never go freely with Beeby onto a train.'

Trinder nodded. 'So could this American have been waiting here when she returned to the station? Or could he have even been following her from Woodford?'

'Both are possible — I perhaps favour him following from Woodford. Beeby suggested that he might have seen this man in the town when he left the cinema early to go home.' Vignoles appeared to smoke his pipe, though it was unlit. 'Of course he was not to know that she was going to return to the station alone, but he seems to be able to react quickly to his sick idea of opportunity.'

Trinder nodded and pulled hard upon his cigarette. 'And finding her alone, he somehow coaxed her into a carriage. If anyone were to see them, they'd just be a couple boarding a train. And in that blizzard they'd be practically invisible. The absolute cad! I want to get this man before...' Trinder stopped short. 'Well, maybe it's too late to save her. Damn him! I want to see him hang.'

Vignoles allowed Trinder's indignation to vent itself before continuing, 'If she was being interfered with during a blizzard on a windswept country station, where would he do that? Clearly not on the platform.' Vignoles was now filling his pipe with fresh tobacco and speaking slowly as he thought aloud. 'In here? Or in the ladies' waiting room? The other is a touch comfier, I imagine.'

They both looked around at the dark-brown-painted wooden dado panelling and the walls painted in a grubby, once glossy, cream paint, now flaking and stained by undulating tide marks of damp. A solitary gas mantle hung from the ceiling on a heavy chain thickly burred by accretions of rust, dirt and dead flies. Faded prints adorned the walls, together with a few browning and dated public information notices about what to do in an air-raid and other emergencies and a couple of ancient posters promoting a bracing Skegness and the delights of Bridlington. All in all, it was a cheerless place that stank of disinfectant, soot, floor polish and mustiness. They shook their heads in unison.

'What cigarettes do you smoke?'

'Sorry? Er, Black Cats out of choice. Some Woodbines and I suppose anything I can get when short. Why do you ask?' Trinder gave a quizzical glance at the inspector and then looked at the cigarette in his hand.

'I'm not sure. There's something nagging in the back of my mind. Can't seem to be able to quite make it a fully formed idea, though. What about the others at the office? Any idea what they favour?'

'You doing a sales survey?' Trinder half laughed, but still indulged Vignoles; he was used to his methods and they could sometimes yield surprising results. 'Much the same, I suppose. I know that Blencowe's a Senior Service man. Though Woodbines are favoured generally, as they're cheap and slightly easier to find.'

'Hmm. It's probably nothing. Let's take a look in at the other waiting room, though if that troop of Land Army girls who've just walked past are going where I presume they are, it's going to be a heck of a squeeze.'

A few minutes later, after passing on his good wishes to Violet, Vignoles accepted a bottle of beer and squeezed onto the bench beside her, Trinder pulling up an empty beer crate and sitting with his back to the queue of Land Army women who were blowing on their hands, stamping snow off their boots and wolfing down bowls of duck soup. There was a low murmur of conversation within the room, but spirits were dampened by the cold, the physical labour and the grim realisation that the girl had still not been found. It didn't take a doctor or a detective to work out that her chances of survival were now minimal.

Vignoles swiftly drank his beer whilst he considered their next move and looked around the room. 'This is the most likely location for a seduction or sex assault to take place. Though it's rather been transformed now and I hardly think we will find any evidence of their presence.'

'You think Katarzyna was here?' Violet asked the question.

Vignoles just nodded. He did not wish to broadcast his theory of a killer on the loose.

Violet thought a moment. 'Look, it may be nothing, but this was on the floor under the bench.' She handed Vignoles the empty lipstick case that she had placed in the ashtray. 'The colour is significant. I remember Katy telling me about it and I agreed that it suited her. I even ran up a blouse to match it, in some fabric I salvaged, and she was thrilled.'

'Did you? Most interesting. Wait a moment.' Vignoles darted out of the room, weaving between the standing and seated women with surprising dexterity. Trinder raised his eyebrows and made a gesture of incomprehension towards Violet. Vignoles soon returned with three cigarette butts resting in the palm of his hand and the screwed-up cigarette packet in the other. 'What do you think? Is that the same colour?' He was peering at the lipstick stain upon the longer butt.

'Hard to say,' Trinder was nodding though. His boss had turned something up again and he was beginning to see the connections. He reached forward, took the packet of Lucky Strikes from Vignoles and turned it over in his hands.

Violet reached into her handbag, pulled out a handkerchief and, after unscrewing the cap of the lipstick she ran one corner of the handkerchief around the edge, collecting a faint smear of colour that was similar in density to that upon the butt. 'A perfect match, and judging by the way this has been scraped almost clean it could just be hers; she had no money to speak of.'

'Ewa Grabowicz might be able to confirm this?' Trinder was looking around the room to see if she were there.

'Assuming that this is hers, then she appears to have shared a smoke with someone. Can we risk saying that he was the killer?' Vignoles was speaking low and the other two were leaning forward towards him.

'It's good enough for me.' Trinder was still looking at the cigarette packet.

'Did you make a note of what trains left the station following that which she and her party arrived on?'

'Yes. Got them here.' Trinder flicked open his black-covered notebook, holding back the open pages with the elastic band attached to the cover. He handed it to the inspector. Trinder then continued to look around for the Polish girl.

'Hmm. Two possibilities.' He shook his head. 'But why go to the trouble? If it is the same man, he is very opportunistic and reacts quickly. He had little time to perform his vile deed with Miss Harding, but still managed it. Would he take time to seduce the girl here, then coax her onto a possibly crowded train to take her somewhere else, the whole time trying to keep her sweet and not raise a hue and cry? Then, and only then, do the evil deed at some other location?'

'Right, why go to that much trouble?' Trinder agreed.

'Maybe he...' Violet dropped her voice to a whisper, '... killed her here?'

'I'm thinking the same way. But assuming so, how did he remove her body?' Vignoles stared at the list on the page of Trinder's notebook. 'Hold on. There might just be a way.' He suddenly stood up; in so doing so surprising those around him that they momentarily stopped eating to look in his direction.

'We need to speak to the stationmaster. Good afternoon Miss McIntyre. Thank you.' He tipped his hat, and strode out of the room. Trinder gave Violet a quick smile, readjusted his hat and followed.

Chapter Twenty-five

'IT'S ALL OVER NOW'
Peggy Lee

Stationmaster Thompson had been completing some urgent railway paperwork in his house, which was set below the station and tucked into the lee of the railway embankment close to the twin metal girder bridges that spanned the A4421. A stand of Scots pine, a trademark of the Great Central Railway, who had constructed his neat, red-brick house to a standard design, were covered in snow and brought a romantic touch to the setting as the last dying embers of the day were being swallowed up by the twin approaches of night and an increasingly threatening bank of cloud.

'To save coal I no longer light a fire in my station office and instead work beside our one source of heat at home: the kitchen range. I have a telephone to hand so that I can quickly be upon the station when needed.'

Vignoles and Trinder were standing in the small porch whilst the stationmaster spoke.

'A commendable use of scarce resources. No thank you, we shall not come in.' Vignoles waved away the invitation to step inside, 'If you could be so kind as to just answer this enquiry, we can be on our way.'

'Of course, whatever I can do to assist.'

'Aside from the two stopping passenger trains, what else left Finmere by, let's say, seven a.m. on the morning of the sixth of February? The odd milk wagon, a newspaper van, perhaps?'

'As I think I may have told you earlier, we had a pick up goods' come through, which dropped off a box van with some animal feed, and the engine crew and guard managed to extricate the hound van that had been holed up here since the last meeting of the Grafton hunt. So the goods' took it away — at last,' he paused, 'and then the milk train collected some churns — the milk was quite frozen solid and they weighed a ton — whilst the empties have been as good as welded to the ground ever since. The farm carts have not been able to get through to collect them nor drop off any more. We're going to run awfully short of milk, I fear.'

'About this hound van?'

'It's Lord Southampton's, he's the master of the hunt.'

Vignoles nodded slightly in acknowledgement of this obvious fact. He knew little or nothing of hunts, let alone their masters. 'They tried a meet on the Sunday previous, but the snow got the better of them and the hounds ended up in a farm somewhere near Hinton-in-the-Hedges and are still there, so I heard. The horses are stabled wherever they could find suitable places. It was quite a debacle in the end and a logistical nightmare to round them all up afterwards. But you don't need to know this. About the van: it brought the hounds down from Helmdon and remained here whilst we awaited further instructions — which we finally received earlier that very same evening the poor Polish girl went missing.'

'It was empty, I presume?'

'Oh goodness, yes. We managed to clean it out, lime it and put in fresh straw ready to convey the dogs back, but of course they never returned.'

'The van was not locked?' Vignoles was already looking impatient, as if he was desperate to be somewhere else. Trinder had caught the sudden change in the inspector's mood and was peering at his watch in the impossibly dim porch light, trying to call to mind the train timetable.

'Never. It conveys live animals, so must be accessible at all times in case they need water or are in distress. There's nothing inside except a water trough.'

'Where was it?'

'We placed it by the cattle dock, as it's easier to get the hounds in and out there. We get so few beasts by rail at this time of year it was not a problem. Oh heavens...' A look of understanding started to creep across the stationmaster's face. 'You don't think that she...?'

'Where is the van now?'

'Lord Southampton wanted it taken back to Brackley Central. He thought they might bring the hounds in there; but the last I heard the van has just been shunted onto a siding and is still as yet unused. There has been far too much snow to get the dogs moved. Are you a follower, inspector? I do so like the hunt.'

'Not in the least.' Vignoles cut him off rather abruptly, his mind already running fast, processing the information and making connections. 'We're going down-line to Brackley now. Telephone ahead and tell them to leave that van alone. They must not touch it under any circumstances. It might be a crime scene.' Vignoles was already at the gate, 'and get a doctor to meet us there. And thank you, you've been most helpful.' He touched his hat brim and then he and Trinder walked quickly below the short overbridge and up the steps that brought them through a glazed wooden structure onto the centre of the island platform.

They hitched a ride on a passing freight train that stopped at their request, using the powers that Vignoles could invoke as detective inspector. The rattling box vans of the train were topped by snow and each was rimed and coated with a heavy frosting. They looked almost magical, with every groove and joint, handle and hinge picked out in pale whites and greys in the lamplight. Despite the rawness of the night and the grim purpose for their journey, Vignoles found something strangely beautiful in the sight.

Trinder gave Violet a quick hug on the platform whilst snow fell around them and a salute to Major Duffy, who was to continue operations at Finmere until instructed to stop. The sense of futility was increasing, but it was considered kinder to keep hope alive for as long as possible.

It was a short ride to Brackley Central, but it could not have passed quickly enough for both men; they sat on a hard wooden bench in the guard's van as close as they could to the roaring stove that was stoked with wood and a few precious lumps of steam coal. The guard said nothing, sensing the tension and foreboding. Both men sat and quietly chewed over the growing realisation that Miss Walentynowicz, with or without her assailant, had probably left Finmere in the hound van. Neither were imagining that she had made the journey willingly, or possibly even alive.

'We need an artist to sit with Beeby and get a likeness. We'll put an alert out the length of the line for a tallish, slim and possibly American, serviceman. It's a pretty poor description and probably covers the few thousand still over here, but it's all we've got right now.' Vignoles spoke quietly, his words inaudible to the guard because of the racket made by the train wheels.

Trinder nodded. 'He's struck twice in less than a month.' He contemplated lighting a cigarette.

'It's as if he's got the taste for death.' Vignoles was thinking aloud. 'Should we get everyone out there looking for him now? Maybe no publicity, so that we don't frighten him into hiding?' Vignoles looked through the little stove door at the brightly-blazing fire within, 'No, I believe we must warn the public. We owe that at least to every woman out there. Our first duty is to stop him striking again.'

'Women should not travel alone. Not on this line, anyway, whilst he's out there.' Trinder looked at Vignoles with a grim expression.

Vignoles felt his stomach turn as a sensation like icy fingers appeared to stir his insides. Anna would soon be going home. He had no means to phone her. He tried to keep his breathing calm. Both men fell silent as they absorbed the terrible threat that was stalking the line and thought about their own loved ones.

'The one small consolation is that he probably has gone to ground because of the weather. I think we're in for another blizzard and no one will be going anywhere. It might buy us time to get a strategy together and make that artist's impression.'

'Yes, we need that time.' Vignoles stood up as the train started to slow down in a series of sharp jerks and jarring squeals as the brakes started to bite on the wheels. 'We're here. I'm not sure if I want my hunch to be right or wrong.'

Stepping out of the guard's van they walked towards three men standing on the deserted platform, one of who was holding a paraffin lantern and wore a band on his arm identifying him as a goods overseer. The stationmaster was unmistakable in his long, dark overcoat and splendid top hat. He was standing ramrod straight, with gloved hands neatly folded behind his back in apparent defiance of the snow, which was already collecting in the brim of his topper and making his eyes smart. He was a man who was going to maintain a proper sense of order and discipline, whatever the weather threw at him. The third member of the group was a smallish man in a well-tailored coat and swaddled in a long knitted scarf of indeterminate colour that covered his chin and mouth, exposing only a red nose and a pair of horn-rimmed spectacles. One hand held his fedora tightly upon his head; a black leather doctor's bag was in the other.

After the briefest of nods and hellos and a grumbled demand from the unhappy doctor that they had 'better have a good reason' to call him out, they trudged through ankle-deep snow along the lengthy platform, heads bowed down against the night. The wind was whistling through some more Scots pines that occupied an elevated position above the running lines and made the telegraph wires sing and wail. Ahead was a yawing expanse of impenetrable blackness and driven snow that concealed the void made by the valley of the Great

Ouse (a remarkably small river despite its name and the wideness of the valley) and the long curving viaduct that their train had crossed only moments before. The station was exposed to the full brunt of the wind and all five men felt the cold like knives through their flesh. At the platform end, close to the huge, cylindrical tank on its solitary metal pillar used for watering the engines, they stepped down off the platform and crossed where a barrow walk lay, though now the tracks were just dark, parallel lines laid across an undulating surface of white with all form and detail obscured. There was no yard lighting and so the lantern proved its worth as they approached a short siding that held a solitary box van.

The wheels were already deeply embedded in snow, which was also collected upon every ledge and in every crevice. Vignoles needed no further assurance that the hound van was undisturbed. They walked up a softly-shaped incline so that they were level with the van doors. In happier times it would be easy to imagine the hounds crowding along this bank, tails wagging and yelps of excitement filling the air as they poured out of the van and down to the muster of men and women in their hunting pinks seated upon their stamping horses in the yard.

'I can assure you that, in accordance with your wishes, the van has not been touched.' The stationmaster had a resonant voice that was easily audible, despite the wind.

Vignoles just nodded whilst Trinder braced himself against the wooden planks as he pulled the heavy metal catch on the door. He heaved at the frozen metal, but the shiny smoothness of the ice that held it fast was clearly visible even in the dim light of the lantern.

'Here, have a go with this.' The goods overseer had stepped away whilst the sergeant was making his attempt upon the door and now returned, handing the lantern to the stationmaster and hefting a long-handled hammer that he had retrieved from somewhere close by. Trinder struggled to swing the heavy tool with accuracy, but managed two hefty clangs upon the frozen clasp and then gave the door and its hinges three mighty thumps, showering ice and snow onto the ground. A mighty heave and a shove and the door screeched open, only to become jammed again when halfway across. But it was sufficient for allow Trinder access. An aroma of straw and dogs filled the air.

'Hand me the lantern.' He rested one foot on the threshold that was white with lime wash, the other remaining on the ground as he leant forward. He extended his hand and the lantern into the dark void. A tense silence fell and, though Trinder's actions took but moments, it seemed to those gathered outside that time stood still. Each man was preoccupied with his own thoughts. Vignoles was struck by a powerful memory of standing in the ex-R.A.F. hut as the girl, her eyes flashing with fury, defiantly threw money onto the kitchen table. He knew that when the sergeant entered the van all hope would die of her being found alive. Vignoles almost wanted the door to remain closed and the dark secret inside to stay just that. Once that Pandora's box van was opened, then the hopes of so many would be shattered and Miss Walentynowicz's life would be at an end.

Trinder looked back over his shoulder and nodded. He then slowly stepped inside. The yellow flame of the lamp now filled the interior, making it glow in stark contrast to the dark exterior and the impenetrable night. It was an oddly beautiful scene, with large flakes of snow caught in a narrow band that illuminated the faces of the watchers. Vignoles, his senses now fully alert, was struck that it was like something by one of his favourite painters Joseph Wright of Derby: all strong contrasts and chiaroscuro, creating almost a latter-day nativity, but with an ugly and shocking twist.

He paused to take a gulp of fresh air before entering the pungent interior. The sight was as he had feared, but was still disturbing. The young woman looked asleep, though her skin was like the purest Chinese porcelain. In the light of day Vignoles was sure that it would have the same slight bluish tone beneath the white. Her limbs were sprawling, an arm resting over her eyes, as if their lantern had just awakened her from a deep and luxurious sleep. She looked almost beautiful. But only if one could forget that once she had been a living person, and neither man could.

A hot anger welled up inside Vignoles. Her coat, presumably the same one that Violet had so expertly made from a blanket, was opened beneath her body revealing a simple but well fitting dress that only partially concealed her perfectly formed legs.

Trinder thumped a fist against the van wall, hurting his knuckles, seeking the pain to help staunch the fury inside him. 'The bastard. The utter bastard! I hope he rots in hell! '

Vignoles turned and leant out of the van. 'Doctor? It will be academic, I fear, but we do require your assistance.' He turned back inside and stood still for a moment, rubbing the bridge of his nose in an attempt to control his own strong emotions, forcing himself to become detached and professional. 'I suppose there is no chance...?' He let the words hang, the sentence unfinished in the still air filled with the foetid stink of dog and urine. The doctor would only confirm the awful truth, and so Vignoles looked down at the straw around his heavy shoes. 'Search the floor for any clues of his presence.' His voice sounded harsh and too loud within the confines of the wagon.

Trinder looked at Vignoles with a faraway expression for a few moments, then nodded. Suspending the lantern upon a hook provided for just that purpose in the curved roof, Trinder crouched down to the left of the body and, with a gloved hand, started to sift through the straw. Vignoles did the same at the other end of the van to allow the doctor space to enter and kneel beside her.

'Any thoughts about how long she's been here?' Vignoles spoke as he brushed the straw aside.

'A fair while, I'd say. She's very cold to the touch. She's as good as frozen, poor thing. And I would say that she's been strangled, those marks on her throat are most disturbing.' The doctor was quietly professional in his manner, placing a stethoscope around his neck before commencing his examination. There was no urgency. 'It is hard for me to hazard a guess...' The doctor was gently touching the girl's wrist and looking at her fingertips, which were an ugly black. 'Frostbite? Now that is a surprise. Then...' and the doctor twisted his head upwards to stare towards Vignoles with a look of intense concentration upon his face.

'Doctor...?' Vignoles sensed something in his expression.

Without answering the question, the doctor quickly pulled open her blouse to expose a curve of breast visible beneath a thin woollen vest, his urgency causing him to abandon any sense of decorum, pressing his stethoscope to her milky-white chest. He shook his head, an action that communicated frustration rather than dismay, as he quickly reached into his bag and pulled out a small ladies' compact, flipping it open and holding the mirror it in front of her slightly parted lips.

'An old trick and still the best. I can't quite dare hope but I do believe... Dammit! Yes! She's alive — just! Quickly, I need blankets and an ambulance. Immediately! There's no time to waste.' He turned back to Kat, 'Come along now…stay with us.'

Trinder leapt to his feet and without a moment's hesitation dashed to the open door and barked orders to the men outside. His voice brooked no dissent and immediately the sound of booted feet could be heard running towards the station.

'If we can just get her to the cottage hospital then we might just save her, though I fear she is horribly weak.' The doctor was rubbing the girl's hands trying to coax some life into her frozen bloodstream whilst Vignoles was wrapping her coat around her and overlaying it with his own, Trinder's and the doctor's.

'She went missing between Tuesday night to Wednesday morning.' Vignoles looked at the doctor, a mixture of hope and fear in his eyes.

'So long ago? It's hardly possible. Her pulse is virtually nothing, just like a poor little bird.' The doctor was shaking his head, 'Hold on, hold on!'

Vignoles forced himself to wait a few moments before making an observation, 'Her undress and the way she is lying suggests that she has been sexually assaulted.'

'I fear you could be correct. If she does pull through, then I am afraid she will have other horrors to face.'

Vignoles closed his eyes momentarily and nodded. He looked away. Time that Kat surely could not afford passed like an age, the doctor doing what he could to coax life back into her ice-cold body, whilst Vignoles looked on, unable to focus on searching the van for clues to her attacker's identity until he could see her removed to the hospital. If she were to survive, then surely she would lead them straight to her assailant. But if she were to die now? How could he forgive himself for wasting so much time?

'Sir?'

Vignoles looked across as Trinder held aloft her handbag with bits of straw dropping from it.

'Looks like everything is still inside. Ration books, some money, rail and cinema tickets and more. It was not a robbery.'

'Nor Beeby's style, either. He prefers to keep such things.'

Both men look at each other, puzzling this realisation.

'Beeby claims that he has seen the man who did this, so he had better start talking and telling us what he really knows or, so help me God, if she dies I'll hold him responsible.' Vignoles spoke quietly but with controlled venom. The sound of the ringing ambulance bell could now be heard approaching followed by the crunch of its tyres upon the access road outside.

'He still might be guilty. He's a damned slippery character and I'm not completely convinced he's innocent.' Trinder watched as a wedge of blue light from the ambulance penetrated the van's interior, their breath coiling and swirling in its path as the sounds of the crew fetching a stretcher grew louder.

'Whoever it is, we'll get him, John. We'll hunt him down, mark my words we will.' The scent of hunting dog filling their nostrils added a piquancy to Vignoles's words that was not ironic.

Chapter Twenty-Six

'THE VERY THOUGHT OF YOU'
Al Bowlly with Ray Noble and his Orchestra

Charles and Anna Vignoles, together with John Trinder and Violet McIntyre, were seated around a table in the one-time ice cream parlour, now a bistro, owned by Anna's parents. The lack of fresh cream had forced a re-alignment of what the Carellis could offer until the supply situation improved, and it had proved a wise choice whilst the country was facing its worst winter since, as some put it, the retreat of the ice-age. Outside it was snowing, the power was off and there was almost nothing on the menu, but the place was still heaving. Thoughtfully, their table was slightly away from the noise and crush caused by extra tables squeezed into the already over-filled room.

'Everyone's buried under the snow or something these days.' Bepe Carelli was complaining. 'I can find almost nothing to cook. Is a big disaster, I tell you'.

But this was not going to stop the Leicester Friday-nighters in their desire for entertainment. These setbacks were no longer seen as such, they were just the normal irritations of daily life and there was little to do but shrug them off, maintain a stiff upper lip and 'get on with it'. And since the outbreak of peace and the long drawn out suffocation of austerity living, there had been an unstoppable rush of people wanting to do just that and get on, go out and live a little.

So, across the land as the evening started, women were reaching for the same 'best dress' that they had been making do with since about 1943 and choosing a newly home-made brooch of painted, dried seed-heads, folded felt and glass-headed pins to go with a crocheted shoulder bag and trying on a hat dextrously constructed from a piece of Axminster carpet and two pheasant feathers picked up on a walk in the woods. They were fretting that their poorly-made, wooden-soled shoes would be ruined by the snow, whilst men were buffing-up the same pair they'd had since the fall of Monte Cassino and had few concerns about their waists fitting into that ancient best suit that reeked of camphor in the back of the wardrobe, as the continual, nagging hunger ensured that braces and an even tighter belt were all that was needed.

The cinemas were just as full, regardless of the programme; the dancehalls thronged and the pubs sold beer as if it were going out of fashion. At least the chancellor, Stafford Cripps, had not rationed that yet. The restaurants had waiting lists for tables where guests could sit and dream of abundant food and long menus, then settle for the one set meal of meagre proportions. And so, Carelli's was crowded and filled by the hubbub of chattering and laughing and the sound of a classic Al Bowlly coming from a massive radiogram in one corner, whilst a thick fug of blue cigarette and pipe smoke hung in the air, gently illuminated by candles in empty wine bottles placed upon each table. The candles suited the evening, whereas they were a serious inconvenience during the working week in gloomy offices and shops.

The table booked by Mr Vignoles boasted two such empty wine bottles. They had started the evening with only the one and its candle, but after finishing off a splendid Bordeaux, the ever-resourceful Violet had produced a spare candle from her handbag and boosted the illumination using the empty. Another bottle, this time a Chianti that had been especially held back by Bepe Carelli, was already half empty and rapidly putting itself forward as a candidate for a further candle. The table was now cleared after they had eaten a spaghetti putaneasca that had been a triumph of how to make practically no ingredients go a long way, though the conversation, as inevitably all conversations had a habit of doing during these times of want, returned to food.

'When did I last have such a tasty meal? It had real flavour.' Violet was smiling.

'I'd forgotten I had taste buds,' Trinder concurred.

'The anchovies in the sauce really give it a kick. And they're not rationed,' Anna replied.

'Anchovies? Then that was the best use ever of those little scallywags!'

'John, what a thing to say.' Violet gave Trinder a look.

'Well I'm not a great one for the anchovy, as a rule. And you have to admit that they can be salty little blighters.' Trinder laughed. 'But if they add flavour like that, then I'll happily review my feelings about them.'

'Whereas I shall not be reviewing my distaste for whale meat, dolphin and, of course, the most odious thing to ever swim in the seven seas...'

'...SNOEK!' Everyone chorused the name in response to Vignoles's prompt. They all collapsed in laughter.

'But really, where did they find that fish? It's just inedible. Quite appalling.' Vignoles then looked at Anna, 'Even your parents couldn't work their magic with that.'

Anna shook her head, smiling as she did so. 'True, very true. Oh Maria, my poor Mama. You should have seen her face when I first brought some home. I thought she was going to get on the next boat back to Italy.'

'I hear that it makes good cat food...' Trinder chimed in.

'And good fishing bait,' added Violet, surprising everyone with her knowledge of angling matters. 'But hang the snoek, how do your parents manage to make such ripping food? They work miracles. I study all the pamphlets and listen to the radio advice shows, but I can't seem to get flavour into anything I make.' Violet shook her head in admiration.

'Anna's parents do have a way. They seem to find a solution to every food crisis and get their hands on choice ingredients. Though,' he glanced at his wife, 'I find it best to just enjoy and not ask too many questions about how exactly they manage this.'

'Eh, what are you saying? They just have the scent for food, that's all'.

'Like a pair of truffle-hounds', interjected Vignoles.

Everyone laughed. 'You're not far off the mark there.' Anna was smiling proudly, 'Though I suggest you don't let your mother-in-law hear you call her that!' Vignoles raised his hands in a gesture of surrender as his wife continued. 'They just know how to find a little something here or there, and then they get a parcel or two sent from home. And Papa is becoming quite adept with his shotgun in the woods, as you will find out with the next course.'

'I shall drink to that and ask no questions.' Trinder lifted his glass and the others joined him.

'And I think you men can forget about being detectives for a while. I sense that you'll be investigating the kitchen any moment.' Violet smiled good-naturedly at Vignoles.

'Hear hear.' Anna chinked her glass against Violet's.

The main course was a roast wild duck that had been shot by her father. It didn't stretch far between the four, but it was again packed with flavour and all agreed that they were feeling something that approximated towards being full.

'And I happen to know…' Anna leant forward, her eyes wide wonder, and she spoke in a soft, and exaggerated stage whisper, '… and I really do not know how on earth they managed it, but we have a very special sweet to follow: a cassata. We must all be a bit hush-hush about it though, as they made it especially just for Vi and John. In their honour. A taste of real Italy, but absolutely not enough to go around the whole place. They all have to make do with cold tinned peaches.' Everyone nodded in agreement that they would help keep the guilty secret. 'You may not be familiar with cassata, but trust me, you'll love it.'

'A cake? Divine…' Violet closed her eyes in anticipation.

'They are spoiling us.' Trinder was patting his stomach.

'But I'm sure I can't manage anything more.' Violet's gentle exaggeration was received gratefully by Anna. At a time when everyone was used to a continual hunger it was a compliment indeed.

'It's rather smaller than she would normally make. And Mama says it falls short of her standards and is nervous that we shan't like it, but I think we have nothing to fear.'

Vignoles sat back in his chair and took a sip of wine, 'and Bepe has promised that he has a half bottle of desert wine to accompany it.'

'Dear me, I shall be quite tipsy.' Violet placed a hand to her mouth.

'Perhaps we all shall, but I think we can afford to let ourselves go, just once in a while. This is an occasion to push the boat out. We've had far too few reasons to celebrate anything recently and it does one the power of good to kick back for an evening.'

'I don't think our gloomy chancellor of the exchequer would agree. He'd have us living off dog biscuits and cold water.'

'But they're served with the coffee.' Anna looked serious.

'Gosh, really?' Violet looked shocked, but then joined in the laughter when she realised that Anna was joking.

'Haha! But even more important than this good food is the reason that we are here this evening. It's not every day that my sergeant gets engaged to be married to — I really must say — such a charming and attractive young woman.' Anna clapped her hands together at her husband's words and Violet blushed.

'I just regret we've had no time to buy a ring yet. It was all a bit sudden, in a way.'

'Time enough for that, John. You can do so just as soon as we can get to London for the day.'

'Another toast. We cannot have too many tonight. Are your glasses charged? To Violet and John. May you have every happiness together and may you not wait too long to tie the knot.'

'And find a nice new home to live in,' Anna added.

'Thank you. That is very kind. Though we might need all the luck we can with that last wish.' Violet blushed again as Trinder placed a light kiss upon her cheek and rested his hand upon hers. 'It is good to have your approval. It means everything.'

'Approval? But of course. John is a very lucky man.' Vignoles sat back again in his chair and looked across at Trinder whilst Anna looked over the rim of her glass at Violet, her eyes sparkling with something that she hoped looked like approval.

'Thank you, sir...um, Charles.' Trinder reached for a cigarette to cover his embarrassment; he was not quite used to the informality of the situation nor was he yet quite accustomed to his emotional attachment to Violet being so openly considered, although he was obviously filled with pride.

Violet looked thoughtful as a cloud appeared to cross her face and her eyes reflected the candle light with a limpid quality that might just have been caused by the cigarette smoke. 'I do so hope getting engaged and married will improve my relationship with the villagers. Some of them don't exactly approve of me at the moment.' She emphasised the word.

'Well, you are amongst friends here.' Anna reached across the table for Violet's other hand.

'Thank you. I wish others could see beyond the rules and regulations of how we are supposed to run our lives and judge the person beneath for who she actually is.'

'Hmm. But I do think things are changing.' Vignoles sensed the mood and spoke quietly so that the group of loud Wrens on the table nearby would not overhear. 'We indeed live in a time increasingly obsessed by rules and regulations, and instructions and do's and don'ts and goodness knows what else, but despite all this controlling and nannying, the war has had a profound effect upon us all. And we have not seen the half of it yet. Attitudes are shifting and society is changing.'

'A Brave New World?' Trinder added.

'So our government hopes, though it's taking a time to

show its brave new face. But I'm thinking more about the shocks and knocks that life has dealt us all. The men returning home from the war have seen and done things that will have an impact. A lot of it will be pretty hard to bear and difficult for them. And society will have to adjust here to cope with their state of mind. Now we, the common working men and women, are all looking for changes and improvements to society and it is coming.'

'You're right. We've all had to change the way we work and how we live our lives. I admit that I am perhaps a bit more...' Anna paused and considered her choice of words, '...open-minded now. I can take life as it actually is, rather than just judge it according to how I was taught it was supposed to be.'

'You've changed your ideas so much?' Violet asked.

'Oh yes. Please don't take this wrongly, as I simply adore you, Vi, and you are amongst friends; but before the war, I suppose I might have thought...' Anna paused a moment, 'Yes, I confess, I too would have judged you rather harshly — like maybe some of the villagers still do? My beliefs would not have given me space and time to understand your situation, nor see you as the person you are.'

Violet nodded sadly. 'It's amazing the scorn that my position can induce.'

'But things change. We've witnessed all manner of horrors and one can't help but look at life differently. And one stops and wonders if all the silly rules really mean anything nowadays. A mother without a husband? It seems trivial compared to... well, to those hateful death camps we read about. And there are many thousands of mothers without husbands now, whatever the reasons might be for that situation. And so I made the decision that I could afford to be less judgemental. And I believe it makes me a better Christian, too, whatever my church might say.'

'But in a small town it'll just take a bit longer. The war largely passed Woodford by. People have not been forced to review their ways of thinking as many others have been.' Vignoles spoke softly and, he hoped, kindly. 'Right now people are more worried about where the next sack of coal is coming from than anything else.' He tried to lift the mood, and it provoked Anna into shooting her husband a reproachful glance. The log pile had diminished considerably and they were fast contemplating a frozen house.

'And it will change, starting from now. If I hear anyone slighting you, then they'll have me to answer to.' Trinder squeezed Violet's hand.

Violet nodded. 'And they are decent people, really. I think coping on my own for so long sometimes gets me down, though I know that I should not be so self-pitying. There are plenty worse off than I am. I'm just happy that we all survived the war. Well, nearly all of us.' Violet was thinking of her father; killed whilst working for the Civil Defence Corps by an incendiary attack upon Leicester in 1941.

They all fell silent for a few moments, the wine encouraging a gentle melancholy to seep into the dark shadows around the room. It was a perfect moment for Mrs Carelli to arrive with the trumpeted cassata, conveyed into the room under wraps and laid quietly upon the table so as not to encourage envious looks from the other diners. Their almost illicit indulgence was safe however, as the table of demob-happy Wrens was cracking open a bottle of champagne whilst laughing and chattering so merrily they were unlikely to notice much beyond their own table.

After suitable expressions of admiration had been exchanged and the cake thoroughly demolished the conversation shifted, as inevitably it always going to, towards police work. Vignoles was doing his utmost that evening to push aside thoughts of the — as yet unsuccessful — manhunt, and of the poor Polish girl lying in a coma and on the edge of death in a hospital in Banbury. She might pull through yet, and this thought encouraged him, but unless she awakened and was in a state to talk it was up to him to find the man who had done this wicked deed. But he needed a night off, as did Trinder. He knew that his tired mind would find renewed energy in the morning, and maybe he might make that big breakthrough in the case. But despite his need for a mental rest, he found that, sitting opposite his sergeant, he just could not help canvass his opinion on police matters.

He was prompted to do so by Anna, who had steered the conversation in that direction because her curiosity was piqued about a problem that, as far as she was aware, had not yet been resolved; namely that of the van laden with coal lying at the bottom of Ruddington Water.

'It seems an awful waste to just leave it lying there under the lake.'

'It's not just lying there, Anna; it's a devil of a job to get it from out under the ice and water. We've scratched our heads for a while over this one, haven't we, John?'

'Oh yes. The army boys are eager to give it a crack, but they're just too busy clearing roads and railways to get essential supplies out and about to have the time. The local civvies are also too busy, and anyway they didn't seem to have much of an idea. The problem is how to attach a rope to the van.'

'There must be a way. You can solve that, I'm quite sure.'

'I think I can muster up the use of a heavy army lorry to drag it out, but we'll also need a small boat.'

'An icebreaker, almost.' Vignoles added.

'Exactly. So I think we must wait for it to melt,' continued Trinder.

'But that could take weeks. The way this winter is going it could even be months.' Anna had really got her teeth into the matter. 'And how much coal is down there? It's criminal to leave it there.'

'Haha, it certainly is criminal, my dear.' Vignoles was lighting his pipe. 'The gang has tried to play down the quantities, but the two lads who hid in the back reckoned about ten or twelve full sacks.' Everyone fell silent and mentally considered the much-needed warmth such a glut could provide. Vignoles looked up from his pipe to see both Anna and Violet looking at him with bright, expectant faces. 'Oh no, if you are thinking what I think you are, then you just stop!' Vignoles shook his head. 'That is simply not an option.'

'But we all need fuel almost more than we need food right now.'

'It's stolen property and crown evidence.'

'And when do they appear in court?'

'Ah. Hum. Well, they already have...' Vignoles hesitated.

'And did the coal make an appearance in court?' Anna's eyes flashed and she gave a wicked grin.

'We offered as evidence the sack of coal obtained in a transaction that one of the uniforms managed to obtain when he was working undercover — though, of course, it didn't actually come into court and give testimony.' Trinder kept his voice free of any expression. He was just stating fact, though his eyes were twinkling.

'You do realise that you are plotting to commit a crime? I really cannot be party to this. I'll hear no more.' Vignoles was laughing but had a serious edge to his voice.

'One could share it equally amongst your department. I can't really see how that is so wrong.' Violet added her contribution.

'Or even sell it. No one suggested that it should be free. You could raise funds for the Police Benevolent Fund.' Anna gave Vignoles her most persuasive look.

'I'm not sure. Though we do need to recover that van before too very long. Enough. I am beginning to feel decidedly uncomfortable.'

Anna winked at Violet, but aimed her comment at her husband and Trinder. 'I'm not trying to turn you both into racketeers, but it's just that it would answer a pressing need.'

Vignoles just puffed upon his pipe and gave his wife a sidelong glance. A tray with a coffee pot and four tiny cups was placed upon the table at that moment, and whilst Anna busied herself pouring and adding a dash of milk from a tiny creamer he held the bowl of his pipe and stared at the ceiling with a look of concentration upon his face.

'Thinking how to effect the recovery?' Trinder asked the question.

'No. It's something else that has been lurking at the back of my mind for days. I just can't quite catch onto it. Something that Anna said has stirred it up. About the spivs.'

'What about them? They're everywhere and they annoy the hell out of me; though they sometimes have their uses, if one is brutally honest.' Trinder looked at Vignoles who continued to puff upon his pipe, nodding sympathetically.

'I really don't like them. But they've at least allowed us a few luxuries. Life is just so...' Anna paused, '...barren without some things.' She spoke softly, not wanting to broadcast her shady dealings with the underworld.

Violet nodded. 'I confess that at times I am so desperate for cloth I'll do anything. And the official suppliers just tie me in knots with their rules and regulations, forms and coupons — they really drive me so mad at times that often I cannot supply my customers unless... Well, I expect you know what. Oh dear. What a dreadful confession.' She looked guiltily at Trinder. 'I think the wine has quite gone to my head and I'm in danger of making a complete fool of myself.' She coloured and looked at the tablecloth.

Trinder just waved her worries away. 'Don't worry. Not our jurisdiction.' He laughed and Vignoles joined in. 'If we are really frank about it we're all just a little guilty of such moments. I cannot pretend that sometimes an offer of some cigarettes or a few sausages comes my way and I reckon that it can't do so much harm...' He let it tail away. 'It's this rotten austerity that's doing it. I'm getting wholeheartedly tired of the endless lack of everything.'

'When will it all end?' Anna asked, rhetorically.

'We all need to live a little.' Trinder paused. 'Though I might just have placed myself on a charge admitting I have had such dealings.' He made a grimace towards Vignoles.

'Fear not. I too am not wholly free of such exchanges, grubby though they are.' Anna stared at her husband and with her fingertips felt the smoothness of the stockings she was wearing beneath her dress, a slight smile formed at the corner of her mouth. 'I'm not proud of myself either. But as you say, sometimes it meets a need. Oh. But wait a minute...that's triggered a memory...' They all looked at Vignoles, sensing that something was preying upon his mind. He toyed with his pipe. 'This tobacco I'm smoking. It's pretty poor stuff and a bit like old dried hedgerow, but y'know, it's all I could find in the tobacconists opposite Central station.' Everyone nodded sympathetically but wondered where this was leading. 'But last week I smoked my last pipe of a rather fine Virginia. Lovely quality and pretty hard to find, and yes, I bought it on the black.'

Anna grinned. 'So you are human? Thank goodness.' A slight relaxing could be sensed around the table, an unloosening of tension as the fellow confessors realised that Vignoles no longer inhabited the highest of moral grounds.

'Of course. But proving my weakness is not the reason for saying this. John? Do you remember I asked you about what brand of cigarettes you smoked?'

'Indeed. Black Cats.' He opened the pack on the table before him to illustrate the point, offering one to Violet and Anna. Violet accepted but Anna politely declined. 'What's this about?'

'The cigarettes we found at Finmere — in the fire bucket. They were American.'

'Yes, Lucky Strikes.'

'And were they not the same brand that you found in some quantity at the Walentynowiczes' place?

'They were.'

'And I seem to recall that Kat said her father bought them off the Yanks.'

'Correct.'

'But what did she say, exactly? I've racked my brains and it's gone. But I sense it's important.'

'She said something about "buying from the American servicemen who would sell anything", but altered that to suggest that it was just someone in particular. Yes... someone who was quite friendly, I think she might have even said that he was "nice". But what is this leading to?'

'A smooth-talking American, wheeling and dealing and being "nice" to girls?'

'Oh, wait a minute. You don't think that he could be the killer? The Yankee spiv?'

'Why not? He had gained Miss Walentynowicz's confidence. He had been "kind" and whatever else to her, and to her friends and family. So she would not be immediately aware that he was a threat. Could he have talked her into sharing a smoke outside the waiting room, then coaxed her inside and moved in for the kill? Or something along those lines.'

'Oh, God. Poor thing.' Violet closed her eyes. 'I just pray that Kat pulls through. But she's still terribly ill, isn't she?'

'Yes. The doctors remain positive, though she's making awfully slow progress. She was starved of oxygen to the brain and then nearly frozen to death. She has suffered frost bite and might lose some toes.' Violet grimaced. Anna reached across and put her hand over Violet's. 'But she is still alive. As the two women spoke, Trinder was nodding vigorously, having considered Vignoles's scenario. 'Yes. It makes sense. Beeby said that we needed to look for a man in U.S.A.F. uniform. It all fits. This American spiv secured the confidence of the Poles at the camp and became a familiar figure around the place, coming and going at odd times of the day, so his presence would not seem strange or particularly memorable.'

'People often fail to notice the familiar,' Anna added.

'And skulking around at odd hours was exactly how they were used to seeing him, so even if they did catch a sight of him, it would hardly attract attention.' Trinder was nodding.

'Which might explain why no one has come forward with a sighting at Finmere station that night.' Anna was suddenly leaning forward and speaking quickly.

'Don't forget that it was also dark and snowing and such a spiv is adept at not being observed.' Violet was breathing slowly and deeply, but knew that she needed to override her emotions and concentrate. If she was going to be a policeman's wife, then she had better start getting used to uncomfortable situations. 'I bet he's also very adept at evading ticket collectors, stationmasters and...'

'...Policemen.' Trinder added with a note of irony in his voice.

Vignoles was nodding. 'But there's more to it than that. I've remembered it all now, it's as if this conversation has broken a dream: I bought that Virginia tobacco from a smooth-talking and actually quite personable American airman on a train ride to Nottingham. We even fell into a short conversation. He was smoking Lucky Strikes.'

'That's him. It's just got to be.'

'Yes, John. I rather fear it might be. He was right in front of me and I could have arrested him on the spot. He didn't just evade the detective department, he sold its top detective some pipe tobacco.' Vignoles spoke with contempt in his voice. 'I even let him go free. I considered nabbing him as we both got off the train at Nottingham Vic. What a fool I am.'

'But he has to be caught for more than black-marketeering. He'd just have got a caution and wriggled away on some slippery bit of legal finessing, and then what?' Anna sought to reassure her husband.

'True.' He nodded sadly, 'But would it have prevented him attacking again?'

'How were you to know at that moment?'

Vignoles nodded at Anna. 'I appreciate the sentiment but it will haunt me nonetheless. And to think I smoked that killer's tobacco. It quite turns my stomach.' He held his pipe and looked at it with some sadness, his enjoyment for the time being spoiled. He certainly didn't have the heart to mention the stockings that Anna was wearing, and to a rather ravishing effect. That was now an unpleasantly inappropriate word. He would have to try to disassociate these from what had happened to the two women, though he wondered if he would be able to do so. It was perhaps a relief that they had indulged in mutually appreciating the glorious effect of Anna in her new stockings before they had left the house that evening and not waited until afterwards.

'We can get him now. That's what matters. You even know what he looks like. And if Kat pulls through, she can ensure that he hangs and we've saved at least one life.' Trinder leant forward in his seat, eyes bright and eager. The two women exchanged glances, Anna, already used to the trials of being the wife of a detective, raised an eyebrow and Violet responded in kind.

'You're right. Now I am allowing myself to become self-pitying.' Vignoles pulled himself upright in his chair, adrenaline flowing through his veins. 'I need to call our artist friend. He and I can improve upon that likeness he made with Beeby. There was something about that artist's impression that seemed vaguely familiar.' Vignoles was nodding as he was speaking. 'Yes. Beeby was not so far off the mark, but I can sharpen up that likeness. We need the picture out there for all to see, as quickly as we can.' He looked at his wristwatch. 'Do artists sit at home on a Friday night?'

'Probably freezing in his garret with his starving girlfriend.' Anna tried a joke.

'Burning his last chair to stay warm like they do in *La Bohème*,' added Violet.

Vignoles smiled briefly and a twinge of guilt stung him as he acknowledged that work was again intruding into his private life, but already he was past the tipping point and he was impatient to move this along. 'I have his telephone number here.' Vignoles was searching through his notebook as he was speaking, 'Ladies, if you will excuse me?'

The evening's frivolities and celebrations suddenly drew to a close.

Chapter Twenty-Seven

'Better Think Twice'

Carol Gibbons & the Savoy Hotel Orpheans

Eddie was feeling down in the dumps. His usual ebullient and cheerful nature was subdued by the combined forces of the never-ending snow, persistent wind and insidious cold that sapped his strength and no amount of standing close to the incandescent heat of the firebox seemed to truly banish it. From the moment he stepped away and climbed down the treacherous steps of his locomotive the cold was back, sucking away any residual heat that he had stored up and, by the time he was swinging the heavy canvas bag of the water column into place and shaken free the many icicles that dropped like crystal daggers to the ground and fought to turn the frozen handle to open the rush of water, he was cold again to his very core. Clambering over locomotives was now a trial, as so much of the machine was now either profoundly cold or painfully hot to touch, constantly inflaming his chilblained hands, whilst each precarious foothold was glassy and insecure. The coal in the bunker was solid and buried beneath feet of snow, all of which needed shovelling away before he could start to smash the mass apart to create a dusty heap of small pieces that did him few favours with his firing.

But, as he leant out of the cab of his diminutive J72 tank loco, waiting for the shunter to raise his hand to signal them forward for another manoeuvre as they cut and re-assembled the vans and wagons in the north yard at Woodford Halse, it was not the cold that was most prominent in his thoughts. What was getting to Eddie and dampening his spirits was the memory of the humiliation that had been the consequence of his and Simon's escapade in the back of the van.

It had been quite the very best adventure ever at the time and initially they had both been filled with a heady mixture of excitement and terror, the adrenaline rushing through their veins and making their hearts pound. Even after their dramatic rescue, whilst they travelled to a nearby farm huddled in an open trailer, they were still exchanging grins and playful prods on each other's arms as they sought to express their enjoyment of the whole adventure. Even the women police officers did not seem excessively put out and were most civil towards them, expressing concern for their well-being.

They lapped up the contact with the two good-looking officers and felt self-important and special, perhaps even crucial to the solving of the case.

These foolish feelings were soon replaced, however, by an abrupt change of mood when they returned to Leicester and were questioned by a furious and cynical sergeant: a man called Trinder. He seemed to find nothing relevant, useful, interesting, brave or intelligent in any of their actions. He rather seemed to want to bawl them out about their 'gross stupidity' and continually harped on about how 'they could have got themselves killed'. When Simon had tried to suggest that they had tracked down the robbers and were on the way towards solving the crime, he had been laughed into a humiliating silence. The sergeant then proceeded to demolish their argument and remind them that they had been impotent fugitives hidden in the back of a van, very nearly crushed by sacks of coal and close to drowning. Rescuing them had been an extra burden upon the police, who, Trinder had made of point of reminding them for perhaps the tenth time, were the ones who had given chase, made the arrests, effected the rescue and got them all safely back home.

Reluctantly, Eddie had to concede that the sergeant was probably right on all counts. He came in for particular criticism when it transpired that he had withheld potentially important information from the police. The fact that he had been manhandled and roughed up by a uniformed officer seemed to cut no ice, and he was forced to concede this point as well.

They both got off with a caution and a clip around the ear by a burly policeman — quite possibly the same one who had arrested him — followed by a sternly worded warning that they had 'better keep their noses out of police affairs from now on or else they'd get far worse!' But this had not been the end of it. Both sets of parents compounded the misery with more angry words and raised voices. That was to be expected and both he and Simon had steeled themselves to ride the storm and looked forward to getting back to work and keeping their heads down for a while. Unfortunately they had not factored in that their employer would also have something to say about the whole sorry affair. A day's wages stopped for time lost being interviewed by the railway police and more words from the shedmaster himself. Mr Saunders had made it clear that they were back on the 'bottom rung of the ladder' of promotion and 'lucky that he didn't just throw them both out, there and then'. They were then given more than their fair share of the most unpleasant jobs and placed on firing duties only when — with obvious reluctance — the shedmaster was short on crews and had to call upon their services to work the shunting engines. No more snowplough duties, pick-up goods and local passenger turns for the foreseeable future. And so, they were placed upon on a daily diet of boiler washing, ashing out and clinker breaking, ash pit emptying and then scraping layers of caked grease and muck and ice from the many connecting rods and virtually inaccessible linkages between the wheels and frames of the locomotives. Only then were they rewarded by a half day's shunting the vast Woodford north yard.

Eddie felt the winter days pass slowly, each filled with the hope for a break in the weather and the return of sunlight and warmth, which would at least make these tasks feel less arduous. But it was not to be. The sky above was, as it so often had been that February, a leaden grey and the wind whistled in from the east across the Fens and straight through his fireman's reefer jacket, overalls, shirt and two vests, all of which had not been washed in many days, for it was almost impossible to get anything properly dry, and dirty seemed preferable to damp.

He reached into the cab and opened the firedoors, allowing a little more heat around his legs; he had plenty of steam and he and the driver were going to be doing little else but shuttle back and forth all day. He then returned to his sentry position leaning out of the cab and nodded to his driver that they had the signal to ease forward.

The driver opened the drain cocks and the little engine snorted steam from beneath its front buffer beam like a dragon, and as the regulator handle was pushed across and then gently eased back, the locomotive breathed, sighed and huffed with a soft, gentle sound, throwing a pillow of steam into the wind, only for it to be pushed ahead and away. The engine slowly chugged forwards, setting off a chain reaction of clattering and banging, punctuated by short screeches of frozen metal complaining, as about half of the train of vans followed behind. Eddie was looking towards the tail of the train, watching for when they passed the lever that controlled the points the shunter would then throw to allow them to back down onto an adjacent road and offer up this selection of vans to those waiting. Backwards and forwards, up and down the parallel lines of sidings, picking up and setting down different combinations of vans and wagons to create trains to be pulled away by the big freight engines to exotic places like Birkenhead or Grimsby, London or Sheffield. Anywhere other than Woodford yard on a bitter winter's afternoon.

As they moved forwards, Eddie glanced across at the huddle of buildings at the north end of the yard, now blanketed by layers of nearly pristine snow. These buildings had been built sometime just before the war for the use of the shunters and crews working this distant part of the yard. They were mess rooms, stores and a place for the yard supervisor to have an office. The railway company, in a rare fit of concern, had deemed the walk back to the 'loco' — as they all called the engine shed and the ramshackle group of dumped carriages, van bodies, wooden sheds, lean-tos and other buildings used by the many railwaymen working at Woodford — as too far for them. But no one had consulted them, of course, and they actually preferred to walk back or hitch a ride on a brake van or flat wagon and join the rest of the gang in their filthy gathering places. They didn't want to be stuck out on a limb, forgotten and out of the way. It wasn't how they were and it wasn't how they worked. And so the buildings had never been used. Abandoned and yet untouched. No one even bothered to look through the windows. Occasionally a railwayman might nip to one side to pee against the wall, but that was it. Why even bother to enter the building and find the toilet? Just use the wall.

So it was unsurprising that Eddie had been mildly intrigued when, the week previously, he had caught a fleeting glimpse of someone ducking into a doorway as he passed on a rare shunting turn. He had seen little more than a flash of a coat tail and a flick of a booted foot, but he was sure that a man had darted inside. He could not have said exactly why, but Eddie sensed that the man was responding to the engine approaching. Had it made the man jump or was he evading being seen?

Eddie had decided that this was just his foolish inquisitiveness getting the better of him. Curiosity had nearly killed them, never mind the cat, and he was not going to entertain the idea that this was of any importance. It was almost certainly a railwayman wanting a piss. So the man went inside? It was cold. Eddie didn't even bother to mention this to Simon nor note it in one of his spotting books. No, he was well and truly off detective work.

But the strange thing was that, early one afternoon a couple of days later, when the shedmaster surprised Eddie by putting him on firing duties again, he noticed another set of tracks leading to the same door, and caught a clear view of a man having a smoke standing at one of the windows, his face illuminated by the reflected light from the snow. The man had stepped backwards into the blue shadows, again acting as though he were evading detection. But Eddie had seen him and their eyes had met. Why had he stepped back and not acknowledged him? Railwaymen were long accustomed to lifting a hand in greeting from the lineside; it was instilled into them as a basic safety requirement that they raise a hand to acknowledge that they had both seen the approach of a train. Even if they were well clear of danger, as this man had been, it was still a common courtesy to acknowledge each other with a wave, a touch to the peak of a cap or just a slight nod of the head; it was part of being in the 'family' that was the railway.

Eddie sensed that this was the same man he had glimpsed before. He was wearing the wrong sort of clothes to be a railwayman, yet he was too clean-shaven, neat and tidy to be a vagrant sleeping rough. Everything about this sighting would normally have excited Eddie's native curiosity and filled his veins with a thrill of intrigue, but he still held his tongue.

As his engine travelled back along the head shunt, he did contemplate mentioning the stranger to his driver, but changed his mind. He was an aggressive little man and not one of Eddie's favourites; he had long since made it clear that messing around with the police was not the way he felt that someone who shared his footplate should behave. Eddie and Simon's escapades were common knowledge around the loco and they were getting used to comments being made, some far from complimentary. So Eddie kept quiet, fearing that he would just invite more scorn and the story might get back to the shedmaster, further damaging what little prospects he might still have.

But today, no amount of effort on his part could stop the sudden rush of adrenaline that hit him like a bad shunting manoeuvre, when, as they slowed to a halt to await permission to set back, he saw the man yet again. It was definitely him. Three times in the same place? This went beyond the simple explanations of a call of nature or a furtive cigarette break. Now Eddie's mind was racing and his senses were on full alert. He had to admit he was glad to have an excuse to no longer suppress his curiosity; now he realised that he had stumbled upon something genuinely strange.

As they had passed the buildings with their line of wagons, Eddie had been trying to fool himself that he had not wanted to look across at the empty buildings to seek the trail of footprints to the door, half hoping that he would see nothing and that the buildings would remain still and silent and unloved. But the other half was seeking any indication of life within, and so it was that his eye caught a tiny movement inside — more of a suggestion of a presence. Eddie only saw this because he knew to look intently into the darkened windows and so caught the shadowy shape move through the gloom like a phantom. But he knew that this was no ghost, no trick of light and shade, but real flesh and blood. He had to have a closer look now that his investigative instincts had kicked in. If only Simon were here to join him.

He could not immediately leave the engine, but as they rumbled and puffed backwards and forwards down the sidings he kept a beady watch upon the buildings for any further signs of life, but saw no other movements. And so, twenty minutes later, when his driver had said the one simple word 'tea' and wound the handbrake on, Eddie took the opportunity to not walk back towards the shed, as his driver and the shunters were doing. Instead, he put the injector on for a few moments to top up the boiler, gave the fire a gentle rake to dampen it down a little, lifted his near-empty enamelled tea can from the metal shelf above the firebox doors and dropped down the cab steps. In answer to his driver's backwards look, he raised his mug in a gesture that suggested that he would mind the engine and drink his tea there, then watched as he walked away between the long lines of coal wagons. Eddie put his tea can down and carefully approached the disused buildings.

He had explored these some years previously, one hot summer's day during the war, when he and Simon had wanted to nose around to see if any enemy parachutists had set up a base camp inside. The memory of this adventure came flooding back and he was feeling a sensation of mounting excitement as he drew closer, scrunching up to knee level with each step he took in the virgin snow. He'd actually found a real parachutist, though the man was unlikely to be a German, more likely a sinister Soviet spy. He knew nothing about Soviet spies, but was pretty sure that observation rather than confrontation would be the best policy, because — and Eddie allowed the realisation to sink in — the man might be dangerous. He paused to consider this possibility, standing stock still in a sea of white. Perhaps he should turn back and tell the others about what he'd seen? Nah. That would be just flunking out of the very adventure he and Simon had waited the whole war to have.

And so he waded forwards until he was up hard against the back wall of the building. He edged around the corner and looked along the wall that had been concealed from his vantage point upon the footplate of the engine. There were more footsteps in the snow here, though perhaps not as many as he might have expected. If the man was coming and going frequently then he would surely have trampled the snow more thoroughly, but instead there was just the one deep and ragged line of prints leading to a side door. Eddie smiled to himself. The spy was clever, for he was stepping into the same footprints each time he came and went, thereby reducing his presence to just one trail, which might easily be ignored or explained away.

Eddie edged closer, keeping close to the wall and stopping just short of the first metal-framed window, and then bent his knees so that his eyes were level with the cill. He slowly peered around and into the room. It was dark, made all the more so by the effect of the brightness of the snow on his eyes and the bright whiteness of the windows on the opposite wall. But slowly his sight readjusted until he could discern shapes within that resolved into a table and chairs, a pile of clothes, a couple of suitcases and a military-style truckle bed with blankets. Someone was living here, of that there was no doubt.

He pulled himself back and thought for a moment. What to do? He felt a wave of nerves flood over him. Should he just advise Mr Saunders of the matter and let the proper authorities investigate? All common sense said that this was the obvious course of action. But who was this man? He did not appear to be damaging the building and, as the L.N.E.R. didn't want the place, why care? But the clothes, the neatness and order that were immediately apparent were most curious. Perhaps it was best that he got a better look at the occupant and then made a decision.

Crouching low, he stumbled forward below the level of the windows until he drew close to the door. His heart was beating fast and he realised that he could do with the courage gained from having Simon close by. Never mind, this was now a solo expedition and he must carry out his duties and report back to HQ.

He listened but could hear nothing from within, the only sounds were those ever-present from the shed: the booming thunder of the coaling tower tippling its wagonloads of coal, the clangs and ringing hammerings and the clatterings and drillings from the workshops and the many toots, crows, whistles and resonant barks of the steam engines, that made them sound like a strange pack of baying hounds impatient to be set free for the chase.

Eddie took a deep breath, stood tall and opened the door. There was nobody in the room, which smelt of cold and damp. But someone had been there, and recently. Sweat, a faint smell of soap powder and damp clothing, wood smoke, cigarettes. Yes, cigarette smoke — a thin layer of pale blue was drifting across the room and its pungent smell immediately struck Eddie. He entered the room, his courage veering wildly from one extreme to another as he tried to walk stealthily so as to remain undetected.

He looked at the open suitcase filled with neatly folded clothes and at two wooden hangers supporting a U.S.A.F. dress uniform, and a swish smoking jacket. A bulled-up pair of military-style boots stood close to the truckle bed. Some tramp. Eddie bit his lower lip. He then felt a prickle of fear down the nape of his neck and his throat went dry as he spied a leather gun holster complete with a pistol slung over a chair back. So, the man was not carrying a gun at that moment — that was some kind of relief — but the fact that this man knew how to handle one did not reassure him. It was one thing imagining a Soviet spy, it was quite another to confront an armed military man. Why was an American airman camping out in this abandoned building? Perhaps he was an undercover spy? Phew, this was serious.

Walking across the room, he approached a second leather suitcase and a large cardboard box bearing stencilled numbers and codes that looked rather official and military. He lifted the lid of the suitcase and his eyes widened as he stared at brand new packets of stockings, cigarettes and pouches of tobacco. He reached in, took a packet of the cigarettes and put them in his reefer jacket pocket. Evidence. After closing the lid quietly he peered into the box and saw cans of food: corned beef, baked beans, tunny fish and anchovies, and some bottled fruit, all good black-marketeering stuff. Maybe this was how he made money? A spiv dressed up as an airman. He knew that he must report what he had found, but for now it was time to get out and back to his engine without meeting the man.

A light cough came from the next room.

Eddie stood completely still and tried to to regulate his breathing, his own throat starting to tickle with nerves. He must not cough, but the more he thought about not doing so, the more it tickled.

The rumbles and whistles of the railway continued, but Eddie could hear no further signs of life from the adjacent room. He quickly stepped back towards the outside door, thankful that the hard concrete floor did not creak, as wood might have done. But there was problem with the door, whereas it had opened easily, now as he started to pull he met with resistance. He tried a little harder and the lower edge of the door gave a slight scrape and then juddered to a halt. Eddie cursed silently.

A heavy train was approaching, making the loud rhythmic clanking and powerful exhaust beat typical of one of the massive Austerity engines as it assaulted the incline out of the station. Once this drew close the noise might just mask that of the door. He grasped the handle with both hands and waited. The noise intensified and Eddie pulled hard, the door making an ugly noise quite different from those of the train as it flew open. He darted through, closed the door behind him and contemplated running, but he could only make slow progress through the deep snow, no matter how hard he tried. Instead he crouched down, just as he had before, and peeked over the window cill into the room. His throat was still tickling like crazy and he must cough at any moment, and so in desperation he scooped up some snow and chewed on its tasteless coldness in the hope that it would salve the irritation. It seemed to work, and not a second too soon, either, as at that very moment Eddie saw a tall man step into the room.

He looked alert, perhaps even tense, and Eddie could see that he was surveying his belongings, eyes flicking from one place to another and a hand gently touching his dress jacket. The man stepped forward in a quick movement, removed the pistol from its holster and held the gun, whilst apparently thinking and weighing up options.

Eddie swallowed and blinked, his throat constricted by fear. This was too much to risk and he ducked down and started to move in an ungainly, crouching shuffle. As he made his escape he felt an odd sensation on the middle of his back, as though something was pointed towards it, boring into him from behind. It was like an itch that needed scratching. No, it was worse, it was if he sensed something directed right at him, something like the barrel of a gun waiting to be fired.

The half-expected shot, however, never came, and when he reached the corner he stood up, pressed himself against the wall and took a few much-needed gulps of air. He could see his little engine steaming quietly just a short distance away. He had only to walk a few yards, and then he could act like he had never left its footplate.

The noisy train had nearly passed, but its smoky trail was still curling and rolling across the yard and partially enveloping him. This was all the encouragement Eddie needed: he started forwards in bounding strides, seeking cover from the smoke screen until he reached the locomotive, at which point he stopped and turned to look towards the buildings whilst swiftly plucking an oilcan from the footplate. He attempted to appear at ease as he idly wiped the nearest section of footplate with an old rag that had been draped over the long, thin spout of the can. As he did so, he glimpsed a head looking around the side of the building, where only moments before he had been catching his breath. The head ducked back almost as quickly as it had appeared, but Eddie knew that he had been seen and followed.

Voices could now be heard as his driver, accompanied by two shunters and a gang of women platelayers, were approaching, their tea break over. He was safe and he had some evidence in his pocket, perhaps even vital information that surely would be appreciated by the railway police.

Chapter Twenty-Eight

'TEXAS AND PACIFIC'
Louis Jordan & his Tympany Five

Eddie's account of his discovery was indeed appreciated and started a rapid escalation of events that seemed to surprise even those involved. Not that Edward Earnshaw had made the connection of whom this man was until Mr Saunders had unrolled the freshly printed posters issued to him by the railway police that were still lying on his desk waiting to be pinned to the noticeboards — an action that was retrospectively accomplished in double-quick time before the police arrived — with a hint that if Eddie was to say nothing about this unfortunate oversight, and in due consideration of his important discovery, the record could be set straight and his place within the shed pecking order reviewed in a more positive light.

Once the likeness on the poster was revealed to him, Eddie immediately made the connection and identified the man. He became conscious that he had been within feet of a monster wanted for double rape and murder. That was pretty gruesome to think about. The only fly in the ointment was that Eddie had waited some hours before plucking up the courage to come forward and tell what he had seen. Valuable time had been lost, exacerbated by the fact that the fugitive was aware that he had been seen. Would he try to escape before the police arrived?

As luck would have it, both Vignoles and Trinder were at Brackley Central station interviewing a witness about a possible, though rather vague, sighting of a man in the vicinity of the hound van when a telegraphed message was brought to them in response to Mr Saunders, the shedmaster, raising the alarm. They immediately flagged down the next train passing through, using Vignoles's special powers of access, and he commanded the surprised footplate crew to power their train of cattle trucks north at a speed more befitting an express fish train. The crew proved more than equal to the challenge, metaphorically whipping their metal steed forwards, aided by the fact that they were driving a Gresley V2, a class of locomotive with a surprising turn of speed and a fine reputation of putting on a performance, no matter how badly maintained it had been. The engine, despite leaking steam in alarming quantities from various glands, stormed up the ruling gradient towards Woodford

Halse, kicking up a cloud of powdery snow in its wake and leaving a powerful smell of alarmed animal and manure that lingered long upon the air. Farm workers standing in the fields near Helmdon watched as this unexpected express hurtled across the magnificent viaduct set against the purple snow clouds on the horizon.

Meanwhile, P.C. Blencowe had been mobilising all the uniformed officers he could muster, posting men on guard at each station along the line and sending a posse of three southwards to meet Vignoles and Trinder at Woodford. The uniforms were accompanied by W.P.C.s Benson and Lansdowne, the latter equipped with two pistols and a pocket full of bullets following the urgently barked orders the inspector had given from the stationmaster's office at Brackley. The Northamptonshire Constabulary, under the command one D.I. Bainbridge, were on their way to help throw a cordon around the town and its vast shunting yards.

The shedmaster had been given instructions for his staff to not approach the man, but to assist only by observing the buildings in a manner that would not arouse suspicion. This was achieved by having no fewer than three locomotives ostensibly engaged in shunting in the north yard, though each engine made only short and intermittent moves followed by protracted periods of gently brewing up steam within view of the buildings, and each was accompanied by more shunters, overseers and wagon number-takers than normal.

The women gangers were put to work on the exit pointwork just to the north of the building, wielding picks, shovels, massive crow bars, lifting tongs and all manner of hefty metal tools that made them a formidable force. Their lookouts placed at each end of the team were especially vigilant, regularly scanning the surrounding area with their red and green signalling flags and hand lamps at the ready. The signal boxes were double-manned, as their commanding positions made them key to the whole exercise.

It was as well an executed plan as they could manage under the circumstances, and as the various teams took their places Vignoles was satisfied that they had done what they could to secure the site. But he could not avoid the stark fact that they had lost quite a few hours between the Earnshaw lad's actually seeing the fugitive and the alarm being raised. Now it was nightfall and heavy snow was falling. Despite the cordon these last two factors would aid the killer's escape, assuming that he had not already fled before anyone knew to stop him.

'No point crying over spilt milk; we do have to accept that the lad was hardly in a mood to rush forward and speak to us after his recent dressing down.'

'Was I too hard on him?' Trinder grimaced.

'Not really. He deserved a jolly good ticking off. It's just that...' Vignoles exhaled, '...who'd have thought that he would have seen the very man we're looking for. What is it about this boy?'

Both men shook their heads in unison and Vignoles sipped some of Mrs Walsh's cocoa.

'So, how shall we play this out?' Trinder was rubbing his palms together to create a warming friction. He was wearing a black woollen balaclava beneath his hat, a practical choice but one that made his face appear oddly disconnected from his body in the gloom of the station lamps. He was humming a jaunty tune between speaking, something that was a bit of habit of his when he needed to settle his nerves.

'Everyone's in place. Upon my signal, the cordon will close in from the north and narrow along both flanks. With the loudspeaker system they use for directing the shunting operations we shall advise him to surrender. Meanwhile, you and I, with Lansdowne armed and ready as cover, will advance and seek to confront him once he realises that the game's up.'

'He's armed.'

'I'm aware of that and there is some risk. But with so many closing in upon him I am trusting that he knows he can never shoot his way out.'

'He might take us out along the way though?'

'That is a possibility. We shall keep a yard or so apart so it is harder for him to get us both, and that's why Lansdowne is primed to be ready to return fire. And I've got this,' he hefted an ancient revolver in his free hand. 'But in this weather and visibility accuracy will be hard.' Vignoles forced a grin.

'I hope you're right.' Trinder drained the last of his cocoa and looked out from under the station awning at the snow falling in ever increasing quantities. 'The weather reports are grim. It's a blessing as he can't get far in all this if he does evade us.'

'That's one way of looking at it.' Vignoles walked over to Stationmaster Markham and a huddle of porters and railway workers gathered nearby ready to act as a kind of 'back stop' cordon in case the man dodged Vignoles and Trinder and made a break towards the station. 'Are the trains still running?'

'At the moment, inspector; but I can tell you that there is very real concern further north. The lines are closed beyond Sheffield and there are fears for closer to home.'

'I see. Are you expecting anything now?'

'Yes, we have two passenger trains due… goodness knows quite when, though I understand that one will be signalled through to us any moment now. And plenty of southbound freight. I understand that you wanted the lines cleared of all traffic, but we really must keep what we can moving tonight.'

That was exactly what Badger had told him on the telephone. Vignoles was not eager to halt services along such a busy line either, but he feared that anything passing Woodford was just an opportunity for the killer to jump aboard.

'Can you even be sure that he's still holed up there?' Badger had bawled down the line.

'No, but it's our belief.'

'Belief? I would need cast-iron, solidly reinforced, concreted bloody proof to allow the whole system to completely shut down. Good God, Vignoles, we can't just grind the country to a halt based upon an unsubstantiated theory!'

He was probably right, and it would have only placed yet another burden of responsibility upon his shoulders, but even so Vignoles was apprehensive. As if to make the point, the signals clanged and a green light winked through the snow.

'That'll be the much delayed five-oh-nine.' Stationmaster Markham was shaking his head and looking at his silver hunter watch. He was the very model of control and calm in the face of adversity, his face betraying just the slightest touch of resigned annoyance that the timetable was shot to pieces. 'Two hours late. It's a crowded one. Troop re-deployment, I understand. I've been told to expect nineteen on the back, maybe twenty.'

Trinder whistled in surprise whilst they all considered this astonishing fact.

'You might just get that complete standstill you wanted if this monster train can't restart.' The stationmaster made a grim smile and Vignoles tried to return it. He appreciated the attempt at humour, even though he felt completely humourless at that moment. Trinder picked up the melody of *Texas and Pacific* as his contribution to the anxious wait.

The train was approaching and they turned to see what was coming. The pale clouds of steam were the first visible signs, followed by the pinpricks of light from the oil lamps on the front buffer beam. A rosy glow flickered around the cab and light spilled from the carriages, kissing the silver rails with a soft yellow. The engine was a magnificent Pacific, one of Nigel Gresley's A3s and a splendid machine that looked almost heroic as it eased into the station with its massive train.

Despite all his immediate concerns, Vignoles took a moment to read the name 'Spion Kop' on the engine's curved brass plate and to look at its crew grimed black as minstrels, their eyes and teeth shining white, with sweat beading their skin and tiredness already etched deep into their faces. Carriage after carriage slowly rumbled into the station, too many for all to fit alongside the platform and the driver was over-running at the far end, glancing back to follow the hand signal of the guard, who was motioning him to continue until he switched his lamp to red to call a full stop.

Vignoles was by now feeling increasingly alarmed and his face had a look of comic incredulity upon it. Trinder had also quickly appreciated the reason for the inspector's look of crazed disbelief; the train was completely filled to bursting, with passengers seated, standing, huddled, sleeping, drinking, laughing, waving and crammed into every spare inch of space. But it was not the over-crowding that had caused their alarm, but the fact that, with few exceptions, American servicemen and women occupied the whole train and the majority were in uniform. Many hundreds in uniforms exactly like those worn by their fugitive. A better cover could not have been imagined and to make the situation worse, the first four carriages were now at rest beyond the platform in the near impenetrable gloom of the snowy night.

Vignoles ran along the platform staring at the many smiling, often slightly drunken faces, all de-mob happy and on the way to Liverpool to catch a boat home, determined to enjoy themselves with copious quantities of beer and spirits. Hands waved from the windows and rubbed condensation from the glass, and curtains were pulled back. People laughed, pointed, and some even cheered at the odd figure of the man running along the platform, gesticulating and apparently deeply concerned about something happening at the front of their train. Doors now swung open, heads were pushed through the small, toplight windows and his anxious face drew comments.

'Say, what's up bud?'

'Some kind of problem there?'

'Cheer up — it may never happen!'

'What gives with that guy? He looks like he's just seen a ghost or something.'

'Where the heck's Woodford Halse?'

'Sure ain't Texas, that I do know.'

Vignoles ignored the banter. He needed to get the operation going and sooner than he had expected, because the sheer size of the massive train was adding an unwelcome dimension to his strategy. It was immediately obvious that if their man were to affect an escape then he would never get a better chance than now. The rowdy and dangerously overcrowded train was going to be released shortly in an attempt to get it as far north as possible before the lines were closed by snow. Vignoles knew enough about steam engines to predict that Spion Kop was going to make a long and slow re-start and would, at best, be merely crawling as it ran beside the north yard. Perfect to be jumped.

'We need the cordon to move in now. Get the tannoy to commence calling for his surrender.' Vignoles blew his whistle and waved towards the signal box. The young signalwoman who was awaiting their signal responded by flashing a hand lamp whilst leaning out of an open window. She then turned to use the lamp to attract the attention of the people forming one edge of the human wall.

'They'll never see the lamp in all this.' Trinder looked worried.

'I fear they won't. The tannoy should alert them, though. Will this snow ever let up?' Vignoles blew again on his whistle. 'Lansdowne! We're moving in.'

As they walked down the end ramp of the platform, the signal was set for the train to pull away and they were swathed in escaping steam as the locomotive's sanders were opened to force the grit between wheel and rail to try and secure a purchase upon the smooth metal. The engine barked and the wheels slipped violently. More steam and loud hissing accompanied a slow sequence of volcanic eruptions from the chimney as the engine inched forwards in a cloud of white, but it gained no momentum and there followed a sequence of wheel slips, each expertly controlled by the driver, but still failing to get the train moving beyond a crawl.

Vignoles was walking beside the carriages that towered above him, trying to peer beneath each to catch sight of anyone attempting to board, but it was now far too dark and the snowfall and steam conspired to render it impossible to see anything. More voices shouted down from the opened windows and cheers accompanied each attempt to restart the train, the whole ensemble creating an odd atmosphere of heightened excitement and jollity, harshly at odds with Vignoles's mood.

'They've used up the sand. He's getting no grip.' Trinder was staring at the locomotive just ahead of him.

'I think you're right. He's stuck. We just don't need this delay.' Vignoles chewed his lip as he watched the steam jetting from the sanding pipes around the massive driving wheels. The locomotive again inched forwards with a series of deafening woofs, but then the wheels spun in an action quite alarming when standing so close.

'We've got to get this away — either that or get everyone off and search the lot of them for our man.'

'No...' Trinder closed his eyes for a second in contemplation of what Vignoles was suggesting.

'They need sand... but wait a tick: the fire buckets on the signal box will do!' Vignoles sprinted forward in the brief lull as the driver shut off the regulator. He crossed the up lines and reached the steps of the signalbox, Trinder following closely behind, whilst two women gangers keeping lookout on that side of the train, who had overheard Vignoles's exclamation, responded with remarkable alacrity and were already unhooking the red-painted metal buckets of sand, handing one to Vignoles and another to Trinder, whilst retaining one each.

'This is dangerous work.' Vignoles blew his whistle and called the driver's attention. 'We'll hand-sand the rails, two of us on each side. We'll cross the line in front of you now and then signal when we're ready.'

'Aye. I'll wait on your hand signal. You can cross over now.'

The driver had immediately understood and was already winding the handbrake on as he spoke. Trinder sprinkled sand along the tops of the rails some way in front of the locomotive, whilst Vignoles drew close and threw handfuls onto the rail beside the front edge of each wheel. He was reaching through and below the massive connecting rods and cranks, his hat being knocked aside by the tempered steel, and any misunderstanding between he and the crew would mean almost certain death. He could see one of the women gangers doing the same on the other side. But would it be enough to restart the train?

He stood back, raised a hand, blew his signal blasts and watched as Trinder stepped back from the track whilst also raising a hand. Vignoles had to trust that the driver would watch out for the women on the other side. He looked up at the fireman, who acknowledged him. He was conscious of Lansdowne standing nearby, pistol at the ready, and gamely trying to survey the area for the fugitive. The A3 again stormed into life and Vignoles took another step back as the great pistons and connecting cranks slowly turned with almost unimaginable power, bracing himself as he awaited the almost inevitable spin of the wheels once the sand ran out. But this time the engine took one revolution and one huge blast of exhaust, then managed a second and then a third. Spion Kop might just do it. Vignoles ran forwards, risking injury by traversing the snowy ground in the dark, and saw the women doing the same, throwing more sand onto the glassy rails. It was foolhardy, but they seemed driven by the same desire to get the train in motion. The engine gave another brief slip, but not as badly as before, and it was now up to a slow walking pace, the crew leaning out the cab and staring into the night with intense concentration.

The tannoy amplified the clear and clipped tones of Detective Bainbridge repeating that the fugitive 'was surrounded and you must come forward and make yourself known to a police officer, with hands raised' whilst the revelling travellers were now cheering and waving as their train gathered speed. Thumbs up signs were made and caps were waved from open windows, creating a strangely surreal sight as the train started to overtake Vignoles, who was now standing and watching its uncertain progress. The tracks groaned, dipped and rose as the carriage bogies passed and the whole railway seemed to sag under its weight. The train was now managing a respectable pace, though it would still be possible for someone to jump aboard. With this in mind, Vignoles started to make a slow jogging run alongside, his glasses continually spotting with snowflakes and rendering him almost blind. This forced him to stop after just a few yards.

'Can you see anything?' Vignoles shouted to Trinder.

'Nothing much.'

Lansdowne and Trinder drew close to Vignoles and watched the train as curtains of snow enveloped it. Their clothes were already collecting a heavy frosting of white and their cheeks and noses were pink with the bitter cold.

'Any sign of movement up there?' Lansdowne was speaking rhetorically as she shaded her eyes from the snow and stared towards the yards indicated by a series of dark shapes of wagons against a black sky. There seemed little point in moving forwards, so they just watched in frustration at the tail lamp receding into the night that appeared to blink as the snow fell across its beam.

'He's going to escape. I just know it.' Trinder was shaking his head, 'So close...'

Vignoles was wiping his glasses with a handkerchief and thinking. 'It seems to me we've got two choices. We have enough men on the ground here to maintain the cordon, so if he hunkers down for the night, we stand a chance of getting him when dawn breaks. But my hunch is that he's jumped that train. It's what we would all do in his situation and it's too good an opportunity to miss. And who's going to see him do it?'

Trinder was nodding in agreement. 'So what are we waiting for?'

'Come on then — we've got to catch that train!' Vignoles started off after the little pinpoint of red light. As if to reinforce Vignoles's reasoning, the train lurched to another unexpected halt as the wheels span in another series of dangerous slips. This at least allowed them to close in on the last carriage before it once again started to move forwards. By trotting beside the vehicle Vignoles just managed to find an uneasy purchase upon the icy wooden footstep and then eased himself upwards to grab hold of the brass door handle and a small handrail. The door opened outwards and he was in danger of falling upon the ground or being struck by a passing signal post, but at the last moment a beefy G.I. reached out a firm hand and pulled Vignoles inside.

'Hey, you nearly missed it there.' The American had a loud and throaty laugh, and practically pushed Vignoles head first into the mass of men squeezed into the tiny lobby. 'Always space for one more! C'mon guys, mind your backs for the latecomer.'

Vignoles muttered a thank you and grimaced as he was squashed and buffeted between a succession of men, kit bags, trunks and knapsacks, all rammed into the confined space. Everyone seemed to be in a state of cheerful carelessness, with bottles of beer in their hands and the smell of cigarettes and booze on their breath.

'Join the party. There's a beer around here someplace...'

'No, but thank you anyway.' Vignoles gave a sheepish grin at the many faces, which were all pressed too close for his liking. There was almost no air to be breathed, though it was at least warmer than outside. He now had the problem of his glasses misting over. He was not normally given to claustrophobia, but felt a few panicky twinges in his stomach and so closed his eyes for a moment to try and regain his composure.

'Hey, your friends are gonna have to take a rain check on this one as they didn't make the jump. Too bad.'

'Ah. I see.'

That was annoying. Vignoles was now alone in the midst of a few hundred Americans on a train with a killer aboard. At least Trinder could oversee things on the ground back at Woodford, but it was still a blow.

Vignoles tried to push his way forwards into the corridor, a manoeuvre that took some minutes and lots of treading upon toes and breathing in deeply and trying to ease into spaces far too small. He was now unsure as to what was best to do. Movement was almost impossible along the train, and yet he could not just stand there surrounded by boozy revellers for the next few hours. He wiped his glasses clear again and looked around. His heart sank to a new low: he had been able to give what he felt was a pretty good description of the killer a few days ago, but now, surrounded by literally hundreds of men in the same looking uniforms and with the same haircuts and similar accents, he realised that he was struggling to retain a clear image of the man he wanted. It was not that everyone actually looked the same when he properly studied their faces, but the very uniformity that military service demanded rendered everyone similar and made him doubt his memory. What part of his I.D. had just been the colour of the clothing and the accent, both elements now lost in a sea of olive greens, khakis and a babble of voices with a similar lilt?

The train was gathering speed now and the engine was meeting the challenge with a spirited attack on the gentle climb toward Charwelton, and the smoky dive into Catesby tunnel. This reminded Vignoles of why he was there. He cast his mind back to the pale, broken body that had been lying in the snow along that very stretch of line, discarded like a forgotten plaything by a man without pity or remorse. A man who still had no name.

Vignoles snapped out of his thoughts and resolved to fight his way the length of the train and to look at the face of each and everyone aboard, no matter how long it took and how many he infuriated and irritated in so doing. Any sense of decorum and politeness would have to wait as he shouldered his way forwards into the first compartment, giving short intense looks at each face that turned his way as he pushed through. Voices were raised and he occasionally received a shove and an elbow in return, but Vignoles just muttered a mantra about having to find someone urgently and hoped that this would be enough to prevent the more drunken and aggressive types from trying to teach him a lesson in manners.

Each compartment was filled to bursting with sleeping, card-playing, drinking, singing and in some cases, when there were women present, kissing, servicemen. And everyone seemed to be in some version of uniform: army, air force and navy — it was a profusion of hats, braiding, epaulettes, helmets, boots, kitbags and weapons. It was like looking for the proverbial needle in a haystack. When Vignoles finally approached the end of the first carriage he was already feeling irritated beyond belief, but he was startled by a sudden change in the sound of the train and a sharp 'whump' as the air pressure changed, signalling that they were entering the tunnel. Coughing and wheezing soon broke out because they were at the trailing end of a heavily stoked engine that had filled the tunnel with dense fumes and the already foul air in the carriage soon soured with the same. Just as Vignoles was beginning to feel a tightening around his chest and some of those around him were rubbing their smarting eyes, the train exited in an exultation of sound like a sudden release of tension, only to be replaced by something far odder and completely unexpected.

After a violent jolt, the brakes were suddenly biting deep in a continuous squeal, as the train started making a sound not unlike that of a speed boat crashing through waves. They were now being buffeted from side to side as the wheels bumped along the rails as if they were no longer made of polished steel. Shouts and cries of surprise went up along the train, and those pressed close to the steamed up windows looked in amazement as the world appeared to turn white outside as a froth of snow pressed hard against the glass like breaking waves. The train was coming to a standstill in a violent series of jerks that threw those standing off balance, sliding men, women and luggage into a confusing jumble against each other as the engine gave one last mournful whistle like a desperate cry for help.

They had stopped dead, and for a few seconds a shocked silence fell.

Then there was an eruption of loud murmuring and chattering, punctuated by a few shouts. There was an even more intense crush of bodies as everyone sought to regain their feet and rush to the windows to see what was up. Vignoles used this as an excuse to continue his slow progress forwards, pushing with diminishing patience towards the end vestibule. If they were stuck fast in a snowdrift — which was what he suspected had happened — and if the killer really was onboard, this was his chance to make an arrest.

A blast of cold air indicated that a door had been forced open and a number of soldiers were half-leaning, half-climbing outside to try and appraise the situation. Even with his restricted view, it was immediately clear that the train was sitting in at least six feet of snow. There were more yells and calls, some urging action and for men to help try to clear it, whilst others more intent upon sleep or their card games were urging the doors and windows to be closed to preserve what little warmth was left onboard. Somewhere ahead steam was escaping in a loud roar — probably from a broken heating pipe between vehicles — this would need shutting off, and then at least part of the train really would soon start to freeze.

Vignoles edged forwards, his movement now slightly improved by the release of pressure caused by some of the men hanging from the outside of the train and dropping down into the deep drift that had been ripped apart by the train. He supposed that was at least the advantage of coming to grief with a trainload of men well used to solving such problems. He shuffled past more faces in a seemingly endless succession of expressions, varying between laughing, joking, scowling or sour, morose or tired and often drunken. As he took in each face he felt his memory dilute to the point that by the time he was at the end vestibule of the third coach, he was exhausted and sure that he could no longer remember the face of the man he was looking for. He leant against a teak partition and closed his eyes for a moment, until his attention was drawn to a bottle of beer being offered him by a man in a pale naval dress uniform, one of a group standing nearby.

'You look bushed. Probably could handle one of these, eh?'

Vignoles gave a rather wan smile but motioned with a hand that he didn't need a beer. Another soldier, who was tall, broad and black, grinned and held out a smaller bottle, 'I ain't in the mood for no beer, neither, but a shot of this'll do you the world of good.' He waved it at Vignoles. 'Go on, sir; we ain't going no place in a hurry.'

Vignoles looked at the whiskey and surprised himself by over-riding his natural inclination to decline. His hand reached out and took it. He was tired, cold and very hungry and could feel his energy dropping; he needed something to give him a lift, so he took a small mouthful and felt the warmth flow inside. 'Thank you. That was good.'

'You're welcome, sir. Take some more. Don't hang back on our account. We got plenty more from where that came from!' Everyone laughed and Vignoles took up the offer with a second and longer swig, but then insisted that the bottle was returned.

Questions followed about whom he was and where he was going, and Vignoles played a careful game of replying with oblique answers that said everything and yet nothing, and he felt inclined to conceal that he was a detective. Most people had a natural aversion to police and he could do without any unnecessary obstruction or antipathy right now. He also did not want word to pass down the train, in case it prompted the killer to bolt. The men decided that Vignoles was some kind of ticket inspector, and he was happy to just leave it like that.

'A fare dodger? And one of us as well. Heck, that's not like an American!' One of the men laughed and the others joined in, with much arm and back slapping. The beer and whiskey were making anything seem amusing. 'We'll sure keep an eye out for him.'

'Hell, I wouldn't pay to travel on this overcrowded heap o' junk, neither.'

Vignoles made an attempt at a description of the man but was soon shouted down by more raucous laughter the moment that he mentioned the U.S.A.F. uniform and American accent.

'You sure chose the right train, buddy! You got a few hundred suspects here, right under your very nose.'

He conceded the point and made an attempt to join in laughing to keep the atmosphere light. There was little point in offending anyone and he could see the funny side of his inexpert description. He made his excuses soon after, then shuffled and squeezed his way into the next carriage.

There was more space and it was far colder, as it appeared that a large detail of soldiers had been marshalled outside into snow-clearing duties, using the foldaway shovels on their backpacks, ably organised by a tough and rugged-looking sergeant with a voice that brooked no dissent. Vignoles stood at the open doorway and looked down at the scene below. Snow was still falling, though the wind had dropped and Vignoles could hear the sound of many shovels cutting into snow and the boiling hiss of escaping steam. He could just make out clouds of white vapour enveloping the stricken A3 that was presumably buried deep in a wall of compacted snow. Looking behind, he could see that the train had just cleared Catesby Tunnel by a few yards, but had ploughed into a heavy slip of snow that had come down the embankment onto the running lines. The snow may not have been so very deep, but as Spion Kop had hit the snow it had built up on either side like a bow wave until the weight had defeated the heavily laden train. It would be possible to bring a locomotive in from behind and pull the coaches out of the drift and back down the tunnel, but the snow first had to be cleared from around the wheels.

Vignoles needed to reassure himself about the safety of the train and to put concerns about the fugitive to one side for a while, and so he swung himself down and out of the door onto the footboard, and then dropped onto the ground. It was a strange and eerie world down here, with the train now oppressively massive to one side and a narrow gap being formed between the train and the snow mountain on the other, and men swinging shovels into the air in a strange ballet of movement occupied this constricted space.

The inspector walked towards the rear of the train, where the build up of snow rapidly diminished as he moved away from the point of impact. There was no activity here, just three or four figures standing in the gloom, the glowing points of orange indicating that they were smoking and stretching their legs. Beyond them, inside Catesby Tunnel, there was a beam of light swinging from side to side, suggesting to Vignoles that the train guard was walking back along the track — hopefully to place warning detonators upon the rails to protect the train.

As he approached the last carriage, the group stepped aside to let him pass; one was a woman, and she gave a slight touch to her cap in a sketch of a salute, whilst the other two murmured something in low but respectful tones. Perhaps it was his ex-service greatcoat that inspired these acts, and Vignoles gave a slight nod in return whilst straining his eyes to make out their features. They were all very young and fresh faced, especially the woman, who could barely have been out of school. The aroma of cigarette smoke mingled with the odour of damp earthiness, bitter soot and acrid coal smoke carried on a bitter draft from the gaping tunnel mouth that loomed in an ominous manner above them.

The fourth figure standing some way apart, looking at the ground so that his face was not illuminated by the carriage lights, his cap pulled low over his brow and his coat collar turned up. He too was smoking, holding a cigarette cupped inside one hand so that the burning tip faced inwards to be protected from the snow. Vignoles noticed that when he took a drag he appeared to place his knuckles to his mouth in a mannerism that was most curious, almost as if he were kissing his hand. Vignoles walked by and for a moment thought that there was something about the shape of his nose that was faintly familiar but upon a second glance he was no longer so sure. The man had looked up. Had there been a flicker of recognition? It was over before he could really say, and so Vignoles continued to follow the faint beam of light into the tunnel.

Vignoles reached into one of his voluminous coat pockets, pulled out a torch and played this upon the ground. But the nagging feeling would not go away and, even as he walked, the sensation increased until he stopped in the middle of the line and furrowed his brow. He heard little sounds of water dripping from long icicles fringing the tunnel opening; the slide of shovels upon snow; occasional calls and the low murmur of voices talking from within the train. He felt an odd tingle down the nape of his neck, inducing him to suddenly spin around upon his heels.

The man with the strange smoking action was staring back. Vignoles flicked his torch upwards to shine it into his face and they exchanged looks for a few moments until the man turned away from the beam, tossing his cigarette to the ground as he spoke.

'Hey, what's with the light?'

Vignoles paced forward, keeping the beam on the man's face whilst his free hand slid into his pocket and felt the shape of the gun, his gloved fingers working themselves around the grip. Vignoles licked his drying lips and assessed the situation.

It was him! He remembered the face from when they had exchanged the contraband, but just as suddenly Vignoles felt a twinge of uncertainty. Could he draw a gun on someone unless he was absolutely sure? To make matters worse, after all the cleaning he had given them, his glasses were smeared and his sight imperfect whilst the torch beam rendered the man's face oddly flat and washed out.

How should he play this? He'd better not get it wrong.

'Could I have a word?'

The man's eyes narrowed as he sized Vignoles up.

'I just need to ask you a few questions.'

'Go to hell!' The tall American suddenly stepped smartly towards the group of smokers reaching inside his coat has he did so.

Vignoles reacted quickly, commanding the man to stop and surrender himself, but it was too late. There was a glint of steel and in an instant the barrel of a gun was pressed to the temple of the woman while a tight arm lock was thrown around her neck. The gunman yelled out a command to stand back then dragged his surprised hostage to one side so that both were up against the rear of the train. Vignoles and the two servicemen stopped in their tracks as they saw the immediate danger. The locomotive's safety valves lifted at this moment in a roar that reverberated around the sloping slides of the cutting and probably rendered their shouts inaudible to those clearing snow.

'Don't move or she gets it in the head, OK?'

'Oh! Aaagh, you let me go right now...' The victim made a choking sound as her head was pulled violently backwards.

'Hey, you leave her alone! Are you crazy?' One of her friends made as if he were about to try and come to the rescue.

'Shut up! Stay where you are and no one gets hurt! I'll kill her if you come any closer. This gun is loaded.'

'You cannot escape. There's nowhere to run and about five hundred armed men around you. You must see that this is hopeless.' Vignoles tried calling out above the sound of the safety valves.

'Drop that bloody light or she gets it. Do it!'

The woman's eyes were wide with alarm and searching frantically from side to side. Vignoles allowed the torch to fall into the snow, where it lay casting a beam skywards and illuminating the hypnotic fall of snow.

'Now don't do anything foolish. Just put the gun down and release her...'

'Cut the crap. Back off or I'll blow you and the girl away.'

Vignoles glanced across at the two men who looked ready to leap upon the gunman and he tried to signal for them to do as advised.

'Listen up. I'm gonna walk down that tunnel and I'm taking this dumb blonde with me. You try anything and it's curtains for her. You got that? So back off and out of my way.'

The roaring safety valves were making Vignoles's ears ring, making it hard to think lucidly. It was probably better to let the man move away from the train and minimise the danger to others, but Vignoles was fearful for the young hostage's safety and for that of the train guard down the line.

'As you wish. I'm not armed. You can pass. Just don't do anything foolish.' He was glad he had kept the pistol concealed and Vignoles now held his arms out whilst stepping to one side.

The man pushed the young woman forwards, allowing her to walk freely but keeping the gun barrel pressed into her back. Vignoles watched them enter the tunnel and, after they had moved some distance away, started to follow. One of the two Americans now ran down the train to raise the alarm, whilst the other reached down towards his boot and pulled out an exotic and wicked looking knife. Vignoles guessed that this was a war trophy and not a tool of the soldier's trade.

'A knife is little use against a gun.'

'It is if I can move up on him in the dark. Who is this crazy jerk, anyway?'

'A rapist and murderer, with a taste for young women.'

His eyes widened momentarily and he swore like a docker. 'We'd better go get him, then.'

Vignoles pulled out his own gun and wished that he could use it more skilfully than his efforts on the practice range suggested. 'There are retreats let into the tunnel wall, we can use these as protection in case he shoots.' With that, Vignoles picked up and switched off his torch and started to run, hugging the curved wall where he knew there would be a reasonably smooth dirt track trodden down by the linesmen. It was now so dark that he could no longer see the two figures and realised that he needed to proceed more slowly and quietly or he might overtake them. The boots of the young soldier fell into the same rhythm as his and he could hear his breathing close behind.

Vignoles trailed his fingertips along the wall, feeling for the edge of the first retreat and then stepped into the narrow recess that gave enough space for two grown men to flatten themselves against the wall if caught by a passing train. Vignoles felt a hand touch his sleeve and hear the solder whispered 'Listen!' They heard stumbling footsteps and small stones making tiny sounds as they bounced off a boot or a rail. There was a sudden curse, as if a toe had been stubbed, followed by a series of grunts and scuffles. Another curse and then a man's voice rang out.

'Don't try anything funny. Damn you, where the hell...?'

Vignoles could see nothing, but they were very close. The soldier tapped his arm again and placed his mouth close to the inspector's ear, 'I'll go the other side. Give me thirty seconds then distract him.' He let Vignoles know that he was now brandishing a gun as well as the knife.

'Righty-o.'

The soldier was gone and made no sound in so doing, but just as Vignoles was feeling confident that their pincer movement might work, a problem arose. It was a distraction but not the one they planned: the train guard, who until now was presumably unaware of the drama unfolding behind him, had set the detonators and was walking back. At that moment his lamp beam illuminated the two figures standing in the centre of the track. The light was weak, as he was some way off, but it was enough to show that the woman was now a yard to one side and out of the grasp of her abductor, who now span around in surprise and without a moment of hesitation, let off a shot straight at the source of the light. The gun flash was spectacularly bright, burning red dots onto Vignoles's eyes. Another shot rang out and the lamp fell to the ground and went out, accompanied by an anguished shout. The guard had gone down.

The woman moved in on the gunman and landed a punch to his kidneys, followed by a hard kick to one of his shins. Another shot, this time showering sparks from the wall above, and Vignoles thought he glimpsed the man staggering backwards and the shape of the young soldier advancing from across the far railway track before blackness enveloped them again, followed by the sound of heavy breathing and the scrabbling of boots on the track ballast.

Vignoles sprinted towards where he thought the gunman was standing, but took a violent collision to his nose that brought him up sharply.

'Aaagh...' He reached out towards his assailant and felt cloth, which he grabbed onto only to find his arm wrenched up and around in a painful twist and a sharp punch was delivered to his ribs. A woman's voice told him to hold still and drop his gun.

'Wrong man! Police...' panted Vignoles, trying to catch his breath.

'Stop!' I'll shoot!' It was the young soldier's voice. A muzzle flash illuminated his face for a moment and there was another ear-splitting explosion. Feet could be heard running hard into the tunnel.

'Aw, shit.'

'Hold your fire, the guard's out there on the track.'

'I hope I didn't hurt you too bad? '

'It's nothing.' He felt his nose, but apart from being sore it was probably unbroken. His arm socket was aching, though. 'Are you hurt?'

'Just a bit shaken up, nothing else. Why did he do this?'

'Shhh! Listen up.' It was the soldier. 'What the hell's that noise?'

Vignoles concentrated on deciphering the various sounds around them. There was the drip of water echoing into a pool and a mounting hubbub from the tunnel entrance, where a major rescue party appeared to be assembling, and the more distant crunch of a pair of booted feet. But there was something else behind all of these; a deep, resonant beat that was increasingly booming around the walls accompanied by a sudden rush of air.

'An engine. Probably come to rescue ours. Get to a refuge, or better still, over to the opposite track.' Vignoles risked his torch and played the beam across the ground to illustrate his point. 'Over there and stick close to the wall. It'll pass by or stop on this track.' He flicked the beam forwards but there was no sign of the killer; reluctant to remain a sitting duck for any longer, he switched off the beam.

'Oh, but the guard! We can't leave him there. I'm going to get him.'

Vignoles's voice echoed around the walls and he tensed, waiting for the bullet that he expected he had drawn towards himself by shouting. Thankfully there was no reaction, so he advanced towards the approaching train with one hand again touching the side wall. He was feeling exposed and vulnerable, despite the pitchy blackness; the sound of the engine grew ever louder and more startling.

'Are you there? Are you hurt?'

He had covered quite some distance and felt sure that he must be close to where the guard had fallen. The noise was now becoming intensely menacing and the oil lamps on the front of the train were approaching like the eyes of some beast. Vignoles had to seek refuge now or he would be struck down. He felt the wall in a sudden fit of panic, tripping over something, sprawling onto the ground and hitting a railway sleeper and a rail fixing as he did so, but as he fell his right arm flailed to one side and felt the open space in the wall that he needed. He quickly drew himself into a crouching position and risked flashing on his light to see what he had tripped over. It was the body of the guard, lying across the track, a livid red wheal on his forehead.

Vignoles dropped the torch and immediately tried to lift the inert weight of the man, a difficult task as his long greatcoat encumbered him and his shoulder was still burning from the American woman's unfortunate assault. He glanced around and could see that the engine was nearly upon him.

Things then happened very quickly.

There were two huge explosions that filled the tunnel with great flashes of light and a noise that left his ears ringing painfully. Vignoles now had the guard by the shoulders and heaved with every ounce of strength he could muster until he was pressed against the wall and could move no further back. He hoped he had managed to move the guard's legs clear of the rails. He laid the railwayman down and looked up as the flashes of light illuminated the shape of someone standing opposite him in the centre of the track. He was tall and gaunt and his eyes were wide and staring with something between confusion and craziness. He was pointing a gun right at Vignoles. It was but the briefest of glimpses and the booming explosions that ricocheted around the curved wall shocked Vignoles so much that he had no time to fully register what this meant. Perhaps he had imagined it.

The gun sparked and a bullet pinged off the wall behind Vignoles. He tasted the bitter tang of brick dust. He dropped to the ground and crouched, one hand holding his hat, the other levelling his gun. There was a shouted command to 'drop your weapon!' from the far side, but this was immediately swallowed up by a clattering roar accompanied by a banshee wail of a whistle.

Vignoles felt the darkness move before his eyes in a whirling, pounding, steaming mass of noise, sucking his hat from under his hand and filling his nostrils with the smell of hot metal and oil as steam poured around him, only to be whipped away again by the rush of air as the engine rolled past. The orange glow of the open firedoors in the engine cab offered relief from the darkness as it illuminated a moving cloud of glowing smoke and steam like some biblical apparition, followed by an aggressive series of clatters and bangs as the train rumbled behind, brakes squealing unpleasantly. Vignoles pushed himself as far back as he could whilst sensing the hard metal passing just inches away from his face.

The train finally came to a standstill and the tunnel was filled with the sizzling fizz of the engine and thick, sulphurous fumes. Many voices and running feet were pounding on the ballast, shouts echoed and torch beams played across the tunnel walls and track. Lights flickering beneath the train between the wheels made strange shadows and patterns. As Vignoles blew his whistle to attract attention and searched for a pulse on the guard's neck, a cry went up that confirmed what he already suspected.

The badly smashed and mangled body of a man was lying beneath the train.

Chapter Twenty-Nine

'MY WOMAN'
Al Bowlly with Lew Stone & his Band

Vignoles and Trinder were each holding enamelled mugs of tea and standing at the corner of the long carriage shed at Woodford. The low sun was casting a well-defined blue shadow of the saw-toothed roofline onto the thin frosting of white that lay all around. The snow was thinner now, and in places was just a few inches deep, though dirty mounds shovelled clear of the running lines littered the yard, and at the edges of this vast arena there remained wind-drifted slopes of virgin white. It was cold, but the sun took the edge off and they could feel its touch upon their faces and enjoyed the soft golden glow it was painting upon the great clouds of steam surrounding the engines on shed, in striking contrast to the clear sky vaulted above.

'Perhaps I am just becoming inured to winter, or is this sun actually feeling warm?' Vignoles squinted to reduce the glare of the sun.

'I reckon as it's got a bit of heat to it. Dare we imagine a break in the weather?'

Vignoles puffed on his pipe and gave Trinder a sidelong glance, 'Better meteorologists than us have been made to look foolish predicting a change and then been proven wrong, but I really do believe that spring is out there somewhere, just waiting...'

'To spring upon us.'

Both men nodded and watched as an engine cautiously propelled a short train of two guard's vans, an ancient passenger coach, a fuel tanker and, at the front, a flat wagon supporting a construction that looked like an anti-aircraft gun on a swivelling base. This monster was actually a jet engine with a long, extended exhaust that formed the barrel. This was now pointed downwards towards the track, whilst the bulk of the engine was swathed in a heavy tarpaulin that allowed just a hint at the complexities that lay beneath in a series of lumps, bulges and glimpses of piping and unidentified apparatus.

'I would like to see this in operation. Far from wishing this damned winter to hang on any longer, I still can't help feeling a touch disappointed that the snow is not deep enough here to fire up this beast!' Vignoles was watching the slow procession intently as it eased its way along the siding.

'I understand that it's being sent up north later. Up Sheffield or Manchester way.'

'I heard that. There's still bad drifting over the Pennines.' Vignoles looked wistful.

'I also heard that it wrecks the track. Might be a mixed blessing, as it not only blows the snow away but blows the track as well! That's no darned use, if you ask me.'

'It's like everything new: it takes time to get to know the nature of the beast and how to best use it, what power and angle of elevation is best and so on. It's really supposed to just punch a way through the very deepest compacted drifts and then normal ploughs follow on to properly clear the actual lines. Apparently it makes the most awful racket.'

Trinder took a deep drag on his cigarette. 'It's pretty amazing what the boffins come up with, isn't it? Makes you wonder what's next. What new-fangled inventions they have waiting.'

'Yes. On that note, whilst it's not quite a new invention as such, I've been advised that as soon as the snow clears they will install an oil re-fuelling depot here and convert some of the steamers to oil. The government has been sufficiently rocked by the lack of coal over the last few months and the unrest down the mines that they are considering converting over to oil.'

'Well that is a turn-about.'

'Yes. I can't quite see it happening, though. Too many people's jobs depend on the railways burning coal and if they just stop, then they're all out of work. The government has so many problems already that I cannot see it surviving such an unpopular move.'

Trinder pulled a face. 'It's all politics, isn't it, in the end? Not what's best for everyone, but what's best for the politicians.'

Vignoles nodded sadly.

The train had now come to a standstill and the crew was uncoupling the engine. A small group of army lads had climbed out of the old coach and were now standing around, stretching their legs and lighting cigarettes.

'We can leave them to guard the jet engine for the time being, so let's see if we can't get a fresh cup of tea.' And with that, Vignoles emptied the dregs from his mug and started to walk towards the engine shed. As they walked, they talked.

'Have we heard anything more from the Yanks about their man?' asked Trinder.

'Yes, I took a call only today from their military police, and it would appear that he was quite a strange character, even before he committed these crimes. He went under a few names in recent months, but he was really Lieutenant Samuel K. Quesada.'

'You're pulling my leg. That sounds made up to me.'

'Yes, well, perhaps. And, though they are being a bit cagey about the whole sorry affair, it seems that he was always rather unstable, even when he was a rookie — I believe that is the term they use. My understanding is that he was probably not good material for combat duties.'

'So he was mad right from the start?' Trinder tossed his cigarette butt away in disgust, twisting his boot on the stub and squashing it onto the frozen ground.

'They are more circumspect than that, but clearly he was a disturbed young man. Of course he then got dropped right into active service during most of 1945, fighting his way towards Berlin, and got pretty much shaken up in a nasty incident along the way. Got injured and was sent home on sick leave, but was posted back after V.E. Day and stayed out in Germany for quite some time.'

'So he was army?'

'Yes, a lieutenant in the U.S. VII Army Corps. And this is where the story starts to go wrong, as apparently there were a couple of incidents in Germany — and they are reluctant to say too much about these — but I get the sense that they involved local girls, and one with a female medical orderly. Complaints were made, but nothing stuck.'

'He killed them?'

'No. But roughed them up and scared them, and tried it on. This was clearly the start of a dangerous shift in his mental well-being.'

Both men walked in silence for a few moments.

'Whatever happened,' continued Vignoles, 'he got away with it, but the army doctor wanted to send him home. Apparently he jumped the transport when in England and never made it to the ship. Went missing.'

'A.W.O.L.' Interjected Trinder.

'Spot on. He was not being treated as a prisoner and they didn't appreciate that he was quite as dangerous as proved to be, so they trusted him. Next thing we hear, he's masquerading as an airman. False papers, passport, uniform, the works. He even gets himself billeted at a camp. Again the military police have been a little unwilling to share the full details with me.'

'I'm not surprised. That was a pretty poor show.'

'A damned disgraceful cock-up, but I suppose in the confusion following the end of the war, it's not impossible to imagine, either. There are servicemen everywhere, moving to and fro, and one clever and devious character can probably fool the system for a while.'

'Perhaps.' Trinder kicked a lump of dirty ice as if it were a football so that it flew forwards, hit a signal post and shattered into fragments. 'So did they rumble him?'

'He moved around and kept one step ahead, but the M.P. was closing in on him, and in recent weeks Quesada vanished and started living off camp — actually in the Woodford offices where the Earnshaw lad spotted him, I presume.'

'But wasn't he trading stuff to raise funds? If he was off camp, how did he keep getting the stores?'

'I suspect he earned a tidy profit in these sales, and then it only takes a bit of charm and a back-hander or two to keep a contact back in the P.X. stores sweet, and he was all right.'

'So, basically he was just crazy? Screwed up by war?'

'Seems that way.' Vignoles fell silent for a moment. 'It's odd, but I feel a bit... dissatisfied by that fact. That poor young woman lost her life and Kat was violated and left in that terrible state simply because a soldier was turned mad.' Vignoles stared into the distance, his voice quiet as he spoke.

Trinder pulled a face as he considered his response. 'Really? But surely you'd not want this man — whatever his name really was — to have calmly planned these attacks and then argue that he knew what he wanted and what he was doing? Is that any better? I mean, you do have to be crazy to do such things?'

'Yes...' Vignoles sounded sad and weary, '...yes, you are of course correct, John. I suppose I try to look for motive and meaning behind each crime we investigate, and sometimes I suppose I must accept that a twisted and disturbed mind is all there is to it. I suppose what is gnawing away at me is a feeling that perhaps one ought to feel sorry for this Quesada. If war and its horrors disturbed him so profoundly and, as I suspect, he received little help for his problems, then was he truly completely to blame? I find forgiveness hard in this instance, but am troubled by a feeling that I should still find it in myself to forgive him. At least young Kat is awake now, and whilst I fear it will take a long time for her to recover from her ordeal, the signs are good. We must take some heart from that.'

'Thanks be to God. And, if I may say so, for some pretty fine detective work on your part.'

'Hardly… I was just doing my job.' Vignoles looked somewhere far into the distance, the bright whiteness of the snow reflecting from the lenses of his spectacles, hiding a slight glassiness to his eyes. Both men fell silent for a moment, the pale vapour of their breath hanging in the air.

Trinder broke the spell. 'That Beeby guy is pretty bonkers, if you ask me.'

'Agreed.' Vignoles managed a slight hint of a wry smile at the sergeant's choice of words. His voice had a lighter note to it. 'Thankfully, he has never crossed the line into rape or murder, though the Notts Constabulary are down on him like a ton of bricks. They are forcing him to report in to the station once a week and are keeping a close eye on his whereabouts. Any woman reporting being pick-pocketed has his movements carefully correlated with hers, and he knows he has a stretch at His Majesty's Pleasure ahead if he is so much as in the same room, bus or train as the victim. A strange fish indeed, but we must acknowledge that he also helped us track down this Lieutenant Quesada.'

'And that's why he got off the pick-pocketing charges with just a warning? A fair compromise, I suppose.' Trinder nodded.

'Enough of the sadder side of life, the sun is shining and it gives me quite a boost. I really do think spring might be on its way.' He looked across the yard towards the still white fields beyond the railway, now kissed by a soft sunlight and at a swirl of snow buntings wheeling and turning in the still air.

'So have you named the day?'

'Violet says that it must be in apple blossom time.'

'As in the song?'

'Exactly. She adores it and says she's dreamt of just that for herself one day.'

'All very romantic.'

'Ye-es,' Trinder winced slightly. 'Of course with the weather as it is, who knows when the apple blossom will be out? But I suggested we go for early May and take our chance on it. We're going to settle everything this coming weekend and then we can think about invitations and all that jazz. I have a slight dread that I am letting myself in for goodness knows how many months of organising and fussing and making of lists and shopping trips and… Well you know all about the confusion that seems to accompany a wedding.'

'Indeed I do!' Vignoles grinned. 'Good luck. And then there is the small matter of accommodation for this happy couple, always assuming they survive the D-Day sized organisational headaches of the wedding plans, that is.'

'Ah, yes. I was rather hoping we could have a bit of a conversation on that subject.'

Vignoles raised an eyebrow, 'Have you put your names down for a prefab?'

'We cannot until we show a marriage certificate. You know how everything works these days. And it's still quite a palaver after that, but we can at least start the process in May.'

'And then how long?'

'A year, perhaps longer.'

'I see. So what shall you both do in the interim?'

'Now that is the issue. We've both talked about it and really the most economical option is for us to live in Woodford. For all its faults, the flat above the shop would serve our needs. But of course this is a fair trek each day to work — though the rail service makes it possible. It can be done and I really don't mind the longer hours.'

Vignoles nodded. 'Good. I was wondering if you might consider that option. She has a business and a pretty large place there, plenty big enough for you both, and it gives Jenny time to decide what she wants to do.'

Trinder visibly breathed out as if he had been holding his breath.

'And actually, I have been thinking about the detective department. We're pretty stretched to cover the whole line as it is, and whilst I cannot see Leicester Central ever ceasing to be our operational centre, and so it would remain your principal base, I can appreciate the advantage of you being further up line. Perhaps if I can convince the penny-pinching finance department, we might be able to connect a telephone into your place. Yes, the more I think it through, I can see that it could work.' Vignoles stopped and looked at Trinder, 'Well, that's settled then.'

Trinder smiled and then looked at the ground, 'Thank you, sir. That is quite splendid news.'

'It's lunchtime, what say we forget the tea and go for a pint of Brackley Bitter at the White Hart?'

~ THE END ~

If you enjoyed this Inspector Vignoles mystery, then you might like to know that the third book in the series will be steaming into the shops in the autumn of 2009. Here is a taste of things to come...

THE TORN CURTAIN
(1948)

PROLOGUE

The Bay of Trieste was bathed with evening sunlight. The sea was the colour of petrol, turning to a silvery grey that sparkled with a million twinkling reflections as it stretched towards the horizon. Not a breath of wind stirred the lazy drifts of smoke curling from the funnels of the ships anchored far out in the deep, shimmering waters, their hulls indistinct at the transition from metal to Adriatic. To his right, across the bay, stood a fairytale castle that gleamed a bright white, burnished by the warm tones of the late sun, its gardens a verdant feast of green foliage and great tumbles of mauve wisteria against the harsh limestone of its promontory. Below a tiny rowing boat made ripples on the bay like a surface-skating insect.

Trieste harbour was crowded; the Molo Audace, a bare, stony finger of a jetty that extended into the bay, was filled with British warships all looking spick and span in freshly-painted grey-and-black with bold numerals on their hulls, each flying limp Union flags at their sterns and crowded against the limestone walls by rusting tender boats unloading coals and provisions. Fishing boats with their red sails drying in the heat of the late afternoon were jostled against smoky cargo vessels in an untidy profusion of masts, nets, crane jibs and drifting steam within the old harbour, whilst the dusky-black passenger steamer approached the Molo Bersaglieri, returning from Cittanova with its deck populated by Yugoslav soldiers and peasant men and women clutching bags and baskets of produce to sell or barter amidst the bustle and noisy confusion of the British zone. A clanking steam engine pulled a motley collection of wagons along the waterfront, its screeching whistle echoing off the towering bulwark of the Karst cliffs behind the city.

Private Paul Brierley was looking down from a magnificent vantage point carved high into this massive escarpment. He was seated on one of the small, fat stone bollards that ringed the base of a tall obelisk set within a small clearing in the Mediterranean pines and bougainvillea beside the winding road and steeply graded tramline. Before him, the Scala Santa fell away in a dizzying drop of worn stone steps, down which an elderly woman, weighed down by bags, was making a slow and painful descent. He wondered why she did not choose to await the return of the little blue tramcar from which he had recently stepped off. It would have reached its terminus in Villa Opicina by now, and if she waited just a quarter of an hour or so it would clank and ring its way back down to the city below.

He had chosen to alight here rather than continue to the end of the line and then walk to the Rossetti Barracks as he normally did, and his heart had been thumping the whole way up the tortuous climb, and not solely due to the effects of too much wine the night before. Though now as he sat and looked somewhat disconsolately down upon the city, he was reminded that he had drunk a lot last night. A tin of N.A.A.F.I. cigarettes bought you a night on the town without a moment's care for the bill and he'd certainly indulged to the limit; now he was wondering what he had got himself into.

Another steam engine puffed along the dock, hustling to collect a fresh cargo of wagons and looking like a little toy train. Despite the great distance, Brierley could recognise it as the little, Italian-built engine that still leaked and dribbled its way each day up and down the quays, shunting and shuffling the wagons of coffee beans, lemons, newly cut timber and other pungent produce, much as it had been doing for a great many years before he and the Royal Transport Corps took over. He'd be on that very engine when he clocked on at four o'clock tomorrow morning. He suddenly felt a stab of something between remorse and longing and wished that he were down there now, shovelling a few rounds of coal in the stifling heat of the cab and joshing and joking with his driver, Curly Lambert, on the footplate.

Why had he agreed meet those two chaps from the Caffè Tergest? Perhaps he should just continue up the hill to Opicina and retreat to the comforting order and regularity of army life. But maybe that was exactly why he had agreed to stick his neck out and do something on his own initiative? The wine had helped convince him of that last night, but the effect had long worn off, and now he was less sure. He felt another flutter in his stomach and failed to quell the realisation that it was fear and not excitement that was causing it.

Brierley rubbed his temples and squinted into the brilliant sun. In so doing he was reminded that his precious Ray-Bans were missing: pilfered no doubt by some light–fingered little bastard in that caffè last night. He'd been warned the place was full of thieves, so he should have been more careful. He began to have a sneaking suspicion that one of his two new drinking companions had taken them. Or maybe it had been the lovely Lola. He snorted and gave a little shake of his head. She could have tried harder to find something more original. Still, he'd told her it was a beautiful name and made some other embarrassing comments in the hope of a squeeze later. Yeah, it had to have been her, she'd been pretty fresh at one point and he remembered her arm around him, and how she pressed herself close. It would have been easy enough and she'd make a good price for those American glasses. He laughed bitterly at the irony of probably buying the very same pair back off one of the dodgy stallholders by the Canal Grande.

He spat into the dry and dusty earth beside his boot, his elbows resting on his thighs as he bent almost double. He lifted his head slightly to look up from under the peak of his cap and watched a young couple stroll in the sun, the woman's head resting on the man's shoulder and his hand on her amply curving hip. He was struck by the girl's sensual figure and how she had a build not unlike that of the temptress Lola. Now he thought about it, what had happened to her at the end of the night? Wasn't he supposed to have had something more out of the evening? He'd bought her enough of that vino and kept her in cigarettes all night, but somehow she'd slipped away into the narrow side streets of the old town with just a couple of quick wet kisses and left just a lingering scent of cheap perfume and a painful yearning as his only reward. His new companions, meanwhile, had been slapping his back or trying to hug him like these foreign types were so eager to do and repeating the time and place of their rendezvous. They had distracted him, and his prize had clattered away on her tottering heels whilst his drunken attempts to call her back had been smothered by dirty laugher, prods to his ribs and heavy arms around his shoulders.

He checked his watch. They'd be here soon. He suddenly felt a wave of agitation and stood up. He pulled the tatty, brown manila envelope out of his pocket and weighed it in his hands, brow furrowed. The money was appealing, well it was almost a king's ransom, but they'd set him up last night, nicked his shades and duped him with Lola. She'd been in on it, for sure. She'd got him all fired up and excited whilst they'd drunk his wine and talked football. Made like they were his friends. Then they'd produced that bottle of grappa that had really finished him off and got him to agree to their demands. Could he really trust them?

He paced around the base of the obelisk, barely registering a man pushing a cycle up the last few yards of the steep hill, his hat pulled low against the sun and head lowered with the effort. Brierley stopped and nodded his head in silent agreement with a decision he'd made. He would leave the envelope tucked under a bush, and that way he could say that he had brought the stuff as agreed and even dropped it off. He could argue the he had been called away suddenly and that there had been no time to wait. Yes, that would work, and then if they went back and found it lying there they'd still give him the money. If it was missing, well, then that was that. He would owe them nothing. But he wouldn't do it all again. No way. He'd be out of it.

He glanced around, then walked to one side of the steps where a few orange-flowered oleanders were growing beside a thick, low bush he didn't recognise. The ground was dry and dusty and worn smooth by many feet, but close to the edge some thin grass masked the narrow space beneath the bush. He bent over, parted the grass with one hand and reached forward to place the envelope underneath in the deep shade. He moved it a little to one side and then the other. He wanted it hidden and yet just visible to someone searching for something they suspected might be there.

Finally he felt satisfied with his work and made to stand up. As he did so, his eye caught a sudden movement, a flash of shadow across the grass. His instinct kicked in and he pulled himself upright whilst trying to twist around and reach out for the arm about to strike him. But he was too late. The cyclist had silently crept up behind and the short metal bar smashed into Brierley's forehead, his legs crumpling and head lolling lifelessly in an instant. It was a crude but skilful execution. The man with the shapely girlfriend had also swiftly moved in on the act, almost catching the falling body and effortlessly hauling him through the bushes as the assailant lifted Brierley's feet. Less than a half a minute later the cyclist was freewheeling at high speed back into town, the envelope in his jacket pocket, and the other man had linked arms again with his girlfriend after exchanging amorous looks and a kiss, as they continued their evening promenade at the edge of the corso along the Passeggiata Napoleonica.

The Inspector Vignoles Mysteries Series

by Stephen Done

SMOKE GETS IN YOUR EYES
(pub. 2007)
ISBN 978-1-904109-1-74
£7.99

THE MURDER OF CROWS
(pub. 2008)
ISBN 978-1-904109-1-98
£8.99

THE TORN CURTAIN
(forthcoming, 2009)
ISBN 978-1-904109-20-4
£8.99

To order books please add £1.50 postage and packing
and send cheques payable to Hastings Press to
21 Silchester Road, St Leonards TN38 0JB

To check availability of books please
email: hastings.press@virgin.net
telephone: 01424 442142
or visit www.hastingspress.co.uk